CW00427784

Gilgarius

J A Tunningley

2QT Limited (Publishing)

First Edition published 2019
2QT Limited (Publishing)
Settle, North Yorkshire BD24 9RH United Kingdom

The author has his own website: http://www.gilgarius.net

Cover by Hilary Pitt
Image Shutterstock.com

Printed in Great Britain by
TJ International Ltd, Padstow, Cornwall

A CIP catalogue record for this book is available
from the British Library

ISBN 978-1-913071-30-1

Dedication

For all children whose lives are blighted by conflict.

"Borders? I have never seen one.
But I have heard they exist in the minds of some people."
Thor Heyerdahl

Gilgarius

A glint of gold saved the traveller.

The two robbers had been watching him from a bank of thorns as he eased his horse into the shallow brown river to drink.

The traveller spun round when he sensed their movements. He saw two men brandishing knives and heard one of them rasping unfamiliar words. The larger of the men, bare chested and entirely toothless, sprang with a grace that belied his size. He grabbed the horse's bridle and pressed the point of his bronze blade against the animal's neck, threateningly close to where its carotid artery pulsed.

The horse snorted and whinnied in protest, hooves dancing.

It was then that the traveller drew the gold coin from his belt pouch and flicked it into the air.

Burnished by strong sunlight, the spinning disc had the robbers blinking as their eyes tried to follow its irresistible arc. Time enough for the traveller to reach over the mare's flank and draw his sword.

He ran the larger man through his bare flesh, twisting the blade as he did so. The gold coin hit the ground a split second ahead of the robber, who landed so heavily that the contents of his pierced gut were forced out onto the mud. The other man, a wiry, sunken-eyed individual, lunged wildly, grunting and stabbing the air with his blade – an ineffectual spasm as he, too, became impaled upon the sword.

The traveller dismounted and retrieved his piece of gold. Kneeling in the muddied water, he scooped some up and washed the intestinal sap off the coin before slipping it back into the goatskin pouch. Blood and gut residue on the sword were cleaned off in the same manner and the weapon dried on a tussock of sun-bleached grass.

The mare dropped her head, wanting to drink more, but the traveller feared the robbers had accomplices. He remounted and eased his horse around the prone men. The big toothless one was groaning but very near to death, flies already arriving to lay their eggs on his spilled innards; the other man was stone dead with hardly a speck of blood on his tunic, even though the sword had clean pierced his heart.

The robbers would have had no idea where the traveller came from on his fine black horse, nor where he was going, but they would have seen how he journeyed alone and perhaps how he paid far more handsomely than he needed to for bed and food at the tavern from which he had not long departed. And they would have assumed from the look of his two fat saddlebags that he carried precious things.

A rich and foolish man they must have thought him.

As he cantered away from the hapless thieves – one dead, one dying – the traveller hoped he would soon be free of living like a prey animal.

He journeyed on, spending five further days alone in the open, eeking out his meagre provisions of flat bread and cheese, seeing only the occasional goat-herder and finding shelter at night in clumps of trees or, once, in the mouth of a cave.

Eventually the traveller fell in with a group of cloth merchants who appeared to know the region well. He accompanied them through a high mountain pass and a plain scarred by dry river beds, where even the meanest grazing for horses was difficult to find.

Where they were heading was also a poor land, the leading merchant told him. Yet people still lived there, scraping an existence out of the dust. He said it was a hard life but still a better one than they used to have. At least they had rain in the mountains for a month each year and irrigation to ensure it reached their crops.

And yes, he had heard of the old man – who hadn't in these parts?

The traveller camped with the merchants and shared their food and histories and tales of hardship and deals well done. They were curious why he travelled alone. He told them he had set out five months earlier with two young and impressionable cousins, who were taken along to keep him company and help him fend off danger.

His cousins had said that they wanted adventure but that desire had only been in their imaginations and the reality of the travelling life bit them severely. They weren't used to enduring hardship as they journeyed day after relentless day, often sleeping out in the cold and rain with bears and wolves and robbers a constant worry.

The traveller admitted he would have been better off hiring a strong servant who could handle a sword, but his cousins had begged to be allowed to join his expedition, proclaiming – or rather exaggerating – the quality of their own swordsmanship.

Their father also entreated on their behalf. 'Take them,' he urged. 'They are strong lads. They will help keep you safe.'

The traveller believed his uncle was glad to see the back of the profligate pair and probably hoped that any robbers they encountered would teach them a lesson while still sparing their

3

lives.

'It won't be easy,' he told his young companions. 'You'll have to travel without any of the comforts you are used to. And there will be danger, for we'll journey through bad places and will have to survive with the aid of our weapons and wits.'

But the lads had never been away from home before and did not appreciate the serious purpose of the journey. To them, it was an excuse to throw off the discipline of their upbringing. They got drunk and tried to seduce village girls, so the pair were often chased on their way by irate fathers, brothers and lovers, who had hatred in their hearts and murder in their eyes. The traveller grew weary of ensuring that these men grasped gold or silver pieces in their fists in place of swords and knives.

Despite their most valiant efforts, his cousins were able to claim hardly any conquests and soon became bored with the business of travel and its attendant discomforts. They had given up and turned back when barely a fifth of the journey had been completed, complaining that their mounts were suffering and one of them had become too lame to continue on such an arduous trek.

The traveller let them go with a sense of relief. They'd proved far more trouble than they were worth, enticing danger rather than keeping it at bay. He believed they would have surely got themselves killed before too long – and probably him, too, as a perceived accessory to their whoring.

So, the traveller told the merchants, he was forced to go on alone and vulnerable, grinding out league after solitary league, falling into the occasional company of other travellers, some of whom pretended friendship but would rob you if they got half a chance. It was an arduous journey, he said, but he did not tell the merchants it was one with a purpose so compelling that he could not allow fear or adversity to deter him.

The traveller described crossing two violent seas, countless malarial swamps and a desert that baked him by day and froze him by night. He risked his life travelling through a bandit-ridden mountain range; he survived by finding safe places to rest during the day and riding only by the light of the moon and stars.

The merchants shook their heads in disbelief and wanted to know what amazing goods he traded in to make such a perilous lone journey worthwhile.

The traveller smiled enigmatically and said, 'I wish to acquire something that is more valuable than cloth and spices.'

The merchants told stories by firelight well into the night. When it came to the traveller's turn, he related a story that had been told him as a young boy by his grandmother, a grandmother he barely remembered yet could never forget.

The merchants listened in silence. It was a good story, they all agreed.

After the traveller said his farewells to the merchants, he departed from the trade route at a canter. He was close now to his destination – another two days at the most.

When he found him, the old man was resting in the shade of a tree, as lean as the exposed root upon which he sat. His hair and beard were white as snow and his skin like cured goat hide. With some difficulty, and the aid of a gnarled stick, the old man rose and greeted the traveller with a friendly wave. He inclined his head slightly and smiled curiously as the visitor dismounted and walked slowly towards him, his mare following obediently.

'Hello, stranger,' the old man said. 'Have you lost your way?'

'I'm not sure,' said the traveller. 'I believe I'm in the land of the Akben people but you will doubtless tell me if I'm wrong.'

'Indeed, you are in Akbenna – and you appear to speak our tongue well enough. But what brings you to this part of the world? You're leagues away from the trade road.'

'I'm seeking a new kind of transaction,' the traveller replied. 'Away from where other traders trudge a worn path with their camel trains and donkeys.'

'I'm afraid you'll not find much of value around here,' said the old man. 'All we do is grow meagre crops and raise goats and chickens. It can be a grim life, though not as bad as it used to be.'

The traveller took in his surroundings, a simple farm of limited extent. The main dwelling was circular, built from mud bricks and thatched with straw. To one side was a stockade and an olive orchard and to the other a much smaller building, also of mud brick. A low circular structure in front of it, which had a boulder rim about waist height, appeared to be the head of a well.

'My name is Han,' the old man was saying. 'Please, join me out of the sun and we can talk awhile.'

The traveller stepped into the shade, his horse dutifully following.

'The autumns are becoming almost as unbearable as the summers,' Han said, returning to his root-bench. 'It's perhaps as well that I'm too old these days to work in the fields, and I certainly don't want to be clambering on to the roof of my house to replace thatch stolen by birds for their nests. I've nothing else to do but sit beneath this chatka tree. But, forgive me, I am jabbering like a jinterbuck and have not even asked your name or where you have travelled from.'

'I am Arkis and I've journeyed from where you see the sun setting,' the traveller said, with a sweeping wave of his arm towards the west. 'I learned to speak your language from merchants who ply the trade routes. It is not so very different from other tongues I've mastered or, indeed, my own.'

'There are many traders these days,' said Han. 'They've brought some wealth to Akbenna, dealing in silk and spices and precious objects that draw the eye and can make some crazed with envy. What kind of trader are you, Arkis?'

'I've yet to determine that. I can only say it's sure to be something captivating. For now, I'm travelling out of curiosity.'

'Curiosity? Now that's a good reason to visit this land. Indeed, any land. If people don't venture abroad, they can become insular and mistrustful.'

'I agree,' said Arkis, 'though travel can be arduous and threatening, as I've learned.'

Han eyed his bulging saddlebags. 'It's a wonder you haven't been robbed.'

'Aye, a wonder indeed,' said Arkis with a wry smile.

'Maybe you would care to rest here for a while,' said Han. 'I'm sure we can find somewhere safe for your possessions.'

'Oh, I carry little of true value,' said Arkis. He smiled and stroked his horse's neck. 'What I value most carries me and I would hate to lose her.'

'Your mount will be safe here.'

'I wouldn't wish to put you to any trouble.'

'It's no trouble. We have very few people passing this way and I get bored with my own company, so you are most welcome to rest here the night. The sun will be sleeping soon.'

Arkis looked to the western sky and nodded. 'Very well.'

'Your horse can stay in the stockade where we keep the goats and hens at night. My granddaughter Pelia will feed her. Once she longed to have a horse of her own and a cart for it to pull, but goats and chickens are enough to contend with. I must say yours is a fine animal and in amazing condition considering how far you must have travelled. Has she a name?'

'She is Rashi, which means the black wind.'

Han patted the horse on her muzzle and she snickered good-naturedly in response. 'I once knew a fine mare whose name declared her to be as swift as the wind.'

He sighed heavily. Arkis detected a distinctive rattle in the old man's chest. His cheeks inflated as if he was suppressing the urge to cough or belch.

'People fade from your memory, but you never forget a fine a horse,' said Arkis.

'You are right, my friend,' Han said. 'I've never forgotten Melemari, even though it was such a long time ago when I embarked on a remarkable journey.' He smiled and closed his eyes, as if conjuring a specific image. 'You see I, too, have done a bit of travelling, though not for many years.'

'You've seen faraway lands?'

'Just one – and it was not so very far away. Now I'm too old for any form of travelling. Reminiscing is all I have the energy for these days. But I can't complain. I'm thankful for my life because I've had a good life, which makes struggling to remember details worth all the effort.'

Han raised his stick and pointed it at a distant volcano that dominated the southern horizon, issuing a wispy plume of smoke. 'See, there is our Mother Mountain. Akben people have worshipped her since the start of time. I've long thought such devotion questionable, yet each day I still offer her my gratitude for allowing me to live so long and fruitfully that I have seen this land finally prosper.'

Arkis couldn't see much that was prospering in such a barren landscape but he held his tongue.

'It's many decades since Mother Mountain last erupted in anger,' Han continued. 'I was only a boy but I will never forget such a momentous event.'

He paused, closing his eyes but still pointing his stick. 'You see her now, Arkis, content to smoulder comfortingly, whispering her wisdom into the blue sky. Her smoke beckons the clouds that bring welcome rain for our crops at just the time they need it. It wasn't always so. Before Gilgarius came, when I was a young boy, we had year upon year of drought and many of us went hungry.'

'Gilgarius?'

'Yes,' said Han. 'Everything changed after that. If you care to sit with me awhile, I can tell you about it.'

'I've no desire to disturb your peace,' said Arkis.

'Nonsense. Please sit here in the shade of the tree. I'm sure my granddaughter will bring bread and beer – and some of her wonderful goat's milk cheese, which she infuses with herbs. Pelia is a beautiful young woman and it's strange that she has never married, though not for want of men from some of the villages around calling and asking her. Well, they used to call and ask her. She has something of an independent spirit. Probably gets it from me.'

Aided by his stick, Han went off to find his granddaughter, who responded quickly to the call of her name. She followed him back to the shade of the tree carrying a newborn kid, which was suckling her finger.

'This is Arkis,' Han told her. 'He's travelled a long way to trade in these parts. He'll be a guest with us tonight.'

Pelia smiled and then seemed to think she shouldn't have and appeared embarrassed. The smile, while it lasted, was wide and warm, though any beauty she might have possessed had been tempered by long days working in the hot sun. Arkis was particularly struck by her high cheekbones and the clarity of her grey eyes and he looked at her with a curious interest.

Pelia allowed their eyes to meet respectfully but almost too briefly as she turned her attention to Rashi, stroking the horse's mane with her free hand as the kid started to bleat and wriggle to be free. 'She's a beautiful horse.'

The mare snickered, as if delighting in the praise.

'True,' said Arkis. 'But more than that, she's a courageous friend. I would trust her with my life.'

Pelia nodded perceptively. 'I can take her into the stockade. She'll be safe and we have hay and water there.'

'Let me first relieve Rashi from the burden she is carrying,' said Arkis.

Once freed from the weight of saddle, saddlebags and bearskin blanket, the mare began to dance with relief, making Pelia laugh.

Later, when Rashi was fed and watered in the stockade, Pelia brought food and drink for Arkis and her grandfather. After Han took his fill, which the traveller noted was very little, the old man settled himself on a comfortable tussock of dry grass in a cosy space between two of the chatka tree's surface roots, over which he draped his arms.

Arkis sat cross-legged on the ground a stride away, resting an elbow on his saddle. 'Now, you were about to tell me of Gilgarius,' he said. 'That is, if you still want to.'

'Ah, yes, indeed,' said Han. 'It's a story I've never tired of telling.'

***

Gilgarius was a huge creature feared by all, said Han, even our priests and elders and our soldiers. I was just a boy when he came and settled on the border between Akbenna and the land of our eastern neighbours, the Bostrati. At first we kept our distance out of respect for Gilgarius's fabled power and for a short while he slumbered, hardly stirring. But all too quickly we felt the wind from his gigantic wingbeats and heard the thundering of his huge feet and the deathly roar of his hunger. Our frightened women wept and some of them hid in caves with their infants and suckling babies as the elders sent armed men to watch Gilgarius's movements.

A few of us children disobeyed our mothers and followed the soldiers, finding a safe place to watch from a hill overlooking Gilgarius's lair in a clump of gorse and dry, twisted trees. We saw our generals nervously approach the creature while awestruck soldiers walked a short distance behind them, some with their broad-bladed spears held high and others nervously fingering slings already charged with stone shot.

Gilgarius sat on his haunches in a flexing cave formed by his huge, fibrous wings. He was slavering and had curled back the soft edge of his scaly mouth to show dripping fangs as yellow as piss and as long and sharp as daggers, which legend said could tear apart a bull elephant. The same legend asserted that Gilgarius's molars could grind that elephant's bones to powder. However, we knew he preferred much smaller fare.

It was the first time any of us had seen the fabled creature in the flesh. We children were all too frit even to slink back to find our mothers; it was as if a spell bound us to Gilgarius.

Our generals halted their approach a hundred strides from the creature and huddled together deciding what to do. At this sight, Gilgarius issued a stenching roar that echoed around the valley until it carried into the distance, transformed into a terrible, mocking laugh. When the awful sound finally dissipated in the wind, Gilgarius tossed his dark-green head and rolled his bulbous eyes.

'So, the Akben have come to sting me with stones and scratch me with pathetic blades,' the creature said. 'You think you can destroy me and stop me consuming your young. You may hide your people in caves so I cannot reach them but I can wait while you sweat with fear in the dark. You will have to come out, and it is only a matter of time before you will offer your children to me. And if you don't, I can always tear down the mountain. You really have no choice but to comply with my desire.'

Gilgarius roared on, threatening us all with an awesomely destructive power, and he became an enormous dark-green shadow over the land. To demonstrate his strength, he tore out a hundred trees from the forest and broke many of them into splinters. Some of those trees had grown for many lifetimes but Gilgarius plucked them from the ancient ground like a farmer plucks weeds from his fields. He tossed them over the border and declared, 'They are now your neighbours' trees, theirs to burn for warmth while they sit and tell the story of Gilgarius's mighty power. You see how I can help your neighbours by giving them what you thought was yours?'

The generals responded to this awesome demonstration with fear and anger. They believed he would tear out all the trees and plunder the meagre stores of grain and give them to our neighbours, and that domestic animals, exposed and untended, would become stock in the creature's larder.

But Gilgarius seemed to mellow after his frenzy and began to talk of compromise. He told the generals, 'I need not take all your young. Only a handful would be required to sate my appetite while I sojourn here. It is not too much to ask.'

'But we do not want to give you any of our children,' said the generals. 'They are our future. Our land is not very good and we need all our young to work hard in the fields alongside their mothers and fathers to ensure we have grain to survive the winter.'

Gilgarius's laugh boomed across the Border Valley. When it subsided, the creature spoke soothingly in a voice that was like a deep, lazy snore.

'My friends, it is not necessary to sacrifice your young without gaining something in return. If you agree to feed me, I will get you better land. I know you have always looked enviously over the domain of the Bostrati. Their fields produce finer corn than you can harvest, and their cattle and goats grow twice as big as your scrawny beasts. This is because their streams flow limitless and pure from the cleansing mountains. Their land is irrigated so the crops thrive and their beasts graze on the lushest grass. If you agree to give me your young, I will move the border line and use my giant claws to gouge irrigation channels from these streams to your arid fields.'

The generals, indeed every one of us, listened in stunned

silence. Gilgarius was offering what we had desired as a people for generations.

'For every three children you offer,' the creature continued, 'I will move the border three leagues into the land of the Bostrati. Think on it and give me your answer at dawn.'

The generals fell into a huddle and we children at the top of the hill shook with fear. Which of us would be consumed by Gilgarius to earn the three leagues of Bostrati land?

The next morning, as an unusually giant sun rose in a shimmering orange glow, the generals went to see Gilgarius.

'We have consulted our elders and priests,' said the appointed spokesman, 'and they have agreed to give you three of our children if you move the border three leagues. But they ask that you lay a line of large rocks along the new boundary to thwart the Bostrati should they decide to retake the land by force.'

'That is too much work in exchange for three children,' Gilgarius grunted. 'But give me five and you shall have your rocks laid.'

Reluctantly, after much debate, it was agreed that five children would be sacrificed to Gilgarius. A meeting of the Great Council was called to select the victims. All the children of the Border Valley were summoned to attend and they gathered in great trepidation at the foot of the Mother Mountain.

In the distance, Gilgarius's thunderous rumbles of hunger could be heard. Tormented by the haunting sound, we children huddled closer together like a herd of young ledbuk detecting the fearful stench of wolves in the wind.

The Akben chief elder, Karmus, fought back his tears as he laid hands on the five children he had decided should be sacrificed. There were three boys and two girls. One was a boy I worked alongside in the fields; he was standing only a stride from me when he caught Karmus's eye. Another was a pretty, pearl-skinned girl who was chosen because she was very young; it was believed her sweetness would particularly please Gilgarius.

They were delivered to the creature by our generals and early the next morning all were consumed. Then, after a satiated slumber, Gilgarius roused himself and flew a league beyond the border, harrying the Bostrati to leave their homes. When none remained, he used his mighty strength to gouge huge rocks from the mountains and place them along a new boundary. Afterwards he used his giant claws to scratch the irrigation channels he had promised.

'There,' he said, when the work was done. 'Gilgarius keeps his word. Now you can give me more of your young.'

General Sperius, who headed our army, was stunned by the creature's words. 'But you said you would go when you were full,' he spluttered.

Gilgarius gave out a deep mocking laugh. 'You are fools to think I can be satisfied by just five of your puny children,' he said, using the finest point of one of his huge claws to pick out the stringy remains of young flesh trapped between his umber teeth. 'They amounted to nothing more than an appetiser, though to be fair the youngest girl was a rare delicacy.'

'But you said—'

'I said no figure, nor a length of time that I might stay here,' growled Gilgarius. 'But I may leave more quickly if I can sample more of your children. Seven will always make a better meal than five.'

General Sperius began to wail his despair and he beat his chest with his shield. He sank to his knees and bellowed to Gilgarius to relent and leave our people in peace. But the creature shifted on his haunches and let out a belch of gas that bathed the generals in the stench of digesting children.

'Go!' roared Gilgarius. 'Do as I say or I shall give the Bostrati their land back – and more besides.'

The general and his fellow commanders returned to the Mother Mountain to consult our elders and priests, leaving Gilgarius once again to his slumber. The elders tore at their long white beards and chanted to the towering peak smouldering above them. Finally, after wailing with despair all night, Karmus decided to call another meeting of the Great Council so that more of the Akben young could be selected for Gilgarius.

'We have no choice,' cried Karmus as the crowd murmured its discontent. 'Gilgarius could destroy everything we have if we do not give him more children.'

Again he walked among us until certain children caught his eye. I was so frit of being chosen, I stared at the ground until Karmus walked by. This time he selected seven girls as sacrifices. The crowd grew restless and some women said it was unfair that no boys had been chosen.

'I dare not diminish our stock of young men,' explained Karmus in a quaking voice. 'I have no choice but to give of our girls. Please, mothers, understand why I do this. If we cannot rid ourselves of Gilgarius this way, then we will have to fight him. Many men may be slain by the creature, hastening the day when these boys become men and have to fight Gilgarius themselves.'

Thus I escaped Gilgarius's jaws once more. The girls who had been chosen were taken by the generals to Gilgarius's lair, but they came across the creature earlier than expected. He was reclining upon a new line of giant rocks – six leagues within the original border. He had driven before him those Akbens who lived there. They were hysterical with fear, Gilgarius having swooped low over their houses, tearing away the roofs with as much ease as a woman pulling a tussock of grass from her meagre vegetable garden.

'What is happening?' cried General Sperius. 'Why have you moved the border?'

Gilgarius issued a putrid belch and rested his claws on his bulging stomach. 'Ah now, my friend, you took too long to bring your young. The Bostrati were quicker and more generous – they brought more children to me than you did.'

Our generals stared at each other in disbelief. Gilgarius had dealt treacherously, agreeing to restore to the Bostrati their land, plus three leagues of ours, in return for seven of their young.

'But we have brought you seven of our own,' said General Sperius. 'What about our agreement?'

'I lost patience with you general,' replied Gilgarius. 'My hunger got the better of me. However, 'twould be a pity to waste such sweet and tender flesh as this you now offer.'

'No, I won't allow you—'

'Very good, keep your scrawny fare. I will wait for the Bostrati to offer more of their succulent young and then I will move the border further into your land.'

'You cannot – you must not,' General Sperius pleaded. 'The elders have sent their sacrifice. Seven tender young girls for your delectation. Please accept them with our goodwill. Only – only move our border back into the land of the Bostrati. Back to where it was defined yesterday.'

'Mmm, 'tis a tempting bargain but I'm not so sure.'

'Be sure, mighty creature. Be sure. Take our young and give us our due.'

Gilgarius slavered as he savoured the prospect of consuming seven of our young girls. The monster's yellow eyes, rolling in eager anticipation, seemed to bulge ever more from their sockets. 'Very well,' the creature said. 'Give me your girls and I will do as you ask.'

And it was done. The girls were consumed and Gilgarius, lumbering more slowly now because of his feasting, pushed back the border line into the land of the Bostrati.

The generals returned to the Mother Mountain to give

thanks, but their gratitude was short lived. Only two days passed before bad news came: Gilgarius had once again restored the border in favour of the Bostrati after they had offered him nine of their most attractive children.

Another meeting of the Great Council was held, at which Karmus wailed his despair to the Mother Mountain. 'How can you stand by and let this happen to your children? Give us a sign that you can bring an end to Gilgarius's greedy double-dealing.'

But Mother Mountain merely smouldered, seeming not to care about our plight, and people were afraid to condemn her. Instead, many believed she was allowing Gilgarius's domination as a punishment and everyone began to ask what evil we had done to deserve it.

Our head priest, Medzurgo, declared it was because many Akbens no longer devoutly worshipped the mountain each morning as the sun rose and in the evening when it set. It was a tradition that had been neglected as our way of life became harder to sustain. Most us went to the bone-dry fields and woods before dawn and came back after dusk; such was the need to work relentlessly, we never found time or were too exhausted for devotion, unlike the Bostrati whose crops and cattle grew effortlessly. They, our spies reported, were able to deliver their rites several times a day.

'That is why their god smiles upon them,' Medzurgo said. 'They are blessed because of their devotions, blessed enough to make Gilgarius favour them over us.'

Yet there were some who dismissed deference to Mother Mountain as a waste of time.

'What use is it to offer our thanks to this deity when she gives us nothing?' cried one farmer. 'This year my crops are stunted and scorched by the relentless sun. It gets worse each year. Unless she gives us more rain, we have nothing to be grateful for.'

The man's outburst was shocking and he was shouted down as a blasphemer, though I saw there were many who did not join in the reprobation but instead lowered their gaze to the ground as if in mute agreement with him.

Karmus shook his head in despair. 'We have no choice but to plead with Gilgarius to leave our land,' he said. 'Soon there will be no young left anyway, and the creature will have to leave or be content to gnaw at our wizened bones and those of our dying beasts.'

It was resolved to select a final sacrifice: twelve more Akben young would be offered to Gilgarius in exchange for the promise that he would go away. To appease the women, boys were also selected. Once again, Karmus walked among the children, nodding silently at each one he favoured as a sacrifice. And this time I didn't escape his stare. My mother grasped me to her bosom, tears washing me in her distress.

General Sperius led me away.

***

Pelia had led the goats to a knoll above the little farm where they were grazing out last bits of nutrition from the spiky scrub, guarded by her two dogs. She sat below the summit, staring down upon the stranger as he reclined against his saddle, listening intently to her grandfather's story.

There was a time when Han had more than a single listener for his tale, a time before Pelia was born. Her mother said people would come from the villages around to hear him and he would sell them beer and hold court like a king, sitting beneath the chatka tree, his rapt listeners arranged around him. People of all ages. Sometimes he would go to the capital, Ejiki, and tell his story from the temple steps.

Pelia, too, had been told the story of Gilgarius. Like Arkis, she had listened alone, sitting at her grandfather's feet, transported into a world which fed months of nightmares. But that was a long time ago before the trouble with her mother and father, which estranged them from her grandfather and which spilled into the other farms around and the village, creating disbelief and resentment. It was a bad time and the nightmares were made worse because of it.

Pelia looked down on the stranger and wondered about him. Where had he come from and why had he ventured so far from the trade road? It had been a long time since any traveller had visited the farm and even longer since it was someone close to her own age. She thought about the stranger and his beautiful horse, and smiled and shook her head before urging the goats down the other side of the knoll where they could spend the dying light foraging on better vegetation.

***

We were loaded onto carts and set off to the creature's lair, said Han.

General Sperius said we would be fed to Gilgarius at dawn the next day. Our mothers sobbed and wailed as they walked a little of the way behind us. Eventually they fell back and we travelled on in a tense, silent trance, decked in hastily made garlands of pathetic scrub flowers.

After a while, as the truth of what loomed before us really sank in, some of the children began to cry for their mothers. I managed to dam my own tears, not wanting to show the fear that was eating me – fear which, in its own way, was as rapacious as Gilgarius's hunger for our young flesh.

We settled for the night within a few hundred strides of the creature's lair and soldiers were set to guard us to prevent escape. Until then it had not occurred to me that liberation was an option but now, the more unlikely it seemed, the more I began to think seriously about it.

For several hours I lay wide awake as the other children slept fitfully, shaking and crying in their dreams. I knew I could not just run away from the guards; they would surely see or hear me and try to stop me. But I was unable to stop thinking, thinking, thinking, until my brain hurt so much I feared that my head would burst.

I tried to distract myself with thoughts of my mother and father. They had a hard life. Although they had tried to have many children, I was the only one who had survived birth – and now even I was to be taken from them. Then, to gain some small comfort, I started to think of a story my mother once told me about a little ledbuk that had been separated from his mother by a pack of hungry wolves and was about to be eaten.

In his fright, the fawn ran into a bog and became stuck. The wolves waited on the edge of the bog, working out how to extract their supper. The pack leader favoured sending some young male wolves in to drag the ledbuk out, but there was a general muttering of discontent. In the end, the wolves decided to hide behind a clump of trees, making the ledbuk think he would be safe to pull himself out of the bog.

In due course he managed to drag himself clear, but the poor animal was exhausted and covered in slimy, black, stinking mud. When the wolves broke their cover and ran towards the ledbuk, he froze with fear. The wolves halted their charge at the behest of their leader, who called to the ledbuk to ask why he would not run to give them some sport and an appetite so they could enjoy the chase before eating him.

The ledbuk said nothing, knowing that he could not run fast enough to escape the wolves. Instead, the little creature resigned himself to death. But then one of the wolves sniffed the air and declared he had begun to feel sick.

The wolf asked the pack leader, 'Why does this ledbuk smell so bad?'

'Because he's been in a stinking bog,' the leader replied.

'Come on, let's get him. I'm sure he'll taste better than he smells.'

But the other wolves hesitated.

'What's the matter with you lot? Are you really afraid of a pong?'

It was then that the ledbuk had his idea.

Although it was difficult and took an immense amount of courage, the fawn managed to unfreeze himself a little from his fear and began to sway this way and that way, buckling his front knees so his head flopped to the ground. He started to moan in the most pathetic ledbuk manner imaginable.

'What is it?' asked the superior wolf. 'Are you afraid of being torn apart and eaten?'

'No,' replied the ledbuk. 'I am already dying. I swallowed some of the bog when I fell in and it is starting to poison me. It is inevitable that I will die a slow, agonising death. Please, wolves, kill and eat me now as quickly as you can to spare me a long, lingering end.'

But the wolves hesitated.

'Maybe I'm not so hungry after all,' said one female.

'This pathetic little ledbuk is hardly worth opening one's jaws for,' remarked another.

There were similar murmurings from the other wolves as one by one they slunk away. None of them actually admitted it was the fear of eating poisoned flesh that had ruined their appetites.

Even the wolf leader was heard to say, as he turned to follow his pack, that they'd all eaten rather too much ledbuk lately and needed to vary their diet a little more.

After the wolves finally disappeared into the forest, the young deer got to his feet and ran off in search of his mother. But when he found her, she did not recognise her child. He did not smell like a ledbuk; in fact, he smelled so terrible that she ran away.

The ledbuk was so upset that he lay on the ground and began to cry. When the mother heard the sobs, she stopped in her tracks, realising this pathetic pongy creature was really her son.

At this point of telling the story, my mother's eyes would always fill with her own tears.

'Why are you so sad when the ledbuk has been reunited with his mother?' I once asked her.

'Because to me this story is about the bane of motherhood,' she said. 'A mother will always recognise her child's cry, no matter how far apart they are. Even if she cannot hear it on the wind, she will feel it in her heart.'

It was a memorable story and I recalled her words vividly as I waited to be consumed by Gilgarius. By then I was desperately tired, yet I could not sleep out of fear. But suddenly, despite my anguish, a wonderful thought occurred to me: if a little ledbuk could outwit a pack of wolves, why couldn't I find a way to do the same to Gilgarius?

**

Pelia sat on a stump of a tree watching the goats feeding. She thought again of the stranger and his fine black horse and admired him.

She had never travelled beyond Ejiki, and had only ever been to the city on feast days when she was a child and her parents still lived at the farm. They would walk all day to reach the capital, carrying what little they could afford to give to the temple priests. And once she went with her grandfather to see the hermit.

That was when she was young, before her mother and father left. They carried food and goat's milk to the hermit's cave in the foothills where he spent his days in silence, staring across a valley of scrub to Mother Mountain.

There was a poor track, and the journey Pelia and Han made entirely on foot was hot and arduous. In those days, Han had the vigour of a much younger man and Pelia found it difficult to keep up. The sun was already beginning its steep decline by the time they reached the cave and there was no choice but to spend the night there.

The hermit had greeted Han like a long-lost brother and they had talked until dawn, while Pelia slept fitfully on a bed of dust. Occasionally she woke and caught snatches of their conversation. Gilgarius was mentioned a number of times, as were the names of her mother and her father.

Later, Han told his granddaughter that he and the hermit had been boys together and had worked alongside each other in the fields in the days before Gilgarius came. Pelia had no idea if the hermit was still alive and still staring at the whispering mountain.

She got up from the tree stump and poked at the somnolent dogs with her crook. There was still some good light, but she felt an urge to go home.

***

Despite my terror, I set about making a plan, said Han. At first my thoughts were confused but gradually a strategy began to form. Later, when one of the guards came to check on us, I used the opportunity to put the first part of my plan into operation. I say the first part because, at that moment, I hadn't thought my plan through to its conclusion.

'Sir,' I said. 'Will you talk with me a while?'

He hesitated, then said, 'Aye, that I will, if it makes you feel better.'

He allowed me to clamber out of the cart and we sat with our backs to one of the wheels, staring towards where Gilgarius was slumbering in his temporary lair.

'Is it that you're frightened?' asked the guard. 'Is that why you want to talk to me?'

'Yes,' I said. 'It's the waiting that makes it worse.'

'Poor child,' said the soldier, shaking his head. 'If only we could beat Gilgarius in a fight. I would gladly take my spear to him if it meant saving your lives. But we have been told not to fight; we are just following orders.'

'I know. The creature would kill you as easily as a woman wrings the neck of a chicken and then it would eat you and use your spear as a toothpick.'

'You are a bright young thing,' said the guard. 'It's a shame you've been selected to die like this. But you may be lucky – the creature doesn't want to eat twelve children. He said eleven will do. Perhaps you will be the one he rejects.'

'Why should I not be selected?' I replied. 'What makes me any more worthy of being saved than any other child of our land?'

'You're a brave one, too. I would be screaming with fear if I were in your situation.'

'What's the point in making a fuss? There's nothing I can do. Gilgarius will eat me along with the others and will be appeased – at least for another few days.'

'And then he will start again,' said the guard, his voice heavy with despondency. 'Your life will have been given in vain.'

'It needn't be so,' I said, seizing the moment to advance my plan.

'What do you mean?'

'I want to go talk to Gilgarius – if you'll let me.'

'Why? How will that save you? The creature would just eat you anyway.'

'I can't know for sure what will happen, but Gilgarius may listen. I want to ask him something.'

'Ask what? How will a question save you – and the rest of us?'

'Please let me go to Gilgarius. If he won't listen to me, he will eat me. If he eats me now, it will end this awful waiting.'

'I'm not sure,' said the guard, staring at the ground. 'How do I know you won't run away?'

'I won't, but I can't do anything other than give you my word.'

The guard thought a little while longer and then slowly nodded his head. 'Go child,' he said. 'Go ask the creature your question. But if he seizes you with his scaly claws and tears your limbs apart, please don't scream for it would wake the other children.'

'I won't,' I said, without any confidence I could fulfil such a promise.

The guard, who was barely able to hold back his tears, grasped my hand and shook it firmly. 'If you are consumed, I'll tell the generals that Gilgarius came in a state of hunger and asked for a child to eat to ease him back to his slumber.'

'Your mind is good,' I said.

'Go quickly,' said the soldier, turning his head away so I couldn't see any change in his face that might reveal the true depth of his anguish.

And so I went alone to Gilgarius's lair, armed only with a lighted torch to find the way – and, of course, my fatuous and as yet incomplete plan.

As I approached, the stench of the slumbering creature silhouetted like a small hill against the pallid glow of the moon was so overpowering that it sent me into a coughing fit. This caused Gilgarius to stir and I froze to the spot just ten strides from the monster as one of his giant eyes opened and embraced me with its evil glare. A powerful rumbling vibrated from the creature's very depths and the ground shook as though in the grip of an earthquake.

'What is this?' Gilgarius asked, his voice rolling out from his giant head like a distant thunder. 'Not yet dawn and my breakfast come already?'

'Yes,' I replied. 'Your breakfast indeed, only—'

Gilgarius snorted and I hesitated, suddenly realising I had committed to a stupid quest. Yet I plucked up the courage to continue. 'Only I wish to talk to you before the others come,' I said.

'Others! How many?'

'There are twelve of us, but I have been told you will only eat eleven.'

'Ah, yes, there's no point in being too greedy,' said Gilgarius. 'Eleven is a good number, a feast indeed. Maybe too much even for me at one sitting.'

'Please, listen to me before you consume us,' I said. 'I wish to ask you things about your life, your ways, where you come from, why you live like this.'

Gilgarius lifted his huge head and snorted again. I was bathed in the warm, damp expulsion from his nostrils. I felt sick, both with fear and repulsion.

The creature shifted on to his haunches so he towered above me. 'What is the point of revealing my life and ways to you, child? When the sun rises, you will be eaten and I will end up digesting all I have told you.' He laughed a resonant, mocking laugh.

I shook my head and said, 'You are right. There's no point. I might as well die right now. Please, Gilgarius, eat me now. Eat me to stop me asking more questions about you.'

'You are a strange child,' said the creature. 'No one has ever offered themselves so willingly before. Come to think of it, no one has ever offered themselves at all.'

'Does the thought of my eagerness to die spoil your appetite?' I responded, walking a little closer.

'No . . . no! But I wish to know why you are happy to give yourself.'

'I won't tell you.'

'Why?'

'Because you won't answer *my* questions.'

Gilgarius lowered his huge head and gave a sigh that rustled through the grass like a wind. 'Ask me again what you want to know,' he said.

I stepped forward until I was but three strides from him. His giant head appeared as craggy as a granite mountain in the flickering light of the torch.

'Why did you come here?' I asked.

'I go everywhere,' said Gilgarius. 'I have no homeland.'

'But you must have come from somewhere.'

Gilgarius grunted. 'Yes, I came from somewhere and I still am somewhere. I am always somewhere.'

'But why here?'

'Because I heard there was envy and mistrust between your people and the Bostrati. Borderlands between bad neighbours make happy hunting grounds for such as me.'

'Why?'

'Because humans are strange creatures. You are supposed to be civilised but you are prepared to destroy your fellow kind to gain a league or two of land and seize its resources. Not just land – I am often used by people to help them achieve wealth and power. Before I came here, I was in a place where men who call themselves priests fed me children in exchange for tearing down mountains to expose the gold hidden beneath.'

Gilgarius paused, as if savouring his usefulness to mankind, then he continued. 'You humans believe you are better than all other animals. You call Gilgarius evil, yet your elders and priests were happy to feed your brothers and sisters to me so I would drive the Bostrati from their homes. So, where is the evil spawned?'

'But we would not have been put in this position if you hadn't come.'

Gilgarius growled. 'I came because I knew your people

would feed me. If you lived in harmony with your neighbours and were not a threat to each other, I would starve. As it is, you saw in me a chance to steal Bostrati land. What made your elders think they could get away with it? Surely they should have known that the Bostrati would be no less determined to defend what is theirs.'

'But why do you demand children to eat?'

Gilgarius emitted a rumbling laugh. 'Because young are always sacrificed by your kind. It is your people's tradition to sacrifice children and therefore my tradition to eat them. Also, children taste better.'

'I don't understand.'

'Think about it, child,' said Gilgarius. 'Who are the first to die in times of famine while soldiers feed in readiness for war? And who are forced to work in the fields as soon as they can walk to produce the stores of grain to fatten the soldiers or to trade to get them swords and spears?'

'We have to help our mothers. It has always been so.'

'Yes, indeed. Those mothers who will pluck a baby from their breast and cast it aside to lie beneath a heated soldier.'

'I don't like what you are saying. My mother would lay down her life for me—'

'Your mother has agreed to lay down *your* life. She has given in to soldiers who cannot call themselves men. Surely in a civilised land soldiers would fight to save their children and ease the anguish of their women?'

My mind was confused. My plan was to get close to Gilgarius to find a weakness in him, something that the soldiers could exploit with their weapons; instead he had shown me the disturbing weaknesses of my own people.

I looked towards the eastern horizon and saw the orange glow as the dome of the sun began to peek above the distant mountains. There was little time left and I had achieved nothing with my foolhardy enterprise.

Everything Gilgarius said was painful to take in, but one phrase more than any other began to dominate my mind: *'If you lived in harmony with your neighbours and were not a threat to each other, I could not survive.'*

That was it, I realised. Gilgarius's weakness.

I returned my eyes to the monster. 'Please Gilgarius,' I said. 'It will be dawn soon and you'll wish to eat me with my brothers and sisters. Would you grant me one favour before I'm devoured?'

'Favours I do not grant.'

'But don't you think I deserve one? After all, I have offered to give myself to you without any fuss.'

Gilgarius moved his head towards me so it was barely the length of an arm away from my face. 'You are a strange child. Different from your kin. Probably tastier, too.'

'So?'

'So, I am minded to grant your favour – depending upon what it is.'

'It's simple. I wish to visit the border which defines the land of the Bostrati to see what it is we are being sacrificed for.'

'But you will run away.'

'No, Gilgarius. I'll not run away. You can come with me if you like to make sure.'

'It is highly irregular.'

'Look, if I was going to escape I wouldn't have walked so boldly into your lair offering my young flesh as a meal.'

'True, strange one. Very well, I will let you go. But be back when the full light comes and the rest of my breakfast is brought to me.'

And so I was able to go in search of the Bostrati. I didn't have to walk far before I came across a group of them who'd gathered at the new border to see what Gilgarius was up to. They expressed surprise when they saw my approaching torch light and were probably afraid someone had come in anger. But they soon saw that I was a child and asked me what Gilgarius was doing. I told them that he was about to make a feast of our children, myself included.

A tall, kindly-faced man stepped forward from the group and put his hand upon my shoulder. 'You are a brave boy, coming into the domain of your enemy like this. What do you want?'

'Sir,' I said, 'all I want is to stop the deaths of my brothers and sisters. And if doing that also saves the lives of your children, then both our people will benefit.'

'But how can you stop Gilgarius?' the man asked. 'He'll eat your brothers and sisters and then turn to us to demand our young. There's nothing anyone can do; he's too powerful.'

'You're wrong,' I responded. Then, not fully understanding where the words came from nor the manner of my expressing them, I continued. 'Gilgarius's power is our willingness to fight, our readiness to give life to appease him. But he can't be satisfied; he'll always demand more. Believe me, the only way to defeat this creature is to open our border.'

'But that's madness! We would not give up what has been so hard won.'

'Sir,' I replied, 'it's madness to give Gilgarius a reason to eat children on both sides of the border. I tell you, if the border goes so will Gilgarius. He's a creature who thrives on disputes between peoples. He's exploited our age-old differences to his own ends but we're the ones who are to blame. We must change our thinking. Can't you see?'

'I don't know,' said the man, shaking his head solemnly. 'I'm the leader of this part of our land and I'm ill with worry about what Gilgarius will demand next.'

Still without a true understanding of where my words came from, I persisted. 'Sir, he will demand nothing if we give him nothing on which to base his demands. If we live in peace and harmony and remove the border, Gilgarius won't have anything to bargain with. He won't be able to gain advantage by promising to realign something that does not exist.'

'Child,' said the man, 'you are wise beyond your years.' He turned to two other men who had stepped forward with him. 'Do you hear what this boy says? If we destroy the border, we destroy Gilgarius.'

'How do we do that?' asked one of the men.

The leader turned back to me. 'What do you propose, boy?'

'Sir, I propose you come with me to our land,' I replied. 'We will walk by Gilgarius's lair and you can meet our generals. I'm sure they will not attempt to harm you; they're more concerned about the creature eating our young.'

'And what will that gain?'

'It will show Gilgarius that we are not enemies,' I responded, though in truth I was not sure how Gilgarius would really react.

And therefore it was agreed that a delegation of Bostrati would come with me. I urged them to hurry, fearing Gilgarius would have already eaten some of my brothers and sisters.

We gave the creature's lair a wide berth, moving down wind from him so as not to alert him to our proximity. The first person we met was the soldier who had let me go just two hours before. He'd been looking out for me, fearing to tell the generals where I had gone. 'You are alive, child,' he said, relieved. 'But who are these people?'

'They are Bostrati,' I said boldly. 'Our allies against Gilgarius – our new friends.'

The Bostrati delegation greeted the soldier formally and he responded cautiously. 'I'm not sure, but you do not appear to be evil,' he said.

'No,' said their leader. 'And you are not a monkey in human form.'

We all laughed and the sound of it brought the generals running.

'What is it?' cried General Sperius. 'And who are they?'

'Bostrati,' said I. 'They have come to help us defeat Gilgarius. They are as distraught as us about the deaths our conflict has caused.'

'I cannot ally us with these creatures,' said the general. 'They are our enemies.'

'Not any more,' said the Bostrati leader. 'We're sick and tired of disputing the border. Gilgarius has exploited our differences. This child says that if we declare there is no border there will be nothing to fight over. If there's nothing to fight over then Gilgarius can't play us off against each other.'

General Sperius thought awhile. 'You may be right,' he said at length. 'But what if the creature becomes angry?'

'Leave Gilgarius to me,' I said precociously. 'But follow a little way behind me and be prepared to speak to him.'

I set out towards the creature's lair for the second time. It was now fully light and Gilgarius was sitting on his gigantic haunches, bathing his huge wings in the strengthening sunshine. 'Ah, child,' he said, upon seeing me. 'You have kept your word. You are a remarkable boy.'

'Thank you, Gilgarius,' I replied. 'And I have praise for you.'

'What is that?'

'You're a good teacher.'

'Why do you say that?' laughed the creature.

'I say it because I have learned a valuable lesson from you this day. You provided the key for our salvation and the salvation of our neighbours.'

'A key you say? But how does it work?'

'It has opened your secret, Gilgarius. I know the truth about you.'

'And what is that?'

'That you are not a hunter and you will not pursue prey. You might be built from the worst parts of the fiercest, ugliest and meanest predators, but you are really no more than a cross between an intestinal parasite and a vulture.'

'But I can kill you with one prick of my smallest claw.'

'Not any more, Gilgarius. You have revealed your secret. You can't survive where men are not in conflict, where people live in harmony. See here behind me: the Bostrati leader and our General Sperius are joined in an alliance to defeat you. There'll be no more wars over this border.'

'The child is right,' said the general. 'We've had enough of your menacing greed. Go from this land.'

'Go!' echoed the Bostrati leader. 'There'll be no more of our young offered to you. We know now you can only take what is offered in sacrifice.'

Gilgarius roared in his anger and spread his fibrous wings. He rolled his yellow eyes and raised himself to his fullest height. 'So you now know how to keep your children safe,' he said. 'It is a lesson a long time in the learning.'

'Go!' repeated General Sperius. 'Find some other border to dwell upon.'

And so Gilgarius rose in the air, at first appearing to accept his defeat, but he soon started to scream in frustration and anger. He circled overhead several times, swooping down to intimidate us, but we would not be bowed by his demonstration.

Finally he flew towards our Mother Mountain and perched upon the edge of the smouldering crater, roaring into the void that we and our neighbours had done him badly. 'Your children do not deserve to survive my hunger,' he thundered. 'You have bred them for me, just as surely as they were cows and goats.'

The Akben people assembled at the base of the mountain and looked up in awe, not understanding the reasons for Gilgarius's distress. As their long hair and beards flowed in Gilgarius's wind, they began to pray to Mother Mountain to save our land.

And it was then that the greatest miracle of all happened.

The Mother Mountain, questioned for being too long silent, woke from her slumber and erupted in the face of Gilgarius, spitting out her potent wisdom so that it engulfed the creature completely.

So loud did Gilgarius scream, the monster's cries must have been heard by many tribes beyond the land of the Akben and the Bostrati. Then, behind the spewing of rock and dust, burst a molten fire from the Mother Mountain's womb. Gilgarius's horrendous screeching issued to the heavens in one last writhing frenzy but was soon ended – silenced by our patient protectress.

***

There was a long silence after Han concluded his story. He stared into the distance towards Mother Mountain, which was whispering a benign plume of smoke into the cloudless, darkening sky, a world away from the violent explosion that had engulfed Gilgarius.

Tears began to bubble from the old man's eyes and he dabbed at them with the sleeve of his tunic. 'Please forgive me,' he said. 'I'm always emotional when I remember those terrible times long ago.'

'It's a remarkable story,' said Arkis. 'Most amazing.'

Han shook his head. 'It is but the start of my tale,' he said. 'Maybe you would care to hear more tomorrow – that is, if you are in no hurry to continue your journey. Although perhaps I have delayed you enough already.'

Arkis looked over to the stockade from where he could hear Rashi whinnying and stamping as if eager to move on. 'I dearly would like to hear more about your life,' he said. 'But you should not tire yourself.'

Han smiled and wiped away a fresh tear with the back of his bony hand. 'I'm sure we're both tired,' he said. 'You from a long journey and I from my long life. I don't know how far you've travelled, but I've no doubt you will have suffered many tribulations. Resting here a while may do you some good. One night, two nights – a whole month, it makes no difference to me.'

'You are generous.'

'No, I am selfish. We rarely have visitors here and it gives me great pleasure to relate the story of my life. Believe me, there's a great deal more to tell.'

Arkis hesitated before responding. 'I wouldn't wish to continue imposing on your hospitality,' he said at length.

'You would not be imposing.'

'I certainly would like learn more about your life and I could use my time here to explore the land around to see what opportunities are to be had.'

'Then stay as long as you like.'

'But I could not do so without making some payment.'

Han shook his head disapprovingly. 'Nonsense. You would be my guest. I have no need of payment.'

'As I say, I would not wish to be a burden.'

'You would be no burden.'

'It's not just me – my horse needs fodder and water. If I'm not allowed to pay, I cannot remain.'

The old man seemed genuinely crestfallen. 'Then you will not be able to hear the rest of my story.'

Another period of awkward silence ensued, punctuated only by the noises of the goats and hens and the occasional whinnying from Arkis's mount.

'Perhaps you should think about it,' said Han at length.

'Yes,' said Arkis. 'Perhaps I should. As for your hospitality tonight, I require no special sleeping place. I can rest beneath the tree here. I've grown used to spending nights with nothing between me and the stars and just my old bear skin to keep out the chilling wind.'

'If you insist.'

'I do.' Arkis paused for a moment, scratching his beard,

thinking. Then he said, 'I may have a solution to the problem of payment for your hospitality, which would make me happy to stay longer.'

'Oh, and what is that?'

'I wish to buy a goat from you.'

'A goat? What would you want with a goat?'

'Perhaps it would make a good companion for Rashi during our onward journey.'

'My friend, a goat would surely slow down your travelling. If you allow the creature to wander in its natural way, it would end up browsing hither and thither, ensuring you would travel just as far backward or sideways as forward.'

'A fair point,' said Arkis with a laugh. 'Yet I still like the idea of buying a goat from you. Perhaps you could keep it here until I decide what to do with it.'

'It's a strange idea.'

'I suppose it is but please hear me out. Because it would be my goat, I could not expect Pelia to look after it without some payment for her trouble. Do you follow me?'

'I'm not at all sure…'

'Well, to ensure you receive the required payment in the event that I can't afford to honour my obligation to settle the debt, you'll have to keep the goat as compensation. That way, I'm neither burdened with a goat nor with debt for its upkeep. What do you think?'

Han responded with a chuckle, but it quickly turned into a coughing fit that took an uncomfortably long time to subside. 'Forgive me,' he said breathlessly when he had begun to recover from his exertion. 'I'm not as resilient in wind as I used to be.'

He wiped his mouth with the sleeve of his tunic and Arkis couldn't help but notice a smudge of blood on the material.

'Your suggested transaction is the oddest thing I've heard in a long time,' Han continued with a smile and a shake of his head.

'The point is, do you accept it?'

'I suppose I have no choice as I desire you to hear the rest of my story.'

'Then that's settled.'

'But I will reveal no more of it tonight,' said Han. 'I'm tired and need to reacquaint myself with my cot.'

'Then you can resume your story when you are rested. Although, as I say, I would like to also spend some time exploring the land around here. Perhaps you could continue on my return.'

'Yes, Arkis, perhaps I could.'

Arkis slept soundly among the roots of the chatka tree, wrapped in his bear skin. The sun was merely a shallow arc nudging over the horizon when he woke to the sound of Han's granddaughter beginning her daily work milking the goats.

Arkis walked over to a clump of scrubby bushes to relieve himself before entering the stockade. Pelia was singing softly, sitting on a stump of wood, her back arched and both hands gently squeezing a nanny's teats. Her face was turned away from him and he could not decide quite what to do. He wished to attract her attention but her voice was incongruously hypnotic among the bleating goats and chuckling hens and he desired the singing to go on.

A dog lying in the shadow growled on his approach and Rashi whinnied and danced, alerting Pelia to his presence. Abruptly, she stopped singing and turned her face to him, still massaging the nanny's teats.

'I didn't mean to disturb you,' he said apologetically. 'Your song is lovely.'

'I merely sing to calm the goats and make the milking easier,' she said with an embarrassed smile.

Arkis crouched by her side. 'Last night, your grandfather agreed to sell me one of your goats.'

Pelia laughed. 'What would a traveller want with a goat?'

'That's what Han said.'

'And the answer?'

Arkis explained his reason behind the convoluted mode of payment.

By this time Pelia had finished milking the nanny and she pushed the animal away, her hide pail almost full. 'Your idea is very odd, but if my grandfather has agreed to it, I suppose I must also.' She got to her feet. 'So, which will you choose?' she said, waving a hand over her animals.

'I thought you would choose one for me.'

'You are perhaps too trusting.'

Arkis reached into his pouch and excavated the same gold piece he had thrown into the air to distract the two robbers. 'Maybe one that is worth this,' he said.

'But that is gold,' Pelia responded with a gasp. 'Enough to buy many goats in Ejiki's market.'

'We are leagues from the city, which makes me a captive buyer,' said Arkis. 'I'm really at your mercy.'

'It's a pity your gold can't buy you a cure for madness,' said Pelia.

'That's true, so I might as well use it to buy a goat.'

***

Arkis was absent from Han's farm for two days and nights. His journey to Ejiki took almost all of the first day because he allowed Rashi to go at her own pace. She picked her way along the easier parts of the track and stopped as she wanted when a scrub bush or bank of dry grass offered a little something to forage on. Occasionally Arkis dismounted to give the mare relief from his weight and she walked companionably at his side as if an equal. Once they stopped at a small settlement with a cluster of mud-brick houses and Arkis bought bread and beer from a man who made earthenware pots. Water was drawn from the well for Rashi and she snickered her gratitude.

Arkis reached the outskirts of Ejiki as night fell and found hospitality at a one-eyed bronze-worker's forge. The man's wife made a goat stew, placing the bronze pot on the same charcoal fire her husband used to melt the ingots of copper and tin. After they had eaten, Arkis watched his host at his work; the man raised the temperature of his forge by forcing air into its heart from goatskin bellows then poured molten metal into sand moulds that offered precise shapes for the objects he wished to fashion.

Arkis learned that a few years before, when the bronze worker was still learning the fundamentals of his craft, a contaminated batch of molten metal had exploded from its crucible. A fiery glob took out one of his eyes, leaving a curdled socket with a black hole at its centre. The eye was so badly disfigured that it could not be blinked and it continually leaked tears, which the man was forced to dab with the folded hem of his cloak.

Arkis and his host talked into the night. The bronze worker was fascinated by anything to do with metal. He delighted in the magic of his craft, especially when working with gold, but he rarely had a chance to do so such was the scarcity of that metal.

Arkis explained the purpose of his visit to Akbenna and the bronze worker said he had heard of Han. 'Now, he is one who knows where to find gold,' he said. 'If he tells you where it's hidden, be sure to let me know.'

Arkis rode into Ejiki before dawn. It was not a big city, but then Akbenna was not a big country. Most of the homes were built from mud bricks but the temple that dominated the main square from a small hill was constructed, at least in part, from blocks of sandstone.

Arkis dismounted to lead Rashi across the city's main square, which was deserted save for one corner where a huddle of traders had camped with their camels and donkeys. The animals had been temporarily relieved of their burdens and the men and beasts had nothing to do but sit or lie about in the dust waiting for the city to waken. Arkis spent time with them, speaking about his own travels and trades. They shared their food generously but had not enough spare for Rashi. Arkis begged his leave and rode the mare back the way he came, letting her meander in search of sustenance.

The second night, Arkis paid for a cot in a tavern. It was the closest village to Han's farm, a village he had deliberately skirted around on his way to Ejiki. The innkeeper was a large man who gave his name as Goman and they talked over beer.

When the conversation got around to Han, the innkeeper shook his head and laughed. 'Next time you see the old man, ask him where the gold is. I'd love to know, and so would many others.'

Arkis said nothing.

The next morning, he returned to Han's little farm and the old man greeted him with a wave of his stick. 'I didn't think you'd come back,' he said.

'Nothing would have kept me from returning,' said Arkis. 'I know there's so much more you can tell me.'

'Then you shall hear it.'

***

It is almost eighty summers since Gilgarius fell into the fiery breath of the Mother Mountain, said Han. That was when childhood ended for me. When Karmus discovered my part in what had happened, he made me sit in a chair made from the finest chatka wood and they got four strong men to lift me high and parade me through Ejiki.

I was feted by cheering crowds and, as you can imagine, my head grew as big as a halibom – and that is a very large gourd of fruit, my friend. Karmus ordered a feast on my behalf to which all the people in the Border Valley came. The Bostrati soldiers who had helped bring about Gilgarius's downfall were also there.

Although our food resources were minimal in those days, everyone brought something to the tables laid out in the square. Wonderful music was played on nose flutes, wood chimes and goatskin drums and much beer and wine were consumed.

My diminutive father, whom nobody ever seemed to notice, was so proud of me. His face became locked in a toothless smile that was still there hours later when he was sleeping off his over-indulgence. My mother, on the other hand, became quiet as if she already knew and feared the consequences of my new fame.

She took me aside and cautioned me to remain humble. 'You are the son of a poor farmer. You have no right to anything beyond working in the fields and being fed for the privilege, if you are lucky. Do not let this feting change your destiny or the destiny of your family, which was pre-ordained by Mother Mountain. She knows fame and fortune are not for the likes of us. We should be happy that we can toil in her shadow and be thankful for whatever she gives us in return.'

My mother's words stung, and hurt me in a terrible way. I looked at her differently for the first time, fleetingly feeling pity and shame. She had always been thin but now she seemed more wizened, diminished, as if wishing to disappear from what was happening to me. As I looked at her, unable to respond to her words, I imagined her vanishing completely until nothing would be left but her dusty bones.

It was the first time I realised that I was as tall as her. Soon she would have to look up to me. My father was not much taller than my mother and he, too, would eventually have to look up to me. I would soon be big enough to speak out my indignation and demand to know what right they had to determine *my* future just because *they* had chosen to remain trapped in such a penurious existence.

At the feast, after everyone had eaten, Karmus waved his robed arms to command silence. He started to address the crowd with me sitting at his side, still on the chatka chair as if it were a throne. 'Today has been a remarkable one in the history of Akbenna,' he began. 'And it is all thanks to this boy.'

The crowd cheered and Karmus turned to me, smiling warmly, his long white beard animated by the warm evening breeze. Then he officially welcomed the Bostrati delegation and said the enmity between our two peoples was now ended. And the crowd cheered again.

I thought that would be the end of the speech and I could go home to bed, for I had been awake for two days and desperately needed sleep. But Karmus had much more to say, particularly about my future. I don't know whether he had consulted the other elders or Medzurgo, the head priest, or had decided to do this on the spur of the moment, encouraged by the excitement of the evening. I sat there, hardly able to keep my eyes open yet wide enough awake to realise my life was to be mapped out for me by the most powerful man in the land.

'Han has held the destiny of our people in his hands,' Karmus declared, his voicing tremulous with emotion. 'He has helped seal peace with our neighbours, the Bostrati.'

The crowd cheered again. Karmus raised a hand to quiet them so he could continue his announcement. 'Now, my friends, I desire Han to make a journey to the land of our northern neighbours, the Polasti, to achieve the same objective by explaining our peaceful aspirations.'

I was not expecting to hear such a declaration – that I would travel to another neighbour's land. I began to shake.

'This boy will be an emissary,' Karmus went on, 'creating good relations between the Akbenna and any other people or tribe willing to live in peace with us. The days of fighting and squabbling must be truly over. Han has shown us what can be achieved when mistrust and fear come up against the wisdom of an innocent child.'

And so he went on beyond the length of the sunset, and the crowd hung on his every word. By the time he had finished, my fate was sealed. Only fleetingly did I hear the echo of my mother's words, which were soon too faint to be taken seriously or even acknowledged.

For all my supposed wisdom, it didn't occur to me that I was about to exchange one form of servitude to my parents for another to my people.

The next morning Karmus and the head priest, Medzurgo, came to my simple home while I was still sleeping. They waited patiently outside beneath this very tree, which was old even then, while my mother silently shook me awake. She did not need to speak; her eyes said everything that she thought was wrong.

My father, still drunk from the night before and with the same slack smile on his face, greeted Karmus with a frenzied handshake and offered him and Medzurgo a gourd of goat's milk, the only sustenance our humble hospitality had to hand. Wisely they declined the offering, leaving my father to slurp the whole down, including the bloated bluebottles that were floating atop the milk.

Then we sat here while Karmus revealed the detail of his plan for my life.

Yes, I hadn't dreamt it. I was to travel to the land of the Polasti to spread the Akben message of peace. I would not travel alone but be escorted by two companions: General Sperius's eldest son Garia, a junior officer in our army, and a much older man called Edbersa, who was to take care of all our practical needs.

For many years Edbersa had served the elders and the priests in the temple at Ejiki, where he'd gained a reputation as a sullen but obedient servant. Rumour had it that he'd never ventured outside the walls of the city, though I was later to find out this was not so.

Karmus said our small expedition was to set off once the hottest part of the year had past – three returns of the full moon – and asked if I had any questions.

'Yes,' I said, casting a glance at Medzurgo. 'Why will no elder or priest travel with us?'

Karmus laughed and stroked his beard as if he were stroking a cat. 'Your precocity is amusing, Han. And I will answer your question by repeating a phrase I used last night – *the wisdom of an innocent child.* It is supposed, generally quite rightly, that wisdom is achieved through age and experience but, as you demonstrated with Gilgarius, we older people can sometimes mistake our various judgements for wisdom.

'We believed we were being wise when we tried to shield ourselves from an outside world we saw as threatening and corrupt. We judged this because our troubled experience with people like the Bostrati told us this was a perfectly sensible position. We believed also that we could buy better land with the sacrifice of our young to Gilgarius, but again this turned out to be a grossly ill-judged position. I thought I was a wise old man but I confess I never would have seen our predicament as you saw it – that it was of our own making. You see, Han, we have been so conditioned by experience that such wisdom that we have has been contaminated.'

All the time he spoke, Medzurgo was standing in his crimson robes, watching me silently with narrowed eyes. I'd never been so close to our leading priest before and felt intimidated by his presence. There was something about him that unnerved me. He must have detected my apprehension for he tried to reassure me with a smile. His beard parted but there was only a sinister black void where the smile should have been.

Karmus, on the other hand, had a genuinely warm disposition. He laughed and his blue eyes, as bright as any young person's, radiated his strange joy that he had been tested by age and experience and found wanting. 'You know, that is probably the only really wise thing I have ever said,' he boomed.

My father laughed too, and urged me to accept Karmus's words even though he hadn't answered my question satisfactorily. But my mother was not happy. She'd been standing quietly by the well, taking it all in but saying nothing until Karmus and Medzurgo prepared to take their leave. Only then did she step forward. 'Why will my son only have two men to protect him? Surely two men are not enough to fight off bandits and hostile tribes.'

Karmus smiled tolerantly while Medzurgo shook his head, frowning.

'Sending a full detachment of soldiers with Han would not, I fear, afford him greater protection,' Karmus said soothingly. 'Indeed, it could put his life in peril. The presence of Akben soldiers in a foreign land without invitation would be viewed as an attempted invasion. It would have precisely the opposite effect to the one intended, which is to cultivate peaceful relations.'

My mother shook her head slowly but said nothing more. She knew my fate was sealed.

The new moon returned twice and we heard nothing more from Karmus, so I carried on my daily grind, helping my mother and father to tend the goats and grow what meagre crops the land would permit. Then one day one of the temple servants came to take me to meet my travelling companions, Garia and Edbersa, in Ejiki.

Garia, a tall fair-haired man who had not lived much

more than twenty years, was dressed in a grey-and-blue tunic, the uniform of our army. He greeted me warmly enough on the steps of the temple but Edbersa, the servant, evaded my hesitant offer of a clasp of arms, scowling through his dark beard. He had little hair on his head, was built like a barrel and wore leather breeks and vest. His bare, hairy arms were long and sinewy. Garia told me later it was from heaving sacks of grain and casks of ale and wine in the temple cellar.

Edbersa didn't seem to be looking forward to the expedition while Garia chattered and clicked like an excited jinterbuck. He showed off the magnificent silver horse he would be riding and the much less impressive, but eminently serviceable, cart for Edbersa and I to travel in that would be pulled by two much less impressive, yet eminently sturdy, brown mares. They were chosen because both had delivered foals that had not survived so we would be able to drink the milk they were still making.

'There will be plenty of provisions for the first month,' Garia declared. 'We have everything we need – dried meat and fish from the Bostrati, goat's milk and cheese, lajtaya tea and flour to make flat bread. That will be Edbersa's duty, in addition to driving the cart and setting up our campfire every night.'

Edbersa continued scowling as he slunk back into the temple and I wondered what trouble this man might cause for us.

I asked Karmus to reconsider his choice of cart driver and cook, but he was adamant. 'For once – and maybe it is the only time I will ask this of you – trust *my* wisdom.'

He gave no reason why I should, but something about the way he said this persuaded me. Maybe this time it was right that age and experience should overrule the instinctive concern of a child, no matter how wise that child appeared to be. It seems I had no choice but to allow Karmus's own wisdom to be tested.

During this meeting I was measured for a fine new tunic

that I would wear on our journey. I also learned what was expected of me in the cause of neighbourly relations.

'All you need to do when you reach Polastia is to tell the king the story of your encounter with Gilgarius and the lessons we can all learn from the experience,' said Karmus. 'Tell the king also that we will welcome emissaries should he wish to send any to accompany you on your return. Garia and Edbersa understand what is necessary and will help you in your role.'

I spent the remaining days working in the fields with my mother and father, gathering in the last of our meagre harvest of grain. On my final night at home after we had eaten, my father sat where I am sitting now and began to cry. My mother just stared at the sun rapidly setting over the horizon. She did not cry then but I had already heard her sobbing that morning at dawn as she milked a goat, drying her tears on the animal's fine coat.

She could not bring herself to speak to me, even as we ate around our fire and later when we worked together for the last time in the fields. It was as if she was anticipating the time when someone would come to tell her I was dead. In a way, I suppose she had already begun her grieving.

The next night I spent in the temple with Garia and Edbersa, sleeping on sacks in the store cellar. Garia was as excited as when I had first met him and Edbersa just as sullen as before.

I changed out of rough attire into my elegant new tunic and we set off as dawn broke. Garia trotted off astride his fine steed, leading our cart through the city gates, with only the Karmus, General Sperius and our stern head priest, Medzurgo, to watch us leave.

As the city walls receded behind us, I felt the sense of excitement changing to unease. For the first time, I wondered why I had not challenged Karmus's plan for me. Although tradition demanded that you never questioned elders on any point, I could not understand why I had blindly accepted the fateful path being mapped out before me. I felt I should have asked Karmus why I had been given no say in my destiny.

I wanted to shout to Garia, who was riding around twenty horse strides ahead of us, to ask if his role had also been forced upon him. But I could see by his proud and purposeful demeanour in the saddle that there was no unwillingness; for him, this was going to be a great adventure.

I turned to Edbersa, wondering how to ask the question of him. His stare was fixed ahead and he noisily worked phlegm into his throat before fluting it into the dull light. Then he flicked the reins to hurry the mares along and grunted as if annoyed at their sluggish response.

'Don't ask me anything,' he said, turning his severe head ever so slightly towards me so he could see me with the almost impenetrably black pupil floating in the cream of his eye. 'I'm not in the mood for prattle.'

How did he know I was about to ask him a question? I thought I detected a smirk on his face, but it was difficult to see beneath his thick, dark beard.

We journeyed in silence for many leagues until I became overwhelmed by homesickness and started to cry for my mother and father. Edbersa grunted something unintelligible, urging the mares on as if to send me a clear message about my wimpishness. I climbed into the back of the cart and tried to sleep off my unhappiness on the flour sacks, but the rattle and bounce of the wheels on the rutted track would not allow it.

Occasionally we halted when we came to a confusing fork in the track. The first time this happened, Garia pulled from his saddlebag a rolled-up piece of cured goatskin with lines and squiggles scratched on it, of which I'd never seen the like before. Garia called it a map and said it showed all the lands around. He stared at it for a while, then glanced at the position of the sun. He seemed confident in his map-reading and consulted it frequently, nodding thoughtfully as he judged our route towards the foothills of the western mountains.

But first we had to cross a dry, dusty basin populated only by isolated Akbenna settlements. Occasionally, we saw families working the land, trying to entreat scrub to produce food; several times we came across children even younger than me herding goats into the arid bushlands where they might find boya berries or cleminia leaves to eat.

At noon we made our first stop for food in the shade of a giant rock, which had been sculpted into an intriguing elephantine shape by our land's abrasive sandstorms. I only knew about elephants because legend said herds of them had roamed our once-verdant land. I'd never seen one and only knew the shape of them because my father had scraped a picture with a stick in our garden dust. He'd said that his father had drawn the same picture, and his father before him, so no one would forget what elephants looked like. But my mother shook her head and said elephants were just a myth like Gilgarius. But, of course, that was before Gilgarius showed himself to be a reality.

We ate strips of dried goat's meat, which Edbersa served on broad panapa leaves along with a thick lumpy paste made from samoya fruit and the root of the tampica. It was more food than I would have had to eat at home, and it lifted my spirits as well as filling my belly until it ached. Garia and I washed our food down with goat's milk while Edbersa gulped something pungent and unfamiliar from the leather flask he carried on his belt.

Soon we were on our way again. The sun beat down upon us and Edbersa cursed beneath his breath. Both he and Garia had to wear leather hats to keep their heads and necks from baking, but I was used to working out in the fields in such fierce heat and needed only my long dark hair to protect me.

By the middle of the afternoon we had begun the gentle climb towards the foothills and it was easier to find rocks to shade us. We stopped for refreshment and let the horses graze some half-decent scrub, their legs hobbled. Again, Garia consulted his map. I asked if I could also see the parchment.

'Aye, of course, lad,' said Garia, rolling it out fully. 'But you will not understand the marks and symbols it shows. I will not pretend I do either. My duty is to read those lines there.' He pointed to some straight lines and some squiggly ones. 'That one is the route we seek. It takes us out of Akbenna, leading us to the land of the Polasti through those foothills and over the mountains.'

The map was busy with unfathomable symbols but there were also little drawings that obviously represented mountains, rivers and forests. At the top, however, was something far more intriguing: a great expanse of blue with little wavy lines randomly marked across it, like birds with their wings outstretched.

'Is that blue country unknown to anyone?' I asked, placing a finger upon that part of the map.

Garia laughed. 'No, Han – have you never heard of the sea?'

I didn't know how to answer Garia, for although I had heard of the sea I was like my mother with elephants and thought it a myth. 'I have heard stories that monsters live in the sea,' I said. 'Creatures even bigger than Gilgarius.'

'It may be true, Han. I have heard that huge sea serpents inhabit the depths. But, as I have never been to the sea, I can't say for certain what we might find there.'

All the time we were talking, Edbersa was sitting with his back against a rock, staring into the distance, occasionally taking a swig of his mysterious liquor and wiping his mouth with the back of his hairy hand. 'That sea has almost as many names as the ships that sail on it,' he said enigmatically in a manner that did not invite a response.

We travelled for the rest of the day through the gently rising land close to the edge of Akbenna, seeing no other people but occasionally hearing the distant barking of wild dogs. As darkness fell, we set up our first night camp and made a fire from what wood and kindling we could find scattered on the dusty ground. Edbersa created the first spark using a mysterious clicking device that he produced from an ebony box. I longed to ask what it was but was too afraid he might snap at me for being insolent.

We made a supper of dried meat and goat's milk as the sun fell behind the mountains. I yawned, exhausted from the day's travelling; it was the longest and most uncomfortable journey I had ever made or thought anyone else could have made.

Garia laughed at me and began to kick earth over our camp fire. 'It is time for sleep,' he said.

'Leave the fire!' Edbersa told him fiercely. 'We need flames to keep wild dogs and wolves at bay.'

Garia hesitated as if he did not know whether to obey Edbersa, who had barked what amounted to an order even though he was no soldier. But Garia finally demurred with a smile and made a little bow to Edbersa. I was confused by the exchange. I thought Garia was our leader; now I did not know which of these two men had the higher authority – the soldier with the fine bearing or the temple servant with all his sullen mysteriousness.

Garia pulled his bed roll from his horse, which he called Melimari, meaning 'spirit of the wind' in old Akbenna. It was a warm night, so he settled a few yards from the fire. I went to sleep on the cart among the sacks of flour. Edbersa stayed awake by the fire, occasionally swigging from his leather flask. I do not know whether he slept at all, for when I woke in the middle of the night to go for a piss behind a rock he was still sitting there, staring at the glowing embers of the fire.

As I climbed back into the cart Edbersa looked up. 'Are you frightened?' he asked in his low, resonant voice.

'Yes,' I said. 'I'm very frightened.'

'You are wise to be so. Fear prepares us so we can handle bad things. You can't always rely on bravery when it comes to danger because it can make us act foolishly but you can trust your fear, for it will tell you when danger should not be confronted.'

He was looking over at Garia, who was fast asleep, his back to the fire. He lobbed another log on the embers, throwing up a cloud of ash and sparks. 'Do not worry,' he said. 'I'll keep the fire going. Go back to sleep.'

'Are there really wild dogs and wolves out there?'

Edbersa lifted his head and I could see him smiling in the fire glow. 'I'm sure there are,' he said.

'Are they really dangerous?'

'Yes, Han, they are – but not as dangerous as the wild men who might be watching us.'

***

Arkis found Pelia some way beyond the farm sitting in the shade of an ancient tree even larger than the chatka he had slept beneath. This tree had gnarled branches reaching out in every direction like the grasping claws of some giant mythical creature. An image of Gilgarius crossed his mind.

Thirty or so goats were also lying in the shade of the tree, stricken motionless by the heat. Pelia's rough dogs were panting and scratching at her feet.

Pelia smiled shyly when she heard Arkis's approach, greeting him with a hesitant wave of a hand. It was clear that her duties on such a hot day had left her exhausted. She would have risen very early to milk the goats and take them on their daily expedition to find whatever meagre pickings of vegetation were out there before the strengthening sun drove her to find shade nearer home.

'I'm sorry if I've disturbed you,' he said.

'You haven't,' she replied. 'I was about to put the goats into the stockade but I can do it later. In this heat they will not wander far.'

Arkis joined her in the shade, employing one of the tree's surface roots as a seat. He cast his eye over the browsing goats. 'Which one is mine?'

Pelia laughed and pointed to one of the nannies which was suckling a young kid. 'See, you are already profiting from your purchase,' she said.

'I may make a trader yet,' Arkis replied with a chuckle. His expression quickly became serious. 'I'm concerned about Han,' he said. 'He is persevering with his remarkable story but I fear he is very weak. And I heard him coughing in the night.'

'It happens nearly every night these days,' said Pelia, getting to her feet. 'He is old and frail now. No one knows exactly how old. My mother, Akona, said he was at least sixty when I was born. He outlived Esta, my grandmother, by many years.'

'He's probably stopped counting the years. Old people do.'

'That's true.' Pelia closed her eyes and swatted away a fly. 'He became ill last winter when the weather was very bad. The snow stayed on Mother Mountain longer than anyone could remember and he began to have coughing fits. But you have made a difference. His days are long and lonely when I have to spend so much time looking after the goats and the crops. Your presence has brightened his life.'

'Your grandfather is a fascinating man,' said Arkis. 'His recollection of those times long ago is so clear.'

Pelia rose to her feet, picked up her staff and began prodding the goats into movement. She said, 'Some people in the village believe that grandfather is an old fool.'

Arkis shook his head. 'I've been to the village,' he said. 'It's clear to me who the fools are.'

***

On our second morning of travelling we rose with the sun and set off with little more than a mouthful of bread and cheese to break our fast, said Han. We started climbing almost immediately as we journeyed into the foothills, which Garia called the Mandas after a tribe that once lived among them. I asked him what had happened to these people and he just shook his head.

The ground was stony and made riding in the cart very uncomfortable. Occasionally I jumped down and trotted alongside because it was easier than having my spine jolted each time the wheel rode over a boulder. Edbersa kept looking into the hills around us and I guessed that he was watching out for wild men.

Eventually we reached a sandy plateau and I rode in the cart for a little while until more stones began to jolt the wheels. Once again I jumped to the ground and ran alongside the cart.

After a hundred strides or so, I noticed the colour of the stones had changed. They were no longer varying shades of orange or brown, nor were they round and smooth; they had become white and were all manner of shapes, many of them with ragged edges. Some were long and more or less straight, others were thin and bowed and many were small and knuckled.

It took me only a little time to realise that these were the bleached bones of dead creatures and they were scattered all across the plateau. But what creatures had they been? Wolves, wild dogs or domestic animals such as goats and cattle? I knew not.

Garia came to a halt just ahead of us. Edbersa pulled up the cart and threw him a look of annoyance. He flicked the reins so they slapped the mares' withers to get them moving again.

'Why don't you tell him what these bones really are, Garia?'

Garia laughed nervously and coaxed Melemari to walk on. 'He is a young boy. He doesn't need to know such bad things.'

'Then *I* shall tell him,' said Edbersa. 'It is important that no truth is kept from him.' He turned to me. 'They are the bones of murdered Mandas people. Hundreds of men, women and children were massacred here.'

I was too stunned to ask why or who had done this, but Edbersa went on to explain anyway. 'A fierce tribe of wild men carried out the deed, Han. Wild men whose descendants still roam these hills.'

Garia started moving again, apparently not wishing to listen to Edbersa's words. I had no such escape. I clambered onto the cart as he spat out what had happened many generations ago in all its gory detail.

'The wild men took their axes and hacked the Mandas to pieces in their huts as they slept. They spared no one, even cutting unborn babies from their mothers' wombs and skewering them to the earth with sharpened stakes to ensure they did not survive and grow. These wild men were rumoured to eat human flesh but, when they massacred the Mandas, there were too many to eat and they left most of the bodies to be consumed as carrion. But even for the vultures and the wolves there were too many dead, and the bodies were left to rot in the hot sun. These are their bleached bones.'

Edbersa urged the mares on, as if he was unnerved by his own story and wanted to be away from there. 'You are seeing it, Han,' he said. 'You are seeing it for yourself, for we are passing through a killing ground and these are the bones of the Mandas.'

We travelled for a while longer then Garia halted his horse by a large white mound of rocks. The young soldier stared at the formation and when we caught up, we could see why he did so. It was a hill built with skulls. Among them I could see the small skulls of the babies, some so tiny they must have been those of the unborn.

'The wild men built this as a warning to everyone, including the few Mandas to escape death here,' said Edbersa solemnly. He laughed humourlessly. 'It says keep away. And here we are riding through the plateau of death with but one soldier to guard us – and he not long out of boyhood into the bargain.'

Garia pulled his rein hard, swirling Melemari to face Edbersa. 'And what good would a brigade of soldiers do when our purpose is to spread words of peace?' asked the young soldier, echoing Karmus's words. 'Men laden with swords and spears would be seen as invaders. We are ambassadors for Akbenna and must not forget it.'

Edbersa grunted something in response that I did not catch, but it made Garia smile. Then, as if we were all drawn by the same thought, the three of us looked beyond the scattered bones and the mound of skulls to the hills around us. I half expected the wild men to emerge from their caves and charge down upon us.

'Come on,' said Garia. 'Enough morbidity. Let us leave this place.'

So we journeyed on through the worst heat of the day to get as far away from the Mandas' bones as we could, stopping only when we needed to rest the horses and give them water.

We left the plateau and travelled along a pass which guided us between two peaks that thrust their jagged rocks high into the sky. Garia consulted his map and concluded that they formed a grand gateway to a new land.

'Have they a name?' I asked.

'They each have a symbol but I can't understand what they mean,' said Garia.

'The Mandas called these mountains the Pillars of Hallas,' said Edbersa.

Garia looked at him thoughtfully. 'You seem to know quite a lot about the Mandas, Edbersa, which is a surprise for one so little travelled.'

Edbersa spat on the ground and grunted. 'I'll make a fire,' he said.

We ate bread and dried meat and drank fresh, sweet

mare's milk as the goat's milk had curdled in the heat and was undrinkable. There was little talking for we were all exhausted.

I fell asleep leaning against a boulder but the position proved uncomfortable and I woke after a little while. Edbersa was sitting hunched by the fire, just like he had been during our first camp, but this time with his eyes closed. Garia was asleep on his bed roll a little away from the fire.

I needed a piss so I clambered up an incline to where I could do it privately.

That's when I saw the wild man.

My instinct was to cry out, but my throat was constricted by fear. He appeared so suddenly before me that I had no time to flee. I could see him clearly for he was no more than four strides away, his oiled body glistening in the moonlight. His skin was daubed with white lines and circles, and bones adorned his entire body. Some had been strung together to make a necklace and were tied into his long hair; some hung from braiding around his waist. Two of the bones dangled either side of his penis which, painted white and with its foreskin removed, also looked like a bone. In one hand he held a spear and in the other a small round shield made from thick hide.

Then, as quickly as he appeared, the wild man was gone.

I ran back to the camp and shook Edbersa awake. 'I've seen a wild man,' I said, my voice squeaking with both fear and excitement.

Garia also woke and jumped up instinctively, grabbing his sword from its scabbard. 'Where was he?'

'Over there.' I pointed to the rocks where I'd gone for a piss.

Garia hesitated. He obviously did not like the idea of going into the shadows where the wild man could be hiding in wait for him.

Edbersa remained sitting, staring at the fire. 'Describe him to me, Han.'

I gave as good a description as I could, emphasising the

frightening nature of the man with his bodily markings and the strange look of his white-painted penis. In those days, I'd not heard of the practice of circumcision.

'This wild man will not harm us,' said Edbersa.

'But how do you know?' I protested. 'You did not see how savage he looked.'

'You have to trust me, Han. Now get on the cart and go to sleep.'

But for many hours I could not sleep; it needed only the slightest noise made by the wings of a swooping bat or a clicking insect to leave me fearing that the wild man was close by, ready to cut my throat. Eventually I did fall asleep, for even a frightened mind cannot fight exhaustion indefinitely. But it was a disturbed sleep during which the wild man and his jangling bones haunted my dreams.

I was jolted awake by the motion of the cart. The sun was hardly visible on the horizon behind us and Edbersa explained that we were making an early start so we could rest longer during the hottest part of the day.

Instead of climbing up beside him, I reclined on the flour sacks, eating a breakfast of flat bread and goat's cheese and still thinking of the wild man. But soon my attention was taken by the landscape which had begun to change around us as we continued our journey into the mountains. The parched vegetation gave way to lush greenery of such variety I could scarcely believe what I was seeing. The trees and bushes grew so close to the track that in some places they hung over it, forming a shading canopy that was as welcome as it was fascinating. There were so many hues of green and shapes of leaves and wonderfully coloured flowers I began to believe we had entered paradise.

Even Edbersa's spirits seem to rise and he began to make whistling noises in response to the bird chorus. Occasionally screeching birds with brightly coloured plumage and flamboyant crests broke from the trees and swooped low over our heads.

We travelled in these conditions for three days before our route departed from the forest into a stepped landscape, which began to rise ever more steeply as we journeyed. On the fourth day, when the sun was at its hottest, we sheltered in the shade of a huge tree that had a trunk ten or more man-strides around, the biggest I had ever seen. That was when I saw the wild man again.

All three of us were sitting on the cart, resting after taking our meal of samoya fruit and tampica. My companions were facing the route we had yet to take while I was looking back towards my home, once again feeling the welling of homesickness within me.

The first hint of the wild man's presence was the spear I saw glinting in the sunlight as it projected from a bright green bush some thirty strides away. Then I saw his savage head with its decorations of white bones. When he realised that I had seen him, he melted back into the vegetation.

My first thought was to marvel at his stamina, for we had travelled many leagues and he had followed us every stride on foot. But why would he do this? Was he waiting for a chance to kill and eat us? Were there others of his kind following on behind who might also like the taste of human flesh?

I anxiously grabbed Edbersa's arm. 'I have seen the wild man again. He's been following us.'

Garia instinctively reached for his sword.

Edbersa laughed. 'I told you – he is no threat to us.'

'You say so but you do not explain,' said Garia.

Edbersa climbed from the cart. 'He is a wild man, certainly. But he has been shunned by his tribe and so is condemned to wander this land alone.'

'How do you know this?'

'That is not important. What is important is that we must

befriend him, entice him into our camp so we can gain some knowledge about the land through which we travel. I have been thinking that we need someone who can speak in tongues with which we are not familiar and find tracks that would otherwise be hidden. He could be that person.'

'And he could be a simple savage with no language and no desire to keep our company,' said Garia.

'Then I shall take great pleasure in proving you wrong.' Edbersa turned to me. 'Han, I want you to walk to where you saw the wild man. Come on, quickly. I don't want him to think we are not interested in him.'

I climbed down from the cart, but hesitated.

'Don't worry. I shall stay with you.'

I felt compelled to obey. I walked nervously along the track with Edbersa at my side, stopping two yards from the bush where the wild man had been. 'I saw him there,' I said, pointing. 'What should we do?'

'We will wait,' said Edbersa.

And wait we did, until my knees hurt with staying in the same position for so long.

Then the wild man appeared, stepping from behind the bush, his spear pointing to the ground as if an indication of his peaceful intentions. I could see he was a man about Garia's age. He raised his shield aloft and spoke in a tongue that was strange to me.

I turned to Edbersa. 'Did you understand what he said?'

'Yes. He does not wish to harm us. He also understands Akben, so you can speak to him in your own tongue.'

'What shall I say?'

'That's up to you – but he should know that we pose no threat.'

I nodded and took several steps towards the wild man. 'My name is Han,' I said. 'I'm from Akbenna and I would like to be your friend.'

The wild man looked serious, stern even, but his words were gentle. 'I am Kairi,' he said. 'I am twenty-one summers and twenty winters. How many are you?'

'Thirteen summers and fourteen winters,' I said, after hesitating briefly to work it out. 'We call it years. In years, I am thirteen.'

'I know years,' he said, stepping forward. He looked at Edbersa, narrowing his eyes. 'You are not Akben.'

I also looked at Edbersa, wondering what the wild man meant.

Edbersa said something in the strange tongue. The wild man laughed loudly, shaking his head. His eyes lit up and he wore broad grin. At that moment he seemed anything but wild.

Then, continuing in the same language, they conversed some more. Of course, I couldn't understand what was being said but I assumed – and it turned out I assumed correctly – that Edbersa was asking Kairi to help us.

As I stood before this wild man whom I had bizarrely asked to be my friend – and was still awaiting a reply on the subject – I felt a sense of exclusion. My head was full of questions I was desperate to have answered. Why, for example, had Edbersa asked me to be the first to talk to Kairi when he could have done so himself? And where had the wild man learned to speak Akben? But perhaps the most intriguing question was why he had been banished from his own tribe.

I had no time to raise these matters with Edbersa, for Garia declared we should resume our journey immediately. Kairi followed us to the cart. While I clambered up, Edbersa took the wild man to one side and they spoke in hushed voices. At one point, Kairi pointed to the west with his spear. Edbersa nodded slowly and I detected concern in his eyes.

After some minutes of speaking solemnly, Edbersa finally smiled. Kairi grinned back at him.

'Right,' said Edbersa. 'We are ready.' He turned to Garia,

who had already mounted Melemari in his impatience to be off. 'Kairi will run ahead of us. There is danger before us. He has agreed be our eyes and ears.'

Garia nodded slowly but, judging by his sullen expression, he was not happy that Kairi had been recruited as a scout as though it represented yet another challenge to his soldierly authority. He whirled Melemari round in a full circle and set her off along the track at a canter. It was obvious that if Kairi was going to be our guide, he would have to be a very swift runner.

In those first days as we journeyed to Polastia, my homesickness remained untempered and I often cried for want of my mother's embrace and my father's kind words. My spirits lifted a little when Kairi joined our little party, for I became distracted by curiosity about him. Edbersa called him a wild man but his spoken manner was gentle and his movements graceful. I was confused exactly why, but I could not help liking Kairi despite his strange appearance.

Garia, on the other hand, behaved strangely towards him. I could see by his set jaw that he was determined to re-assert himself as the guide to our mission. But our new companion was equally determined and refused to be outrun by a horse.

The day after joining us, Kairi rose long before dawn to run ahead and ensure our route was safe. Garia cantered Melemari all morning and never got ahead of him. In the end, he gave up and walked the mare the usual distance in front of the cart. 'The horse is a little lame,' he said by way of excuse.

Melemari appeared to be in no discomfort, which prompted Edbersa to remark, 'Garia thinks he is a man, Han, but today he is acting like your younger brother.'

After three more days of arduous journeying, a cool wind started to blow across the foothills enabling us to make better progress. Again I was amazed at Kairi's stamina as he ran without fatigue the same distance that we travelled by hoof and wheel. We only caught up with him as the sun began to fall low in the sky.

We camped that night a little way from the track in a woodland clearing, through which ran a small stream. The ready supply of water meant we could refill all our spare gourds and flasks and wash ourselves for the first time. Such was the pleasure and convenience of the location, Garia proposed we remain there the whole of the next day to rest the horses and ourselves.

Edbersa readily agreed. He had been tired and irascible all day, having drunk more of his liquor than was usual the previous night. He had gone to sleep so drunk that Garia had found it difficult to rouse him at dawn. Once we were under way, Edbersa pushed the cart mares hard, as if they were to blame for the wretched state of his head.

As Garia and I collected wood for our campfire, Edbersa propped himself against a tree and dozed. Kairi disappeared into the trees and came back when the sun had almost set, carrying a dead ledbuk across his shoulders. He dropped the young deer to the ground by the fire and I could see the spear wound that had dispatched it clean through the heart.

Edbersa woke when he heard the fuss we made over the kill. As if completely restored by his brief sleep, he sprang forward eagerly to butcher the animal.

The meat was the best I had ever tasted and it restored all our spirits. We thanked Kairi, whose face beamed with pleasure because he had made us happy and full. The kill was timely because our food was beginning to run low and Edbersa had already warned we would have to start catching animals to eat. Now we knew that Kairi could hunt well, it seemed we had little to worry about.

The rest of the meat was cut into strips, which Edbersa said he would salt and suspend around the cart to dry in the sun as we travelled. He cut lengths of parasitic vine from a tree, which he threaded through the strips of the salted ledbuk meat and tied to the cart. 'It is the only way to do this on the move,' he told me. 'It will be up to you, Han, to make sure no wild dogs run up and steal the meat.'

'How shall I do that?'

'You will throw rocks at them. Make sure you load plenty on the cart.'

The next day Kairi once again ran ahead as we journeyed mostly in silence over gently rising land until we came to the edge of a thick forest, where our new friend was waiting for us. He and Edbersa held a huddled conversation. By the expression upon Garia's face, I could see that he was annoyed at being left out of the deliberation.

Then Edbersa turned to us. 'We cannot risk entering the forest,' he said. 'Kairi says it is very dense in places and we would have to abandon the cart. We have no choice but to skirt around its edge. It is a longer route but may be quicker in the end.'

We followed the edge of the forest, the side upon which the sun shone. I observed with wonder the amazing variety of birds that kept flying in and out of the trees. I saw no other animals, but I feared wild dogs – maybe even wolves and bears – could be lurking at the forest's edge, ready to pounce upon the strips of drying ledbuk. I kept a rock in my hand at all times, ready to hurl it at any creature that dared come near.

We continued our journey until the sun began to disappear over the distant hills. Kairi was waiting for us by a small river which would have to be forded. He pointed along its bank to a clump of trees isolated from the rest of the forest. 'We can find shelter there for the night,' he said. 'We can cross the river tomorrow.'

The following day we all woke later than usual and Garia and I spent some time washing our clothes in the river. I was not used to being naked in front of anyone save my mother and father, so I sat in the water's shallow edge as I scoured my breeches and tunic on a smooth boulder.

Garia stretched out his pants and soldier's tunic on a broad rock so they would dry quickly in the sun then he reclined in the stream, letting the cooling water run over his long naked body.

I dressed while my clothes were still wet and busied myself making a fishing line from a spare length of Edbersa's vine, stealing a small piece of meat to use as bait. I sat on the bank of the stream, dangling the meat in the water in the vain hope of catching a freshwater crab.

Kairi, who had gone off into the woods earlier with an empty flour sack, returned with it slung across his shoulder, weighed down and bulging with intriguing contents. He emptied it onto the bank of the stream and smiled broadly. Edbersa's beard parted in a grateful grin and I squealed with delight. Only Garia was grudging in his reaction to the haul, which comprised of figs and a type of breadfruit Akbens call a cabinom.

I hoped this gesture, on top of last night's ledbuk feast, would help to improve matters between Garia and Kairi. It was obvious, even to a thirteen year old, that there was a masculine rivalry fermenting just below the surface. Both were warriors in their own ways, each one tall, lean and muscular with a proud, finely-boned face. It was inevitable there would be wariness, even mistrust. I desperately hoped this would not develop into serious antipathy but instead they would become true friends.

When we finally got under way, we travelled more miles than on any afternoon previously, the breeze blowing from the mountains encouraging our progress by keeping us cool. As usual Kairi ran ahead, and we came upon him when the sun was at its highest. He was crouched on the shelf of a large rock rising steeply above the track. Immediately we stopped, he climbed down and spoke in a low voice to Edbersa, pointing with his spear to the way ahead.

Annoyed once more at being excluded, Garia interrupted their intimate conference. 'If you have anything to impart, you can say it to me also.'

Kairi looked questioningly at Edbersa, who nodded. 'Garia is right, Kairi; you must speak openly to us all. Even Han, as young as he is, has to be told of the threat we face.'

'We must be careful at all times,' said Kairi, looking to the mountains. 'There are men in these parts who would do us harm.'

'Are they wild men like you?' I asked as quietly as I could without actually whispering.

Kairi smiled. 'You need not be afraid of my fellow wild men, Han,' he said. 'They live way beyond those hills we have already passed. That is why you have seen only me. No, these people I fear are not wild, though they are capable of great savagery.'

'They are the Castra, whose home is way beyond the mountains,' Edbersa said grimly. 'They travel far to perform their ill deeds and are known to ambush travellers. Kairi believes it would be foolish to stay long on this track.'

'What alternative have we?' asked Garia.

'There is a way,' said Kairi. 'But it will add two or more days to our journey. Even then we cannot be sure to avoid these people. The Castra are the reason very few people travel this route into Polastia. They rob travellers of their horses and carts and everything they carry. If they feel well-disposed, they might strip the clothes from the backs of those they rob and send them on their way naked. If not, they have been known to stock their meat caves with salted human flesh, much like my own ancestors did in times long ago.'

'Then we have little choice,' Edbersa said in his most solemn voice. 'We must take the longer route to give ourselves a chance.'

We travelled on towards the mountain pass for two more leagues, Kairi running ahead again to ensure the way was safe. We caught up with him on the bank of a broad river into which the track disappeared.

'This is where travellers used to cross but it leads into the narrowest part of the mountain pass where there is the greatest danger of ambush,' said Kairi. 'We must stay on this bank and follow the river's flow to find a safer crossing. From there we will head over the broad shoulder of those mountains.'

We tracked his gaze towards a range of majestic peaks in the distance; they had forested skirts and above them jagged cliffs so steep I could not imagine a human being able to scale them.

The horses were tired and needed to rest but Edbersa said we should keep moving to find somewhere less exposed. Garia led the mares to the river where they drank thirstily. Kairi, too, knelt at its edge and gulped the cool water down before throwing off his bone adornments and dousing his entire body in the river. Then he scrubbed himself with coarse grass until all the paint that decorated his torso and limbs was removed so he no longer looked like a wild man. I did not detect any weariness in his movements but he had run hard throughout the afternoon and must have begun to tire because, after he had finished washing, he sat on the grassy bank for several minutes, breathing deeply and gently massaging his long legs. Then he fashioned a garment from one of our empty food sacks and wrapped it around his naked loins, tying it with a belt made from dexterously plaited grasses. After Kairi had finished this, I knelt by him and took my own fill of fresh water.

He looked at me and smiled. 'Edbersa told me the purpose of your travels,' he said quietly. 'You are a brave boy to make such an arduous and dangerous journey.'

'I am not brave really,' I responded. 'It's just that I am sent personally by our chief elder and he is not to be disobeyed.'

'That may be true, Han, but you will need to find courage as your travels become trials. Your journey so far has been uneventful but don't believe it will remain so. There is danger at every turn.'

'I'm afraid of death,' I confessed. 'Even though my people believe I'm a brave boy for something I did, I'm still very frightened. I wish I was still at home looking after the goats or working in the fields alongside my mother and father.'

Kairi smiled reassuringly. 'If it is within my powers, Han, you will be returned safely to your parents.' He retrieved his spear and shield from the riverbank and rose to his feet. 'By the way, I did not call you brave simply to make you feel good. I know what you did in Akbenna – that your courage and wisdom defeated Gilgarius.'

'Who told you? Edbersa?'

'No one here, Han. It was whispered to me by the wind.'

I was intrigued by his answer but left it at that because I had another pressing question. 'Why did the wild men banish you, Kairi? Is it because you are a sorcerer?' Although the words came from my own lips, the audacity of the question still took me by surprise.

Kairi laughed. 'What makes you think I am a sorcerer?'

'You are not like other men.'

He laughed again and put a finger to his lips. 'One day, Han, you might learn what kind of man I am. Meanwhile, I'm happy for you to think of me as a sorcerer.' With that, he set off and it took but a few strides before he was settled into his elegant loping run.

As Kairi disappeared into the distance, Edbersa slapped the reins on the rumps of the cart mares to urge them into action. 'Come on,' he said. 'Let us get out of here. The air is full of bad smells.'

We travelled for half a day longer, following the course of the river. Sometimes the easy way was along its bank but occasionally, when it descended into an impassable gorge, we had to veer away and climb higher to find a way around. Once I thought I glimpsed Kairi ahead, watching to ensure we went the right way, but by the time I had focused my eyes properly he was gone.

Finally, just as it was getting too dark to see our way, we made a welcome descent to a clearing by the river. Kairi was waiting for us, a fire ready for lighting and two large fish, gutted and prepared for cooking.

Edbersa greeted him, smiling. 'Brother, you are proving a useful scout,' he said in his gruffest voice, as if begrudging the idea of paying a compliment.

I looked at Garia and saw that he, too, smiled with gratitude at the prospect of a fish dinner, though I suspected he tried very hard not to.

Edbersa baked the fish slowly in clay dug from the riverbank. By the time we ate, the sun had been replaced by one of the largest and brightest moons I'd ever seen. Afterwards we sat round the fire, mostly imprisoned in our own thoughts. Very soon, lulled by the slap of the river against the bank and the crackle of the fire, I fell asleep.

What made me wake a few hours later when everyone else was sleeping I still, even after all these years, cannot properly explain. I was dreaming about my mother, who was crying because she believed I was going to die. I stood next to her in our home and watched her wailing for the loss of her only son. My father was not in my vision but I knew he was close by. My mother cursed Karmus, who suddenly appeared at her side. I was standing before her but she could not see me. I was crying because I could not make her hear me and all she could do was wail to Karmus that I would be killed.

Then, for several moments, she did see me; she saw me crying out for her and she stopped her own crying and reached out her arms to cup my face with her hands. Her eyes were bright and reflected the embers of the fire in the grate. 'You must wake up, Han,' she said. 'You must wake this moment, for there are people in the trees who mean to kill you.'

That was when I jumped out of my sleep. Without thinking, I was on my feet and shouting for Garia and Edbersa. The horses began to scuff their hooves and whinny and Kairi, who was sleeping a little way from the fire, sprang up spear already in hand. Garia was a little slower to pick up his sword but even he was ready by the time the men broke from the trees.

Everything that followed remains vivid in my memory. There was confused shouting and the clashing of blades and the squealing of horses. To my right, Garia had sprung forward and was thrusting his sword towards two shapeless forms that lunged from the blackness between the trees. To my left, Kairi had speared a similarly shapeless assailant as cleanly as he had dispatched the ledbuk. The attacker had raised an axe, which he was about to bring down on Kairi's head, but the wild man was too quick for him and his assailant fell in a heavy lump, stabbed in the heart.

But soon others came. More dark forms broke from the trees, driving Kairi and Garia back towards the river. Suddenly I found myself lifted from the ground and carried backwards. It was Edbersa, conveying me towards the river as if I was no more than a baby.

'You must swim for your life,' he said. 'Let the current take you. But don't go too far. We'll come and find you when we have dealt with these savages.'

'I cannot swim,' I protested.

'You have no choice, Han. You must swim or drown. And believe me, it will be better to drown than be taken alive by these men.' With that, he lowered me into the water and pushed me away from the bank.

I was frightened, for it was true I had not learned to swim. As far as I knew, no child in Akbenna could swim for there was never enough water in the rivers and streams in those days. But, for all my lack of experience, I knew instinctively that I would sink if I did not kick my legs and sweep my arms through the water. It did not work at first, and I sank beneath the surface, but I kept kicking and sweeping as hard as I could so that, although spluttering and floundering, I managed to keep my head above water as the current swept me away.

My eyes were filled with tears as well as river water, for I could hear the clash of the weapons and the terrible cries of those who were being slain. These sounds and the haunting squeals of the horses followed me as I was carried along on the surface of the river, accompanying me to what I thought was going to be my death.

Then the noises suddenly stopped and all I could hear was the gurgling current and the water slapping against the riverbank close to my left. Once again I kicked my legs and swept my arms and was soon crawling over mud and tree roots to find a place to hide.

I stumbled around until I found a grassy bed between two large and diverging roots. I lay down and curled up as tightly as I could, like a spiky yurtzhog rolling into a ball to protect itself from a wild dog. I tried not to think that Garia, Kairi and Edbersa could be dead. I dared not, for my despair would have been too much to bear and I might have chosen to throw myself back into the river, to be carried away to oblivion in the strong current.

It was in such a disturbed frame of mind that I finally fell into an exhausted asleep. Once again, my mother appeared in my dream. She had finished abusing Karmus and was now abusing my father as a weak and obsequious man for allowing me to be taken away. But my father appeared his usual imperturbable self, his face lit in a toothless smile. He looked beyond my mother over the many miles of unfamiliar land until his eyes found me.

In my dream, I was sitting in the stream, washing my clothes. I waved at my father and he laughed and waved back. Then he faded into the distance.

'Father! Father!' I shouted. 'Please don't leave me.'

'I will not leave you, Han.' The words were delivered in a now-familiar growl.

I opened my eyes to find Edbersa staring down at me, blood oozing from a gash in his head. 'You are wounded.'

'You are very observant, Han.'

'Where are Garia and Kairi – are they dead?'

'They are alive, my young friend. We are all alive but still in mortal danger. We must leave now before other Castra come.'

Edbersa pulled me to my feet and led me through the trees to a small clearing where Garia and Kairi were waiting, holding the three mares by their halters. Both men appeared to have dispatched their assailants without incurring injury.

The only wound was the one inflicted on Edbersa; I learned later that the gash above his right eye was caused by a Castra axe. After sending me off into the river, he had turned just in time to see the blade glinting in the moonlight as it was brought down to cleave his head in two. With a lightning instinct, he thrust his long sinewy arm towards the axe handle, managing to deter the blow so that it caused only a glancing wound. Then he pulled the Castran towards him, jerking his knee hard into the man's groin as he did so. He tore the axe from the man's suddenly loosened hands and reversed the assault, driving the bronze blade deep into the man's skull so that, as Edbersa later recalled, his head resembled two halves of a grotesque mask.

'Come, Han. We must move quickly while we still have moonlight to see by,' said Garia as he urged Melemari into the trees. 'You will ride with Edbersa.'

We were leaving the cart and most of our possessions to give us more speed. The two cart mares were now our steeds and I could sense as Kairi lifted me up behind Edbersa that our mare, Nera, resented our combined weight upon her back. The second cart mare, Fermansa, was laden with three of the grain sacks filled with food and other essential items to ensure our survival.

We travelled through the thick woodland for a while until we found ourselves once again descending to a small clearing by the river. By this time the sun had risen and Kairi waded in to determine if it was a suitable place to ford. The water was soon lapping his chin. 'I think we can cross here but only by swimming,' he said after returning to the bank.

The horses did not like the river other than as a place to drink, but Garia skilfully coaxed Melemari into the water, stroking her elegant neck and gently urging her with soothing words. Once she was half way, with Garia swimming alongside, Edbersa, Kairi and I led the other mares in. I clung on to Fermansa's halter and let her drag me across. Soon we were all on the far bank, drying ourselves in the warming sunshine as we ate a meagre breakfast of cheese and tampica.

Kairi hurried us over the meal for he was impatient to leave the exposed riverbank and head to higher ground. 'Those Castra we slew last night might have been just a scouting group,' he said. 'When the bodies are found, their companions will continue to hunt us down.'

Even I, with all the naivety of a thirteen year old, knew three horses would make an easy trail to follow so it was with relief that we began to ascend to stonier ground, where the imprints of the horses' hooves would not be so discernible. Our route was also strewn with large boulders, which provided us with cover in what was an otherwise exposed mountainside.

Eventually, after almost a full day's trekking, Kairi considered it safe enough for us to find a place to camp. 'There is a cave here where I have sometimes sheltered,' he said. 'I believe the Castra may not know this place for, although it must have been used by ancient peoples, I have never seen any sign that man has been there in new times. But if I'm wrong and the Castra come, it will be easy to defend.'

As the sun fell rapidly, we followed him along a narrow track which snaked its way around many large rocks. We only just made it to the cave before dark descended upon us.

'We will make no fire tonight,' said Edbersa. 'And we must make the best of what food we have.'

'Dried ledbuk then,' said Garia grimly.

Edbersa nodded and I felt my heart and my spirits sink even further. Our food would not last long and we had little water, perhaps enough to last only one more day if we failed to find a stream or spring.

The cave was entered through a narrow squeeze between two long tooth-like stones, which seemed to me to have been deliberately placed there. The opening was too narrow for the mares so Garia hobbled them among the rocks where all they had to browse on was hardly more than scrub grass.

The ledbuk was not completely dried and we ate it enthusiastically, along with a little of the goat's cheese and the last of the bread. When we had finished, Edbersa went out to check the horses. A few minutes later he came back with half a gourd of mare's milk, which we shared in silence.

For a while light from the rising moon streamed into the cave, but it failed to illuminate more than the first part of it. I found the least uncomfortable place I could on the earthen floor, close by the entrance, and soon fell asleep with the others still talking quietly.

The next day I woke to find myself alone. The cave was only a few strides long. There was sufficient light for me to see what a special place it had been for its previous human occupiers. On the roof and along one wall were pictures of animals being chased by people with spears and bows and arrows. One picture showed a tall, thin man with long hair being speared by a short, fat man.

Fear struck me, for the picture made me think the Castra had come in the night and taken my companions. Then I heard Edbersa outside, singing a strange foreign song in his deep, resonant voice. I emerged to find him loading the pack mare, Fermansa. 'What is the song you are singing, Edbersa?'

He patted the mare's neck and smiled. 'It is an old song my mother used to sing when I was a child. Did your mother not sing to you?'

In truth, I could not remember. If she did it must have been when I was very small. 'She sometimes told me stories but I've never heard her sing,' I said, unable to hide the regret in my voice. Then I added quickly, 'Every day, she works very hard.'

'Yes, well – life is like that in Akbenna these days.'

'Your song wasn't an Akben song,' I pointed out.

Edbersa did not look at me. 'No, Han. It is a song from another people.'

'Is Kairi right, that you are not from Akbenna?'

Edbersa did not answer but busied himself roping our diminished supplies on to Fermansa's back as if he had not heard my question. 'I hope you are not hungry, Han, for we can't break our fast just yet,' he said as he worked. 'We must move quickly from here.'

'Where are Garia and Kairi?'

'Garia has gone back to see if we are being followed and Kairi is scouting ahead.'

My expression must have shown fear or fatigue or both, for Edbersa added, 'Don't worry, Han. The first Polasti settlements are only a few days' travel away. They are a wary, mistrustful people, but not as savage as the Castra.'

By the time Garia returned, Fermansa was laden with our supplies and Nera was saddled and ready to travel. He took Edbersa to one side and spoke to him briefly in a hushed voice. I guessed the Castra were indeed following us but Garia had no wish to alarm me with the news.

He came over and playfully slapped my back. 'Come, Han,' he said with forced cheerfulness. 'I will put you up behind Edbersa. I hope you are ready for another long ride, my young friend.'

'Where is Kairi?' I asked.

'Don't worry about Kairi,' Edbersa said. 'I'm sure he will be waiting for us ahead somewhere.'

'But how will we know which trail to take?'

'There is only one way, Han,' said Garia, laughing. 'And that is upwards. Come on, climb up; we must leave this place.'

We did not see Kairi at all that morning but he left us signs along the trail – thin branches resting on rocks which pointed the way we should go. Garia knocked each one off with his sword as we passed in case any pursuing Castra would see their significance. What we did not realise was that the Castra must have known all along where we were.

By noon the horses were snorting and sweating with fatigue and Garia decided we must find somewhere to stop. Soon we would be above where trees could live and it would be much more difficult to find cover and shade. So when we came across a clump of bayatki pines, Garia declared it an ideal place to rest.

We had barely stopped and had not even dismounted when the Castra launched their next vicious attack upon us.

I had never heard a speeding arrow before but I know now that they whoosh and whistle if they pass close to your head. I have no idea how many were fired during the ambush but they were coming from somewhere below, whooshing and whistling and cracking and sparking as their bronze tips hit the boulders around us. Fermansa reared and whinnied pitifully as an arrow cut across her rump and ended lodged almost entirely in a food sack.

One arrow grazed my head and embedded itself with a thud in Edbersa's shoulder. He did not even flinch but drove Nera straight into a canter by kicking her hard with his heels, with me hanging on for my life. How we avoided being fatally hit I will never know, but we had no time to dwell upon anything but flight.

It seems the Castra had been circling us and an advance foot party had anticipated our trail and scaled the mountain's steep cliffs to catch us unawares. But after their attack they did not pursue us for long, not even with their arrows, for we made good speed. When we were a league or more distant we stopped, the mares snorting with excitement and Edbersa visibly wincing with what by now must have been the most terrible pain. He slid from Nera, leaving me holding the reins.

Garia examined the arrow protruding from his shoulder. 'If it is barbed, it will be difficult to remove – at least without causing you great pain and further injury. The only way to get a barbed arrowhead out without tearing your flesh apart is to force it all the way through your chest.'

'You must first probe with your knife,' said Edbersa. 'Then I shall have to take my chance.'

It was then that I remembered the arrow embedded in the food sack. I reached over to Nera and pulled it out. The arrow was liberated cleanly without tearing the sack. 'Garia, there is no barb,' I declared triumphantly. 'See.' I thrust the arrow towards him, showing the slender bronze tip.

Garia took it from me and examined the head closely. 'Let us hope it is the same for *your* arrow Edbersa,' he said.

'Just get on with it,' Edbersa growled.

Garia worked slowly, pulling out the arrow a little at a time until it came out cleanly. He examined the bloody wound closely through the gash in Edbersa's leather tunic. 'It is deep and will become bad unless it is cleaned and the blood staunched,' he said.

'And what do you propose, Garia? We have little water to waste and hardly enough time before the Castra will be upon us.'

'In the army, we are taught to cleanse wounds by pissing on them,' said Garia. 'Not that I have ever done so personally.'

Edbersa laughed bitterly. 'And what makes you think I will allow you to piss on me?'

'If you don't then the wound will surely become bad and poison you, maybe not right away but in a few days. The poison will spread around your body and you will die.'

'You must let him piss on you, Edbersa,' I pleaded.

'And I suppose if he hasn't enough piss, you will add yours to my wound,' Edbersa answered.

'If it is needed to save your life, then yes,' I said.

Edbersa laughed again but not so bitterly this time. 'You would do that to save my life, Han?'

'Now you are making fun of me,' I said.

'Maybe I am, but that does not mean your offer is not appreciated. Come on, Garia, help me off with my tunic. If this is to be done, let it be done quickly.'

When his upper body was exposed, Edbersa sank slowly and painfully to his knees.

Garia nodded to me. 'You go first, Han. I'm not ready.'

I looked at him and then Edbersa. 'I am not sure…'

'Hurry!' said Edbersa. 'If we do not get this done quickly, the Castra will be here to piss on all of us.'

Self-consciously, I pushed down my breeches and hovered my penis over Edbersa's shoulder. Nothing happened.

'Concentrate,' said Garia. 'It will come.'

I closed my eyes and tried to imagine the sound of running water. After a few moments, I felt the piss coming but it turned out to be just a trickle of strong yellow urine, which dribbled on to Edbersa's shoulder. Only the tiniest amount actually made contact with the wound. I realised this was not going to be easy, for none of us had been drinking enough water.

'Move away. I will try,' said Garia. 'I think I can do it.'

I stepped aside and Garia stood astride Edbersa, a look of grim concentration on his face. Then his expression turned to joy as a spout of urine surged from his penis, completely drowning the wound. 'That will do to start with,' he said after finishing. 'But we must do this again later to ensure your survival.'

'That is very nice to know,' Edbersa replied with undisguised irony. 'You are both very caring companions.'

'You can have my piss also!'

In one movement, we all spun around to see Kairi step from between two elephantine rocks. 'But I think you will probably live without it, Edbersa,' he said.

I ran to Kairi. 'We were attacked by the Castra,' I said excitedly.

'I know – and it seems they will keep doing so until they kill most of us,' Kairi said sombrely.

'I thought you were supposed to be our eyes and ears,' snapped Garia. 'Why did you not warn us?'

Kairi strode towards Garia, holding his spear aloft. 'The answer is that I did not anticipate their manoeuvre. I am not a soldier.'

'If that is the case, I shall be the scout from now on,' said Garia, thrusting out his chest assertively.

'Then you will have no need of my company,' said Kairi.

'Stop it!' snapped Edbersa. 'We have no time for fighting among ourselves. You will continue to scout for us, Kairi.' He turned to Garia. 'And you will stop bearing grudges. No one could have known the Castra would catch up with us so quickly. But they did and we have thankfully survived.'

'But we're still in danger,' said Kairi. 'We must move quickly to find safety, for they will continue to pursue us.'

'Why?' I asked. 'What do they want from us?'

'It is because we have humiliated them,' said Garia. 'They are seeking to avenge the deaths of their companions and restore their pride as a savage people.'

'It is more than that,' said Kairi. 'Doubtless they have a wish for revenge but they have a more intriguing reason to follow us.'

'And what is that?' Garia asked.

'To make themselves rich. For some reason I do not yet understand, the Castra leader has been promised gold to take young Han here captive.'

***

'Do you find me a good story teller?'

Arkis laughed. 'The finest I've heard. You certainly know how to keep me waiting to know what happens when you come to the most suspenseful moments.'

'A practised art, my young friend – from which I now need a rest. I can't keep going as I used to do.'

'And I must give Rashi some exercise. Unlike you, Han, she's getting exceedingly restless.'

Arkis went to retrieve the mare from the otherwise deserted stockade and led her back to saddle her. Han appeared to have fallen asleep but stirred when he heard them.

'Please, you must rest,' insisted Arkis.

'I will as soon as you have gone,' said Han. 'But first I'd like to ask you a question.'

'Of course. Ask whatever you want.'

'Why did you take on such a hazardous journey to this part of our land when there are so many more fruitful places to visit, where trade can be transacted with greater ease and, dare I say it, pleasure?'

'As I have already told you, I'm searching for inspiration.'

'That is a very vague word, Arkis.'

'It is a vague quest.' Arkis hoped his expression would not give away some of the guilt he felt at the deceit he was breeding.

'We don't have much here to interest the trader,' Han continued. 'It's true we are close to an important trade route along which men of many guises – of black, pale or yellow skin in all manner of costumes, drab or vibrant with many colours – ply their wares. But no one comes this way unless they are badly lost. Are you lost, my friend?'

'A lost cause, perhaps,' Arkis replied with a chuckle.

'That is an intriguing answer. But what I want to know is why you came to trade with nothing but a horse and two saddlebags?'

'I do not wish to trade in cloth or spices. I have come to acquire something I consider to be of far greater value.'

'Can you tell me more?'

'It's complicated.'

'I'm sure it is. I'm also sure you'll tell me when you're ready.' Arkis looked away. 'Perhaps.'

Han closed his eyes but continued speaking as if relating a dream. 'I sometimes spend nights out here beneath the stars, looking at Mother Mountain. Sometimes, when it is a moonlit night, I see the smoke rising from her crater as if she is using it to whisper to me and me alone. It is like she is reminding me of the part I played in defeating Gilgarius. Sometimes she whispers nice things but occasionally she spits flaming lava into the night sky, as if chastising me for a bad thing I've done or unkind thought I've had. But mostly she whispers about Gilgarius and the wonderful way we both devised, albeit independently, to strike such a blow against the terrible creature.

'Mother Mountain is especially interesting in the cold season when we have nights so crisp you can almost feel the air with your fingers and she dominates the horizon, the jagged rocks around her crater silhouetted against the moon glow as sharp as Gilgarius's fangs. I used not to mind sleeping out here in the cold when I was younger and stronger. There was something cleansing about it. Last night I trust you were warm, Arkis.'

'I was indeed.'

'Where will you go today?'

'I don't know. Maybe I'll let Rashi decide.' The mare pranced impatiently. 'You must rest,' Arkis continued. 'I promise I shall return to hear more of your story.'

'Be sure to tell my neighbours I'm still alive,' said Han.

Arkis found he could not meet the old man's eyes.

He saddled Rashi and walked her to the stockade where Pelia was examining a pair of new-born kids. One was on its feet, sturdy and sure, calling for its mother; the other, bleating pathetically, could barely get off its knees.

Pelia looked up as she heard his approach. 'This one will not live beyond the high sun,' she predicted in answer to Arkis's unasked question. 'Goats are good mothers. She is making enough milk for two but this little one is not suckling. Not to worry, the kid will make a nice stew.'

'Your grandfather is tired,' said Arkis.

Pelia nodded, smiling sadly. 'Although your presence has lifted him, he still needs to rest. When are you to leave us?'

'Not today but soon. I have business in Ejiki, but it is not pressing.'

'I hope you don't mind me saying but you seem to have spent a lot of time listening to my grandfather and probably not enough time trading. What is it exactly that you deal in? Shiny stones that rich women like to adorn themselves with?'

Arkis laughed. 'No, Pelia, something far more valuable than shiny stones. At least to me.'

Arkis rode away, guilt weighing heavily upon him.

***

What a story it has become, said Han. There we were, a band of travellers far from our homes in a hostile land being told there was a golden price upon my head.

'How do you know this?' Garia had demanded of Kairi. 'How do we know you are not lying to deflect my criticism of your scouting abilities?'

Kairi laughed scornfully and turned to address Edbersa as if Garia no longer existed. 'My scouting may not please some, but it was sufficient to get me close enough to the Castra who had been sent to intercept us – the ones who fired their arrows upon you.'

Garia sniffed dismissively. 'And how did you do that? No, don't tell me – you made yourself invisible and walked right into their camp.'

'That is not far from the truth,' Kairi responded with more than a hint of defiance in his voice. 'But maybe I ought not to reveal my spying secrets to you, Garia, in case you try copy them ineptly and end up a meal for the enemy.'

'That's enough,' said Edbersa. 'You're bickering like two old women in the market.'

Garia grew sullen but Kairi shrugged off Edbersa's reprimand. He explained how that morning, after setting the trail of branches to guide us, he'd climbed to a rocky outcrop above the pines to get a better view of the mountainside. He had been settled in his crouch for about an hour when he saw us coming along an exposed section of the track. Then, almost immediately, he had spied a small party of Castra with bows and arrows who were climbing a steep cliff to cut us off. Kairi said he scrambled from his vantage point and set off to try and warn us but was too late.

'I saw them fire their arrows and feared the worst,' he said. 'I did not want to leave you at their mercy, but I confess the speed of their pursuit took me by surprise.'

Kairi then climbed a tree to get a better view of the attackers.

'They had not many arrows with them because they were

forced to assail such a steep rock face to intercept you, so it was no surprise that they fired them all so quickly. Concerned that you were all dead, I climbed almost to the top of the tree. You can imagine how relieved I was to see that you had survived the assault and were in full flight.'

Kairi smiled and looked directly at Garia. 'Even your survival pleased me Garia, despite your arrogance.'

Garia stiffened, as though about to react, but he shot a glance towards a stern-looking Edbersa and thought better of it.

'It was then I found that I, too, was in a difficult situation,' said Kairi. 'The Castra climbed to where you had been to see what damage they had done and to recover their arrows. To get there, they had to pass beneath the tree in which I hid. That is when I overheard their talk of gold.'

'Did they reveal who was to give the reward and why?' asked Edbersa.

'Not who was to give the gold but it was clearly to do with Han. It was something one of the Castra said. He looked like their leader. He was a much bigger man than the others, with flowing red hair and a beard down to his chest. He was the only one who wore gold and bronze adornments, including an elaborate belt around his tunic, and that made me think he was important. I could not make it out clearly but he seemed angry. I thought it was because they had failed to kill you all but it soon became clear that the leader was angry because they had not captured Han alive – instead they had put his life at risk. He waved his arms about and said someone would not be happy if the boy had been killed in their wild arrow-firing. He said he would make them suffer if he did not get his gold. Again, Han, your name was mentioned. Then they moved out of my hearing.'

'Well, well,' said Edbersa. 'This certainly stirs things up.'

'You must have run like the wind to catch us, Kairi,' said

Garia with a sarcastic edge to his voice.

'I used my brain before employing my legs,' Kairi retorted, revealing that he crossed the mountain summit to intercept us, using the arduous climb to shorten his journey by what must have been half a league. 'It was just like intercepting a lame ledbuk,' he said with a hint of contempt in his voice.

Garia was about to respond when Edbersa interrupted. 'Come,' he said, as he hauled himself awkwardly on to Nera's back. 'We'd better get moving or we'll end up like *dead* ledbuk.'

We pushed hard for the remainder of the day, descending into a broad valley before rising again to assail yet another mountain. This one had a dense skirt of trees which offered a safer hiding place than the more open mountain we'd just left.

We camped for the night in a small clearing by a narrow stream. The horses drank the brown water thirstily and Edbersa risked making a fire to bake flat bread, which we ate with more of the dried ledbuk, washed down with mare's milk and as much of the bitter stream water as we could stomach.

Edbersa sat apart from us, his back to a tree, occasionally taking a swig of liquor. This was the first time he'd touched his flask in days and I assumed he was trying to deaden the pain of his arrow wound.

I went to sit with him, resting my back against a neighbouring tree. 'How is your shoulder?'

'It is aching – do you want to piss on it?'

'If it will keep you alive.'

Edbersa growled a laugh. 'It will not be necessary. The wound is clean enough.' He took another drink from his flask. 'You are a good boy, Han,' he said with an appreciative nod of his bald head. 'You care about others and you still cry for your mother. But you will not remain a boy for long and then you will care only about satisfying your own wants and desires.'

He nodded towards Garia and Kairi, who were occupying their own thoughts, staring into the dying flames of the camp fire. 'They are at the confused stage in their lives,' he said enigmatically.

'I worry about them both,' I said. 'I want them to be friends but they are always angry with each other.'

'That is because they are not yet true men. Yes, they have grown tall and strong and have the fire of warriors in their bellies, but their minds have yet to catch up.'

'Do you think they will try to kill each other?'

'If they do, who would you want to win?'

'I like them both. I don't want either of them to die.'

'Then you must make sure never to let them fight.'

I was undoubtedly frightened as we journeyed to find the first Polasti village but I tried to make myself a little braver by remembering the stories my mother used to tell me when I was small – like the little ledbuk and the wolves. This was the story I recalled most vividly while we travelled though that dangerous land into the plains of Polastia. It left me wondering if my mother could detect my own desperate anguish across all the miles that lay between us.

You see, Arkis, I was but an innocent, frightened child despite what I had achieved with Gilgarius and what Karmus had thought of my wisdom. I was just a young boy desperately missing his mother and father.

That was especially so after the Castra's attacks upon us, when I was left in mortal fear. It is true I was travelling with three strong, resourceful men, who had proved they could handle themselves against an enemy, but I believed the Castra would ultimately prove too strong even for them and we would be hunted down and killed or, in my case, enslaved.

I imagined the enemy hiding behind every tree, crouching in every shadow. Each creaking bough of the forest was a drawn bow and the rustle of the leaves in the wind was the whispered command of their leader. When a bird took flight, I believed it had been spooked by a Castra scout; the distant rumble of thunder became a drumbeat which betrayed our path.

Thus I travelled for three days in total fear. This only began to subside when we finally saw our first signs of the Polasti. The tracks and paths we travelled on appeared to be well-used and in the forest clearings we encountered wicker huts, which Kairi said were overnight shelters for their forest hunters.

'What do they hunt?' I asked him.

Detecting the reason for the nervousness in my voice, Kairi gave kindly laugh. 'Do not worry, Han, they are hunters of animals not humans.'

More at ease, I began to wonder what kind of people the Polasti were and whether they would be as mistrustful of strangers as my own people had traditionally been.

I thought I caught occasional glimpses of the hunters moving through the trees at the edge of the forest. Several times a wild boar or some other creature broke from the canopy as if in flight from a hunter's spear, but we saw no human until we finally left the forest behind and descended onto a grassy plain. There we began to observe cattle and goats that were obviously domesticated. They did not run away as we approached; as we came closer, we saw that some wore bronze bells around their necks which tinkled as they browsed, tended by four or five boys around my age. Their skin colour was paler than mine, their hair longer, and they wore loincloths rather than tunics. They did not run away at our approach but neither did they speak to us. The nearest to us, who was tending a herd of goats, simply leaned against his crook, watching our movements very carefully.

Kairi went over to speak to him and the boy gesticulated towards where the sun was now quickly falling. They spoke a little more before Kairi returned to us. 'We are close to his village but not so close that we can get there before the sun sets. Bathlaya, the city which is our destination, is quite a bit further along the valley.'

'We should press on,' said Garia. 'Night or day, I'm sure they will welcome us the same.'

'I disagree,' said Kairi. 'It would be better if we arrived in the daytime.'

Both he and Garia looked at Edbersa, who scratched his beard. 'Why do I always have to deal with your disagreements?' He paused and patted me on the shoulder. 'Maybe Han should decide – after all, he was chosen to be the official emissary of Akbenna.'

They all looked at me. 'You are making fun of me again, Edbersa,' I said.

'But you are the wise one, Han,' he responded. 'This is an opportunity to demonstrate your wisdom.'

I did not believe wisdom came into it. My mind and my body told me the best thing to do was to keep going, guided by moon and starlight, until we found Bathlaya or some other settlement.

I looked at Garia. 'Why do you think we should continue, Garia?' I asked.

'It's simple, young Han,' he said. 'Although I'm weary from the day's travelling, I'm desperate for a filling meal of kaya stew and a warm, comfortable bed of straw to sleep on. We should find both in a Polasti settlement. I am also worried about spending a night on the open plain where the Castra might once again launch an attack upon us.'

It was a convincing argument that persuaded me to rule in favour of pressing on. However, out of courtesy I decided to ask Kairi to explain why he thought we should wait until morning.

'It is because I know the Polasti,' he said. 'They are a superstitious people who believe it is bad luck to travel after the sun sets. That is why they build shelters in the forest clearings, to protect themselves from evil spirits they believe are always active in the night. The boys who care for the cattle and goats use them, as well as those who hunt. In Polasti lore, the animals they hunt by day become the hunters of men's spirits at night.'

I looked at Edbersa and he nodded. 'What Kairi says is true, Han. I can vouch for it.'

I was about to ask him what he meant when Kairi grabbed my arm and pointed to where the sun was already close to disappearing behind the peak of a distant mountain.

'If we were to arrive at Bathlaya after dark, they will see it as a bad omen, that we are bringing the night spirits into their midst. It is most certainly not a wise thing to do. While I believe they would not use it as an excuse to kill us, they would certainly drive us away and we would end up having to sleep out in the open anyway. No, I think it would be better to find somewhere sheltered to make our camp and continue our journey at first light.'

'So, there you have it, Han,' said Edbersa, working spittle into his mouth and fluting it over Fermansa's head. 'You have both sides of the argument. Now you must make your choice.'

It was then that I realised Edbersa was teaching me a lesson – that making wise decisions is not easy, especially when you have to make them quickly.

I looked from one to the other, settling my eyes a little longer on Garia than on the others. I, too, wanted to eat kaya stew and sleep on a soft straw bed. I also wanted to be away from this plain and the danger pursuing us. Just one more push – maybe only half an hour's hard riding – and we could make the herd boy's village. We would be safe for the first time in days. Unless, that is, we were driven away.

Then I looked at Kairi and saw in his eyes that he already possessed more instinctive wisdom than I could ever hope to have, no matter how long I lived. He knew that displeasing the Polasti at the very outset would blight us as we journeyed through their land. We would stand no chance of achieving the peaceful treaty that Karmus desired. What we thought of the Polasti superstitions did not matter; more important was showing we had respect for them and their beliefs, even if that meant putting our own lives at risk by setting up camp on the open plain.

Kairi knew I had made my decision in his favour and he allowed his lips to part in a subtle smile.

I turned back to Garia. 'I'm sorry. We can't afford to offend people who we would wish to be our hosts.'

Garia shook his head and shot Kairi a mean glance but said nothing.

Edbersa dug his heels into Nera's belly. 'Come on, then. We'd better find somewhere safe to camp before it's too black to see our horses' ears.'

Believe me, Arkis, trying to be a wise child was not an easy thing. Issuing wisdom ought to make you feel worthy or happy but all I felt was a gnawing in the pit of my stomach. If the Castra attacked and killed us in the night, it would be my fault.

To find shelter first we had to cross an open plain where we were at our most vulnerable. At the plain's rocky edge, Kairi warned us to travel as quietly as possible and walk the horses rather than canter. 'The Castra are close,' he said. 'I know it.'

We continued travelling after the sun had set, guided by Kairi. Occasionally he stopped to look at the sky, as if seeking some heavenly guidance. After a while the ground began to rise and, from the silhouetted shapes ahead, I could see we had reached the edge of a forest.

'We will camp here,' Edbersa said after we had travelled only a little way into the trees.

Garia and Kairi went off in different directions to scavenge fodder for the horses, returning with armfuls of dry grass from the forest edge. We made no fire and shared only the smallest amount of food and some mare's milk before we tried to sleep.

I made a soft bed of pine needles and lay listening to the noises of the night but I must have disturbed a natural community of insects in the making of my bed, for agitated creatures crawled all over me, some of them climbing inside my ears to exclaim their annoyance with so many buzzes and clicks and painful bites.

It was not easy to sleep, even though I was exhausted. My mind was a jumble of thoughts and fears about my mother and father, about Garia and Kairi's rivalry but, above all, about the Castra and what lay ahead of us. All these images jumped around in my head and, when I finally fell into a restless sleep, they became my dreams.

Edbersa shook me awake before dawn. 'Get up, Han. There's no time to waste – not even to break our fast.'

'But I'm hungry,' I protested.

'It is not a bad thing that you should give your stomach a rest. The Polasti of Bathlaya are noted for their feasting and you will be expected to eat everything they put before you. After a while you will yearn to be hungry again.'

'How do you know this about the Polasti, Edbersa? Have you been to this land before?'

Edbersa scowled but didn't answer; instead he busied himself loading our own meagre supply of food on to Fermansa's back. The horse whinnied and kicked up a flurry of dusty pine needles. 'Steady girl,' he soothed. Then he turned to me. 'You will ride the pack mare and not with me. My shoulder can't stand any more of your tugging at my arm in fright every time a baby ledbuk makes a squeak.'

We kept close to the forest edge until the sun was fully in the sky, then we headed out across the plain once more, ever fearful and watchful lest we encounter the Castra. Soon we came across small settlements consisting of clusters of mud dwellings with straw thatch, not unlike our own in Akbenna. There appeared to be no men, only women and a few very small children who stopped to watch us go by but gave us no greeting.

We halted on the brow of a hill to take some mare's milk and a little flat bread. Kairi pointed across two leagues of forested valley to a rocky outcrop in the distance, which projected at different levels from a small mountain like gigantic stone steps. 'Yonder is Bathlaya where the local tribal leader lives,' said Kairi. 'He is known as Mulenda.'

Edbersa scratched his beard and appeared deep in thought.

'Pediv, who rules Polastia from its most important city, Dhagani, does not always like or trust Mulenda because he is quarrelsome and sometimes unduly harsh with his people,' Kairi continued. 'But he guards the southern border fiercely and the king turns a blind eye to many things.'

It was decided that Kairi should go ahead and alert Mulenda to our arrival. I could not hide my concern. 'Is it not dangerous to travel alone among these people, Kairi?'

'I know the Polasti well,' he replied. 'They will not harm me.'

After Kairi set off, employing that easy loping stride of his, we coaxed the horses carefully down the hill, following a track to a river where we let the animals drink and eat a little grass. Then we accompanied the river as it passed by several Polasti villages. Again, women and children came out of their huts to stare at us as if we were creatures they had never encountered before, yet without any obvious surprise at our presence. By the time we were leaving the river and climbing the final stretch of track to the giant rocky steps, the thought was firmly lodged in my mind that these people had somehow been expecting us.

The city of Bathlaya was not how I imagined it would be. In those days Bathlayans did not live in huts or houses but in caves hewn out of the mountainside. The huge steps were terraces stretching half a league along the valley side and upwards to the very top of the mountain. There were so many caves that they could not be counted. But the entire place appeared to be deserted and because there was no sign of Kairi, I feared something bad had happened to him. Maybe the Castra had taken him prisoner – or worse!

Edbersa detected my fear. 'Don't be afraid, Han. Kairi can look after himself.'

'But where are the Bathlayans? If he has told them we are coming, why has no one come to greet us?'

'The ordinary Bathlayans are notoriously shy until they get to know you,' Edbersa said.

Once again, I was tempted to ask him why he knew so much about these people but decided it could wait.

We dismounted and led our horses along the lowest terrace until we reached a large, neatly cut slab of stone perhaps the height and breadth of five men, which had strange symbols and animal figures carved upon it. It was at this moment that a horn sounded and many people – men, women and children – emerged from the caves. They were chanting in a strange tongue that appeared not to be a language but was like the sound of gathering thunder.

When their chanting died away, the people stood silently, unsmiling, staring intently. Then there was another blast of the horn and the formality evaporated. The people's faces opened up; they began to engage with each other, talking and laughing.

Three priests wearing long white garments edged with gold thread that set them apart from the rest of the crowd approached with Kairi at their side. I waved to him, relieved that he was safe.

The tallest of the priests stepped forward. He was a thin man with a dark beard that was so long it made Karmus's beard look like the beard of a goat. He reached an arm out to Edbersa. 'Welcome to you all,' he said in almost perfect Akben. He looked at me. 'Especially to you, young Han.'

Edbersa grasped the man's arm with both hands and bowed his head. 'We are glad to be here, to deliver greetings and good wishes from the elders and people of Akbenna,' he said gravely.

The tall man then revealed his name was Asdur and that he was Bathlaya's head priest. He introduced the other priests as Estil and Gresda.

Edbersa greeted them in the same arm-grasping manner. Then he asked, 'What of Mulenda, your leader?'

'He is away hunting but he will return before the sun sleeps. Then there will be a feast to celebrate the forest deities.'

Asdur signalled to three men who were hovering in the background. He pointed to the horses and issued a terse instruction in Polasti. I didn't find it difficult to understand some of the words he said; they were similar to my own. I realised later that we belonged to the same family of languages.

Garia became agitated. He was reluctant to let Melemari be looked after by strangers and was hanging on to her bridle with one hand while gripping the hilt of his sword with his other.

'Don't worry about the mare,' said Edbersa. 'She will be well cared for. The Polasti have a reputation for being lovers of fine horses.'

'That's what worries me,' said Garia.

Following a hard stare from Edbersa, he relented and the horses were taken away. We were led further along the terrace until we reached a flight of stone steps that took us to the next level. Here we were ushered into a cave which was so magnificent I could scarcely believe what I saw.

Inside it was not like a cave at all but a long, high room lit by a wonderful array of bronze oil lamps. The floor was covered in the finest silk rugs interwoven with golden thread. Cut into the walls were recessed seats where people could sit in comfort on fabrics of so many patterns and hues that I could not grasp the richness and industry of them all. From smaller alcoves at the height of a man's head shone glistering statues of animals and humans. There were golden birds that were also beasts, and elegant human figures carved from what I now know to be jade, decorated with gold and silver adornments. The walls and ceiling were richly painted, depicting hunting scenes where Polasti men pursued all manner of prey. I could not hold my eyes in one place for more than a moment such was the splendour of all I beheld.

My three companions were also bewitched by the scene. Garia was so entranced that he kept repeating almost in a whisper, 'It cannot be real. It is like a dream.'

I did not know then but learned later that many of those gold and silver objects were made from the precious ores stolen from Akbenna in those far-off days when we were the envy of all our neighbours. The Polasti were among the most fervent of the raiders, returning time and again until we had nothing of value left in our mountains.

The priest Asdur beckoned us to sit in one of the larger recesses. 'You will doubtless be hungry from your travels,' he said. 'And it is our tradition that anyone who sojourns here should receive our finest hospitality.'

And so Mulenda's servants brought us a feast of fruits the like of which I had never seen before, let alone tasted. It was a succulent harvest representing all manner of nature's textures, colours and tastes. There were fruits with perfectly smooth, pliable skins that you could peel with your fingers, and fruits with skins so soft the whole of them melted in your mouth. Yet some of the offerings were so hard and knuckled you could have been forgiven for thinking they were lumps of rock but, once prised open with a knife, all of them fleshy and juicy inside.

It was then that I realised how deprived we Akben had become. In my family a halibom was the most luxurious fruit we could expect. Even then it was a rarity, served up only on feast days to honour the Mother Mountain. My father would cut a halibom in half with his axe and we would eagerly scoop out the scarlet flesh with our fingers. I had always considered its taste to be luscious and sweet but, as I devoured the Polasti fruit, I decided I had been persuaded of the halibom's sweetness by everyone else in Akbenna saying how sweet it was. Compared to what I was tasting now, it was pungent, bitter. No matter how hard I tried, I could not help feeling that I had been deceived by my own people and, worst of all, by my own mother and father.

After we had eaten our fill of fruit, Asdur ordered one of the servants to take us to our quarters. We were led back to the lower terrace where Edbersa and I were shown a small, simple cave that we would share. It had no adornments and the only concession to comfort was a pile of sacks filled with straw upon which we were to sleep.

'We are not the honoured guests I would have liked us to be,' Edbersa growled beneath his beard.

Garia and Kairi both reacted petulantly on realising they were also expected to share a cave further along the terrace.

'Is there no place where I can sleep alone?' Garia asked the servant. The man shrugged his shoulders and mumbled something as if to indicate he could not understand the question.

Kairi said nothing but appeared deep in thought.

I tugged Edbersa's tunic. 'Edbersa,' I whispered, 'I am worried that Garia and Kairi will fight if they are forced to sleep together in such a small space.'

'Then you must watch them carefully,' he whispered.

Garia went off moodily to find where Melemari and the other mares were being kept and Edbersa declared he wanted to sleep off an excess of fruit.

I must have looked a little lost because Kairi took pity on me. 'Come, Han, together we will explore Bathlaya.'

By now it was the hottest part of the day and, given the exposed position of the terraces, the Bathlayans had wisely returned to shelter in their caves. The only sign of human life was an occasional servant hurriedly going about his master's business; the only animals were rough-haired dogs lying across some of the cave entrances like somnolent guards.

We climbed to the highest terrace so we could get a better view over the densely wooded valley to the range of mountains that formed Polasti's western border.

'Beyond those mountains is the sea, a body of water so vast and rich in life it provides food for the peoples of all the lands surrounding it.'

'Shall I go there, Kairi?'

'I truly do not know, for those matters were decided before I joined you and I have not been taken fully into your companions' confidence.'

'Are you sad?'

He laughed. 'No, I am not sad. But I am annoyed that Garia does not trust me enough to tell me anything important.' There was a resentful tone to his voice.

'You do not like him, do you?'

Kairi laughed and gently squeezed my shoulder. 'That is correct, Han. I do not like him. Garia is surly and thinks far too much of himself. But I have agreed to help you on this part of your journey and I am a man of my word.'

'But *why* are you helping us?'

Kairi smiled but then grew serious. 'As you've already seen, I live a lonely, nomadic life which I've become used to, but even I sometimes yearn for the company of others. You are unknowing travellers who would harm no one except to defend yourselves, but perhaps you are too unknowing to make such a journey as this. Even Edbersa's experience of life and Garia's arrogance are not enough to ensure success. I decided that you needed my guidance and protection, for which you are exchanging your companionship. That is fair, is it not, Han?'

'It is very fair.'

We explored Bathlaya further, encountering more people

as the afternoon cooled. They appeared curious about us and some stopped working on their pot making or basket weaving to question what we were doing in Bathlaya. Their accents were thick and I could not understand everything they said, but Kairi translated their questions so I could explain my role as an emissary of peace for Akbenna. Most appeared not to take me seriously, shaking their heads dismissively or laughing as if I had made a joke.

'What do they find so funny?' I asked.

'They believe you are *pocnu*, Han, which roughly translated into Akben means a crazy fool. I told them it was most certainly true that the elders of Akbenna had sent you on a great journey to neighbouring lands to create new bonds of friendship.' He laughed. 'Now they think I am also *pocnu* for believing you.'

We inspected every terrace but each appeared much the same as the next. We soon returned to the magnificent cave where we found Asdur and his fellow priests waiting outside to greet the tribal chief Mulenda upon his return from hunting.

The sun had begun to fall over the western hills and Asdur said the hunters had to make it back before dark or they would be hunted by the spirits of the forest animals. Then, just before the sun plunged completely out of sight, Mulenda and his men appeared along the stone road. They were greeted immediately by cheers from a relieved crowd of Bathlayans.

The noise abruptly roused Edbersa from his sleep. He joined us on the main terrace, still rubbing his eyes and not in a good humour.

Asdur explained to us that this had been no ordinary hunting expedition but the precursor to an important night of feasting. The Polasti did not worship a lifeless mountain like the Akben, he said with an ill-disguised sneer; their devotions were to the mysterious and powerful deities of the forest. The animals killed by Mulenda and his men would be ceremoniously prepared, cooked and eaten in such a way that their spirits would enter those who consumed them.

The Polasti hunted all manner of creatures, Asdur said, even those they could not eat. In this way, the hunters would adopt the most important characteristics of the animals, like the speed and grace of the ledbuk, the cunning and pack instinct of the wild dog and the ferocity and power of the tiger.

Mulenda reached the first terrace ahead of his men who were labouring under the weight of many dead creatures. There must have been a hundred or more men, almost all of them walking in pairs, shouldering poles from which the animals were suspended. I had never seen so many dead creatures and almost all of them of them I could not name.

Mulenda, who wore a leather tunic not dissimilar to Edbersa's, carried a bow which he raised above his head as he approached the crowd. Everyone cheered. Judging by their reception, they undoubtedly held him in great esteem – or perhaps I should say in awe.

Mulenda wore his thinning hair gathered up in a top-knot. His bearded face with its fleshy nose was marked, as if it had been ravaged by a pox. He was not small but neither was he a big man; indeed, he was perhaps a little less than the height and build of most of those who followed him. I thought at first that he was weary from his hunting for he walked with a pronounced stoop. It was only when he turned to receive his men that I saw beneath his tunic he carried a huge hump like a rock upon his back. I had never seen the like of it before and a feeling of repulsion overtook me.

As usual, Edbersa sensed my emotion. 'He is not some kind of monster, Han. It is merely a physical deformity. An uncle of mine had a very similar hump.'

This remark prompted me to ask more about Edbersa's family. I was about to engage him on the subject when Asdur urged us forward so we could greet Mulenda and explain the purpose of our journey to Polasti and that, with their approval, we could then journey on to their Dhagani capital to meet the king, Pediv.

The crowd became silent as Edbersa stepped towards the chief and addressed him in fluent Polasti. It appeared to be an answer to my unasked question about Edbersa's past: he must have come from this land.

Mulenda listened intently. Then he looked at me and smiled. In heavily accented Akben he said, 'Greetings to you, Han the Emissary. You are most welcome in Polasti. I trust you are being well taken care of.'

I nodded. 'Yes, thank you,' I said brightly, despite my nervousness. 'Bathlaya is the most wonderful city and your people are very kind.'

'You have yet to witness how generous we can truly be,' Mulenda replied. 'It is a long time since anyone from Akbenna came here.' He laughed. 'We were beginning to think you did not like us.'

Asdur, who was standing beside me, placed an arm across my shoulders. His long beard tickled my face. 'I think Han will see there is much to respect in Polasti.'

'Indeed, Asdur,' Mulenda affirmed. 'We must make sure he sees what a friendly people we are.'

Once again he raised his bow above his head and the crowd responded with more cheers. A horn sounded as if to declare the feasting should begin. The crowd fell upon the slaughtered animals and dragged them off to be butchered or cooked whole on the many roasting spits that had been set up over fire pits along the terrace.

Asdur bade me follow him as he visited each one. He carried a small sack; from it he extracted handfuls of aromatic herbs and spices which he sprinkled on to each carcass. Soon all the fires were roaring and the fat from the slain animals was spitting into the flames.

'We call this feast Caldic Asturta,' Asdur explained. 'It

means the feast of flesh. We will eat nothing but meat for a whole night and day. Every edible part of every animal must be eaten; the rest of the creature will be turned into many different objects or used to make potions to keep our men virile and our women fertile. Nothing must be wasted – to do so would show disrespect for the spirits of the animals we have killed. It is our belief that we must live in harmony with all the creatures of the forest. Whenever we kill and eat them, we offer our prayers of gratitude. Our devotions ensure the forest creatures thrive. In Akbenna, you offered your gratitude to a lifeless mountain and look what you got in return – a lifeless country.'

'But you are wrong,' I protested. 'Mother Mountain was there when we needed her. She destroyed Gilgarius.' The comment was out before I realised that I was even thinking it.

Asdur frowned and grunted something unintelligible. I lowered my head in humility. I had offended my hosts with my precocity. But he smiled benevolently. 'I have heard of your part in Gilgarius's downfall, although some say it really did not happen and the creature could not have been destroyed so easily by a mere boy.'

'I did not destroy the creature,' I retorted, my voice piping with indignation. 'Mother Mountain did that. I only got him angry.'

'Whatever you claim, or is claimed on your behalf, the truth will always come out. And when it does, do not expect it will always come out in your favour.'

Asdur's benevolent smile had by now evaporated. His words confused me. What did he mean?

He placed a hand upon my shoulder and squeezed it, as if regretting his words. 'The truth is that the people of all lands must find ways of worship that are best for them,' he said, his voice now less strident. 'Those who live by the sea offer their devotions to the fish and the turtles and the crabs to ensure the sea keeps providing them. We survive because we harvest the riches of the forest, so it is natural that we worship the forest spirits. You worship your sleeping mountain because once it attracted rain clouds from far away and the rain that fell upon her slopes ran into your lands so you could grow the finest crops. But the clouds stopped coming and your land became a desert. I'm sorry to have to say this, Han, but you must have failed in your devotions. There is no other explanation. It is the only way it could have happened.'

Asdur's words, although spoken more gently, troubled me. It had often been mumbled in Akbenna that we had sown the seeds of our own desperate situation but hearing it from a priest in another land made it seem more of a truth.

Instinctively I became combative. 'At least we are not likely to kill every living creature in our land. We nurture our animals and they feed us, albeit modestly. My parents have but twenty goats from which we get our milk. We give animals life and you give them death.' From where those words came, I do not know; it was as if I was compelled to speak whatever jumped into my head. I had no time to think about it.

Asdur retained his composure despite my provocation. 'Ours may seem a one-sided form of worship, where we take all the forest creatures and give nothing in return,' he said. 'Except that we Polasti are happy to offer ourselves to the spirits when our natural time comes or other circumstances dictate it must be so. You see, Han, when Polasti die their bodies are not burned or hidden in tombs or buried deep in the ground so only the worms can eat them. Our dead are taken into the forest and laid upon the ground so all the creatures that desire to do so can feed upon them.'

Asdur's words chilled my heart. I tried to block out the invading image of the Polasti dead being carried into the forest to be torn apart by wild animals.

The priest could see that I was disturbed and he placed his large bony hand upon my shoulder in a gesture of reassurance.

'It has been our tradition for many generations,' he said quietly. 'To give yourself back to Nature is the greatest thanks you can express for your life.'

But it was not just the giving of the dead to the animals that concerned me.

***

Pelia was intrigued by the routine Arkis had established. He would sit for a while with her grandfather, listening to a little more of his story, then he would saddle Rashi and ride off, but not always in the same direction. Mostly he would be back before dark, to share their food and sleep wrapped in his bear skin under the chatka tree, but sometimes he stayed away a whole night.

Pelia was curious about where their visitor went and to whom he spoke but Arkis never volunteered the information. And she did not have the courage to ask about his journeys or all the other things she desired to know about him and the land he had travelled from.

Visitors rarely came to their little farm. When Pelia was young and her parents lived there, they grew all their own grain to make beer and bread and provide extra feed for their many goats. In those days there were farms scattered all along the Border Valley and everyone helped out at harvest time. But gradually the farms were abandoned as old people died and their sons and daughters moved away to find better lives. Even though irrigation from the Bostrati mountains made the crop fields viable, few wanted to take them on. The farmers' sons left to become soldiers, traders and artisans and the farmers' daughters followed them to become the wives of soldiers, traders and artisans.

Ejiki had grown in size and importance, though Pelia never went to see how large and important it had actually become.

She knew its growth was due to the trade road, which brought the outside world to Akbenna. But while the city provided opportunity for many, it had left Pelia and her grandfather isolated.

They were able to grow only a few crops after her parents left the farm during that angry time. They needed to trade milk and cheese and eggs to get enough grain to make bread and beer and provide extra feed for their animals. Pelia also harvested what olives she could from their little grove. A trader called Petris would come with sacks of grain slung over the backs of three donkeys; he exchanged these for some of Pelia's produce and her unwanted billy kids.

Petris, a widower, was not as old as Han although he was at least the age of Pelia's father. Her grandfather had once said that Pelia should consider marrying him but she was insulted by the suggestion. Even though she had sometimes wondered what it would be like to share a man's bed, Pelia had grown contented with her isolated life.

At least, she thought she had.

Things had grown more confused since the arrival of the traveller. She wanted to know more about him, about the land he came from. Maybe when her grandfather's story was done, Arkis would spend a little more time talking to her. Although he sometimes sought her out, their exchanges were fleeting or at best punctuated too much by hesitation. When Arkis was not listening to her grandfather's story, he was happy to saddle Rashi and explore the land around.

He was free and bold and curious. Pelia wished she could be the same.

***

'When our natural time comes or other circumstances dictate it must be so.'

Asdur's words rang in my ears, said Han. I wanted to understand what he meant by 'other circumstances' but could not bring myself to ask him.

I left the priest to continue his blessing of the roasting carcasses and went to search for Garia. The animosity between Kairi and he had become my greatest worry now that we had been delivered safely from the Castra. I needed to talk to Garia to persuade him that Kairi was a good man who deserved our companionship.

I found him sitting on a slab of rock, some distance from the feasting Polastians, his face shining in the flames of a torch that had been wedged into a crevice in the rock.

'How is Melemari?' I asked.

'She has a cave of her own,' Garia said bitterly. 'I may go there to sleep in her company tonight. It will be better than that of an ignorant wild man.'

'Please do not think badly of Kairi,' I pleaded. 'He just wants to be a friend to us all.'

'You always think the best of people, Han, and that is a good thing most of the time. But Kairi is a bad one. I don't trust him.'

'That is unfair. He put his life in danger to save us when the Castra attacked us by the river.'

'He had to fight the Castra to save himself. It was not for us. He is just staying with us because we have things he wants.'

'Like what?'

'Food, Han. He would be starving without our provisions.'

'He killed a ledbuk and caught fish for us,' I countered.

'Well, maybe not food – but he is after something. A horse maybe. I have seen him eyeing Melemari with envy in his eyes.'

'He can run so fast he has no need of a horse,' I said.

Garia pulled a face. 'Anyway, I simply do not like him,' he said. 'Kairi is arrogant and is full of himself.'

I laughed.

'What's so funny?'

'It is not the first time today I've heard words like those.'

I left Garia to his sulk and went in search of Edbersa. I found him close to our cave, cutting a slice of meat from a small animal that was being roasted on a spit by two women. They were dressed in smocks that appeared to have been woven from the strands of palm leaves. Edbersa was speaking in their language, making them laugh. I recognised some of the words because they were not so different from Akben, but because they were so strongly accented – or perhaps due to my immaturity – I failed to understand their meaning.

'Ah, Han!' Edbersa exclaimed. 'These fine women are cooking up some tasty flesh. Come and join us. There is plenty for all.' He was in unusually good spirits, red faced and waving his arms at me in an exaggerated fashion. I suspected he had been drinking his liquor or some potent grog supplied by Mulenda.

'Now Han,' he said. 'I was just telling Bakiba and Lapeda about our run-ins with the Castra and that you and Garia saved my life by pissing on me.'

I reddened and the two women laughed. I realised that in this frivolous mood Edbersa would be no company for me. I accepted a sliver of meat out of politeness and set off in search of Kairi.

I could not find him in the crowd of feasters but it did not matter, for my attention was soon attracted by music being played further along the terrace. Following the sound, I wove in and out of the feasting Bathlayans who were squatting in small groups. Some of the impatient ones were devouring rats they had cooked in the fire embers while waiting for the larger carcasses to roast. Most of the men were drinking wine from clay cups; the more that they consumed, the louder their laughter and banter became.

The musicians were in no ordered group but were scattered

among the revellers, blowing horns, striking bones or plucking gut strings that had been stretched tightly across wooden frames. Some of the men were dancing to the music, frenziedly whirling around each other, while the women and children clapped and cheered them on.

All these sights and sounds, combined with the redolence of roasted flesh, mesmerised my senses. I had never experienced the like of it before. In Akbenna I was used to festivals that were much quieter, more respectful affairs. Prayers were offered to Mother Mountain in hushed tones, as though raising our voices in a chant would cause her to erupt in anger. We did not feast in the sense of devouring large amounts of food or drink, for such was not available to us. Our devotions were quite timid; indeed, we were a timid, anxious people in those days, always fearful of our neighbours.

I was a typical Akben. Anxiety blighted my life. Although only a child, I was possessed by worries that normally afflicted people much older than me. In this regard I took after my mother, whose life was blighted by woes, both real and imagined.

So you can guess, Arkis, how much anxiety I felt after being chosen as an emissary by Karmus. From the very start, I believed his faith in me and his expectations of me had been wildly misplaced. I was like a whimpering child, afraid at every turn. Was this the same child who had saved his people from Gilgarius?

I have thought about this often over the years and have arrived at the belief that within the child lies the man. We do not acquire wisdom as if it is a new cloak to be worn; we are born with its capacity already within us. Indeed, we come into this world with many powers, which sometimes come to the fore when we are faced with life's most desperate challenges. Wisdom is one of these. It is not acquired by experience but revealed by it.

But where was I, Arkis? Ah yes, the celebrations in Bathlaya. I was describing to you the sights and the sounds of the Polasti feast. It went on through the night and, though tired, I was determined to remain awake until dawn.

I wandered around looking for Kairi and was offered meat at every spit I encountered. Out of respect for the Polasti tradition I did not dare refuse any of it, even though I soon became full. Eventually I returned to Edbersa and the two Polasti women and found Kairi sharing meat and drink with them.

'Ah Han!' Edbersa exclaimed. 'You must eat some *musdor*. It is most succulent. I have not tasted such flesh for many years.'

I accepted a little of the meat out of politeness but was more interested in pressing Edbersa about his past. 'Is Polasti your homeland, Edbersa?' I asked as I ate without enthusiasm.

He fixed me with his dense eyes, which were like black beans in a blood soup. 'I suppose this is a homecoming of sorts,' he said enigmatically. 'Some welcome, don't you think, lad?' He waved a hand towards Bakiba and Lapeda who were carving meat from a dog-sized animal. 'It's so long since I have been in this land that I'd forgotten how fine looking Polasti women are, Han.'

I did not think Bakiba and Lapeda were fine looking. One was too fat and the other too thin. The fat one had no teeth and the thin one had dark hair growing on her upper lip like a man.

Edbersa put his hand on my shoulder and pulled me close to him, conspiratorially. 'I'm not sure if you know about how things are between men and women, Han,' he whispered. 'But I would like to sleep with one of these two before the dawn comes.' His black beard parted, revealing a crooked smile. 'In truth, I would like to sleep with both of them.'

Of course, at thirteen I had barely started to grow into a man so I did not fully understand what he meant. In my confusion, I thought he was simply rejecting my companionship. I did not know what to say, so I said nothing.

Edbersa continued, 'I'm telling you this, Han, because if I don't return to our cave to sleep then you know that I will be with one of these women.' He looked over to Bakiba and Lapeda and licked his lips. 'Both are widowed and I think they crave a man.' He took a long swig of his grog and wiped his mouth with the back of his hand before adding, 'And I certainly crave a woman.'

At this point Garia arrived and I jumped up to greet him, relieved at the welcome diversion. Edbersa nodded a greeting but said nothing.

Garia cast a mean eye over to Kairi, who was sitting quietly watching some of the festive ribaldry further along the terrace, and poured himself a generous measure of liquor into a clay cup. 'Cut me some meat, Han,' he said. 'My hunger has got the better of me.'

Far from being in a festive mood, the night left me feeling despondent. Edbersa remained preoccupied with Bakiba and Lapeda, enticing them to sit on straw sacks on each side of him. He pulled them both close, talking to them in a low growl. I saw him try to kiss the thin one but she pulled her face away, laughing. The fat one was not so bashful and allowed Edbersa to lick her neck. The thin woman responded by placing a hand upon Edbersa's knee. He shifted his position slightly and her hand slipped between his legs.

Confused and embarrassed, I turned for companionship to Garia and Kairi but both were brooding in their own inaccessible worlds. Their attitude to each other upset me but there was nothing I could do about it. All I could do was hope they would not fight.

Thankfully there was the feasting with its heady atmosphere of music and smoke and laughter to distract me. Leaving Garia and Kairi to their moods, I once again lost myself among the celebrating Bathlayans.

As I moved among the throng, I compared these people with my own. As I have already told you, Arkis, in those days we Akbenna were a quiet, timid folk, certainly in comparison to the animated Polasti. But there in Bathlaya another difference struck me: there was an absence of old people in public places. In my land, we did not hide our elderly but revered and celebrated their lives openly. Asdur was the oldest Bathlayan I had seen, and he could have been little more than fifty years old. So where did the old people live? And why were they not in attendance at the feasting? I decided these were questions I would have to ask Asdur the next day.

After a while I returned to where I'd left my companions, only to find my worst fears realised: Garia and Kairi were standing almost toe to toe, involved in an argument. Edbersa was too distracted by Bakiba and Lapeda to see what was unfolding only a few strides away.

I pushed myself between the adversaries just as Garia grabbed the hilt of his sword. Kairi, who was not in possession of his spear, sneered at him dismissively.

'Please, do not fight,' I pleaded.

On hearing my voice, Edbersa looked up. 'Leave them to it, Han. If they're stupid enough to want to kill each other, let them get on with it.'

'You are drunk, Edbersa,' I shouted. 'You don't know what you are saying.'

Edbersa shrugged his shoulders and returned his attention to the women.

I looked up at Garia. 'Please stop this.'

'I cannot,' he replied firmly. 'It has gone too far.'

'Why? Why are you two always falling out?'

'Ask him.'

I turned to Kairi. 'Why can't you be friends?'

'It is impossible to be friends with one who thinks so much of himself.'

Garia issued a husky laugh. 'And not without reason.' He started to unsheathe his sword.

'Stop it! Stop it!' I began to sob. 'Please, Garia. Please do not kill Kairi.'

Garia released his hand from the sword hilt, issuing a laugh of bravado. 'For your sake, Han, I will not kill him. But I can never be the friend of a wild man.'

I looked at Kairi. He was smiling wryly. 'For your sake, Han, I will try to be Garia's friend.' He raised a hand as a gesture of companionship.

I fixed Garia with a determined look through my tears. 'What about you, Garia? Can you not take Kairi's hand?'

He hesitated a few moments before reaching out. Their touch was fleeting but it was a relief to see it. I swear I also saw a flash of triumph in Kairi's eyes.

You can imagine, Arkis, how much I longed to go home, for all this was too difficult for such a young, innocent mind. It was not the experience I had expected when Karmus sent me on my journey. He wanted me to be an ambassador for peace and harmony yet those I travelled with were anything but peaceful or harmonious.

I continued to miss my mother and my father; it was an ache that would not go away. I was acutely aware of the stress that my mother, in particular, would be feeling. Once again the story of the muddy young ledbuk and the wolves came into my mind. I believed my mother was suffering just as I was; somehow she could hear my mental cries, which were carried to her on the wind. And I knew she would not believe anything – even the goal of a greater good for Akbenna – was worth the sacrifice of a son.

And I already doubted the wisdom of our journey. Since leaving home I had encountered only discomfort and danger. It had made me realise that, even if our mission was successful and a treaty of peace was agreed between Akbenna and

Polastia, the achievement would surely be undermined by the Castra. If a trade route was opened, for example, no one could travel freely or safely between Akbenna and Polasti because the Castra would not allow it. For whatever reason, they had been determined to stop us reaching Bathlaya. Although they had failed, I had a feeling we had not heard the last of them.

My head was still full of all these doubts and worries when I fell asleep beside the dying embers of the terrace fire, lulled by the music and the unintelligible Polasti chatter. When I awoke with the first spears of dawn, all was silent.

Many of the Bathlayans had chosen to sleep among the remains of their feasting, incapable of movement after so much meat and drink. Edbersa, Garia and Kairi were nowhere to be seen.

I shivered. A cold wind had got up along the valley and I decided to continue my sleep in the cave. Of course I was concerned what I might find there. I did not know whether Edbersa might be there with Bakiba or Lapeda, perhaps even both of them. I was also anxious about Garia and Kairi. How sincere was their promise not to fight? I had no way of knowing.

Yawning, I set off for the sleeping cave. To reach it I had to pass the cave allotted to Garia and Kairi and I approached it apprehensively. As I came closer to the entrance, my worst fears were realised when I heard a cry of pain, as if someone had been run through with a sword.

Instinctively I ran to the cave's mouth and looked inside though I hesitated to enter. There was another cry, even more agonising, which both frightened and emboldened me. I stepped inside.

An oil lamp gave off only the dimmest, flickering light but it was enough to see Garia's attack upon Kairi. A naked, sweat-glistering collection of flesh and limbs were interlocked in an implausible wrestling hold. Kairi was on his knees with Garia laid across his back, biting his neck. Kairi gave another cry of pain as if he had been stabbed by a dagger but there were no weapons in Garia's hands.

Then Kairi half-turned his head so I could see his face, and instead of fear and pain I saw only joy. His mouth parted and he whispered something. Garia lifted his head from Kairi's neck and their lips met in the tenderest of kisses.

I wanted to cry out in my confusion but gulped back the sound and tumbled out of the cave. I fled, shocked and troubled and failing to understand the reality of the strange combat I had witnessed. Disoriented, I climbed to the topmost terrace of the city and sat waiting for the sun to rise. I was exhausted but my head was full of so many confusions, I felt I would not be able to sleep.

My concerns were not just related to Garia and Kairi but also to Bathlaya, its citizens, their leaders and their beliefs and rituals. In particular, I worried about the strange absence of older people.

I desperately wished dawn would come so I could leave this place of evil, for I was sure that is what it was. I faced the direction from which we had come towards Mother Mountain and began to pray to her. I begged her to send my father to find me. He would know what to do. He was resourceful, despite all the names my mother called him, and would find a way to come for me.

Eventually I slept, curled up next to the fading embers of one of the cooking fires. It was a fitful, dream-laden sleep in which I once again searched desperately for my mother and father. I swear I heard them calling my name, their desperate cries carrying across the desert and the mountains. I woke, my face drenched in tears.

What was I to do, Arkis? Whatever Edbersa and the others decided, I believed I could not stay a moment longer in such a place. And I had no inclination to venture a further distance from Akbenna. Yet could I go back alone into a hostile land where the evil Castra seemed to roam at will? Indeed, could I ever find my way home without the help of my companions?

I felt wretched and almost completely drained of life. When eventually Kairi came to find me, after the sun was well risen, I could not look him in the eye. 'What is troubling you, Han?' he asked.

I did not reply but stared towards the rising sun from whence we had come. Nothing Kairi could say would appease me and he left, shaking his head.

Eventually Edbersa appeared, I know not whether he was alerted by Kairi but he came to find me nonetheless. He wasn't the Edbersa I knew. His eyes were as red as the embers of a bread fire; his demeanour hunched and leaden. 'I'm sorry, Han,' he said. 'I have behaved badly. I have been charged with your protection and became distracted.'

I did not ask him if he, too, had been involved in some strange form of combat. If he had, it looked like he had lost. Instead I remained silent, staring into the distance, desperately homesick and feeling completely alone despite Edbersa's apparent concern for my welfare.

For a while we sat without acknowledging each other as Bathlaya slowly came to life beneath us. Still I could see no older people. The matter troubled me so much I was compelled to end the spell of dumbness and put the question to Edbersa.

He growled a little, as if struggling with an answer. Then he turned to face me, trying to deliver a smile out of his dense beard. 'The reason you can see no old people in Bathlaya is because there are none.'

He belched loudly, emitting a smell so putrid from a night of drinking and meat-eating I was forced to turn my head away. 'Do I have to spell it out to you, Han,' he continued. 'Or can you guess?'

I suppose I knew all along but did not want to admit it to myself. Asdur had almost said as much: *'When our natural time comes or other circumstances dictate it must be so.'* So that was it. The Bathlayans disposed of their old people by driving them into the forest so they could be eaten by the wild animals. 'They kill them,' I said.

Edbersa growled and shook his head. 'No, they would not do that, but they do leave them to fend for themselves. And inevitably the older and more infirm they are, the more they become vulnerable to preying animals.'

I felt a stab of pain and anger. How could they do this? How could young Bathlayans allow their mothers and fathers to be driven away? I imagined my own parents growing old back in Akbenna and knew I could never allow such a fate to befall them. 'Why don't the old people resist?' I found myself asking.

Edbersa laughed humourlessly. 'You must realise, Han, that those who are being driven away were once young people who did the same to their own parents, and their parents to their grandparents. They accept it is the way of things that those who cannot bear children or hunt or fight are no longer useful.'

'Do they never see each other again?'

'Look, Han, it is not as bad as it seems. The old people go to live in their own communities, fending for themselves. Although they face danger, they're probably glad to be away from this place, for Bathlaya is a place for the young and vigorous.' He laughed, more like a grunt.

'What's funny?'

'I suppose I should feel out of place here at my age.'

Edbersa grunted some more. He always grunted when he was uncomfortable and growled when he was angry. Perhaps he carried guilt that he had once been one of these people and therefore was part of this terrible culture. He must have known all along that this is what happened to Bathlayans when they reached a certain age. Maybe he had driven his own parents away.

I got to my feet. Edbersa reached out a hand and gripped my arm. 'Sit down, Han,' he ordered. 'I know what you're thinking and it is time I explained about … about my past.'

I hesitated.

'Please, Han. Sit down and listen. Don't judge me until you have heard all I have to say.'

Edbersa's voice was even more croaky than usual, parched by too much liquor and, I suspected, emotion. He had, after all, returned to his homeland after many years; in his own way he must have felt as lost and confused as I did. I sat and waited while my companion composed himself to speak.

'Yes, you are right about my past, Han,' he said at length. 'I was not born here in Bathlaya but much further along the valley in a farming community that valued its independence. Like Bathlayans are of the Polasti people, so are my people, the Caylan, but we always considered ourselves independent spirited. We certainly did not want to have anything to do with the Bathlaya Polastians, whom we always considered to be bad people. You can see why. Our communities were vastly different. We were farmers, not hunters. We worshipped the sun and the winds and the rain because they helped our crops pollenate and grow.

'One day, when I was a young man, Bathlayan warriors sent by Mulenda's father, Utakok, came to our town to try and force our elders to accept him as provincial ruler. We resisted because we knew that their alien rituals would be imposed upon us, especially driving out the old when they were no longer useful. Our society was so different. Like the people of Akbenna, we revered our elders. They taught us everything about growing crops and caring for livestock. They knew the value of every plant in the meadows and forests. They could make concoctions to ease any malady. They nurtured and propagated and respected every salub of ground. Even older people who could no longer work the fields or take care of the animals led useful lives, making the concoctions or helping to produce the cheese and ale that kept us fed and happy.

'But the Bathlayans came and destroyed all we had. They drove away our old people, just like they did their own. They took our young women and killed most of the men. Thus, I was forced to flee my home. We pleaded with the Polasti king to send an army to retake our home and rescue our young women but our entreaties fell upon a barren heart. The king was preoccupied with combatting enemies at our northern and western borders. All he cared was that Utakok guarded the southern border against Akbenna and kept the Castra at bay. The king did not care to hear about what evil acts Utakok chose to carry out within his own domain.'

As Edbersa looked at me, tears drowned his bloodshot eyes. He hung his head. 'My mother and my father resisted and were among those killed. My sister, Leandra, was one of the young women taken by Utakok for his own pleasure.'

He turned his head away and I wondered if he was ashamed of his tears. We sat in silence for a while, staring beyond the Bathlayan terraces to the dense forest that cloaked the distant hills.

'You are probably wondering why I consented to return to this place, given all that has happened,' Edbersa said at length. 'And you may also wonder why I have been able to deal in such a measured way with Mulenda when I should have driven a spear through his heart because of what his father did to my family.'

'Yes, Edbersa,' I said. 'I was wondering those things exactly.'

'Well,' he parted his beard in a crooked smile. 'For all the evil Utakok did to us, there is a fact that cannot be escaped – his son, Mulenda, is my blood nephew.'

The question was barely on my lips when Edbersa answered it. 'Mulenda, the leader of the Bathlayans, is the son my sister Leandra.' He turned his head to face me and I could see the flood of tears disappearing into his dense beard like a mountain stream into the forest. 'Leandra did not live long. She died delivering a male heir to Utakok.'

'Do you hate Mulenda?' I found myself asking.

Edbersa dabbed his eyes with his leather sleeve. 'Oh yes, I have hatred in my heart all right. I hate what Mulenda represents, what he and his people believe in. But the hatred is tempered by knowing he is of my blood.'

'Does he know you are his uncle?'

Edbersa shook his head slowly. 'And nor should he, Han.' He attempted a laugh. It came out like a toad's croak. 'So I don't want you running off and telling him.'

We sat some more in silence as Edbersa's revelation sank in. He then told me how he came secretly to Bathlaya and tried to rescue Leandra from Utakok's clutches. But by then she had become his wife and was bearing his child, so she refused to leave. That is when Edbersa abandoned the land of the Polasti and made his way to Akbenna to begin a new life.

He did not know of his sister's fate until many years later, when a rare Polasti traveller passed through our capital Ejiki and sought shelter in our temple. Charged with administering hospitality, Edbersa could not resist asking news of his homeland. That was how he discovered Leandra had died giving birth to Mulenda.

He placed a companionable arm around my shoulders. 'So, there you have it, young Han. My family secret is out.' He sniffled and wiped away a last remaining tear with his sleeve. 'And while we are revealing secrets, I would like to know why you chose to hide yourself away up here. Kairi said you are troubled by something.'

'Edbersa, I am troubled by many things.'

'Then please tell me. If I can help ease your mind, I will surely try to do so.'

But how could I tell him all that which made me confused

and afraid?

Edbersa prompted me. 'Are you still afraid Garia and Kairi will kill each other?'

Now it was the turn of my eyes to fill with tears. 'No … I am not afraid of that any more. But there is something I saw…' I hesitated to respond, struggling put into words what I had witnessed, unable to understand the most confusing change in two men who only hours before had been deadly enemies prepared to kill each other.

I was silent for a good time but Edbersa was patient with me. We watched Bathlaya continue awakening from its heavy, feast-induced sleep. The sun was beginning to climb above hills behind us and in our exposed position we would soon bake. Yet I did not wish to move until I had explained all to Edbersa. So I told him about the scene I had stumbled upon in the night.

'You are right to be confused,' said Edbersa. 'I would not have forecast such an outcome, yet I confess that I am not surprised.' He began to laugh.

'You are mocking me,' I said with indignation.

'You have to admit, Han, it is very amusing.' Edbersa swallowed hard to supress another laugh. With an effort, he straightened his face. 'I am not mocking you, Han. I am merely amused that I failed to see what could happen between Garia and Kairi.'

He hesitated a little as if to gather his thoughts, then said, 'Please allow me to explain.'

He said he knew that Kairi had been driven from his tribe because of his desire for other men. The wild man had not confessed this directly, but Edbersa was certain it was so because Kairi's tribe was renowned for mutilating the penises of young men who preferred congress with their own sex. Thus marked, they were then banished into the wilderness.

'As Kairi's manhood has been disfigured and he wanders alone, it is obvious what his true nature is,' said Edbersa sombrely. 'Men of Kairi's persuasion also whiten their bodies and paint them with recognisable patterns. These markings set them apart and identify them to other wanderers in the wilderness who also prefer the company of men to that of women.'

Despite Edbersa's explanation, I remained confused that the two of them should behave so intimately with each other, How could a manly soldier like Garia have been seduced into such an act by someone he seemed to hate so much? But I resisted further questions. Of course, I now know all about such matters but back then the episode I witnessed and Edbersa's observations proved rather embarrassing for such a young boy as I.

I knew, however, that neither of us should dwell on it. 'Please, Edbersa,' I said. 'We must not let Kairi and Garia know that I saw what I did. I fear it would make our continuing journey awkward.'

'Good point, lad.' Edbersa slapped me on the back and rose to his feet. 'But it will certainly be interesting to see whether our friends continue to pretend that they hate each other,' he added, summoning a mischievous laugh.

Thankfully we were to stay not a day longer in Bathlaya. Our true destiny was the Polasti capital, Dhagani, where it was expected that I would meet the king, Pediv.

We collected our meagre possessions and strapped them to our mounts, together with some of the leftover meat from the night's feasting. Garia and Kairi gave nothing away that suggested either enmity or intimacy as Mulenda and the priest Asdur gathered to bid us farewell, along with a small crowd of Bathlayan townsfolk.

Bakiba and Lapeda also appeared to wave farewell to Edbersa, bleary eyed and looking uglier than ever. It was no surprise that he tried not to notice them.

'I have sent ahead so other Polastian settlements beyond

the forest know of your journey,' said Mulenda, 'to ensure you will be welcomed with food and shelter should you need it.'

Knowing now that he was Edbersa's nephew, I examined the Bathlayan leader more closely to see if I could identify a family resemblance. The obvious difference between them was the large hump on Mulenda's back, which Edbersa did not have. There was something in their faces, however, that indicated a blood link: their deep, dark eyes and dense beards naturally drew comparison, as did their fleshy noses and hue of skin. At the very least, it was obvious they were both of the same people.

Mulenda thrust out a strong sinewy arm and Edbersa twined it firmly in a snake grip. 'We thank you for your excellent Bathlayan hospitality,' he said.

There was something in Edbersa's expression, the timbre of his voice, that suggested he was supressing an emotion as active as leavening dough in his gut. Mulenda, too, must have detected such a resonance. He hesitated to let go of the other man's arm, inclining his head slightly to one side as if to view Edbersa from a more revealing angle.

He was about to make an observation when Asdur interposed. 'So, my friends, your journey of diplomacy continues and I'm sure we all wish you well.' He looked at me; he was smiling but his eyes held menace. 'And you have a fine emissary in young Han here. He is not afraid to question and criticise, despite his lack of worldly knowledge.'

For me, we could not ride out of Bathlaya quickly enough. To subdued waves and unenthusiastic shouts of farewell, we finally began our journey onward to Dhagani, Kairi running ahead of us in his usual graceful manner. I could not imagine being more pleased to leave a place.

We travelled the remainder of the morning in silence and without incident as we passed through some of the small villages that skirted the forest's edge. I knew that soon we would have to enter the trees. Kairi indicated this would be done at the forest's narrowest point, making our journey to the plain on its far side as short as possible. Even so, we faced spending at least one night in the dense and dangerous place as it would take two days or more to reach the open land beyond.

In each community we encountered, the people came out to watch us silently and without expressing any emotion. We did not stop to avail ourselves of their hospitality or even exchange talk with them.

Only once did we see an old person and it was a fleeting encounter at the very edge of the forest. I saw her first, a tiny woman with grey hair down to her waist. She was bent double, plucking some sort of plant from the undergrowth and placing it in a wicker basket. She looked up upon our approach and I smiled and gave her a wave because I wanted to assure her that we were friends and did not behave meanly towards elderly people like her Bathlayan kin. But the woman looked aghast, as if ashamed at being seen; dropping her basket, she hurried into the forest. She was an outcast in her own land and I dearly wished I could do something so that this terrible shunning of the old would be ended once and for all.

As the sun reached its highest point, Kairi found a suitable place where we could enter the forest. The shade provided by the canopy was a welcome relief from the draining heat of the day but there was no respite for my heart, which pounded against my rib cage at the thought of the wild creatures we might encounter.

Every sound or sudden movement startled me; each swooping bird, or scurrying rodent caused me to cling on more tightly to Edbersa.

'Easy lad,' he said. 'Save your fright for when we come across truly savage creatures – and I'm not talking about those of the animal kind.' His words were to prove prophetic.

Even though Kairi had found us a well-used trail to follow,

progress was slow because the horses had to pick their way over tree roots and vines that ran along the surface of the ground. There were also boggy areas our mounts had to be coaxed through carefully and we had to ford streams, which were sometimes wide enough to be called a river though none were deeper than half the height of a full-grown man. Occasionally there were clearings where we stopped to let the horses graze and take our own relief and refreshment.

It was in one of these clearings that we decided to halt for the night. Garia took care of the horses while Kairi prepared a fire, not for cooking on but to ward off dangerous animals. Mulenda had furnished us with bread and leftover meat from the feast and our gourds had been replenished with fresh goat's milk and we set to eating as soon as we could.

The fire crackled and spat out its embers while we sat in silence. We all of us had reasons not to speak. I was too embarrassed to address either Garia or Kairi, and they were probably too embarrassed or afraid to address each other. Edbersa seemed to withdraw so far into himself, assisted by swigs of strong liquor, that he could not be reached.

As the sun fell, the already forbidding forest was as black as the night that embraced it. Around us the canopy blocked out many of the star patterns that helped us to know our place on the earth and in the heavens. I could, of course, see some of the familiar ones directly above our clearing. Such star shapes had meanings which we learned in stories.

In Akbenna, we followed the traditional belief – encouraged by the elders – that the stars were the celestial children of Mother Mountain, hurled into the heavens during her fiery eruptions. The elders said many things about Mother Mountain, with one story often contradicting another. Some said the eruptions were a punishment for our bad ways; others said they were to be celebrated as a sign that she loved us because for generations she had also showered our land with rich red earth upon which we could grow anything we wanted. That is, before the water stopped flowing out of the hills.

I tried to believe the stars had been created by Mother Mountain because she wanted to give us comforting light when the sun went to sleep, but I realised all the skies above every land were lit by stars at night. Either Mother Mountain was a very generous deity in her giving, or the stars – at least those shining upon other lands – were not her children at all.

Together, the stars made the shapes of exotic creatures and godlike men. They hunted each other, but in our stories the men always triumphed. Some carried spears and pursued lions and elephants with tamed wolves at their heels. There were stars that looked like leaping ledbuk and stars that were beautiful maidens, all manner of shapes that inspired lots of stories. My favourite story was about the star children, which my mother used to remind me of whenever I misbehaved.

Like children on the land, star children can be disobedient, my mother said. One particular star mother had given birth to so many star children over so many years that no one could count them. But this star mother's children were so disobedient they wouldn't do a thing their mother told them.

One thing the stars do, as you know, is to form patterns in the sky so that people down here can recognise them. Sailors and other travellers need these patterns to see which direction they should go. But these star children decided they did not wish to be told what patterns to make. They danced about the night sky, doing whatever they wanted without a care for the feelings of other more obedient stars or for the people down here who need to be guided by them.

This went on for a long time and the mischievous little stars remained unpunished. They believed that their antics were actually appreciated by the other stars as well as humans and other creatures and that they made our lives more interesting. But the great god of the stars grew tired of their behaviour and called upon their mother star to explain why they couldn't lead settled star lives.

'You cannot have any more star children until you learn how to control them,' the star god told her.

'But I've tried everything to keep them orderly,' the star mother protested. 'It's not my fault they don't take any notice.'

'Then I shall have to deal with the situation myself,' said the indignant star god. 'I shall banish your children from the heavens – and you also, if you attempt to have any more of them.'

The star god is not an unkind god, and it troubled him terribly to have to be so harsh with the star mother, but he felt there was nothing else he could do. She was not capable of bringing up responsible children who would behave in a proper manner and take predictable positions in the night sky. The children were impossible to control.

The star mother replied, 'You might as well banish me anyway for if I can't have any more children, I have no purpose. Producing little stars to grow into big stars is all I exist for.'

This upset the star god. He attempted a direct approach to the errant star children to get them to behave but they were never still for long enough to hear his demands. They just carried on their crazy antics, flitting about the heavens, causing chaos and confusion.

The star children were so preoccupied that they never noticed their distressed star mother weeping tears of light into the night sky. All, that is, but the youngest star child. 'Why are you so sad, mother?' he asked.

'Because we all have to leave the heavens.'

'Why?'

'I have borne too many star children who simply won't behave. You and your brothers and sisters are far too unruly. We are all to be banished because I can't control you.'

The little star child began to cry his own tears of light. 'But

I don't want to be banished,' he wailed.

But the star mother said there was no choice. 'Go to your brothers and sisters,' she said, fighting back more light tears. 'Tell them we must prepare to leave the night sky forever.'

The little star flew off to do as he was told, but he was so tearful he had to stop to have his cry. Soon his brothers and sisters gathered round him, asking why he was so sad when there was nothing else to do in the heavens but have fun.

'I'm sad because we are all going to be banished for being disobedient,' he said. 'Even our star mother has to leave the night sky because she can't control us.'

'Is she sad, too?' asked a star sister.

'Yes. She's weeping so many tears of light, she could soon disappear completely.'

'Then we must do something to stop her crying and cheer her up,' said one of the other star children.

'What can we do?' asked another.

'I know, let's make some interesting light shapes,' said the eldest of all the star children.

'Like earth children draw pictures in the dust?' asked another.

'Yes. Like pictures in the dust.'

So all the errant star children started to dance about the night sky and make different pictures. They made so many – shapes of bulls and bears and giant fish and crabs and boats and ploughs and many other creatures and objects. They even made a picture of a man hunting with a bow and arrow, which they thought particularly amusing.

When all the pictures were complete, the youngest star child went to find his star mother and said to her, 'Look what my brothers and sisters have done.'

And when she saw the pictures, she stopped weeping tears of light and smiled, shining brightly and so clearly that she became the brightest star in the night sky.

The star god saw the pictures and shapes, too, and began to laugh heartily. 'Now that's the sort of thing you should have been doing all along,' he said. Then he grew serious again and said, 'But I am not hopeful they can stay like that.'

However, the star children were so pleased with what they had done and how it cheered up their star mother that they promised to remain in their new positions so their creations would be seen forever in the night sky. That's when the star god forgave them and said that they and their star mother would no longer be banished from the heavens.

And that is why stars form pictures of creatures and objects that never change how they appear to us.

I fell asleep in the clearing, thinking of the star children and other stories until they became my dreams.

I woke to the sound of our horses whinnying pitifully. Something in the forest had disturbed them. Dawn was casting its first dim light and I could see Garia and Kairi were already on their feet, their weapons raised. Edbersa was kicking earth over the fire he'd kept going through the night. He placed a finger to his mouth to signal that I should remain silent. But nothing could quiet our horses and they continued their fearful whinnying, as if they could smell fierce forest creatures that had gathered on the edge of the clearing to attack us.

Garia and Kairi whispered urgently to each other while Edbersa tried to calm the horses. Fear froze me as I imagined the hungry animals lurking on the clearing's edge: wolves, wild dogs, mountain lions with their umber fangs as sharp as daggers. They were all capable of killing humans. I wanted to cry but resisted. This was no time to be a blubbering burden on my companions.

I forced myself to my feet and plucked a smouldering tree branch from the remains of the fire. If any wild animal came to attack me, I would burn out its eyes.

The creatures that finally broke into the forest clearing were of the two-legged human kind, however. I could only see their shapes in the still-dull light, but there were many of them, too many this time for us to fight. The silence was broken by their shouts, the clash of metal against metal and the cries of pain.

From behind, a large calloused hand was clamped over my mouth. The smouldering branch was plucked from my feeble grasp and I was lifted clear of the ground by a sinewy arm. Edbersa jumped to defend me but two men just as powerfully built were quickly upon him, wrestling him to the ground.

The sound of the fight in the clearing subsided as I was borne into the forest.

***

Han stopped speaking and closed his eyes. Arkis said nothing, respecting the old man's need for silent reflection. After some time went by, he began to worry. Han's head had slumped on to his chest and he was so still that he appeared not to be breathing.

Arkis reached out to touch his arm. Han opened his eyes, blinked and looked around as if he could not believe where he was. 'I'm sorry,' he said, slowly lifting his head. 'I must have fallen asleep.'

'Tell me no more today,' Arkis said. 'You are too tired.'

'But I have come to a very important part of my story,' said Han. 'I must reveal what happened.'

'Of course – and I'm desperate to hear it, believe me. But for now it's time for you to rest.'

'Yes, I suppose you're right,' said Han, smiling weakly.

Arkis left the old man with his silence and went off to find Pelia. She was busy making curd cheese. He watched from a distance as she poured the curdled goat's milk into a muslin cloth from which she would squeeze the watery whey. She stopped working when she saw him approaching.

'Please, carry on,' Arkis said. 'The light is fading and I know you need to complete your work. We can talk while you do so.'

'Is he asleep?'

'Yes. He seems to be getting weaker. Maybe it's not good that I'm here. Telling his story is tiring him out. He can recall so much.'

'It does take quite a long time to tell but it is too much for him to tell it in one go.'

'Do you know his story well?'

By this time Pelia had ladled all the curdled milk into the muslin sack and she tied the open end with strands of dry grass she had plaited. 'Yes, I've heard him telling the story to different people,' she said as she continued her work. 'But I've never known him speak as much as he's spoken to you. In recent months he hasn't been able to move about much. He's just been sitting day after day in his porch or under the tree, hardly moving, staring into the distance. He must have been waiting for you to come along.'

Arkis found himself intrigued by the observation. 'I'm worried,' he said. 'Han is fading yet he's desperate to carry on. I can see everything is taking a real effort. I've said that he should stop if he finds it too difficult, too painful. But he resists, although it is sometimes hard for him to continue. Even so, every word, every image is presented to me so clearly it's as if all of it has only just happened.'

They stood there in silence as Pelia hung the sack on a tree branch and pressed it hard with strong, expert fingers, squeezing out the whey through the hessian. Suddenly she stopped and stared at Arkis in an odd, quizzical way. 'You have been very patient with him. Why? A lot of people would have tired of an old man's ramblings after just one day.'

'It is a fascinating story.'

'He's not always clear about everything,' she said, resuming her curd squeezing. 'And memory can deceive.'

***

I had become, as you might already have guessed, a prisoner of the Castra, said Han. It was obvious to me as soon as I was taken that the men who bore me away were not Bathlayans, for they would never venture into the forest at night. Also, those who carried me – and there were maybe three or four of them – grunted urgent comments to each other in a language that I had never heard before.

It was the lowest, most terrible moment of my young life. From the cries and clashes behind me, I feared my companions were being slaughtered by Castra fighters. It did not occur to me then to try to work out why I was being carried away rather than being killed.

I was hauled along, passed from man to man and sometimes carried between two men, but for how long I don't know. I also didn't how my captors could see to make their way in the dark of the forest. These men had no fear of wild animals – or other men, for that matter.

After a while they made me run with them or, more accurately, they dragged me along between them. I couldn't see and stumbled over exposed tree roots and felt my skin pricked and scratched by needle-sharp thorns and stung by the night insects we disturbed.

We did not stop until well after daylight when the sun was a good distance along its arc in the sky. Then we rested at a camp that had already been set up just beyond the forest's edge. Gauging the position of the sun to determine which direction we had travelled, I realised that my journey of the previous day had been reversed and we were back on the Bathlayan side of the forest.

My hands and feet were tied with vine and, for good measure, I was also bound to a tree. There were many Castra in the camp. Some of the men who arrived after us nursed wounds that I assumed had been inflicted by my companions, but none of their injuries seemed severe. Indeed, the men appeared in very good spirits, occasionally looking over towards me and laughing as if they had captured some great prize.

They soon lost interest as they made cooking fires and turned their attention to food. I began to cry but no one took any notice. If I was a prize, it was one that held no human value.

Eventually I was offered a morsel of meat and a little milk, almost as an afterthought when they had filled their own bellies. I accepted what they gave me because I knew I had to do so to survive. Their offer of food also gave me hope that I was not to be killed – at least not so quickly.

I began to assess the nature of the danger I faced. My Castra captors appeared not to be in any haste to leave the land of the Bathlayans. They laughed and conversed unhurriedly with each other and some even dozed in the warming sunshine. I realised they were confident that neither my companions nor the Bathlayans would interfere with them.

The two frightening conclusions I could draw from this were that Edbersa, Garia and Kairi were either severely wounded or already dead and would not come to find me, and that the Bathlayans or other Polastians had somehow been complicit in my kidnapping by allowing the Castra to operate freely in their land. At this realisation, I stopped eating and started to cry, which made my captors laugh.

I was still crying quietly when camp was broken, despite the heat being too stupefying for travelling. Two Castra hoisted me onto a small horse, strapping me so tightly onto the animal I could not lift my head from its hot neck.

Then began a most fretful journey.

I could not see where we were going but knew we had left the remnants of Bathlaya's forest behind us, for there was no shade. We were climbing relentlessly up a rock-strewn mountainside. I had no respite from the sun and not a drop of drink to make travelling bearable. My mouth became so parched I was forced to suckle sweat from the horse's neck.

After the sun disappeared we still kept going. When we finally stopped, I was barely conscious.

I was unstrapped and dragged roughly from the horse. Opening my eyes, I saw that we had arrived at a larger camp occupied by more Castra. Several fires had been lit and the air was filled with the smell of roasting flesh.

Two of the Castra took me into a cave at the edge of the camp, pushing me roughly onto the hard floor. I felt a strange sense that other people also occupied the cave, although I could not see or hear them. There was nothing I could determine, but do you understand what I mean, Arkis, when I say the place stank of fear? I was too exhausted to react with any more fear of my own, so I curled into a protective ball and fell into a terrible sleep.

When dawn came, the sunlight streamed far enough into my cave prison to bathe my face. I sat up and rubbed the salty wet sleep from my eyes so I could take in my surroundings. Close to the entrance to the cave, their backs resting against the rock, sat three Castra guards, two of them dozing with their heads on their chests. The third guard saw I had woken and immediately reached for his spear as if I might attempt escape.

But his attention was quickly taken by something further inside the cave. I followed his stare and froze with fear as I saw a pile of bones picked out by the shards of penetrating sunlight. I thought the bones must be from animals that had been eaten until I saw that there were human skulls among the pyramid of remains, just like the ones I had seen early in the journey to Polastia. A large rat was perched at the top of this pile of bones and this must have been what had attracted the guard's attention.

Then, as if animated by a ghostly force, the skull began to rock from side to side. I imagined an entire skeleton about to rise out of the mound and edged my way towards the guards. But I froze to the spot as the skull rolled down the slope to the cave floor and another rat's head peered curiously out of the human eye socket.

The guard laughed and lowered his spear. He barked some comment at me that I took as a warning to stay where I was. I shuffled backwards on my rump and rested my quivering body against the cave wall.

Were these bones left over from Castra victims who had been eaten? Kairi had warned that they carried out cannibalistic rituals. Maybe this was proof of it – and I was going to be their next meal.

The morning passed. I was offered no food or water and I dared not ask for any. After a while I was visited by the Castra leader, whom Kairi had described to us. It was true that he was a much bigger man than the others, with flowing red hair and a beard down to his chest. His bronze adornments shimmered in the sunlight, including the elaborate belt Kairi suggested was an indication of his importance. He spoke no words to me but grunted something to the guard before walking off.

It was then I remembered Kairi's talk of a gold payment the Castra had been expecting. Clearly it was a reward for my capture but who was to pay it? And what was it about me that accounted for such a gilded valuation?

As the sun reached its zenith, all the Castra gathered at the camp's centre. Their attentive demeanour indicated they were expecting something to happen – and soon it did.

I heard the sound of horses approaching and saw the dust rising as the animals crunched their way along the stone track to the camp. My view of the visiting party was obscured by rocks at the side of the cave entrance, but I could hear words of greeting in a familiar language, not my own but one I had heard spoken so recently: Polasti. Then a guard came and dragged me from my prison. My head was forced down so I could only see the ground and the Castra legs shuffling out of the way to allow my passage.

They were replaced in my vision by the stamping hooves of a large horse. I could feel its foul, steamy breath on my neck and hear the creak of taut leather on its back. One of the Castra grabbed my hair, jerking my head upwards. The rider's eyes looked down upon me, gleaming triumphantly, and the thin bearded face broke into a humourless smile.

'So, this is where your reputed wisdom has led you, Han!' It was Asdur.

My first thought, Arkis, was that the Bathlayan priest had come to rescue me and my heart jumped. But it took only a few moments to realise the truth, that Asdur was complicit in my capture.

He had not arrived alone; two of his priests had ridden with him. On Asdur's order, one dismounted and took me by the arm. I tried to resist but a Castra guard helped the priest to restrain me. My mind raced with many confusing thoughts, one dominating above all: why me?

I'm not ashamed to say it, Arkis, but once again I began to cry, sobbing and shivering with both fear and despair. I would have sunk to my knees had I not been held up by strong, mean arms.

Asdur slid from his horse and the leading Castran greeted him with an exaggerated wave, declaring something unintelligible but undoubtedly triumphal in his own tongue.

Asdur looked me up and down and placed a bony hand upon my shoulder. He shook his head and attempted a smile of consolation. It did not appease me. I wriggled my shoulder in a vain attempt to dislodge his unwelcome touch. The Castra leader laughed at my struggle, muttering a comment that encouraged some of his followers to also laugh.

Asdur squeezed my shoulder and smiled his most menacing smile. 'Gostopo cannot see why such a scrawny boy is worth so much trouble,' he said. 'But that's the Castra for you. They have always been short-sighted people, just living for today. Even so, they have served me well.' He patted my head as if I were a favoured son.

'I might as well tell you, Han, that you have cost a deal of gold,' he went on. 'A great deal of gold – fifty horses' worth, to be exact. Why do you think you could be possibly worth such a sum, young man?'

I bowed my head. I did not want to engage in conversation with this terrible priest yet I was truly curious to know the answer to the question he had posed.

Something prompted me to respond with defiance. I lifted my head and stuck out my chin. 'You have wasted your gold,' I said, charging my voice with anger so it was as strident as I could make it. 'For Edbersa will come with Garia and Kairi to find me. Then they will know of your treachery and all the gold which could buy all the horses in Polastia will not save you.'

Asdur laughed. 'You have spirit, boy, I'll give you that, but I doubt you are as wise as your precious Karmus asserts.'

He lifted his hand from my shoulder and waved it at the Castra chief. 'Get your men to strap the boy to a horse, Gostopo. It's a shame you and your people will not be able to feast on his precocious flesh but we have a more interesting fate in store for him. Then again, you might be relieved, for Han's balls might prove surprisingly tough for one so young.'

So I wasn't going to be cooked and eaten – at least not immediately. Instead of stoking up their cooking fire, the Castra threw earth upon it and broke their camp. I was placed upon the same horse as before and, with Asdur and his priests following on their horses, we set off on another arduous trek.

Again I was strapped tightly to the mount and could not ascertain from the sun which direction we travelled in, but at times it was a steep climb. The horse snorted and sweated and stumbled along the rocky track, which sometimes narrowed to barely the width of the animal with a sheer drop into a river gorge on one side of it. Unable to lift my head, my frightened eyes hovered above this terrifying abyss, which was a sure grave for any carelessly footed animal or human.

A thunderstorm came to compound my despair. I had little experience of such a force of water for, as you now know, Arkis, Akbenna had endured years of drought. Even as my companions and I travelled through Polastia there had been barely enough rain to dampen our hair. But on this mountainside, as we reached the highest point of our climb and began to descend, the sky darkened to an oppressive grey as if the fleece of the fabled sheep Arios had been draped across it. The thunder growled and then cracked. The sky flashed and I could see the gorge below me glow with fire as if a thousand torches had been ignited so some god of the underworld could light the way to my terrible fate.

When eventually the storm clouds released their burden of rain, the power of it almost pounded the breath from me. So dense was the downpour, I was convinced it could not be penetrated by any earthly creature's vision. We were still on a narrow track and I feared the horse that bore me would lose its direction or its footing and I would be plunged into the gorge. But as quickly as the storm came so it disappeared, and the sun's heat once again bore down upon us. I could not see it but I could smell the steam rising from both man and animal as the relentless trek continued.

I fell into a despairing sleep and only woke when our journey halted as daylight faded. I was unstrapped from the horse and carried into yet another cave, where some meat and water were given to me. Otherwise I was left to fret alone. I slept deeply and it was one of the rare times in my travels that I don't remember dreaming.

The next day I was woken by one of Gostopo's men shaking my arm. As other Castra looked on, he dragged me to my feet and pushed me roughly towards his leader. Gostopo stood in the cave entrance, looking me over critically as if he could not understand why anyone would want to pay fifty horses' worth of gold for such a puny human specimen. His interest soon evaporated and he spun round with an order grunted to one of his men.

This Castra prodded me with his spear, forcing me to move into the daylight. When my eyes adjusted to the bright sun, I looked around to see I was at the elevated head of a lush valley surrounded by mountainous peaks. In the distance a magnificent waterfall cascaded from a cleft in the rock into a narrow river. In the lower part of the hills I could see cave entrances, over some of which hung curtains of vegetation. Unlike the caves of Bathlaya, they appeared to have been made by nature for there were no formal edges to indicate that man and his tools had been at work.

Stone steps rose to some of the caves and wooden ladders to those that had no natural incline to employ. The small valley was crossed by well-worn paths and tumbling streams, over which bridges of both stone and wood had been constructed. The whole seemed how you would imagine paradise to be.

I was prodded by the spear again to make me move forward along one of the paths. When we reached the central part of the valley, it opened out into a broad meadow upon which goats and cattle grazed and an abundance of fowl scratched and pecked for insects.

In the distance I saw a large building growing out of a rocky mountain. As we got nearer, I discerned the tall figure of Asdur. He bowed his head so our eyes were no more than the span of a hand apart. His eyes were cold and distant and I felt them boring into my heart.

'What place is this?' I plucked up the courage to ask.

'Why, it is Havilon,' said Asdur. 'It is the home of Polastia's most eminent priest. Kolak will find you an interesting proposition, I have no doubt.'

Asdur led the way and the guard pushed me to ensure I kept up. We walked no more than two hundred strides along the valley before we came to a large square paved in stone flags, upon which sets of stone seats had been constructed, one resting on a plinth so it dominated the rest. Beyond this square a lake stretched towards a sheer rock wall – the base of the mountain – out of which, to our right, the large building grew. I later learned that this was a temple.

Asdur indicated that everyone should remain standing. All eyes, including mine, became fixed upon the building's entrance.

A group of men slowly emerged from it to the sound of chanting, similar to what we had heard upon our arrival in Bathlaya. These men were of great age, with long grey hair and billowing beards. One priest in the centre, the tallest, appeared to be the most significant; he held a long wooden staff upon the end of which was a golden orb studded with precious stones that glinted in the bright sunlight. I assumed him to be the one referred to as Kolak.

Despite my distressing situation, I couldn't help but wonder why a priest would be named after a timid burrowing creature with large back legs and long ears, for that's what kolaki are in Akbenna.

After the old men came a group of younger men, each tall and handsome with long, fair hair and dressed identically in rich blue smocks tied at the waist with golden cord. They walked slowly in a regimented way, exactly the same distance apart; when they halted it was like gazing upon a row of statues, such was the stillness and rigidity of their posture. Eventually I learned that these young men were the priests' dutiful servers, but in what various manners they served I was not to find out until later.

The chanting, which had come from somewhere within the temple, ceased and the chief priest pointed his staff with its twinkling orb towards me. 'So, this is the great young mind of our times.' He spoke almost perfect Akben, in a voice incongruously firm for one who appeared so old. Whether he smiled or frowned, I could not see, for the priest's hair and beard obscured almost all his face.

He waved his staff over the gathering. 'Please, Han, you may sit. You must have had a tiring journey.'

I remained standing, oddly defiant. Kolak was about to pronounce something but stopped when he saw me stabbing a finger towards Asdur. 'This man is a bad priest for he has made an evil trade of me,' I shouted. 'I am brought here in exchange for fifty horses' worth of gold. Brought here to die – to be eaten! At the very least I deserve to know why.'

Kolak's eyes widened, evidence that he had probably broken into a broad smile though it was difficult to see beneath so much facial hair. He addressed Asdur. 'You were correct in your assessment; the boy does possess a precocious spirit.'

He stroked his long beard and turned his attention to me. 'How are matters in Akbenna these days? They tell me Karmus is on his last legs. Is it true? Of course, he may already be dead.'

Although my body was trembling with fear, my blood boiled with fury. How could he expect to engage with me in such an easy manner when I was being held against my will? I became combative, though tears of defeat were already welling behind my eyes. 'If anyone is at death's door, it is you,' I said, jabbing my trembling finger at the whole assembly of priests and their human statues.

Asdur growled, 'You should show respect, boy, or you will suffer for it.'

I inflated my chest and indulged in more finger jabbing. 'What difference will it make if I'm going to die anyway?' I said.

Kolak waved his staff as if to ward off my anger. 'The manner of your death will be swift or it will be slow – but in any event it will be painful.'

'Do your worst for I don't care,' I hurled back. 'I wasn't afraid of Gilgarius and I'm not afraid of you.'

Kolak stepped towards me. I feared he was about to order my immediate slaughter but instead he let out a great roar of a laugh that belied his aged appearance.

At that moment, something occurred to me. Why I had not realised it before I can't tell you, Arkis, but it suddenly occurred to me that these elders were very elderly indeed, perhaps older than I am now – and that should not have been possible. If they were so old, why were they still alive?

'You should be dead, all of you,' I said, hearing the words issuing from my lips but not believing that I was speaking them. 'If you were in Bathlaya, you would not have been allowed to live so long. You would have been driven out to die in the forest. And that would be no bad thing.'

I pointed to Kolak. 'You are old and ugly and have a stupid name. In my land, kolaki are timid creatures that are so little esteemed they have to live deep in the ground, hiding away for fear of being eaten. Polastia and everywhere else in the world would be better off if you were dead.'

The priest laughed again and jabbed at the ground with his staff. 'It is true, Asdur – he's not like any other child I have encountered.'

Asdur waved an arm in my direction. 'There is more than a little fight in the boy, I grant you, but it will soon dissipate when he learns his fate.'

'Then let us not waste time, Asdur. He must be made ready to meet our other guest.'

Asdur smiled without parting his lips so his expression appeared more of a smirk. 'It is always good when old friends meet up again,' he said.

Although inside I was shaking like a young ledbuk confronted by a hungry pack of wolves, outwardly I was defiant. I drew myself to my full height and jabbed my fist at this arrogant old man, telling him he had a stupid name. Then I turned on Asdur, denouncing him as an evil priest who would die a horrible death for arranging my capture.

I called them mad, I called them old and ugly, but they didn't seem to care what I said. Kolak waved over two of the human statues, their faces devoid of emotion, and they grabbed my arms to stop me jabbing and pointing. Somewhere behind me horns and drums sounded.

Kolak waved his staff and looked skyward. From over the temple came a large bird, an eagle with a white tail, which swooped low over us before settling on the priest's outstretched arm. He gave an instruction to his servers with a nod of his head and two of them came to me and took my arms.

As I was led away I looked around to see Kolak with his eagle, Asdur and some of the other priests following at a distance, and the other priests playing their instruments at the rear. It was a strange procession and, looking back, must have been an oddly comical. I was there at its head, trying to feign defiance while I was as frightened as I had ever been. There was no doubt in my mind that I was to be sacrificed to some god I didn't believe in and, therefore, I was determined not to go meekly but defiantly.

We processed away from the temple and across a lush pasture where goats and cattle grazed unconcerned at our presence or the loud music that accompanied us. At the far edge of the pasture rose a high cliff of white stone with jagged pinnacles piercing the sky. At its centre the rock was cleaved from top to bottom, narrowing dramatically towards the ground but still wide enough for our procession to pass through. Beyond, the path broadened into a dramatic gorge that was completely enclosed by the walls of sheer rock and through which a stream tumbled over a series of cataracts before disappearing into the ground. It felt like a natural prison and I was soon to learn that is exactly what it was.

We halted.

'Are you not curious to know your fate, Han?' This was Asdur, who by this time was leaning so close to my shoulder that I could feel the tickle of his long beard upon my neck. From behind me, I heard Kolak rasping an order to the human statues to release their grip upon me.

Once my arms were free, I turned to address both priests. 'It can't be a fate worse than being in your mad company,' I heard myself saying, as if I had no way of stopping these ill-advised words.

Kolak didn't hear, or was deliberately ignoring me, for he drew the eagle closer to him and spoke quietly to it. After just a few moments of this, the bird launched itself skyward, flying swiftly towards a huge pinnacle of rock that rose out of a clump of trees at the furthest point of the gorge. The eagle circled the rock, issuing a strange, haunting cry before disappearing.

Kolak bent his face towards me. 'Are you not curious about what will happen to you?'

'I expect I'm to be sacrificed.'

Kolak nodded and smiled. 'You are correct, Han – but not to any god. Your precocious being would be wasted on a deity.' He straightened and lifted his head, staring to the horizon, in the direction his eagle had flown.

By now I was struggling really hard to control my shaking. I shut my eyes tightly so I could conjure up images of my mother and father, as if seeing them in my mind's eye would bolster my courage and dispel all the fears that were consuming me.

No one spoke and I sensed the tension rise in those around me. Whatever awaited me was so powerful, so terrible, that it put everyone in fear of its impending presence.

Eventually Kolak spoke and I opened my eyes to see him raising his staff to the sky. 'There, he is coming,' said the priest.

I followed his indication and saw something huge and ominous rising above the rocky pinnacles like a black storm cloud. Seemingly bidden by Kolak's eagle was a beast as large and fierce as the one I had outwitted in Akbenna. Creating a great wind, the creature settled upon the rim of the gorge, wings spread, blocking out the sun. The monster's body was so big he was able to remain perched at the top of the cliff and still rest his head upon the gorge's rocky floor.

Asdur placed a long bony hand upon my shoulder. 'I said you would meet an old friend, Han, and here he is. The famed adversary you and your elders so arrogantly thought had been disposed of.'

***

Barely half a league into the scrub, Arkis dismounted and led Rashi on foot through a stand of decaying trees, many gnarled and twisted into grotesque shapes. They halted at a clearing where the earth hollowed out and a rough circle of jagged rocks protruded around its perimeter. At the centre was a single flat stone, raised knee height from the ground.

Arkis relieved Rashi from the weight of the saddlebags and let her browse without being hobbled. From the larger bag he extracted a scroll made from dried animal skin, a bundle or reeds cut short and shaped at the ends and a gourd filled with ink.

He rolled out the parchment and weighted down its edges with small stones. Then he carefully selected a reed stylus, bringing it close to his eye to examine the point before scratching it across the back of his hand to confirm its soundness. After removing a wooden stopper from the gourd, he dipped in the stylus but hesitated before applying it to the parchment. These marks had to be right if they were to represent accurately what Han had told him so far. Not everything, for that would be impossible, but the essence of Han's story.

Arkis had long ago memorised the shapes of the symbols that could be used to represent key events. He had also devised pictorial depictions he would use for the mountains, the forests, the rivers and where the sun rose and set.

He had been to this place on previous days and would return again as more of Han's story was revealed. And it had to be done in secret; too much was at stake to risk otherwise. There would be a time to reveal the truth, to apologise for the deceit, but first he must hear all Han had to say, to check it against what he already knew so he could complete the story as accurately as possible.

After the ink was dried, he carefully scrolled up the parchment before restoring it and the writing paraphernalia to the saddlebag. Then he called Rashi.

As Arkis mounted the mare, he wasn't the only one practising a deceit. From a hill overlooking the gnarled, decaying trees and the circle of jagged stones where he had scratched his symbols, someone was watching him.

The sun had almost set when he returned to Han's farm to find him awake on the porch, nibbling at a piece of bread.

The old man smiled. 'I wondered where you were. I was worried that you'd become bored and had decided to leave us. Are you hungry? There is some bread and Pelia has made some kaya stew.'

Arkis declined the food with a raised hand and shake of the head. 'Your story is sustenance enough for the time being,' he said.

'Some beer then.'

He accepted the beer. 'Are you feeling better?'

'Yes, yes – of course,' said Han. 'I'm happy to continue, that is if you are sure you are not bored with an old man's rambling.'

'I most certainly am not.' Arkis could have added that it was also utterly important that he heard the tale to its end. But he didn't.

***

I'm sure you have guessed it, said Han. Gilgarius did not perish, as I had supposed, but was alive and free to ravish other lands with his demands for young flesh.

It was obvious that Kolak was taking great delight in my horror at this realisation. He prodded me hard in the back with his staff and I stumbled forward.

'I imagine you are keen to know how he survived that great belching mountain of yours,' said Kolak. 'Well, he'll no doubt tell you that himself, for it is time you two adversaries renewed your acquaintance.'

I hesitated as if in a trance but, against my natural fear, I took a few steps forward before my entire being froze. I could not move my legs nor lift my arms. I fell to my knees. Kolak's eagle descended upon the ground before me, issuing a haunting screech, prodding the space between us with its menacing beak.

'Stand up,' ordered Kolak. 'Let your old adversary see you.'

But I remained upon my knees, my brain racing as I tried to work out whether it would be better to risk being beaten to death by the priest's staff than succumb to the monstrous fangs of Gilgarius.

'Get on your feet,' shouted Asdur. 'Be prepared to face your fate, for it cannot be avoided.'

Then Gilgarius's roar echoed around the gorge. 'Where is the boy you promised?'

'He is here,' shouted Kolak, pointing with his staff. 'Here upon the ground.'

'I cannot see him,' said Gilgarius. 'If I cannot see him, I

cannot consume him. Expose him to me.'

'Stand up boy!' ordered the priest.

'I cannot see him,' roared Gilgarius. 'But I can smell his fear.'

From the corner of my eye I could see Asdur and Kolak and the human statues appearing to hold no fear of the monster for they did not move. Just as unconcerned was the priest's eagle, which was now happily preening itself.

Gilgarius lowered his head into the gorge. I could feel his hot breath upon my neck. 'I see you now,' he said in that sonorous voice of his, rumbling like an earthquake. 'Stand up so we can address each other in a proper manner.'

I raised my head.

'Go on, I won't eat you.' Gilgarius laughed. 'At least not yet.'

For a reason I couldn't fathom, I got to my feet. 'What are you going to do with me?'

'Make a breakfast of you when I'm ready. What else is a young boy good for? Are you afraid?'

'No, but I am confused. I thought you were dead.'

'As you see, I am very much alive. No thanks to you. Now it is time for my revenge.'

'Will you eat me now?'

'No, I am still full from three young girls I had for breakfast. Anyway, I wish to savour the prospect of consuming your precocious flesh. I have no doubt Kolak here will see to it that you are appropriately fattened up in the coming days. In any event, I'll end up digesting you.'

'Please can we talk a little before I am eaten.'

'Oh, you are a wily little creature. You want to talk to distract me from my purpose, and therefore your destiny, while you work out a plan to deceive me, just as you did before.'

'No, Gilgarius. I accept my fate. All I want to know is how you survived falling into the depths of our Mother Mountain. I don't wish to die without knowing the truth.'

'Well, if you put it like that.'

The creature raised his head so it hung over the gorge. He furled in his wings so we were once again bathed in sunlight. Then Gilgarius sat upon his giant haunches, picking at yellow teeth with the hook of his long foreclaw. He belched and the expelled breath which seemed always to carry with it the stench of digesting humans.

'You see, Han, while every other creature in this world can be destroyed by fire, I am immune. Indeed, you could say I was forged from fire and nurtured in the molten belly of such a mountain. Your deity's heat barely raised my temperature. I simply feigned my death and remained inside her until night fell and the stars beckoned me to new lands. If it helps you picture the scene, I can tell you that I spent my time happily snoozing, occasionally shitting out child waste. I may add that your Mother Mountain seemed not to mind one bit, making me very comfortable indeed.'

'Why didn't you emerge and fight back against us? Why didn't you hunt me down for my trickery?'

Gilgarius snorted. 'If you remember, Han, I can only take what is offered in sacrifice by priests and elders. No more Akben young were offered – nor Bostrati, for that matter – so in that regard you won a small battle. But I was determined to wreak my revenge upon you and your people. No doubt you could learn from your hosts here how this has come about and why they are eager to give children. From me, you only need to know that I shall savour crunching your young bones and picking out your brains as a delicacy.'

I shook my head to defend my brains from the terrible image Gilgarius's words conjured up. I needed to remain calm and strong. 'Is it because of your desire for revenge that gold is being paid for my capture?'

Gilgarius snorted. 'These Polasti priests wanted me to help them and were only too eager to offer the Castra gold so you could be part of my reward,' he said. 'And I wanted you more than any other child because you made a fool of me. Nobody has ever made a fool of Gilgarius before and I have to admit it rather threw me. Made me question my invincibility.'

'And what was your conclusion?'

'That I should never engage in verbal combat with upstart boys.'

'Isn't that what you are doing now?'

Gilgarius growled, 'No, because there will be no bargaining this time. No allowing you to wander around the place pitting everyone against me. I am wise to your tricks.'

'Then eat me now.'

The creature issued a low, rumbling laugh. 'There you go again. *Eat me now, if you please. I'm not afraid to die.*'

'Well?'

'I'm not hungry at present. You must wait with the other children.'

I didn't understand what he meant. 'What other children?'

Gilgarius ignored my question. 'I'll call for you when I'm good and ready.'

With that, he raised his ugly head and unfolded his giant wings and, expelling another foul blast of putridity, took to the air. The force of his wingbeats created a great wind that blew me off my feet, although the priests and their guards managed to remain standing against the force of it.

Kolak stepped forward and prodded my prone form with his staff. I sat up, glaring at him defiantly. 'What did he mean about the other children?'

'You are about to find out,' said the priest.

With that, he reached out and hauled me to my feet as though I were nothing more than a tiny kid goat. Kolak then pointed with his staff. 'See there, Han.'

I followed the indication until my eyes rested upon a narrow opening cleaved into the rock close to where the stream emerged.

'Go,' the priest ordered, once again prodding me with his infuriating staff.

I stumbled forward, oddly enthusiastic to see what I would find. I entered the opening in the rock to see, like the gorge behind me, that it opened up into a smaller area mostly covered by two overhangs of rock reaching across to each other, almost forming the space into a cave. Light penetrated where the overhangs failed to meet so I could see clearly enough what was before me. Or, more precisely, who was before me.

The children.

They were bound together on the dusty ground in frightened little groups, silent but for an occasional cry or sob that could not be stifled.

'Does what you see disturb you, Han?'

'Who are these children? Why are they so frightened?'

Kolak smiled. 'That's what children are like. It is natural for them to be frightened when they no longer have their mothers and fathers to comfort them. You are barely more than a child yourself so you will understand.'

'Perhaps Han doesn't know what fear is,' Asdur offered with a laugh.

'Perhaps he doesn't,' said Kolak. 'But I am sure he will soon learn.'

'What will happen to them?'

'They will endure the same fate as you, Han.'

Then, as if following an order from its master, the eagle gave a squawk and jabbed its beak at me, forcing me towards the huddled children. Although I wished not to be obedient, I moved willingly. My only desire was to talk to the frightened children.

As I got closer, I could see they weren't just huddled together through fear, although afraid they most certainly were. They were sitting on beds of dry moss, bound together in small groups. Their bonds were strips of hide lashed around their wrists and ankles. They were ragged, frightened, bare-footed, their hair long and matted – even longer than my own – and wearing filthy smocks. But though they looked frightened and dishevelled, their bodies in no way appeared wasted. Whatever deprivations these children were forced to endure, starvation was not one of them.

I did not count their number then, but was to soon learn there were fourteen of them. They were tied together in groups of three, except for a boy and a girl who were bound as a pair. An order was barked and I was made to sit with these two and have my hands and ankles lashed to theirs.

The priest lowered his head to mine. 'Now, Han,' he said in almost a whisper. 'These children will, I am sure, tell you their story. But I would advise you to refrain from revealing your previous experience with Gilgarius for it might raise their hopes of deliverance when really no hope exists.'

The priest raised his staff and said to all the children, 'For two days you will be spared sacrifice. For some reason known only to the creature, he will not eat when the moon reaches its fullest, as happens to be the case at present. But when it wanes – well, that's another story. In the meantime, we must keep you all nice and plump in readiness to please him. I expect every one of you to feast well to ensure Gilgarius is fully nourished when he consumes you. Those who don't eat all before them will be painfully punished.'

Kolak waved a hand towards the guards as if that was the signal for food to be served, then he turned to me. 'Please do not let any fear of your impending death dull your appetite, Han. It will be a pity to serve our honoured guest scrawny fare, especially when he has been so looking forward to devouring you.'

Although I was quite hungry by this point, the prospect of being forced to eat against my will to please Gilgarius made me defiant. 'I have beaten that creature once and I shall beat him again,' I said.

Kolak prodded the small of my back with his staff. 'There is nothing you can do to save yourself. Gilgarius will eat you and all the other children – that's a fact.'

With that, he and Asdur and the other priests departed. I was now able to address the boy and girl to whom I had been bound. 'My name is Han. I'm from Akbenna,' I said, not sure whether they would understand my words.

'I am Arkemis,' said the boy in an unfamiliar but perfectly understandable version of my own tongue. 'And this is my sister, Nyxes. We were taken from our homes many leagues away.' He shook his head mournfully. 'The Castra raided every village between the sea of the Caspi and the border of Polastia, taking as many children as they could. Then they marched us, half-starving, for many days until we came here. Now they insist upon fattening us up.'

'Were you told why you were being taken?'

'No. Only that we would serve a great master.'

'We believed we would be sold as slaves,' said the girl. 'Anyway, Han, what did you mean when you said you'd beaten Gilgarius once before?' Although in a fearful situation, Nyxes managed to ask this while attempting a smile despite her striking grey eyes radiating a terrible sadness. My heart warmed to her immediately.

'It is complicated to explain,' I said. 'But I promise you I'll endeavour to do so. For now, all you need to know is that it's possible to outwit this monster.'

'Have you a plan?' asked Nyxes.

I attempted my own version of a smile to reassure her. 'No. But that doesn't mean one won't come to me.'

By this time the children around us had all but ceased their wailing and sobbing and were listening intently to our conversation.

I lifted my head proudly and declared my name to them all. 'In case you did not hear, I'm Han from Akbenna. I've encountered Gilgarius before and believe he can be defeated. I urge you not to despair.'

'Rubbish!' exclaimed one of the other boys, not three strides from me. 'He's already eaten most of us, my sister included. All you offer is words. Words are worth nothing when such a monster is licking his lips.'

The boy was bound to two small girls who could not have been more than eight. One of them started sobbing and the other girl spoke hushed words of comfort.

I attempted a reassuring, friendly tone in my response, sweeping my gaze around the captive children and trying to bolster my voice with something resembling self-belief. 'All I ask is that you retain some hope that you can be saved. It's not impossible.'

'Kyros is right,' said Arkemis. 'You can say what you like but we're bound together and held in a place from which there's no chance of escape.'

'Yes,' said Kyros. 'We are guarded day and night and when Gilgarius settles on the ridge and calls for food, some of us will be dragged off to be eaten. It's been like this since the day we arrived when there were many more of us. He's been feeding steadily upon us from that day, except when there's been a full moon. There's no hope. Even if we tried to escape, we would be speared to death and fed to the creature.'

I could understand their despair, the resignation to their fate, yet it wasn't within me to give up on hope. I'd survived too many threats to lose my faith so easily. I turned to Arkemis. 'What of those who guard you? What kind of men are they?'

He thought for a few moments, then said, 'The servers? Well, they don't speak. It's as if they have no minds. I'm not sure if they understand us very much. They only seem to respond to the priests, mainly the one who calls himself Kolak.'

I couldn't resist a smile. 'I told him his name was stupid,' I said. 'In Akbenna, kolaki are timid creatures that hide under the ground.'

'In our land, too,' said Arkemis. 'But kolaki are worshipped in many places, including the land of the Caspi. People aren't allowed to eat them. Perhaps it is different in Akbenna.'

I nodded. We would never have had enough meat had we not had kolaki to trap. 'They don't seem human,' I said.

'Kolaki aren't human, Han,' said Nyxes, smiling.

'I mean the servers. They behave as if they're not quite human, like they're moving statues.'

'They're human all right,' said Nyxes. 'Or two of them are. There's one guard who usually brings us food. He never speaks and tries to look stern all the time, but when you look into his eyes you see only kindness. And there's another who I saw reach out to steady one of the little ones when she stumbled as she was taken to be eaten by Gilgarius. You could clearly see he was sad.'

'That's just two,' said Arkemis. 'All the others are not so human. They can be quite frightening, the way they stare at you and push you when you have to go into the trees for a shit.'

'That's interesting,' I said.

At that moment, four of the servers appeared carrying food. I must confess, Arkis, that by this time I was very hungry. Even the prospect of being fed to Gilgarius didn't dull my appetite. They brought gourds of goat's milk, a good variety of Polasti fruits that I'd now become familiar with, as well as bread and cold meat – though probably not the flesh of a kolaki.

The one who brought food to our little group must have been one of the less human guards because his stare was cold. Indeed, he made no eye contact with us at all.

The food was placed within reach of our bound hands but I recognised right away that eating was going to be something of a problem.

'We can only put food to our mouths in turn, Han,' said Arkemis. 'Our own hands must follow the food to another eater's mouth. It's not easy but you'll get used to it. As our new friend, you can go first.'

I picked a piece of meat, pulling two other pairs of hands with me, then I raised it to my lips and the hands came too.

'Be careful not to bite my fingers,' said Nyxes.

I soon got the hang of eating in this strange manner. We took it in turns to eat meat, then bread and finally fruit, finishing off with the goat's milk.

Each of the other groups employed a similar system of feeding, where the chief virtue was obviously patience. Despite the prospect of a terrible death, all the children ate well. But then a thought occurred to me – if we have to eat and drink like a three-headed creature, how would we answer nature's call? I decided to delay my enquiry, assuming that an answer would come when the need arose. Instead, I asked Arkemis to tell me more about their capture and the ordeal of their journey.

He said their villages were close to a large sea and the Castra raiders came and took them and other Caspi children when their fathers were out on their boats fishing and their mothers were in the fields tending crops.

The raiders beat the children with sticks and tied their hands behind their backs, forcing them on relentlessly until they reached the next village, where they stole more children. This went on, village after village, until two hundred or more Caspi young were gathered together. The Castra moved so swiftly that the villagers had no chance to warn the next community that their children were in danger of being taken.

'We knew our fathers would follow to try to free us,' said Arkemis. 'But they are fishermen, not fierce warriors like the Castra.'

'Yes,' said Nyxes. 'The men of the Caspi villages can use

weapons but only for spearing fish or hunting animals in the forest. They would have little chance against so many wild men. I can't say for certain, but I fear our fathers would have been killed by the Castra had they tried to rescue us.'

After days of forced marching, during which some of the younger children died and were left to rot where they fell, the young prisoners were finally met by Kolak, his priests and their strange guards.

'We could see the Castra being given gold in exchange for us,' Arkemis said. 'But we did not know why, or what fate awaited us. We were crowded into this place and bound together like animals, as we are now. But it was soon clear what would become of us.'

'Had you heard of Gilgarius?' I asked.

'Yes, of course,' said Arkemis. 'Our parents used stories about the creature to frighten us into being good. They'd say that if we disobeyed them Gilgarius would come to eat us. Every mother and father threatened us with the creature to ensure our obedience.'

'But we never believed he was real,' said Nyxes. 'I'm not sure even our parents believed the creature *really* existed.'

'Gilgarius only exists because we allow it,' I said. 'But as I say, he can be outwitted.' Then something occurred to me. 'Arkemis, can you tell me why we are all tied together in groups of three? Is this how Gilgarius is fed – three children at a time?'

'No. Sometimes it's just one child, sometimes he takes three. Once he took five children for one meal, although possibly because they were the youngest and smallest.'

'But he never eats two children together?'

'No. At least I don't think so.'

'Or four?'

Arkemis hesitated, trying to recall.

'I know he hasn't,' said Nyxes. 'He's never eaten two or four or six children together. Only in those numbers that can't be shared equally between two without causing one of the numbers to be cut in half. And you know you cannot cut numbers in half. It would be bad luck.'

'In Caspi they are known as caltri numbers after a plant whose shoots only grow three leaves,' said Arkemis. 'Why do you ask this?'

I was still trying to work that one out, casting my mind back to when Gilgarius came to Akbenna and how many children he had called for each time he made his demands of us.

I was silent for a while, thinking hard, while Arkemis, Nyxes, Kyros and all the other children looked on intently, with only an occasional sob from one of the younger children to break the silence. Then it came back to me. In Akbenna, Gilgarius had first insisted on having three children to eat, then five, then seven, then nine. Why, I wondered, did he not ask for two, four, six or eight?

'Arkemis, in your village stories of Gilgarius was anything ever said about the creature other than he would come to eat you if you misbehaved?'

'What do you mean?'

'I mean, were there things that people said he would do or not do, perhaps to bring himself luck?'

'No – I don't…'

'We know Gilgarius never eats children when there is a full moon,' said Nyxes. 'That terrible old priest said so.'

'It would seem the creature is wary of full moons and numbers that are even,' said Arkemis. 'In case you don't know, Han, an even number is one that can be divided cleanly without ending up with bits of broken numbers.'

'Do you know much about numbers, Arkemis?' I asked.

'I once listened to a scholar speak of these things, a man who was passing through our village on a long journey to where the sun rises. We gave him food and shelter and he stayed for three days, talking to our elders about many wonderful things, such as how we can predict where and when the sun and moon will be in the sky. He scratched strange symbols on wet clay, which he said preserved important stories. The marks were still there when the clay dried and could not be removed. He played games with me and the other children, using pebbles to show us how to count and work out different number puzzles. I quickly learned how to make numbers bigger or smaller.'

I was suitably impressed and said so. Despite our difficult situation, Nyxes beamed with pride for her brother.

'I would like to be a scholar and learn more about the symbols and numbers,' said Arkemis, before adding with a heavy sigh, 'but it is not possible now.'

'You will be a scholar, Arkemis,' I insisted, 'if we can only work out a way of using our new knowledge about Gilgarius to gain an advantage over him.'

I realised, however, that we would have to put further deliberations to one side for it became apparent that several of the children were shuffling about in some discomfort. Straight away, I understood what was happening; indeed, I was beginning to feel an early sign of nature's call myself.

'What do we do about having a shit?' I asked.

Arkemis said, 'You call a server who takes you to where the shitting place is.' He indicated a narrow gap in the cliff wall I had not noticed before. 'It leads along a passage and out to a wood.'

'He watches you while you do what you have to do,' said Nyxes. 'There are pools where you can wash because Gilgarius doesn't like eating shitty children. Then your guard escorts you back.'

'You mean they untie us and let us go on our own?'

'We're not exactly left on our own,' said Arkemis. 'There's no real chance you can escape, if that's what you think. The passage is always guarded.'

'They don't let you all go together,' said Nyxes. 'It would

mean untying too many children. No more than two at a time.'

The first of the children called out to the nearest server and was untied and led away. This happened perhaps three or four times before I called out my own need.

'He's the one with the kind eyes,' Nyxes whispered as one of the servers responded.

I didn't have a chance to confirm if what she said was true, for he didn't look directly at me. 'I know you are not allowed to speak,' I said as he released me from my new companions, 'but I would like to know if you actually can – speak, I mean.'

Both Arkemis and Nyxes appeared shocked that I spoke to him in such a way but the server gave no response.

I got to my feet and headed for the gap in the wall that led into the dark passage, A little way ahead I could see daylight. I turned to address my escort. 'What do you think of your leader, Kolak?' Again, there was just stone-faced silence. 'Are you brain dead?' Nothing.

We had almost reached the light when I halted so suddenly my guard was unable to prevent himself from walking into me. I let out a cry of pain, partly genuine, and fell to my knees. 'That hurt. Can't you be more careful?'

The server remained motionless.

I rubbed the back of my ankles, feigning worse pain than I was actually experiencing. 'Gilgarius will not like to eat a battered and bruised child,' I said. 'I've a good mind to complain to your stupid leader.'

Again nothing. By this time, we had emerged into the light. 'Surely, you must agree with me that he is stupid,' I persisted, turning my head to gauge his reaction. It was then I detected something – some tiny sparkle of mischief flashing across the guard's eyes. 'Do *you* have a name?' I asked.

This time he reached out both his arms to push me on. I stumbled over a rock and ended up sprawled on the ground. He stared down at me and I wondered if he would inflict some vicious punishment for my insolence.

'I only asked if you have a name,' I said. 'Why is everyone so grumpy round here?' I got to my feet and carried on walking slowly, the guard following close behind.

'*I am Osbin.*' He said this in almost a whisper. I swivelled my head to see a worried face. 'Please don't tell anyone I have spoken to you,' he continued urgently. 'It is not permitted. I will be killed – or worse.'

'So, you *are* more human than statue.'

'As human as you, only…' His voice trailed off.

I waited a moment or two for him to continue. When he didn't, I said in an urgent voice, barely above a whisper, 'I need to talk to you about this place and learn why your priests are feeding children to Gilgarius. There are so many things I need to know.'

'I cannot tell you anything,' said Osbin. 'I will be tortured if the priests find out I have spoken. I cannot risk it.'

'You don't belong here, Osbin. Maybe I can help you. Maybe we can all get out of here.'

'Please be quiet. Others will hear.'

Another guard had appeared along the track, returning two girls from shitting. As they passed, the girls smiled weakly at me but Osbin and the other guard offered no acknowledgement of each other.

The shitting place was a small clearing in the trees. As you can imagine, Arkis, such an area for so many children really did stink. I plucked a handful of dry grass from the edge of the clearing and found a spot beneath a low hanging tree branch, close to a small stream. With Osbin standing a few yards away, I carried out my business and washed myself in one of the rock pools.

As we returned, we met no other guards or children so I felt emboldened to engage Osbin in further conversation. 'Osbin – is that a Polasti or a Caspi name?' I asked.

'I – we – are from a land further away even than Caspi,' he said, still in a hushed, almost fearful voice. 'We were brought here as young children, but not by the Castra or any other kidnappers. Our fathers sold us to the priests for a lifetime of servitude.'

He reached out and placed a hand on my arm, gently squeezing it as if in a gesture of friendship. I looked at his face. He was smiling nervously, truly human. 'Please don't ask me anything more.'

By this time other guards and children were coming our way so Osbin resumed an attitude of cold authority, pushing me roughly onward, a vacant stare displacing his smile as if it had never existed.

After my return, a number of other children, including Arkemis and Nyxes, were escorted in small groups to the shitting place. The last of them returned before the sun set and the full bright moon appeared over the forest where Gilgarius appeared to have made his lair. He must be slumbering, I thought, believing his bound and guarded fodder had no possible means of escape. But I was determined to confound such a belief and began to formulate a plan.

Meanwhile I decided to delay revealing my conversation with Osbin to Arkemis and Nyxes, preferring instead to contemplate how I could build upon our exchange. We would have no chance of escape without the help of the servers and I needed to think of a way of getting Osbin on his own again so I could gauge the strength of his loyalty to the priests. It would not be easy.

After the sun fell beyond the rim of the gorge, my captive companions settled down to sleep, despite the inconvenience of being tied to each other. Fortunately the leather bonds allowed some movement and the dried moss was comfortable to lie on, but it was an awkward sleeping arrangement.

The groups had been tied together for so long that they

had managed to fashion solutions to the problem. Most lay on their sides, legs stretched out like the spokes of a cartwheel, their bound wrists meeting behind their heads, as if the boss of the wheel. After some difficult contortions, which appeared not to have been improved with practice, Kyros's group settled to sleep in a sitting position with their backs resting against each other, arms and hands tucked into the space afforded by the curved shape of the lower back. I could not imagine this arrangement leading to much sleep.

Arkemis detected what I was thinking. 'I think we have a problem,' he said. 'You see, Nyxes and I are used to the two of us being together. We usually sleep facing each other.'

'None of the other ways look comfortable,' said Nyxes.

I agreed. 'Perhaps you and Arkemis should sleep facing each other as you are used to. Try it before we decide how I shall sleep.'

The brother and sister assumed their usual sleeping position. Despite the short length of the tether between them, they appeared to be reasonably comfortable. However, I was now attached to them both.

'Why not lie behind me?' said Nyxes. 'Lift your arms and I'll go under them.'

'I don't want to strangle you,' I said.

'Let's try. You don't know until you try it.'

Nyxes sat up and I shuffled behind her. She moved her head behind my bound wrists and up between my arms. Arkemis's arms were forced to follow our manoeuvre. We slumped awkwardly to the ground.

'How does it feel?' I asked her. 'Can you breathe?'

'Don't pull, Han. You're pulling my head back. Move closer.'

I did as she bade.

'That's better. I can breathe now. How about you?'

I was closer to Nyxes than I expected to be, with my body moulded tight against her back. It felt strange.

'Get any closer, Han, and she'll be calling you husband.'

'Shut up,' snapped Nyxes.

'I'm sorry,' I said. 'Maybe this isn't such a good idea.'

'Don't worry. At least we can keep each other warm if it's a cold night.'

'Come on, let's try and sleep,' said Arkemis.

You're obviously a man of the world, Arkis, and you may well wonder what was going through my mind as I lay there, my young body nestled against Nyxes. Well, I can tell you it was a confusing experience and I could not find sleep at all. For a while, Nyxes lay perfectly still save for the occasional movement of her head but after a time, she began to shuffle her body as if to settle it more comfortably into our mossy bed. As you might imagine, the effect upon me was quite profound.

I'll not embarrass either of us further, save to say that I hoped dearly that Nyxes was sound asleep and unable to detect my emotions. Comforted by her closeness, I eventually fell asleep. But it was not to be a long sleep.

Well before dawn, I was woken by a hand pressing hard upon my shoulder. I blinked and looked up to see the guard Osbin crouching over me, clearly illuminated by the moon which was directly overhead. He urged silence by placing a finger across his lips.

'I will free you,' he whispered. 'Wait a little while then crawl into the shadows over there.' He pointed to where he meant. 'Then we can talk.'

Osbin moved quickly with his knife to cut the leather thongs that bound me to them. Arkemis stirred a little, though Nyxes remained in what seemed to be a deep sleep. I quickly glanced around the stockade to see if any other guards were about but there was not one within sight. Osbin slipped into the shadows and I waited for a short while as instructed, still lying close to Nyxes, before beginning my slow crawl.

I found Osbin crouched on his haunches and looking

around nervously. 'Where are the other guards?' I asked.

'They are where they usually are at night, with the priests. I was left with one other to guard you – Drago is his name. He is someone you can trust. I cannot explain more now because we have not much time. Others will come soon.'

I said, 'I have so many questions about this place – about you, about why the priests are feeding children to Gilgarius instead of protecting them.'

'Please be patient. For now, all you need to know is that I will try to help you. I have seen too many children devoured by Gilgarius and done nothing to try to save them. It must stop.'

'I have a plan,' I said.

'That is good to know,' said Osbin. 'After one more night, when the new day dawns, the creature will want to feed again. The problem is that the other servers are not to be relied upon to help, apart from Drago. They are completely loyal to the priests.'

I said, 'My plan means we will make our escape when Gilgarius comes. Can you arrange that it is you and Drago who are guarding us when the creature arrives for his breakfast?'

'I cannot be certain but I will try.'

'My plan is risky because it involves angering Gilgarius,' I said. 'There is no way of knowing how he will react. But for it to succeed, it has to be when he comes for his meal.'

'Then you'd better explain what it is you intend to do.'

This I did quickly, adding that it was not yet a complete plan but one which required further thought. Osbin said it was crazy and risky but he would give it some thought to see if there was anything that he could do to improve upon it. We spent a little while more talking, mostly me explaining how I had come to be captured by the Castra and my fear about the fate of my companions.

'The Castra are particularly evil,' Osbin observed with a solemn shake of his head.

'Then why do the priests use them?'

'Because they are evil, too, and evil feeds on evil.' There was a terrible bitterness in his voice.

No more was exchanged between us. I slipped back to try and resume my sleep with Arkemis and Nyxes but I could not rest. My escape idea had begun to grow in complexity as I tried to imagine all that could go wrong and what we could do to combat each potential problem.

When Nyxes awoke, she gave a little gasp of surprise upon finding I was no longer tied to her. I smiled and shrugged my shoulders. 'These human statues are not very good at tying knots,' I said by way of excuse.

'But this looks like it has been cut with a knife,' she said. 'What's going on, Han?'

Again, I smiled. 'I'll explain later. For now, I have to re-attach myself to you and your brother. No one must know about this.'

I could see Arkemis was now waking. 'Know about what?' he asked, blinking the sleep from his eyes.

Nyxes dug an elbow into his ribs. 'Keep your voice down, brother. Han will tell us when he's good and ready.'

By this time all the children were awake and Osbin and some other guards were preparing to bring food. I managed to re-tie myself to my companions in such a way that the thong would slip free if I pulled my hands in a certain direction. Thankfully, it was Osbin who brought our food so I was no longer worried about being discovered.

Understandably he did not smile but, when he looked fleetingly at me, his eyes showed a flicker of warmth and I was reassured he was truly on our side.

When the sun was well risen, we received a visit from Kolak and some of the other priests, including Asdur. I wondered if the Bathlayan was extending his stay there just for the satisfaction of seeing me eaten.

'Well, Han,' said Kolak. 'I trust you spent a comfortable night with your new companions.'

I did not answer, even though I was desperate to ask why he was helping Gilgarius by feeding children to him. I decided silence would stop me being distracted while I was still working on my plan.

The priest appeared not to appreciate my taciturn reaction. He glowered and jabbed his staff in the air between us. 'I hope you are prepared to die. After one more night Gilgarius will come for his feast – and I suspect you will be the first morsel he will wish to taste.'

There was more silence from me, which further annoyed the priest. I could see it in his severe eyes.

'Very well,' he said, turning away. 'Your subdued demeanour is a welcome change. Fear of death, I suspect, has finally found a way of tempering your arrogance.' With that, Kolak and his entourage departed, leaving us to contemplate our impending fate.

Most of the children, myself included, could not face food but Kyros tucked into bread and cheese as if he was at a feast. 'Well, you lot can starve if you want,' he said. 'More for me.'

I admired his spirit and said so.

'There's no point in worrying,' he responded. 'There's nothing we can do about Gilgarius. Anyway, I don't care to think about the creature, except that I hope I give him a bad case of the shits.'

'Nicely put, Kyros,' I said. 'But you're wrong – there *is* something we can do.'

'Yeah, and what is that precisely?'

'I have worked out a plan to save us.'

***

Not for the first time, Pelia lay awake in the middle of the night listening anxiously to her grandfather's unconscious breathing. Earlier he had made peculiar gurgling noises which turned into a coughing fit. Pelia had hurried from her cot to comfort him. She sat him up and gave him a drink of beer, most of which dribbled down his beard. Moonlight streamed through the un-shuttered window and she could see in his eyes a faint glistering of tears. She took his hand, squeezing it reassuringly. He looked at her, blinking forlornly, saying nothing.

After a while he settled into back into his cot, nestling his head into the sack of straw, mumbling unintelligible words that seemed to articulate the measure of his distress. When unconsciousness finally overcame him, his breathing returned to normal but Pelia could not sleep.

She lay awake thinking about the traveller.

***

It was to be a slow and stressful day for us all, said Han. I certainly feared that for some of us the coming night could be the last. The only joy was being so close to Nyxes throughout those long hours, talking about our own lands, our families and how we missed our old lives.

Later in the day, Osbin brought more food to us. Before he moved on, he glanced around quickly to see if any of the other guards might be watching then he whispered, 'We will talk again tonight. I'll give you a signal; you must listen carefully for it.'

Arkemis looked surprised to see Osbin communicating with me and was about to say something when Nyxes nudged him with her elbow. 'Shush, brother. Han knows what he is doing.'

When Osbin was out of our hearing, she turned to me. 'What are you planning?'

'To get us all out of here alive. And we have to rely on

Osbin to help us.'

Nyxes looked at me, her large eyes wide open, trusting. She glanced at my hands, now only loosely bound to hers. Then she looked at me, rather sternly I thought. 'Is that why you freed yourself in the night – to make your plan with one of our guards?'

'I didn't exactly free myself,' I replied defensively. 'But I can't say more at the moment. Before long everything will become clear. And when the time comes, you'll all be told what you need to do.'

'How do you know you can trust him?' asked Arkemis. 'It could be a trap.'

'What would he gain by making a trap against us when we are already trapped?'

Arkemis frowned. 'I don't know. It was just a thought.'

'Best not to think then, brother,' said Nyxes. 'I trust Han knows what he is doing. You should, too.'

'All right, Han,' said Arkemis. 'What great plan have you made to save us from that monster?'

'I'll tell you later. For now, we must think about getting good rest.'

'We've done nothing but rest since we came here,' said Arkemis.

'We must pretend to go to sleep to stop the other guards becoming suspicious,' said Nyxes.

I did not believe the guards would care whether any of us slept or not, but I said, 'If you think it is for the best.'

Later, we settled as we had done the previous night, although this time my freed arms were placed around Nyxes' waist and she settled against me.

Arkemis suddenly sat up issuing a painful cry, pulling Nyxes away from me as he did so. 'What are you doing, brother?' she whispered hoarsely.

'I've got a cramp in my leg,' he groaned. 'I have to stand.'

'No,' said Nyxes. 'The guards will see you. You must stretch out and keep quiet.'

Arkemis obeyed the instruction, wriggling about in the dust until his pain eased.

As dark descended, the children fell asleep or just lay motionless with fear. Anyway, they were all perfectly still and silent, save for an occasional cough or croaky sob. As the moon rose, I picked out two guards patrolling the perimeter of our prison. At times one of them would stop to stare at us. I could not tell if it was Osbin or Drago or one of the others. All I knew is that, when the time came, I would have to time my movements very carefully so as not to be detected.

It was after the moon had moved over the rim of the gorge that I heard a sound in the shadows – tap, tap, tap. Then a short silence and again – tap, tap, tap. I slipped my hands from the bonds and rolled over to check quickly for watching guards. When I was sure there were none, I crawled to where the sound came from.

Osbin was there as promised, crouched in the shadows. 'Drago is patrolling over there so we have no fear of being discovered,' he said. 'But we have little time. What of the other children?'

'I've said nothing yet,' I replied. 'But they have to be prepared for the morning. I must set them free from their bonds before dawn and explain what they need to do.'

Osbin reached out a hand, which held the same blade he had used to cut me free the previous day. 'Use this. It will be quicker. And keep it upon your person – you may need it.'

I took the knife and slipped it into the waistband of my breeches.

'Are you still sure of your plan?' asked Osbin. 'It is very risky.'

'Yes, I know. But I have decided. I only hope the others will go along with it. But what about you? Will you be able to help us?'

'Don't worry. I have also made a plan. There is a place – a safe and secret place to which I will guide you. From there it will be easier to make your escape. But you must heed everything I am about to tell you for it will be dangerous.'

I listened in silence, occasionally nodding in agreement as Osbin outlined what he had in mind. When he finished, I smiled. It was as good as I had hoped. 'Thank you, friend,' I said. 'Your mind is good. I only hope that my plan works so that yours will not be frustrated and we can all get out of this evil place.'

Osbin placed a strong hand upon my shoulder. 'We must be brave for both our plans to work. You must not tell the other children too much, otherwise they will be frightened and may freeze at a crucial time.'

I crawled back to the children and began my night's work. First, I woke Nyxes and Arkemis and cut them free. Nyxes had the sense to be silent, trusting that I knew what I was doing, but Arkemis wanted to know what was going on. 'When do we run? How do we overcome the guards? What do we…'

'Patience, Arkemis,' I whispered. 'I shall explain when everyone is free.'

I commenced to crawl around the groups of sleeping children, whispering them awake and urging silence as I cut through their bonds. I whispered the same instruction to each group as I loosely retied the thongs in such a way that they could be slipped off easily.

'You must make it look like you are still bound together. When dawn comes, food will be brought by two of the guards who will not look too closely at your wrists. You can trust them.'

I then explained the signal they should listen for and what to do when it was given. It is fair to say that my words were received with suspicion among some of the older children, though the younger ones appeared to trust me without question.

Kyros, who was a little older than me, was particularly mistrustful. I suspected he was rather put out that someone younger had taken command of the situation. 'This is a mad idea,' he whispered hoarsely after I outlined what would unfold when light came.

'It truly is,' I agreed. 'But it is the only way we're going to get out of here. Are you with me?'

There was a worrying moment of hesitation as he contemplated my words. Then his face broke into a pleasant, reassuring smile. 'I would be mad not to be,' he said.

'Good,' I said. 'Because come the morning you will play an important part in our salvation.'

'I'm relishing it already,' said Kyros.

I returned to Arkemis and Nyxes and the other children settled down to try and sleep, although I suspected most would lay awake thinking about what lay ahead of us. I did not tell them every element of my plan, just sufficient so they would know what to do upon the given signal. Kyros, Nyxes and Arkemis, however, were to play a more crucial role and therefore needed to know more than the rest. I had already explained matters to Kyros; now I had to do the same to the other two.

'But that's crazy.' Arkemis's reaction was not surprising. Osbin had thought it crazy, Kyros had thought it crazy, and even I thought it crazy. I turned to Nyxes, believing she would, too. In the moonlight, I could see her smiling and slowly shaking her head. Her eyes shone as bright as the moon itself.

I leant closer to her. 'What's so funny.'

'You, Han. Everything about you makes me smile. Even in this terrible place with this horrible threat to our lives, you are not diminished. I'm impressed.' She kissed me gently on the cheek.

'What's that for?'

'For saving us all.'

'I haven't saved anyone yet.'

'No, but you will.'

Such faith worried me. What if my plan failed? Then I thought we would still be killed and eaten anyway – no different to the fate we already faced. Not to try to fight back and give us at least a chance of survival would be a folly; if it led to just one child escaping, I would deem our effort a success.

We all settled as best we could, waiting for the long terrifying night to be over. I could not sleep and neither, I suspected, could Nyxes. She did not emit that deep sonorous breathing you would expect from someone asleep but instead lay perfectly still against me, hardly breathing at all.

Sometime in the night our little group was joined by Kyros, who had slipped free from the two small girls as pre-arranged. We were now four.

When at last the sun began to rise, we sat up and waited for Gilgarius to come. We were bound together tightly in silence, if not by leather thongs, staring towards the rim of the gorge. I could see the tall figures of Kolak and Asdur standing with other priests, staring down upon us from the rim of the gorge, the sun rising behind their backs. There was one other person there too – the Castra leader, the man Asdur had called Gostopo.

Kolak thrust his orbed staff towards me. 'Make ready to meet your fate, Han,' boomed the priest, his deep voice even more resonant in the natural amphitheatre.

I did not reply. Any words from my reedy throat would have been wasted, carried away by the wind.

'Your silence is understandable,' Kolak continued. 'It is perhaps wise to spend such remaining time as you have in quiet contemplation of your death. And I trust we will not have long to wait; I suspect Gilgarius will be quite ravenous following his fasting.'

Barely was this said when we heard the creature stirring in

his forest lair. His giant wings vibrated great draughts of air as he rose above the trees, bending their trunks and branches as if they had been caught in a violent tempest. Gilgarius circled twice before he came our way, his gigantic body almost blotting out the sun. He flew directly over us, like an enormous dark storm cloud, and landed upon the opposite ridge to where Kolak and Asdur were standing. The priests' long robes billowed in Gilgarius's gale and they were forced to move back towards the shelter of the rocks to avoid being blown over.

Gilgarius glowered at us over the rim of the gorge. Behind him the cone of a distant peak thrust itself into the sky, making it look like there was a pointed hat upon his ugly head. The creature spread his huge wings to form a giant cave, inside which red eyes flashed. He emitted a low, grumbling sound from deep within his hollow, hungry belly. Eyes rolling, he yawned, showing off teeth as sharp as daggers and yellow as gold.

He spied me and thrust a hooked claw in my direction. 'Ah! There I see my breakfast,' Gilgarius roared. 'Come, Han. It is time to be consumed.'

At that point, two guards entered our prison. I was relieved to see that one of them was Osbin and hoped that the other was the one he called Drago. Without their help, my plan would surely fail.

I indicated to Nyxes, Arkemis and Kyros that we should now stand while still making it appear that we were bound together. As we did so, Gilgarius rose into the air and circled the gorge before returning to the ridge above us.

He boomed his breakfast order. 'Five children shall I eat this morning. Take the boy, Han, and four others to my feasting place.'

Osbin, knowing there would only be four of us, indicated with a nod that we should move towards the narrow passage leading to the shitting place. It was not easy to walk while pretending our hands were bound together. We turned into something resembling a human crab.

We emerged into the brightening light, Osbin leading the way, while the other guard – the one I assumed was Drago – stayed to guard the remaining children. At least, that is what the priests expected him to do.

I had been warned about Gilgarius's feasting area, fringed by thick forest in a wide clearing beyond the shitting place. Osbin had described it to me but all the same I was stunned by it, for the ground was littered with leftover bones from the creature's previous meals.

The sight of so many child skulls visibly shocked my companions, especially Nyxes. These were the bones of the children they had known, the play friends they had grown up with and been captured with and suffered alongside. Many of the skulls were broken apart so Gilgarius could pick out the brains with his sharp claws; the leg and arm bones were crunched or cracked open in his desire to feast upon the marrow inside them.

Osbin held back as we walked to the centre of this terrible place. Although they were fearful steps, we knew what we had to do to prepare ourselves for our confrontation with Gilgarius.

I looked around to see that Kolak and Asdur had made it to the feeding place by some other route and were standing upon the flat summit of a huge rock which cleaved the trees to one side of us. They were obviously expecting to enjoy watching our terrible end. I, on the other hand, was expecting them to be mightily disappointed.

I turned to my companions. 'Are you ready?'

Nervously, they murmured that they were.

Almost in one movement, we slipped free from the loose bonds which bound us and lined up to face Gilgarius, now arm in arm, with me and Kyros on each flank.

By this time the creature had lifted himself from the ridge, circling high above before swooping towards us then settling maybe thirty strides away. We were standing firm, arms locked ever tighter in response to the fear that was understandably fermenting inside us.

We waited silently. Gilgarius was about to extend a large hooked claw to pick out one of us – most likely me – but he suddenly halted, letting out a low grumbling sound which vibrated the earth beneath us. 'What is this?'

He lowered his huge head so close to the ground that it was almost resting on some of the child bones. He viewed us menacingly with eyes the colour of burning embers, blinking them as he mentally counted our number. Then he lifted his head and roared towards the priests on the ridge. 'Four! You send me four when I ask for five?'

The priests looked at each other. Kolak bellowed something at Osbin but this time his words were lost on the wind. Gilgarius stamped his giant feet and ground shook like it sometimes does here in Akbenna when Mother Mountain is angry.

Nyxes began to shiver uncontrollably with fear. I squeezed my arm more tightly around hers. 'Don't be afraid. He's angry, but as long as we stay together the creature's fear of even numbers will protect us.'

Gilgarius ceased his stamping and turned to me. 'One of you must leave. Not you, Han. I have looked forward to this day since our time in Akbenna. Send the girl away; she will give me indigestion her body is shaking so much.'

'No, Gilgarius, we stay together,' I shouted. 'If you want to eat one, you must eat us all.'

The creature snorted so fiercely with anger and indignation that he almost blew us over. The effect of the snorting must have given him an idea, for his ruby eyes widened as if with joy. He stamped his feet again and drew to his full height, blowing his foul breath so fiercely upon us that it felt we were being buffeted by a violent storm.

'Stand firm,' I urged, gripping Nyxes ever more tightly. 'The monster will not take us if we hold on to each other.'

But we could not resist the power of Gilgarius's breath and all four of us were buffeted so fiercely we were unable to stay on our feet. Yet even as we were blown onto our backs, we did not let go of each other.

Gilgarius took to the air, using his giant wings to create an even greater wind. The force pounded us relentlessly, hurling us across the ground where the dust choked us and sharp stones and child bones cut into our arms and legs. Yet we held to each other firmly.

Gilgarius settled again and shook his mighty head, breathing heavily as if over-exerted by his attempt to separate us.

We managed to sit up, our arms still interlocked.

'Now you are really starting to annoy me,' said the creature. 'But I am prepared to bide my time. You cannot remain fixed like that forever.'

'Why wait?' I shouted. 'Why can you not eat us now? I am ready. My friends are, too. We have come to be consumed, yet you insist upon playing games with us.'

'Games? It is you, boy, who are playing games. I asked for five children and have been served four. Any Gilgarius would get annoyed. It stands to reason – four can never be as good as five.'

'But you wanted the girl to go, leaving just three of us. Therefore, three must also be better than four.'

'Three is a good number, I grant you.'

'And four isn't?'

Gilgarius snorted in a sneering way. 'I haven't time to play number games. Detach the girl and let's get on with this. My patience is ended.'

'No, Gilgarius. We are four. We come as four and must

be eaten together. Or maybe four is too much at one sitting. Maybe we should split in half and you can eat two of us now and two later.'

'Enough!' roared the creature. 'Enough of this nonsense. It is three or nothing.'

'Then nothing it shall be.'

'No, I did not mean that. I meant…' The creature did not finish his sentence. Instead he sat upon his haunches grumbling something under his foul breath.

'Why, Gilgarius?' I asked, determined to pursue a reaction from the creature.

'Why what?'

'Why do you fear even numbers?'

'What do you mean? Do not accuse me of being frightened. I fear nothing: no human or animal or fiery mountain.'

'But you fear twos and fours and sixes. I want to know why, because such a fear does not make sense.'

'I told you, I fear nothing,' growled Gilgarius. 'Numbers do not frighten me. Don't say they do when they do not.'

'Even numbers make me feel calm,' said Arkemis. 'They are gentle; no awkward edges. Don't you think they are gentle, Han?'

'Yes, I agree. Even numbers are about balance and fairness; they are about peace and order and everyone being treated equally. Evenly.'

Gilgarius snorted dismissively. 'Why should I like numbers to be calm and gentle and peaceful? A three-legged stool will always sit firmly on the roughest ground, while one with four legs will never be steady. Anyway, numbers should have sharp edges – as sharp as daggers.'

'Sharp like your teeth, Gilgarius?' I said.

'Yes, my teeth are sharp as you will soon discover when they tear into your precocious flesh.'

'What do you think, Arkemis? How many dagger teeth do

you think Gilgarius has?'

'I can't count them from here, Han,' said Arkemis. 'Though I suspect there will be an even number of them. All creatures are the same when it comes to teeth, surely even a Gilgarius. There are no odd numbers when it comes to teeth.'

'Unless some fall out, like three of mine have,' said Kyros.

Gilgarius rose again on its haunches and thrust out a claw. 'Stop this now!' He stretched out his huge wings. 'You think you can beat me again with talk, Han,' he boomed. 'You think you can resist being eaten because you are clever. But I shall have a meal of you yet.'

With that, he took to the air, the power of his beating wings almost forcing our separation. But we clung together, watching him rise with a terrible screech and head across the valley to where the priests were observing from their vantage point, presumably to vent his frustration.

Gilgarius rose high above them, twisting and turning as he roared out his anger. Then the roar turned into a mighty screech as if the creature had been mortally wounded and he swooped low over the priests' heads, almost blowing them over with the force of his giant wing beats. The priests and the Castra leader hurried into the rocks to escape Gilgarius's wrath.

This was our moment.

'You must follow Osbin,' I shouted, as the four of us separated.

'What about you, Han?' This was Nyxes.

'Don't worry, I'll be close behind you. I have to be sure we are not going to be followed by any of the other guards – or Gilgarius, once he discovers we have escaped his clutches. Hurry,' I said. 'You must waste no time. You can trust Osbin to take you to safety. He, too, is desperate to escape this place.'

Nyxes held back. She took my arm. 'You must come now, Han. Do not put yourself in further danger.' Her eyes were bubbling tears. 'Please, Han.'

I pulled her close to me and kissed away the salty wetness from her cheeks. 'Don't worry. I will follow quickly. I just want to see what Gilgarius does.' In truth, I hoped to witness him killing the priests out of his frustration, but I did not wish to reveal such murderous thoughts to my new friends.

Reluctantly Nyxes drew herself from me. She hurried to join Arkemis and Kyros who were already disappearing into the forest, led by Osbin.

I found refuge behind a large bush at the edge of the trees. Although now alone, I had no fear at that moment because my plan was working.

Gilgarius continued his screeching as he flew high and low in his anger, swooping over the rocks where the priests and their guards had hidden themselves. After a while he gave up his violent ranting and settled upon the sloping rock, wings outstretched and panting, as if exhausted by hunger and exertion. He ranged his eyes over the now-deserted eating place then he realised what had truly happened. 'Gone!' he cried. 'I am deceived and my breakfast is gone.'

The monster had been outwitted and, although he had not killed the priests in his anger, his violent reaction had forced them to seek cover, thereby delaying any effort to order our recapture.

I hoped the children had been given a good start to gain their freedom. With the priests distracted by Gilgarius's eruption of anger, they would all now be able to escape and be guided into the forest by Osbin. For his part, Drago would feign being distracted by the creature's wrath as an excuse for not preventing the children's escape.

Unfortunately, I hadn't realised how precarious my own situation would become once Gilgarius discovered the true state of affairs. He rose into the air once more then descended to the feeding ground where he landed heavily, causing the very earth to shudder. From deep within him emanated a rumbling sound prompted by hunger or anger – or perhaps a combination of the two.

He lowered his head, flaring his nostrils and sniffing the ground, and began to move slowly towards my hiding place. I should have run. Yes, I know I should have fled with the others to find safety but I must have been deceived by my own cleverness, believing nothing now could harm me. If Gilgarius can't see me, he can't eat me, I convinced myself. What I did not appreciate was how strongly he held within him the memory of my odour.

By this time the creature was even more agitated, gouging the earth with his claws and stamping his huge feet hard upon the ground so that clouds of choking dust rose. 'I smell you, Han,' he growled. 'Smell you as good as if I'm already crunching your bones.'

Realising it was high time to make my escape I turned to run into the forest, but for some unfathomable reason my legs would hardly move. And the closer the creature got to me, the more transfixed I became, as if intoxicated by his foul breath. Although he could not see me, he knew where I was; he could smell my person and my fear. Nyxes had been right; I should have fled with her and the other children, instead of hanging back to watch Gilgarius out of idiotic curiosity.

'You are close, boy,' said Gilgarius. 'So very close, I could reach you with my tongue. I am sure of it. And just one prod of my foreclaw is all it will take to impale you.'

I was but five strides from the creature, well within his reach, and could see a claw penetrating the bushes to find me. I dropped to my knees and tried to crawl away but Gilgarius hooked me by the legs and dragged me from the bushes.

'Ah, Han – my young breakfast,' said the creature.

I lay prone upon the ground. Gilgarius brought his head close to mine and I was bathed in his foulness. Although petrified, I assumed a combative attitude. 'What are you afraid of, Gilgarius?'

The creature seemed surprised at my question. 'I am afraid of nothing.'

'Except even numbers.'

'Irrelevant! You are now the odd one, Han. On your own and ready to be consumed. I know it. My digestive juices know it.'

'But there's still something stopping you from eating me, isn't there?'

Gilgarius blinked his huge eyes in puzzlement. 'Like what?'

'I cannot be consumed because I am not given.'

'On the contrary, I think you are very much given.'

'No! I am not. To be consumed, I have to be offered in sacrifice by a priest. Where are the priests?'

'They've already offered you, as they have offered all the children.'

'You rejected me because there were four of us. Once rejected, I have to be offered again. Where are the priests to offer me? They are hiding out of fear.'

'Once given, never not given.'

'No. You must go to them and ask them to offer me again.'

'Do you think I'm an idiot? By the time I return you will be gone, and I shall have missed out on the revenge I have been savouring. Now stop this nonsense, boy. Play the game and let me crunch your bones.'

'No! I have not been given anew and I refuse to offer myself.'

'Then I shall eat you anyway.'

'You cannot eat me,' I screeched. 'You told me the rule yourself. I insist that I am no longer given in sacrifice.'

I could see the creature hesitate, as if unsure. He blinked his eyes, now fiery red as the rocks which sometimes spewed from Mother Mountain's belly. He shook his head from side to side, all the time growling and snorting his foulness upon me.

'Take him! Take him, Gilgarius!' The booming voice of Kolak

was the last thing I wanted to hear. I looked to the ridge beyond the eating place to see that he and Asdur had emerged from their frighty holes and were looking down upon us.

'*Eat him!*' boomed Kolak, waving his orbed staff.

'*Eat him!*' echoed Asdur, though much less commandingly.

Gilgarius's eyes widened, demonstrating his delight. 'Well, boy – if there was doubt before, there is no doubt now. You are most assuredly given. Now, prepare to acquaint yourself with my digestive juices.'

As you can guess, Arkis, I was in a terrible hole and it was all my own doing. The creature curled his claws around my body and lifted me towards his cavernous mouth, suspending me in mid-air as if to heighten my fright. I was so close to Gilgarius's teeth, I could see beyond the forest of green fur that grew on his tongue to his huge quivering clacker. The stench from in there was so noxious that I began to wretch.

It was then that I remembered Osbin's knife.

My hands were not restrained and I could still feel it there, tucked into my breeches. I clasped my fingers around the hilt as firmly as I could and plucked it free. I had only a fraction of a second to act and did so with no fear of the consequences. Even if Gilgarius only reacted to the plunging blade as I might twitch at the bite the of an ant, I was at least fighting back and not submitting with a mere whimper.

I did not have time to think what part of Gilgarius's head I should strike. The decision was instinctive; just as the monster's dagger teeth prepared to sink themselves into my body, I plunged the blade with as much force as I could summon into his eye.

There was a great roar as the pain of the strike registered. Then, in his reaction, Gilgarius began to squeeze so tightly with his claws that I felt my innards would burst forth. As he stamped and wailed, a combination of his poisonous breath and the grip of his claws rendered me almost unconscious.

Now, Arkis, you may imagine my fear. I had possibly made the most foolish mistake of my young life but inflicting harm upon this terrible creature while hovering so close to his jaws. Yet he did not thrust me into them to swiftly crunch me in the manner of revenge; instead he suddenly and inexplicably released his grip upon me.

As I fell, I heard shouting: frenzied human voices quite close by. I hit the ground next to one of Gilgarius's stamping feet and would have surely been crushed into the earth had not strong hands grabbed my legs and dragged me into the bushes.

By then all was chaos. Gilgarius continued to roar and stamp as spears and arrows rained down upon him. He rose into the air, all the time raging as the missiles assailed him. Some of the spears managed to embed themselves in his softer parts but most of them just bounced off his thick hide. It seemed that I had found the most vulnerable part of him when I had thrust Osbin's dagger into his eye.

I sat up and turned to thank Osbin for rescuing me from the monster, for I believed it was he who had returned from helping to hide the other children to drag me clear. But when I looked up, it wasn't Osbin crouching over me.

Oh, Arkis! Can you imagine the great joy that surged through my pain-wracked young body upon discovering my saviour to be none other than Garia? My brave companion was alive and had come to save me.

'Hello, my young friend,' said Garia, before adding with the broadest smile, 'Next time you decide to fight, I'd suggest you pick someone your own size.'

I could not hold back the tears and blubbed with both joy and relief. There were so many questions I needed answers to, principal among them whether Edbersa and Kairi had survived the Castra attack which had led to my kidnapping.

Garia hauled me to my feet and dragged me further into the forest. 'No time for talk,' he said, obviously aware of my urgent desire for information. 'There are those who'll keep the creature occupied while we find safety.'

I took his reluctance to explain as an indication that our Edbersa and Kairi were no longer alive. The joy at being rescued by Garia started to subside. But I had no time for mourning.

Despite the pain, I managed to keep on my feet as Garia pulled me along through the thick foliage. After we had made what must have been half a league, we halted to take breath. I gripped the side of my body in a feeble attempt to squeeze out the pain. I looked down to see blood oozing through my fingers.

'Let me take a look,' said Garia, lifting my arm away. There was a large gash in my tunic. 'We've got to stem the bleeding,' he said.

He ripped a length of cloth from his own tunic and tied it around my middle so tightly that I cried out with the pain.

Garia placed a kind hand upon my shoulder. 'I am sorry but it has to be done. We must get you somewhere safe quickly to clean the wound and apply whatever healing plant we can find.'

'Will you have to piss on it?'

'Maybe. But I might not have enough piss on my own. I haven't had chance to drink much water lately.' Then he smiled. 'But don't worry. I have two travelling companions who will no doubt be willing to help.'

It took me several moments to work out who he meant. 'Kairi and Edbersa!' I exclaimed. 'They are alive!'

'Yes, my young friend. Very much alive and both just as annoying as ever.'

'Where are they?'

'Helping to distract Gilgarius. Come on, we don't want their efforts to be wasted.'

Garia grabbed my arm and we set off again through the thick undergrowth. It was not easy. We kept tripping over exposed tree roots, and the branches Garia pushed aside to allow our passage had the habit of thwacking back into my head and body, including my already painful wound.

Finally, breathless, we made it to a clearing. As soon I burst gasping into the open space, I saw the solitary figure of Osbin emerging from the trees at the far side, looking worried. 'Han!' he exclaimed.

Garia looked ready to grab the hilt of his sword. I reached out to stay his hand. 'He's a friend,' I said.

Osbin ran towards us. 'What were you playing at? Why did you not follow the other children? I've been worried sick. And who is this fellow?'

'He's Garia, one of the travelling companions I told you about. He's just rescued me from Gilgarius.'

'You are wounded.'

'A little. Where are the others?'

'They're safe – for now – waiting in the thickest part of the forest. But they cannot stay long. We must move quickly.'

I sank to the ground, exhausted and still in great pain. I looked up at Garia, whose expression showed he had his own questions and concerns. 'Garia, there are other children,' I started to explain. 'Osbin helped them to escape from Gilgarius.'

'You can tell him all that later, Han' said Osbin. 'Now we must move before Kolak sends an army of Castra to find us.'

He was right. Although there were so many questions to be answered from every side, this was not the time. The urgent thing was to get everyone to safety, including Edbersa and Kairi.

'I have to go back to help my companions,' Garia told Osbin, as if reading my mind.

Osbin reached down and helped me to my feet. 'If they are still alive, bring them here,' he told Garia. 'But you must ensure you are not followed. I'll take the boy to safety and come back to meet you here when the sun is at its highest.'

I can remember no other words. Having lost so much blood by this time, I began to feel nauseous and sensed the forest spinning around me. I sank to my knees as consciousness drained away.

It was told to me later that I raged with a fever for two days and nights, yet the only thing I can remember was having the most vivid dreams imaginable – if indeed they were dreams.

In this state, I was able to return to my home where I saw my father sitting here beneath the chatka tree, shaking his head and staring into the distance where the sun sets, as if trying to imagine where I had gone. And over there by the stockade, my mother was making cheese, muttering to herself and weeping gently. In another dream, I found myself in Ejiki, pleading with Karmus and Medzurgo to let me go home. They ignored me as if I wasn't there, despite my shouts and curses for what they had done to me.

Yet another dream saw me once again confronting Gilgarius in a desert so barren that it left me feeling we were all that existed in the living world. His growl had become more like the purr of a cat, albeit a giant one; he told me he did not really want to eat me but it was what he had been created to do. 'No hard feelings,' he said, 'but we all have to go sometime.' I jabbed a finger at the creature and said I would ensure his time would come before mine. He just laughed, but it was a laugh like thunder.

In the most vivid dream, the one I remember in greatest detail, I was in a place I had never been to before where the sky glowed with gold and the ground was carpeted with flowers of vibrant blues and reds and yellows and all the hues in between. A stream ran through the pasture as the freshest spring water, filtered through the finest grains of sand. I was bathed in a light that had a clarity the like of which surely does not exist in any land known to humans.

And the music, Arkis. Yes, the music I heard was the most beautiful that could be produced by any instrument. As a child, I'd never heard anything other than the sounds of coarse instruments like those played by villagers on feast days, sounds – you could hardly call them music – made by drums of boar hide, horns from dead cattle or strings of goat-gut pulled taut across a bowed branch.

Nothing in my experience prepared me for the joy that unfolded during my time of unconsciousness. And not just instruments, Arkis; there were voices singing, powerfully deep, achingly high and every shade of sound in between, and all in perfect harmony. Yet nowhere could I see anyone playing an instrument or singing. I searched, of course.

I rose from the softest fern bed and wandered around this place, hearing everything but seeing no one. Then I came upon the spring of the clearest water. I knelt and cupped some of it into my mouth and more of it I splashed on to my face. I could feel it refreshing me as sure as if I had been awake but I remained in a dream I did not wish to leave.

Although I could see no humans, there were animals of every kind imaginable. Kolakis were everywhere, prompting me to smile, and ledbuk, of course. There were many such prey animals, frightened scurrying creatures, as well as the creatures that habitually prey upon them such as wolves and bears. But no prey animal was laid low by a bear's powerful blow or ripped apart by a wolf's dagger teeth.

We all dream, Arkis. All my life I have experienced the most vivid dreams imaginable but nothing, before or since, has come close to what I experienced in my time of dying. I wandered through this beautiful land among the creatures who showed no fear of each other or of me. I sat for a while upon a small hill, overlooking a shimmering lake of the most striking green. The water sparkled in the sunlight and I could see fish breaking the surface with little leaps.

Then I saw a human form approaching the far shore of the lake, a solitary man walking steadily towards the water's edge, a small figure whose gait was achingly familiar to me.

It was my father.

I had not noticed it, but at the far water's edge was a small rowing boat with oars laid inside it. I had never seen the like of this before. In Akbenna, we barely had enough water to bathe in, let alone float a vessel. So it was surprising to see my father clamber into it and operate the boat's oars easily, smoothly dipping them into the still water to propel himself towards me.

I rushed into the water to greet him as he stepped from the boat. I hauled him to me in a powerful hug, tears streaming down my face and soaking his hair. I realised that I was now much taller than him. He felt so slight in my embrace and I eased my grip for fear of hurting him.

He looked up at me, tears washing his sad eyes.

'Father,' I said. 'You answered my call. You came to save me.'

'No, my son,' he said, smiling weakly through the tears. 'You are strong and brave enough to save yourself. I came to say goodbye.'

His words devastated me. What could he mean? I did not want to say goodbye, so I clung to my father to prevent him from leaving me, only to feel his body dissolving from my embrace.

Oh, Arkis! Can you imagine my distress? I had found my father only to lose him once more. He suddenly reappeared upon the far shore of the lake and, though his voice was distant, he spoke words that came to me clearly, borne across the water. 'You will live a long life and have remarkable things to relate, my son,' he said. 'But remember this, Han – remarkable stories should never be dressed in simple clothes.'

It was a strange thing for a poor, uneducated man like my father to say. I had no doubt there was wisdom hidden in what he said. Yes, I was sure of it, but I have to admit that I did not understand then what he truly meant or what lesson he wished me to learn. All I truly know is that he faded from me, lost forever.

'Don't leave me,' I implored. 'Please don't leave me.'

I sank to my knees and sobbed into the beautiful flowers that carpeted my dream. Then I heard another voice behind me. I turned my head to see a small, slender figure in the distance, beckoning me away from the water. All I remember after that is rising to my feet and following this new voice, which returned me to the life I had so nearly lost. I awoke from my dream, bathed in perspiration and still pleading with my father not to leave me.

'Don't worry, Han,' the voice was saying as I blinked open my drowning eyes. 'I won't leave you.'

It was Nyxes.

***

Han paused. With a sniffle, he turned his gaze from Arkis so his visitor would be unable to see the distress in his eyes. He wiped his nose with his sleeve and made as if to continue his story, but though his lips attempted to form a word no sound accompanied it.

Arkis waited, unwilling to prompt and unable to say what he really wanted to say, even though time was running out and Han visibly weakening with every twist and turn of his tale.

The old man continued staring silently into the distance but this time not towards Mother Mountain, his habitual source of comfort. Instead, his eyes followed the decline of the sun over scanty patches of corn, as though he was observing the final setting of his own days on earth.

After a while, and still staring into the sunset, Han turned to Arkis. 'Forgive me,' he said. 'Whenever I think of dear Nyxes and how she cared for me as I fought to recover from my wound, I realise how much time has taken from me.'

'You became close to Nyxes?'

'Yes. From the very first moment I saw her, there was something that happened to me. I can't explain it exactly, but though we were young it was as if I had known her for an eternity.'

'And you believe she saved your life?'

'Nyxes stayed by my side almost the whole time I was in a fever. If not for her I would have died, I'm sure of it.' Han fell into silence again.

'Do you wish to rest?' Arkis asked.

The old man shook his head. 'I am not yet ready for resting,' he said. 'For now, I must continue my story.'

'Very well, but on condition that you stop when you feel too tired. It is no problem for me. I have plenty of time.'

'I wish I could say the same,' said Han with the saddest smile of resignation.

***

I suppose this would be an appropriate point to describe the place I found myself in, said Han. The place where Nyxes, Arkemis and all the other children had been led by Osbin and where I was also carried in my unconscious state.

In the midst of the forest was a gorge so deep that it was almost impenetrable, save by those who knew its secrets. At the head of this gorge was an abandoned structure that had been made by the hands of men in times long forgotten. Osbin believed it was some kind of temple but it was largely overgrown with trees, vines and other vegetation. It was difficult to see exactly what it could have been because so much of it was hidden, but he showed us where huge blocks of stone could be glimpsed. It was clear they had been hewn and chiselled smooth with tools.

How Osbin knew about this place I was to find out later. He believed its existence was known only to him and Drago, otherwise he would not have risked taking us there.

Anyway, beyond the ruin a mountain rose upon which grew stunted trees and giant ferns. Hidden behind this vegetation was the entrance to a cave and it was in here I woke from my fever to find myself being nursed and comforted by Nyxes.

I could see the look of relief in her eyes as I regained consciousness. Those same eyes were red from crying. I attempted to lift myself into a sitting position.

Nyxes pressed both hands gently upon my breast. 'No, Han – stay still. You must keep resting.'

I relented and relaxed.

'We nearly lost you. Your wound – we feared it was turning bad.'

I could see fresh tears starting to glisten in her eyes. 'I owe you my life,' I said.

'No, no – not me, Han. I just stayed with you and trickled water into your mouth and mopped the perspiration from your brow. It was that fierce-looking man who saved you. The one they call Edbersa.'

My heart lifted. It was true: Edbersa was alive.

Nyxes continued, 'He staunched the bleeding and cleansed and bound the wound with a poultice made from forest plants, which I would not have been able to do. I was useless – all I could do was watch.'

I decided not to ask Nyxes if Edbersa had pissed on me. 'You helped save me in another way,' I said. 'You were the one who brought me back after my father left me by the lake. It was you – I followed a vision of you.'

'Your father? Lake?'

'In my dream my father crossed a lake to say goodbye. Then I saw you beckoning me.'

'My heart did beckon you, Han. I didn't want you to die and

I kept talking just to let you know I was here, caring for you.'

'And you brought me back.'

'Sometimes in your fever you tried to tell me things, as if you knew I was here. Your voice was weak and I couldn't understand what you were saying. All I knew is that you were trying to come back. I never believed you were going to die.'

I reached up to take her hand. 'I will never forget you, Nyxes.'

She turned her head away, as if to hide a blush.

It was then that I began to take in my surroundings. The cave we were in was lit partly by natural light penetrating from outside and partly by a fire just inside the entrance. Although I could not gauge its full extent, the cave was big enough to accommodate maybe forty or fifty people. All the children who had escaped Gilgarius were there, whispering nervously to each other or curled up asleep on fern leaves.

'Osbin says this place is not known to the priests,' said Nyxes. 'I don't know if that's true but, even if it is, we can't stay here forever. We will never be safe while Gilgarius is searching for us.'

'Doesn't he ever give up?'

'The creature is angry to have been tricked by you again and because you half-blinded him; he is scouring the land seeking revenge. But you must not worry. Edbersa and your other companions have soldiers to help them. You must regain your strength. Are you hungry?'

'A little.'

'That is perhaps as well, as there's only a little food to offer. Osbin found provisions but they are fast running out.'

Nyxes was right. I needed rest. I ate a little flat bread, then closed my eyes and soon fell into a dreamless, healing sleep. I don't know how long I remained thus, but when Nyxes woke me gently from my slumber I realised she was not the only one staring down at me.

'Well, young Han, you gave us all a scare,' a gruff voice, achingly familiar, was saying. 'But the one you scared most of all was that half-blind monster out there.'

It was Edbersa. He was standing behind Nyxes, who by now was preparing to feed me some kind of porridge from a wood bowl. She placed the bowl on the ground to help me sit up with my back resting against the cave wall.

'Edbersa – I knew you would come and find me.'

'I needed to know what all the fuss was about. You seem to be worth a lot of gold, lad.' Edbersa sank to his knees and placed a hand upon my shoulder.

I placed my own hand over his. 'Garia told me you were alive,' I said. 'But I don't know anything else – how you escaped the Castra and found me here.'

'It is an interesting story, Han. Probably not as exciting as your adventure, but fascinating in its own way.'

'Will you tell me?'

'Of course, but you must eat first. You need to build up your strength for the danger has not passed and soon we must prepare to move on.'

Edbersa's words worried me but he smiled reassuringly. We fell into silence as Nyxes fed me a little porridge and water. Afterwards, Edbersa told me what happened in the hours following my abduction.

***

As you were being carried away through the forest, said Edbersa, some of the Castra remained behind to prevent us following. Kairi took a blow to the side of his head in the combat that ensued – fortunately it was not the sharp side of the axe that made the contact. He fell to the ground but before his assailant could finish him off with the blade, Garia leaped between them and ran his sword into the Castran's gut.

I was busy fighting my own battle with two other axemen and did not know of Kairi's predicament. I learned later that Garia showed the mettle of a true warrior as he stood guard over our unconscious companion, dealing death upon any Castran who dared to come close and taking a slight shoulder wound into the bargain.

These Castra were dumb to continue fighting and dying after their prize – that is you, my young friend – had already been gained. We killed five of them before they realised fighting us was fruitless. The remainder fled, leaving Kairi unconscious but all three of us undefeated and relatively unscathed.

But I was angry that Garia and I had failed in our sworn duty to keep you safe, betraying the trust placed in us by Karmus. Garia was determined to make amends by setting off in immediate pursuit of the Castra, but Kairi was too dazed to even stand.

'We must think about this,' I told him. 'We can't simply rush after them like idiots. They are too many. We must form a plan.'

'But what if they are intent upon killing Han?' Garia said.

'Think about it,' I countered. 'They have gone to a great deal of trouble to take the boy. If they simply wanted him dead, they could have struck the fatal blow here. No, they want him alive for some reason.'

Understanding this allowed us time to recover from the attack and devise a plan to find and rescue you. But we were just three and the Castra were many; we would have to use our wits and have a great deal of luck.

After Kairi recovered and it was light enough, we set out to search for the horses. They had run off when the fighting started but Melimari and Fermansa came quickly to Garia's calls and whistles. We had no idea what had happened to Nera and presumed the Castra had taken her. But at least we could now follow the Castra with more speed.

With his skills, Kairi had no difficulty finding the tracks through the forest and even out on the open plain, but our progress was slower on stony ground. We did not rest until the sun set and it was too difficult to continue. We found shelter among large rocks strewn across a grassy hillside where the horses could feed. We hardly slept and ate very little, such was our concern about your fate.

The next day we continued to track the Castra, but it was a slow task as Kairi was still affected by the blow to his head and at times felt dizzy or could only see through blurred vision. We had to stop frequently to rest, which meant our journey to find you cost us two more nights in the open. On our third morning Kairi rose feeling much better; we set off when it was still hardly light, halting to rest only when the sun was at its highest.

It was then that Kairi noticed a cloud of dust billowing over the ridge of a distant hill. 'I fear we have company,' he said.

Soon, from out of the dust emerged a phalanx of horses and riders – warriors. Their spears could be seen glinting in the sun. 'Castra!' exclaimed Garia. 'They have returned with an army to finish us off.'

'They are not Castra,' said Kairi.

It soon became obvious what this army was. I recognised at their head the distinctive, hunch-backed figure of Mulenda, leader of the Bathlayans. With him were thirty or more of his warriors, all armed with swords and spears. Some also carried shields and had bows and quivers of arrows slung over their shoulders.

Mulenda held his men back and approached us on his large white horse. He came so close, I could hear the creaking of leather and feel the animal's hot, snorting breath from the hard ride on my cheek.

Mulenda held me in a severe stare. 'I know who you are,' he said.

'Of course,' said Garia with an incredulous laugh. 'We are from Akbenna. We were your guests but three nights ago.'

'I'm talking about him!' Mulenda's eyes had remained fixed on me. Then, with just the barest hint of a smile, he said, 'Well, uncle, what have you to say for yourself?'

I said nothing – at least not immediately. Not that I had nothing to say but because I was trying to work out how Mulenda could have possibly known.

The Bathlayan leader dismounted. 'Well, uncle,' he said again.

I tried hard not to smile – I was in no frame of mind for a joyful reunion – but a smile somehow forced itself on to my face.

'I suppose I should have known,' said Mulenda. Holding his horse's rein with one leather-gloved hand, he reached out to me with the other. There was a moment's hesitation – hardly enough time for a flea to jump from one head to another – before I reached out my own hand, grasping my nephew's wrist in the true manner of brethren.

Mulenda drew close, releasing his mount's rein to enclose me in his strong embrace. 'I never suspected, not for a moment,' he said almost in a whisper, as if he did not want his men to witness anything resembling an emotional state.

'I did not want you to know,' I replied.

Mulenda looked at me questioningly but chose not to put his thoughts into words except to say, 'We have much to talk about, uncle, but that is for later. I believe we have a more pressing problem to deal with.' He looked around. 'You seem to have lost the boy.'

'The Castra took him,' Garia said. 'We don't know why, but they wanted him alive. We are tracking them.'

'I believe I know why,' said Mulenda. 'But I haven't time to explain now, for we must cover as much distance as possible before nightfall.'

'You are pursuing the Castra?' This was Kairi, who added, 'For what purpose?'

'There is treachery afoot but, as I say, there's no time to explain now. We must ride. If you want to find the boy, you must ride with us.' Mulenda pulled away from me and hauled himself back on to his horse.

'But we have no idea where Han has been taken,' said Garia. 'Kairi has done his best to track the Castra over this poor ground but it is slow work.'

'It is clear to me where the boy is,' said Mulenda, pointing towards distant mountains. 'We must move with all haste to gain as much ground as possible while daylight lasts.'

So, with Mulenda at the head of his warriors and we three making up the rear, we set off at a gallop. The horses were driven so fast even Kairi could not have kept up, so Garia hauled him up on Melemari.

I could not help smiling as I saw our two companions sharing the same mount, Kairi's arms wrapped around Garia's waist. I could not help but imagine what you, Han, might think of such a situation. If you remember, friendship was what you desired between them, I think you might agree with me that some aspects of their new bond would be better not spoken of.

And so we found ourselves galloping in the wake of Mulenda and his men as they pursued the Castra. We kept up a relentless pace until the sun began its steep fall below the horizon. When we reached the bank of a narrow river, Mulenda pulled up to allow his horse to drink. Like all the others, the animal was dripping with sweat and snorting from the exertion of the ride. 'We must find shelter now dark is nearly upon us,' he said.

But Garia was contrary. He whirled Melemari round to face Mulenda. 'We have to press on. Han is in grave danger. We can waste no time.'

Mulenda raised himself angrily, standing in his stirrups. He jabbed a fist at Garia. 'I do not countenance insubordination in my own soldiers – I'm certainly not going to stand for it from a wet Akben.'

Garia was about to say something else but I stopped him with a severe stare. 'You know Bathlayans will not remain out in the open at night,' I reminded him quietly. 'They have to seek shelter.'

'But *we* don't, Edbersa,' argued Garia. 'There is good moonlight to see by. We can ride on.'

'Aye, we could if we knew where we were supposed to be going.'

Garia said nothing more and Mulenda settled back into his saddle. 'There are places among the rocks in these parts where we can shelter until the morning,' he said.

With no difficulty, we found one small gorge with a spring running through it. The horses were hobbled in a nearby clump of trees and the Bathlayans lit fires. In silence we settled to eat some of the provisions Mulenda's men had carried with them, mostly left-over meat from the night of feasting, which seemed such a long time ago given all that had happened.

Although my body was still hurting from fighting Castra and weary from the hard ride, I could not settle my mind to make way for sleep. I sat on a tuft of grass, my back resting against a rock, contemplating all that had befallen us since leaving Akbenna and fearing that it might already be too late to save you.

Then, just as I was about to nod off, Mulenda, who had been holding close counsel with his senior men, came and sat beside me. For a moment, there was an awkward silence.

'You must forgive Garia, he's anxious about the lad,' I said at length. 'He would happily ride through the night – even at the risk of not knowing where he's going.'

Mulenda raised his eyes to the night sky. 'It is true we could have kept going as there is a good moon and plenty of stars to guide us. But you will know better than most that Bathlayans, like many tribes in Polastia, are afraid of the night spirits. But we are not afraid of other men, especially Castra.'

'Polasti tribes have always been fine warriors,' I said. 'Fearing spirits is understandable – we can never be sure what harm they might bring, only imagine it. On the other hand, we know men are full of blood and shit, making them easy to command or kill.'

Mulenda nodded. There was another period of silence, both of us lost in our own thoughts. It was finally broken by my nephew. 'You and I have much to talk about, uncle,' said Mulenda. 'No one in Bathlaya ever spoke of my mother and her family. All I knew is that she died giving me life and that my father grieved terribly for her.'

'Leandra – your mother – was a wonderful sister to me,' I said. 'She had the sweetest smile and kindest disposition.'

It was an awkward moment. I could have so easily said the words I truly felt, condemning Mulenda's father for imprisoning and raping Leandra, forcing her to be his wife. I could have told him that I had long harboured a desire for revenge. But faced with a dire situation, knowing that Mulenda could help to save you, Han, I fought to suppress the hate that had eaten away at me all these years.

I had to remember that Leandra had, of her own free will, chosen to stay with Utakok when she could have escaped with her brother to Akbenna. And there was a further undeniable truth: although Mulenda was the son of a rapist tyrant, he also happened to be my own flesh and blood.

I looked straight into my nephew's eyes, watching the firelight reflected in them, trying to see something hopeful, some clue about Mulenda's true nature – perhaps whether he possessed more of his mother's goodness than his father's vileness. In the firelight, I saw nothing but steely resolve.

We sat silently, occasionally feeding the fire with brush and listening to the horses whinnying as they fed among the trees. 'How did you know?' I asked at length.

Mulenda smiled, shaking his head. 'You mean how did I know you are my mother's brother?'

I nodded. 'You have a loose tongue,' said Mulenda.

You'll no doubt recall, Han, the two women I befriended at the Bathlayan feast. Well, the one called Lapeda was rather free with her womanly ways – more than a little persuasive, if you get my drift. It seems I said far more to her as we lay together than perhaps was wise. I assure you I did not confess my link to Mulenda to impress her; believe me, it's not the sort of thing I would do, even in drink. But the truth is I can remember very little of what was said between us; she must have forced it out of me like squeezing juice from a calcipod. That night she drained both my body and my brain, although I'm sure I would have sworn her to secrecy on the matter of Mulenda being my nephew.

But it is fortunate for you, Han, that Lapeda was incapable of keeping such a secret otherwise you would have surely ended up being expelled as Gilgarius shit.

This is how it transpired: Lapeda has a son who serves the priests – a weak lad, both in mind and body. He would never make a hunter or a warrior and most things go straight in and out of his brain. But when his mother let slip that Mulenda was my nephew, it was a particular piece of information that stuck. And a good job, too, as it turned out.

The lad, keen to fawn favour, went blabbing to Asdur about me and told him who I was. Later, he overheard Asdur talking to one of the assistant priests. 'How does this affect our plans?' asked the priest.

'It certainly complicates matters,' Asdur replied. 'If Mulenda finds out about Edbersa – who he really is – and the Castra kill him, it could be difficult for us.'

Now Lapeda's son – Basilla, I think his name is – might be

as brainless as a de-juiced calcipod but it seems he's not totally stupid. He told his mother what he had overheard, that it was likely I would be killed by the Castra. For her part, Lapeda had no desire to see me slain so she sought out Mulenda to tell him what Basilla had overheard. In doing so, she was forced to reveal to him my true origins. He insisted upon interrogating Basilla to find out more and the lad had plenty more to tell.

It is fortuitous that Basilla is held in such low regard by those he serves; he's almost invisible to them. He told Mulenda that some time before, as he went about his lowly duties, he overheard a conversation involving Asdur and some of the other priests. During one of these exchanges, while he was clearing up after a meal, he heard mention of Gilgarius for the first time.

And what is interesting about this talk of Gilgarius is that your name, Han, was uttered almost in the same breath. Perhaps just as fascinating is that this conversation took place some days before we even arrived in Bathlaya.

Mulenda, like the rest of us, thought Gilgarius no longer existed, but Basilla said knowledge of the creature's resurrection and his whereabouts had been brought to Asdur by a messenger sent in secret from the highest, most powerful Polasti priest – one who is known as Kolak. I believe you, Han, have already had the displeasure of meeting him. The messenger revealed Gilgarius had a lair in a forest close to Kolak's enclave in the Valley of Havilon and was making certain demands, which prompted the priest to seek help from Asdur. The messenger asked Asdur to use his influence with those mercenaries, the Castra, to help appease Gilgarius.

The creature was demanding large numbers of children to eat but the one child he wanted above all others was you, Han, in revenge for his humiliation in Akbenna. Asdur sent back the messenger with an assurance that he would deliver you. But how did Asdur know he could do this? Did he somehow know you were preparing to venture into the land of the Polasti? It's a very important question that has yet to be answered.

Another question is why did Asdur and the Castra end up so very thick with each other. It's an alliance Mulenda was blissfully ignorant of, otherwise he would have put a stop to it. Mulenda is a sworn enemy of the Castra; discovering that Asdur could be in league with them had his nostrils flaring. His response was to gather together his finest warriors and set off to hunt down the disloyal priest. And that's when we encountered them.

Mulenda and I talked through most of the night, despite knowing we would almost certainly be fighting a battle in the coming hours. At one point I asked what Mulenda intended to do with the treacherous Asdur and the other priests.

'They will be killed, of course,' Mulenda replied. 'Priests have become too powerful in our land. Kolak is the worst example. He has carved out his own dominion and has become untouchable. It is happening all over Polastia. Priests have grown rich by commanding all the land and people around them. Kolak's treasure house is full to overflowing with gold. He is not afraid to use force against anyone who stands against him. He has created complex doctrines to mystify and frighten people – and not just simple people. He and his followers can enslave all minds and bodies.'

'How has this been allowed to happen?' I asked. 'It was not so during my time in Polastia in the days of my youth.'

'It is the fault of weak leadership. Even the most powerful generals have been afraid to challenge the dominance of the priests for fear they will be damned in some kind of hell. Aye, and that included my father, Utakok, and now me. But it is time someone stood up to them. I've been watching Asdur closely and seen his influence growing among my people. He has obviously been influenced in turn by Kolak, but no people's destiny should be determined by power-hungry priests.'

We finally managed to get some sleep until we were woken by the restless activity around us as the first spears of sunlight appeared and the Bathlayan warriors noisily readied for another hard ride. But this time it would be a short one, as we had spent the night just a few leagues away from Havilon.

This was the morning Gilgarius was intent on consuming you and your new friends for breakfast.

Mulenda drew us to a halt on the ridge of a hill overlooking the Valley of Havilon, ranging his eyes over the broad valley spread out before him. Suddenly we saw Gilgarius rising into view over one of the opposing peaks, screeching with anger, before settling out of sight.

Mulenda called to me, 'What do you make of that?'

'It's Gilgarius for sure. I'd like to know what made the monster so angry.'

'Maybe Han has been upsetting him again,' said Garia. We had no idea how close to the truth that was.

No more was said and Mulenda began to coax his mount down the hill. The route he chose was steep and strewn with scree, putting the party and their mounts at risk of serious injury or death, but all made it safely into the valley. We were still a league or more from Kolak's temple. We did not realise as we spurred our horses into a gallop that we would first have to pass through Gilgarius's eating place with its terrible piles of child bones. And where you were about to have your own bones crunched.

As soon as Mulenda saw your predicament, he ordered his men to attack the monster with a hail of spears and arrows, thus saving your life.

***

'So, there you have it, Han,' said Edbersa. 'You now know as much as I do.'

'Except you haven't said what happened to Gilgarius,' I replied anxiously.

Edbersa shook his head despondently and stared into the fire. 'Mulenda's men managed to drive the creature away with their weapons but it seems he was not badly wounded.'

'What about Asdur and the other priests?'

'Mulenda has yet to deal with them. He rode with some of his men to find Kolak but was repulsed by Castra mercenaries. He had not brought enough men to start with and lost some of them fighting Gilgarius. He will need to work out what it is best to do.'

'Then it is not over,' I said, shaking my head.

Nyxes put a hand upon my shoulder and looked up at Edbersa. 'You must let Han rest now,' she said. 'His wound is not fully healed.'

But I knew I could never rest with everything that was whirling around in my head. After Edbersa left the cave – he said he needed to talk to Mulenda who was camped with his men in the temple ruin – I settled down and closed my eyes, pretending sleep to please Nyxes. But my mind was still churning over all that Edbersa had revealed.

From what Edbersa had said, it seemed Asdur knew about Karmus's decision to send me as an emissary to the king of Polastia before we left Akbenna. Then I remembered that Kairi also knew of my first encounter with Gilgarius – that it had been whispered to him 'by the wind'.

Intriguing indeed. I resolved to ask Kairi to explain more about this strange whispering which appeared able to send stories in every direction.

I did sleep eventually and when I awoke Nyxes was nowhere to be seen. I looked anxiously around and saw Osbin kneeling by the solitary fire, preparing several rush plants to make torches. I watched quietly as he greased the dried pith of the plants with animal fat before thrusting one into the embers of the fire to bring it to life. Satisfied with the result, he smothered the torch with a fern leaf.

I sat up, groaning from the pain in my side. Osbin looked over. 'Your wound might hurt but I'm sure it's healing well,' he said. 'Which is good, for we will soon have to leave here.'

'Why are you making torches?'

'In case we travel by night. The forest is so dense, no moonlight or starlight will penetrate it.'

'Will Mulenda and his men travel with us?'

'I'm not sure. Mulenda has yet to confront Asdur and Kolak. There are many Castra about and they will no doubt be willing to fight for the priests in exchange for more gold. Defeating them in battle will not be easy.'

'What of Gilgarius?'

'It seems he is gaining in strength with every passing day. He has been forced to eat the flesh of anything he can find – goats, cattle, Mulenda's dead soldiers. The lack of children has left him feeling very much cheated.'

There were some moments' silence between us as I digested this confirmation that Gilgarius was still a threat. I feared his desire to wreak revenge upon me would have grown a hundredfold and endeavoured not to think more about it.

Osbin went on to explain that Drago, who would hopefully not be implicated in our escape, was remaining in Havilon to continue monitoring reaction to our disappearance before seeking an opportunity to effect his own escape.

'Do you know where Nyxes is?' I asked Osbin.

'She is sleeping over there.' Osbin indicated with a nod of his head a dark area of the cave. I can't explain it but somehow the idea that she had left my side to find a private sleeping place tied my stomach in a knot.

'She hardly slept while you were fighting your fever,' said Osbin, as if appreciating how I felt. 'She needs rest to recover.'

I understood, of course. I was doing well now and she

had no need to keep cleansing my wound, mopping my brow or feeding me water and porridge. Yet still I was left with a strange sense of emptiness that she had not slept by my side.

'Osbin, will you tell me how you came to be here?' I asked by way of a distraction from my negative thoughts.

He pondered my question for a few moments. 'It is not an easy subject to talk about,' he said at length. 'Especially to one so young.' He looked away as though he didn't wish my eyes to meet his. 'Yet you appear wise beyond your years, Han.'

'You're not the first person to say that about me.'

'Really?'

'Yes, really.'

'Then perhaps it will be all right to explain – to explain things about my experiences so you can understand what a truly evil place this is.'

***

I was very young when the priests came, said Osbin.

I'll never forget that day in high summer. Normally at that time of year the weather was fine and we children would play out in the fields and woods all the daylight hours or perhaps help our mothers in the vegetable gardens.

Our fathers were herders and in the spring and summer they stayed with the sheep and cattle in the high pasture. But this day I'm talking about began differently to all the other summer days I had known.

I woke to find my father had returned from the high land with some of the other men; that was the first strange thing. The second the sky, which at that time of year should have been almost totally devoid of clouds, but was dark and foreboding. Rain had fallen in the night and more of it threatened. There was a harsh wind getting up and a feeling of dread about the village.

My father did not greet me as I rose and rubbed the sleep from my eyes. His gaze did not meet mine and I noticed his bronzed, bony hands were shaking so much he had to grip them together.

My mother, too, seemed nervous and she acknowledged me only with an embarrassed smile. My sister – my beautiful older sister, whom I adored more than anyone – was sitting on the earth by the door, quietly weeping.

This was the scene which greeted me when I rose from my sleep on the day the priests came.

My father and mother did not say why they let the priests take me but I was not the first from our village to be sold in this way and would not be the last. I did not see the gold pieces the priests paid for me, nor did I know how many of them my parents received – but I knew what they would mean to their lives.

My people are poor and know little other than hard toil for scant reward. Sheep and cattle are their wealth. They provide most of the things needed by my village: leather and cloth for cloaks and blankets, meat to keep us alive in the harshest days of winter, and milk and cheese for our regular sustenance.

Even at such a young age I helped my parents, pulling new young from inside struggling ewes or assisting in a lame sheep's slaughter to give us meat. Bringing life, ending life. And that day the priests came was like my own life ending.

Although I should have done, I did not fight it. You see, total obedience to your parents was expected and I would never have dreamt of going against them. I was taken to the centre of our village where four other young boys were already gathered – Temad, Belik, Ortho and Drago. All of them looked as bemused as I felt.

Then the priests came, three of them on horseback. They were with another man, not a priest, who was driving a cart pulled by two donkeys.

The priest with the longest beard, who appeared to be the eldest, dismounted and addressed the gathering. 'You boys are the blessed ones,' he said, using our tribal language but with a heavy Polasti accent. 'Your wise parents wish us to take you into our care where you will be educated and nurtured into fine young men.'

He said something about our mothers and fathers having only our best interests at heart by making this decision, even though it would make their lives harder to give up strong sons in this way. That is why they were being rewarded in gold.

I turned to my father and thought I glimpsed tears forming in the corners of his bloodshot eyes. My mother turned her face away as if she could not bear to see me taken away. The other fathers stood stern-faced while their wives wept openly.

I cannot remember much more about what was said, only the words my father spoke when he finally plucked up the courage to address me. 'It is for the best, Osbin. One day you will realise what we have done is for the best.'

But for whom? This I have long wondered. If my father had known the fate that we five boys and many others like us were to endure, I am sure he would never have soiled his honest hands with the priests' gold.

It is true the priests wanted to educate us, and it was also true they wanted to feed and nurture us, but for what end? What purpose do you suppose they had in mind?

When I first came here with my four friends, we were treated kindly. We were taken with boys from the other villages – perhaps a dozen of us – to meet Kolak. At that time he was already an old man, but I noticed there was something strange about this oldness.

Each of us was allocated a priest to be our mentor who would teach us the rituals of the priesthood. We were told that one day we, too, would become priests but that would be many years away.

We were told that age was to be revered, that not only knowledge and wisdom increased with age but also physical strength. Yes, Han – the priests in Havilon get stronger as they get older. You may think I am crazy for saying so, but it is true. Even though I am very strong and have exercised each day since I arrived here, I cannot beat one of these priests in a wrestling bout or any other trial of strength you care to mention. And the strongest of them all is Kolak.

The priests' beards may be long and grey, their skin like goat hide and their voices hoarse with age, but their long robes hide bodies as hard as bronze. And through these bodies runs blood as cold and unfeeling as ice.

You asked me, Han, if I was human or a statue and I said I was human. That is true, but over time I was meant to become hard and unfeeling like these priests. It was always clear that, when my current purpose was served, I should become one of them. But I could never face such a prospect and so decided I should cling to my humanity as long as humanly possible. Drago, too, felt as I do. Yet we knew we could never displease the priests, for to do so would make our lives terrible to endure.

***

After Osbin stopped speaking, he turned his face from the firelight as if to hide his despair. The silence was broken only by the echo of laughter from several of the other children in a far corner of the cave.

I was trying to take in everything he had told me, though still failing to understand the true nature of these priests. 'They are so old,' I said, when I could bear the silence no longer. 'Surely they will die then you can be free.'

'Very few priests have died since I've been here, Han. Mostly they only grow older and stronger and ever more desirous of power.'

'But where do they get this strength and power from?'

Osbin looked away again. He would not or could not let his eyes meet mine.

'What is their secret?' I asked again.

Osbin gave a little shake of his head. 'Think about it, Han. Why do you think they are prepared to pay gold for village boys?' There was a pause as he distractedly poked the fire with a stick.

'I don't know,' I said. 'I'm confused. The priests paid gold to your father and Drago's father and said they would teach you to be priests. Yet they've also paid gold to the Castra to bring children to feed to Gilgarius. Why were you brought here and not fed to Gilgarius, Osbin?'

He smiled and slowly shook his head. 'I suppose it is because we were seen by the priests as special. We have fair hair and skin and blue eyes. Not every child is like that among our people; most are dark with brown eyes. But because we are different the priests are attracted to us and that is why we were selected to serve them.'

'I still can't understand how you make them stronger. What do you do?' There was another long silence, both us staring at the dancing flames of the fire. A breeze from outside wafted smoke into my face, stinging my eyes.

'The priests are subtle – at first,' Osbin said after a while. 'They appear genuine in their desire to teach young boys in their charge. I was allocated to a young priest called Calbor. When I say young, I mean in the sense of this place and not the outside world. He was probably sixty years old. His beard was already greying and long, down to his chest, yet the strength of his body was immense.

'Fortunately, he was kind to me. He seemed a little different to the other priests, not so demanding. Sadly, he suffered for his kindness. While other boys were expected to attend to a priest's every need at any time of day or night, I was spared much of it.'

'What do you mean by "every need"?'

'It is not easy for me to tell you, Han. You are young and I suspect you don't understand some of the more distasteful ways of the world. At least, I hope you don't.'

'I'm learning fast,' I said.

'Then you'll probably know that the Bathlayans and some of the other Polasti tribes believe that by killing a wild creature you can obtain its power. Well, in much the same way these priests believe that taking boys and young men to their beds sustains their strength and virility. They also believe that their own wisdom and knowledge is given in exchange. They see it as noble and pure to treat boys and young men this way.'

I didn't fully understand what Osbin was talking about but, having already witnessed what can happen between men when they think no one is watching, I had a fair idea. 'What happened to him, this priest Calbor?'

'He was punished for not being so devoted to his duties – for sparing those in his charge much of the humiliation that the other priests delighted in. It was a terrible punishment inflicted personally by Kolak, which I and the others witnessed. I do not wish to dwell on it. It is sufficient to say that Calbor no longer remained as I knew him.'

I looked around me. 'How did you know about this cave?'

'I discovered the temple ruins and this cave by chance when, still a young boy, I tried to escape from my miserable life. Yes, Han, I did once try to get away. One morning, I rose very early. Taking a little food, I headed alone into the forest, even though I knew I might encounter bears and other fearsome creatures. I walked while there was light to see by, but it became dark early under the forest canopy and I lost my way among the dense trees and vines. Eventually I stumbled upon this cave and hid inside it until the following morning. That's how I knew it existed.'

'Did the priests find you here?'

'They sent out searchers, thinking I'd simply wandered off and got lost. They had no idea it was a deliberate attempt to escape them. I left the shelter of the cave when it was light enough to see and set off once again to find my way through the forest. Soon I heard voices shouting my name. By then, I was so desperately afraid, I followed the sound until I came across one of the priests and my friend Drago. I pretended to be so overwhelmed at being found that I fell to the ground and kissed the priest's feet.'

'But Osbin, did you tell anyone about this place?'

'No, I did not then, nor at any time afterwards. Only to Drago when I knew he was of the same mind as me. I am sure the priests do not know this cave exists, hidden as it is so deep in the forest. Anyway, there is no gold to be found on this side of the valley so they would never be curious.'

'Did they ever suspect that you ran away?'

'No, otherwise I think it would have been very bad for me. Others who had tried and been caught were never seen again – or only seen again much altered.'

'What do you mean?'

'Their minds were taken from them.'

'How can someone do that?'

'Well, you see, this is another power the priests have. They know how to make strong potions from special plants that grow in the forest. The priests take some of them in the night to withstand sleep and help them find greater power, and they give certain of the potions to those that they take to their beds. If enough are administered, those who take them lose their free will. Sometimes the potions are strong enough to take away someone's mind completely. That is what happened to Calbor.'

'Have you been given them?'

'Sometimes, but I wish to forget those things now that

I have a chance to regain my life. Anyway, I have told you enough about what the priests do.'

I said nothing and there was quite a long silence before Osbin spoke again. 'I suppose you are wondering why I never tried to escape again.'

I nodded because that is precisely what I was wondering.

'I always planned to. I always knew that one day I would be free of the priests. I knew also that I first needed to grow in strength and knowledge. But I suppose what I needed most was courage. You helped me find it, Han.'

'I don't understand.'

'It's simple. The defiant way you addressed the priests put me to shame – I had never experienced the like of it before. And what I learned about your bravery in the face of Gilgarius, well, that too was an inspiration. You are but a boy, yet you showed the courage and resourcefulness of a man.'

I have to say I was flattered by Osbin's words, and I had no reason to doubt they were genuine, but I never would have considered myself an inspiration. It is true I could be defiant and could sometimes think up clever plans to outwit vicious creatures, but everything I did was born out of fear rather than courage.

'You look puzzled, Han,' Osbin said with a smile.

'I am – very much,' I confessed.

'Perhaps you should just accept that all I have said is true.'

'Very well. But there is something else that confuses me: how Gilgarius fits into all this. Why do the priests tolerate such a creature in their midst? If the they did not feed children to him, he would surely not stay here.'

'The creature has been very useful to the priests. The children are his reward.'

'Useful? What does he do for them?'

'Gilgarius came here, like he goes everywhere, to exploit humans. He arrived one day and was encouraged to stay because of one thing – gold. It is no secret that the priests here have plenty of it but they always want more; thanks to Gilgarius, they will always be able to replenish their stocks. If there was no benefit to the priests, it would seem a waste of riches to pay the Castra to steal children just to have that monster eat them.'

'But where does the gold come from? And how exactly does Gilgarius help the priests?'

Osbin paused to gather his thoughts. I waited patiently, saying nothing, unable even to guess how disturbing my new friend's testimony would be.

'There are veins in the mountains on yonder side of the Valley of Havilon that run rich with gold,' said Osbin. 'This pernicious metal is very important to the priests because it allows them to dominate all the lands and people around. But to get the gold in the large amounts they desire, they employ the evil power of Gilgarius.

'When I first came here, there were villages scattered in valleys around those mountains full of life, full of children. Then Gilgarius came, offering his services to the priests in exchange for those children. The creature ate many because the priests offered many; in return, Gilgarius used his monstrous limbs and claws to gouge the rock from the hills above the villages where the priests believed the gold would be found. And it was true, gold was there in abundance – but all the villages were destroyed in the process of extracting it. First, Gilgarius uprooted a vast area of the forest that clung to the mountainsides, destroying the people's hunting grounds. Then he gouged out huge amounts of rock to locate the seams of precious metal.

'For their part, the priests cared nothing for the devastation wreaked upon the villages. Indeed, they heaped more of it upon them, forcing the men and women – whether fit, old or crippled – to descend into the clawed-out tunnels to extract whatever gold ore they could find. And all the while the spoil from the mine was poisoning village water, killing many of those who survived the hard labour. When it rained heavily, the waste slid down the mountainside in great rivers of mud to bury entire villages. Many thousands died, including those children who had been spared Gilgarius's jaws, and the rest of the villagers were forced to flee to save their lives. It was merciless, and not one priest gave the people any pity.

'When no one remained to work the mines and there were no children left to eat, Gilgarius flew away. He roamed the skies far and wide to find people willing to sacrifice their young to keep him appeased.'

'That's probably when he came to Akbenna,' I said, 'when I first encountered Gilgarius and got the better of him.'

'We heard what happened, Han, even before Gilgarius reappeared. You were very brave.'

'How did you know? How does everybody in Polastia seem to know about something that happened so far away.'

Osbin laughed. 'Do you know what spies are, Han?'

'I've heard of them, yes, but what has that to do with Gilgarius?'

'Akbenna is spied upon by Polastia, and I dare say Polastia is spied upon by Akbenna.'

'A Polasti spy would have to disguise himself very well in Akbenna, Osbin. It is a small land and anyone from a foreign place would be detected quickly.'

'Very true – unless he is Akben. Then he wouldn't have to disguise himself at all.'

'What do you mean?'

'I mean, Han, that the person in question may have been as much a traitor as a spy.'

***

Han yawned and pulled his blanket tight around his shoulders. 'Is it me, Arkis, or are the nights getting colder?'

'It is not as warm as yesterday. I fear winter will soon be upon us.'

'Yes, winter is always coming. I hope you don't mind but I'm tired and must go inside to sleep. I know I've come to another intriguing part of my story and I would dearly like to carry on, but I feel we both need to rest awhile. You can see the sun is setting fast.'

Arkis smiled and patted the old man's shoulder. 'It is important you should rest. Although I am fascinated by your story, I can wait until tomorrow to hear more of it. Do you want me to ask Pelia for anything?'

'I would like beer and a piece of bread. That will do. I'm sure you'd like beer and bread, too. Perhaps a little cheese.'

Arkis found Pelia about to stockade the goats and offered to help.

'I can manage, they're quite obedient,' she said.

After the animals were enclosed and given fresh water, Pelia gave her grandfather the meagre sustenance he had requested. After Han retired to his cot, she and Arkis sat a little apart beneath the chatka tree and ate their own supper.

'Your grandfather is a remarkable man,' Arkis said. 'He is determined that I should hear all his story, and he tells it in remarkable detail.'

'I'm sure you're finding some of it hard to believe,' said Pelia.

'It certainly is incredible.'

'With grandfather's stories, you have to give your imagination wings.'

'A nice way of putting it.'

'There's more beer if you want it.'

'Thank you. It's very good.'

'My grandfather showed me how to make it when I was young. He showed me many things. I grew up very quickly.'

'What happened to your mother and father? Are they dead?'

'I suppose they might be.'

'Now you're confusing me.'

'My grandfather argued with my father. He ordered him to leave and my mother went too.'

'Why?'

'There were horrible things said, which led to a fight. They fought, and my father beat my grandfather. It was terrible. I remember my mother called my grandfather – her own father – a liar, then she and my father left. They didn't ask if I wanted to go with them, but I would have stayed anyway because I couldn't bear to leave an old man on his own.'

'What makes you think they might be dead?'

'Oh nothing, really. I decided to imagine they were so I wouldn't have to think about them coming back.'

***

'All this remembering,' said Han. 'I'm not sure it's a good thing.'

'But you said you enjoyed telling your story, that remembering the past makes everything worthwhile. It was a good thing to say and I hope I can do the same when I'm older. That's if I have anything worthwhile to remember.'

Han did not answer right away but slowly shook his head. He lifted his thin parchment hands, bringing them to his face and examining them closely. 'I suppose I remember my childhood so clearly because I've been deceiving myself and I haven't been able to face growing old. But I am older than I ever wanted to be and finally dying.'

'We all die.'

'Yes, some of us more than once.'

Han returned his bony hands to his lap and looked up at Arkis. 'I have lost Nyxes,' he said, blinking away tears. 'I fear I shall never see her again.'

There was silence for a while, during which the old man closed his eyes and seemed to fall asleep. Arkis made to reach out to gently shake his arm but Han looked up before he made contact, his face pain-etched and eyes bloodshot and sorrowful.

'I dreamt last night, as I often do,' he said. 'Mostly about times long gone by. Sometimes the present intrudes upon my dreams but I always know that, even in the present, I'm young again. Never in any of my dreams have I been a man, let alone an old man.

'In last night's dream, I was walking across a flower meadow where goats and cattle were grazing in the bright sunshine. It is nothing unusual; scenes like that I dream about often, which could be something to do with growing up in a barren land.

'Anyway, some of the animals wore bells that jingled as they browsed. The place was alive to all my senses, just as if I was wide awake and walking through a real meadow, and I began to feel intoxicated by what I saw. You would scarcely believe such a rich conjuring could be at work in an old man's unconscious mind.

'I knew the dream had taken me back to my long-ago childhood and that I was searching as I have done many times before.

'I kept walking until I came upon a river, hearing its thunderous roar before seeing it. Then, as I stood transfixed, unsure whether I was expected to cross this treacherous water, the children appeared on the far bank as if from nowhere – my friends from all those years ago. The friends I had escaped with from the jaws of Gilgarius. Except they were no longer children. Every one of them I recognised, even though they were fully-grown men and women. They smiled and waved at me and, although I could not remember all their names, I shouted out to those I knew as I waved back.

'There was Arkemis, as serious as ever, and standing next to him Kyros with his broad, cheeky grin. And I could also see

Lejo, Celion, Kiyem, Iasoph, Verilo and Lemis. All happy and smiling. But the one person I desired to see most of all was not among them.

'All I wanted, Arkis, was to get across the river to find her. I looked up and down the bank to see if there was a boat as there had been that time in the throes of my fever, when I dreamt that I saw my father row across a placid lake. But there was no boat to be seen.

'I shouted above the roar of the river, imploring Arkemis to tell me where Nyxes was and why had she not come into my dream. But Arkemis and all the others faded to nothing before me without giving me an answer, leaving me bereft.

'I've dreamt of Nyxes many times and probably called her name out in my sleep. I could always conjure her into my unconsciousness almost on a whim. And every time I would wake crying because I knew I would never see her again in my waking time. But now, Arkis, I fear she is lost even to my dreams.'

Arkis did not know what to say, even though he knew he could find words to ease Han's distress. And why should he not say it? Why had he decided to play such a game with the old man, such a cruel game?

'I'm sorry for being so maudlin over the past, Arkis,' Han was saying, wiping a tear from his cheek.

'It's understandable. They were terrible times.'

Han shivered a little. He hitched the goatskin cloak tighter around his shoulders. 'Shall I continue? Yes, of course. Where was I in my story? Ah, yes, Osbin's talk of spies and traitors.'

***

I didn't understand about spying and traitoring and wanted to know more, said Han. But Osbin placed a hand upon my shoulder and urged patience. 'I must go now,' he said. 'I have to help Mulenda's men find food. I shall return as soon as I can.'

'When will we be able to leave this place?' I asked, knowing we were still in much danger.

'That's something I need to find out. The question is whether it is safe for us to make a move just yet.'

'But surely it would be better not to delay,' I told him. 'I'm well enough to walk now and time is not on our side.'

'You are right. Gilgarius is still out there and will want his revenge. But we'll have to think carefully about where we go from here.'

'Will Mulenda not help us?'

'Mulenda wishes to fight the priests but they have the Castra to help them and he has not enough men. He is sending two of his soldiers back to Bathlaya for reinforcements.'

I'd yawned several times during this conversation and Osbin insisted I should rest. I said I would, though I did not speak true. Rather than rest, I wished to be reunited with Nyxes.

When Osbin had gone, with some difficulty I got on to my knees and crawled over to where he'd indicated Nyxes was sleeping. Although little natural light penetrated so far into the cave, I could make out where she was, lying on her side on the bare cave floor without the comfort of ferns or any other cushion for her body. Yet she looked so peaceful.

I settled on the ground close by, watching her. Then I, too, fell asleep. I've no idea how long I slept but I was woken by a movement next to me. Straight away I knew it was night time, for the only light was a little insipid moonlight. I could just make out Nyxes' shape. She had brought the ferns used to make my previous bed and was kneeling, spreading them out next to me.

'It will be better if we both lie on these,' she said, when she realised that I was awake.

'I don't know if I can sleep again,' I said.

'Then we can talk,' said Nyxes.

So, we just lay on the fern bed and talked. We talked about everything we could think of – about ourselves, our families, the homes we longed to return to.

Nyxes said nineteen children had been taken from her village but only she, her brother, Arkemis, and six others had not been eaten by Gilgarius – Lejo, Kyros, the cousins Iasoph and Celion, and two young boys, Verilo and Lemis. These six, along with nine of the youngest children from other villages, were the only ones still alive from the Castra raids.

'But we are still not out of danger,' Nyxes said. 'We could be eaten yet.'

'We will survive,' I said with as much conviction as I could muster. 'We have friends now to help us, and Mulenda with his men. Gilgarius and those foul priests will not stand a chance.'

Nyxes laughed. 'You are always so optimistic, Han.'

'Why shouldn't I be? There's no sense in just giving up.'

We talked through the night, returning in our imaginations to fondly remembered places so we could avoid having to think of the deadly fate that might still await us. Eventually we fell into an exhausted sleep, arms wrapped around each other to keep warm.

We woke as the dawn light probed the cave entrance, by which time the other children were also stirring from their slumber. At first, everything seemed calm. The children stretched and yawned and several shuffled off to find somewhere in the cave to relieve themselves.

I could see the crouching forms of Kyros and Arkemis deep in conversation, occasionally looking in our direction. I wondered if they were speculating about what we might have been doing. Nyxes didn't seem to care and reached out to hold my hand. After a while, Arkemis came over.

'Hello brother,' Nyxes said. 'Did you managed to get some sleep?'

'I reckon more than you did,' Arkemis replied.

'We did a lot of talking,' I said.

'I'm sure you did,' he said. He waved a hand at the cave entrance. 'Do you know when we will get to leave this place?'

I said, 'Soon, I'm certain.' Although, to be honest, I had no idea. I told Arkemis that Mulenda was waiting for more men to come from Bathlaya to fight the priests and the Castra.

'We also should fight,' he said. 'Kyros would be up for it and Lejo, too. How about you?'

'Han is in no fit state to fight,' Nyxes said, draping an arm protectively around my shoulders. 'And you, my brother, have no experience as a warrior. Nor have Lejo and Kyros.'

'We must do something to help,' replied Arkemis petulantly. 'It's so frustrating just sitting around waiting for something to happen.'

'We've been doing that ever since we arrived in Havilon,' Nyxes pointed out. 'Anyway, the other children need us to stick together now there's a real chance to escape.'

This observation silenced Arkemis and he returned to Kyros and the others. It was obvious that Nyxes was the stronger character of the two. It occurred to me for the first time that I had no idea how old they were and who was the eldest. I asked her.

'We were born on the same day,' she said with a smile. 'We are twins.' Nyxes told me she was the first to make an appearance and it was quite some time later that Arkemis emerged. She started out ahead of her brother when it came to learning about the world around them and it seemed she'd maintained the advantage ever since.

We remained sitting there, again talking about anything and everything to do with our lives. Strangely we did not dwell on the dangers we had just escaped from, nor those we yet faced, but instead, as in the night, upon our lives before those terrible days.

Nyxes was curious to know about my mother and father

and why I was an only child when most families had as many children as possible and kept having them, even though they knew many would die very young. In truth, I had no answer for Nyxes, although in some ways I was not happy at being an only child. I sometimes even thought my only-ness was some kind of punishment and I often wished for a brother or a sister, which would make me like most other children. I could never understand why my parents did not provide me with one or the other. I told Nyxes that if I dwelt on this too much it would make me sad.

She reached out and took my hand. 'Don't worry, Han,' she said. 'I can be your sister.' This made me feel strangely deflated.

After a while, we both yawned. We lay at each other's side as we had done in the night; all the talking had exhausted us and we fell asleep.

We were woken suddenly by the sound of shouting from outside the entrance to the cave. Suddenly Osbin appeared, breathing heavily as if from a hard run. 'We must prepare to leave,' he said. 'The Castra are burning the forest.'

Nyxes helped me to my feet and put an arm around my waist as if to steady me. Although I had no real need of support, the comforting feel of her was special.

By this time, Mulenda's men – those who had survived the battle with Gilgarius – were also piling into the cave. Edbersa emerged from among them. 'They have us trapped,' he said.

We were joined by Garia, his eyes stinging with smoke and fiery with rage.

'Have you seen Kairi?' I asked.

I saw tears start to streak down his blackened cheeks. Garia smudged soot into them as he wiped his face with the back of his hand. 'Kairi was with the horses when the fire came,' he said. 'It was like the wind, burning everything between us. I tried to go back…' His voice trailed off.

'Kairi will survive,' I said. 'He's resourceful and brave and swift and sure. If he can keep up with Melemari with you on her back, he can outrun fire.'

Mulenda was the last to arrive at the cave, his men parting to allow him through. By this time I could see smoke from the fire swirling around outside the entrance. The Bathlayan leader beckoned Edbersa and Osbin and the three were soon embroiled in conversation. Distracted and agitated, Garia seemed not to care that he was excluded from their deliberations.

All the while Nyxes held me close, saying nothing. Arkemis and Kyros re-joined the other children who had become restless, some of them sobbing out of fear.

By now we could smell the smoke and hear the deafening roar of flames as the fire engulfed the gorge beneath us. We would have little time to save ourselves. The children were acutely aware of the danger and huddled together in fright. They had escaped one deadly fate only to face another. Many began to cough as smoke penetrated the cave.

Nyxes and I moved closer to hear the exchange between Mulenda, Osbin and Edbersa. Osbin was waving a hand towards the cave's black interior. 'A passage leads from this cave,' he said. 'I have explored it a little in the past. It may provide a way of escape through the mountain.'

'And it may not,' said Mulenda gruffly.

'What have we to lose?' asked Edbersa. 'We will burn to death if we venture outside and we'll be suffocated by smoke if we stay where we are.'

'Very well,' said Mulenda. 'Osbin, you must lead. Edbersa and his companions will follow with the children. My men and I will take up the rear.'

Garia grabbed Edbersa's arm. 'I must go back to find Kairi.'

'Don't be foolish,' growled Edbersa. 'You will perish for certain. Anyway, Han is right – Kairi is fast enough to outrun fire. Come on, let's get moving before we all choke to death.'

Reluctantly, Garia allowed Edbersa to lead him to where Osbin was bringing some of the rush lights to life in the embers of the cooking fire before handing them around.

Osbin retained one of the torches and headed towards the back of the cave. Nyxes and I followed, the others filing behind us in the order Mulenda had suggested.

At first the passage was wide enough for two people to walk side by side. Nyxes stayed close by me and put her arm through mine as the ground began to fall steeply. Where it grew too narrow, she walked behind but was quick to reach out whenever she detected that I had hesitated or was in danger of stumbling.

I soon realised that Osbin might be right about where this route led. The air was not as stale as you might imagine in such a tight space. That encouraged me to believe there must truly be a way out of the mountain somewhere ahead of us.

Gradually the passage widened and Nyxes resumed her place by my side. We walked maybe half a league before we heard what I thought was the distant rumble of thunder. Osbin halted and waited for everyone to catch up.

'What is that noise?' I asked.

'It is an underground river,' said Osbin. 'Many of Havilon's mountains have water flowing through them.'

He led us onward, the sound of the river ever more deafening, until we rounded a slight curve in the passage and entered a large cavern. The flame of Osbin's rush light revealed the source of the thunderous roar: a great wall of water that burst from the rock high above to our left and plunged into a circular pool, sending a fine spray towards us. The overflow from the pool swirled and tumbled across our path before it was funnelled into a passage directly ahead of us.

By now Mulenda had come to the fore. For several moments he surveyed the torrent impeding our route then he waved his arms to indicate we should go back along the passage where he could better make himself heard. Once away from the roar of the waterfall, Mulenda drew Osbin close. 'Is there no other way out of here?'

'No, the river would seem to be the only way unless we go back,' said Osbin. 'It will convey us safely out of the mountain. I'm convinced of it.'

'Or drown us all in the process,' I heard Edbersa growl behind me.

By this time the urgency of our situation was becoming increasingly apparent as, one by one, the rush lights began to die. Although Mulenda's men carried spare torches that could be lit from those already aflame, it was clear they would not last long.

Mulenda went into a huddle with three of his key soldiers. Then he turned to the rest of us. 'We have no time to waste and we have no choice. If this cavern is not to be our tomb, we must take our chance with the river.'

'What about the smallest children?' I piped up. 'It may be too deep for them.'

'I cannot help that,' said Mulenda. 'You must make sure they keep their heads above the water.'

'Then use the shields your men carry,' I responded. 'They are made of bronze and will surely float. Maybe the youngest children can sit on them.'

'The lad has a point,' said Edbersa. 'The shields are like shallow boats and certainly big enough to carry a small child.'

Mulenda scratched his beard and glanced over to where the youngest children, some of them sobbing quietly, were being comforted by the older ones. 'Very well,' he said. He barked an order to his men and enough shields to accommodate all those children who might need them were handed to Osbin and Edbersa.

For his part, Garia still appeared to be in something of a daze. I feared for his state of mind and that he might not be able to respond properly to the dangers we had still to face. I placed a hand upon his shoulder. 'Please don't worry about Kairi,' I said. 'He's strong and resourceful and I'm sure he will have found safety. It is we who are in danger.'

'You may be right, wise Han,' said Garia, attempting a smile. He reached to take one of the shields from Edbersa and beckoned one of the youngest children, a timid girl called Shami, who was clinging to Kyros. She hesitated but Kyros ushered her forward.

Reassuringly, Garia ruffled her hair. 'Don't fret, little one. We'll get through this.' It seemed to me that Garia was talking as much to himself as he was to his new charge.

Mulenda selected the other children who would be conveyed the same way. Meanwhile, Edbersa and Osbin took two of the rush lights and waded into the river to explore potential dangers and determine if it was passable.

We waited anxiously for their return, sitting on the cold rock floor with our backs to the cave wall, no one daring to speak. Our remaining torches were dying one by one; the obvious fear was that they would all burn out before we reached the outside.

Perhaps my thought was shared by Mulenda, for he suddenly sprang up. 'We can afford to wait no longer,' he shouted, urging his men to their feet. 'We must take our chances, for good or ill.'

But the words were barely out of his mouth when Edbersa and Osbin reappeared, soaking wet and with just one pitiful light between them.

'What dangers did you encounter?' Mulenda demanded. 'Can you say for certain that this is the way?'

'We came across a pool that is deep and will have to be swum,' said Edbersa. 'But otherwise there appear to be no serious obstacles to our escape.'

'Did you see daylight?'

'No, nephew, I did not see daylight.'

Mulenda growled, sounding just like Edbersa in a grumpy mood, and his uncle draped an arm over his shoulders. 'Do not despair,' Edbersa said mischievously. 'I saw no daylight because it is night time.'

Mulenda scowled but there was no annoyed riposte. Instead he instantly became purposeful. 'There is no time to lose,' he said. 'We must get out while we still have lights to see by.'

And so we embarked upon our escape from that inhospitable hole in the mountain.

Mulenda and two of his key warriors entered the water first, then Garia and Kyros followed with the little girl, Shami, crouching upon the floating shield. Garia murmured words of reassurance to her as she reached out and clung both fearfully and faithfully to his strong arms. But they had barely made any headway when the makeshift raft began wobble and threatened to sink. I despaired that my idea of using shields as boats was a failure until Garia and Kyros managed to steady the improvised craft and keep it floating.

Next were Edbersa and Osbin who entered the water with the little boy, Lemis, upon a shield. Again, it would have proved unstable were it not for the strong arms of those who steadied it. Employing the other shields in the same manner, Mulenda's warriors conveyed the remainder of the youngest and smallest children.

We older ones followed them, with Nyxes and I the very last to enter the biting cold water. Nyxes took a firm hold of my arm as we gasped for breath and struggled to keep on our feet in the swirling current. Treacherous boulders and jagged stones impaired our every step.

The deep pool presented no serious impediment. Although I was no swimmer, with Nyxes' help I managed to keep afloat. But we could only see a single dim light ahead of us and this frequently dipped out of view, leaving us in total darkness.

We finally emerged into the night to find Mulenda's men

had already started to make fires so we could dry ourselves and cook what little food they had managed to carry. The children huddled together beneath a rocky overhang, sitting on tussocks of damp grass, shivering from the cold. Fortunately the very youngest had stayed largely dry thanks to the shield rafts, and I felt proud that I had thought of the idea.

I took in our surroundings but could see very little. The moon was now behind the mountain from which we had just emerged and most of the starlight was obscured by trees. It seemed, from what little I could discern, that the river carried on tumbling into what appeared to be a forested gorge.

Later I was to find that, within very few leagues, it flowed into a sea.

***

They sat in a silence. The goats were bleating in the stockade behind them, Rashi occasionally snorting. Arkis and Pelia were almost close enough to touch but there was safety in the space between them. Safety and uncertainty occupying the same void.

Pelia broke the silence. 'Your goat is lame,' she said. The tone of her voice was apologetic, as if she had personally caused the animal's injury.

'I hadn't noticed,' said Arkis.

'But her kid is growing stronger. You still have value.'

They did not look at each other.

'The rains will soon fall in the hills,' Pelia said, lifting her head to see the clouds already gathering over Mother Mountain. 'You must leave before they come. Rivers will flow from the high ground and flood all the tracks.'

Arkis glanced to the hills. Did she want him to leave? Then he heard Rashi, stamping impatiently. *Soon, Rashi*, he said to himself.

Pelia turned to him. 'Can I ask you something?'

'Ask anything you like.'

She paused as if unsure how to frame her question. Then she said, almost inaudibly, 'Have you a wife?'

Pelia's question surprised Arkis and there was a momentary hesitation before he answered. That may have come across as an unwilling confession because Pelia looked away. Arkis kicked at the dusty ground, sending a flurry of leaf litter into the air. 'No, I've never been married,' he said. 'Why do you ask?'

It was Pelia's turn to hesitate. Arkis smiled, though she did not see it; instead she returned her gaze to the clouds, which were beginning to obscure the summit of the sacred mountain.

'I used to be asked the same question,' she said at length. 'Men who didn't know me would ask if I was a wife and, when I said I was not, they would ask if I wanted to become one. I never did. Now no one asks me either question.'

Arkis detected an edgy sadness in her voice. 'I never married because I've never found anyone I wished to be married to,' he said. 'Maybe that's been the same for you and we've both been too particular.'

Pelia stared at the ground. 'There were a few good men. The best went off to Ejiki to be soldiers or traders. Those left behind just wanted to drink in taverns and let the women and children do all the work.'

'You must have had many admirers.'

'I've had my chances. I'm sure you must have had, too. You're not an old man.'

Arkis laughed. 'Perhaps. But the truth is, I like the freedom I have. If I had a wife I couldn't travel. I wouldn't be hearing Han's fascinating story and sitting here next to you.' He thought maybe he shouldn't have said that last bit.

There was more silence, not awkward but somehow charged with anticipation. Pelia broke it. 'Where will you go next?'

'I don't know. It depends.'

'Upon what?'

Arkis hesitated, unsure what to keep concealed and what to reveal. He turned to Pelia and put a hand on her lower arm, squeezing gently. 'I wish there was something I could do to help your grandfather.'

'There is nothing anyone can do. His body is failing.'

'I know,' he said. 'But his mind is good.'

Pelia continued staring at the ground, shaking her head as if rejecting any thought that her grandfather's life was ebbing away. 'You have been very patient with him,' she said. 'Listening to him when most people would have grown bored and moved on.'

'I believe my presence here has helped him. Telling his story in such detail is a reason for him to keep going.'

'You may be right. Where has he got to?'

'The part where he and his companions escaped from the forest fire set by the Castra. Did he ever tell you about this?'

'Yes.'

'Then that's where we are. They have found a way through the mountain.'

Arkis's hand was still resting upon Pelia's arm. She made no effort to pull away from him.

'Then you are not too far from the end,' she said.

***

We had emerged from the mountain, all of us safe but wet, cold and hungry, said Han. Mulenda's men lit four or five separate fires to cook a little food and enable us to dry ourselves.

We were all exhausted but I found it hard to sleep, even on a soft bed of ferns and moss. I stayed awake half the night while Nyxes lay next to me on her side, dead to the world and with one arm draped over my chest.

When I did fall asleep, it was deep and I woke with a

heavy head as dawn broke. The fires that had been kept going through the night were doused so their smoke wouldn't attract the attention of Gilgarius or the Castra, who would surely be looking for us in the daylight.

It was clear we couldn't remain where we were much longer; with the forest burnt, the cave we had hidden in on the other side of the mountain would surely be exposed. It wouldn't take a great deal of imagination on the part of our pursuers to work out how we had made our escape.

Mulenda's men gathered together their shields and weapons and Osbin urged the rest of us to our feet to begin our trek to find a new place of safety. Because of the steep terrain, we had no choice but to follow the course of the river, which for some distance cascaded over a series of cataracts as it ran through a deep gorge.

When the sun was at its highest, we came to the final and highest waterfall at the end of the gorge. From there we could see the river running wide and shallow across an open plain. It was at this point, where there were still steep gorge walls to shelter us, we stopped to rest.

Mulenda dispatched some of his men to hunt for meat and forage for fruit and I noticed Garia go off with them. I was pleased; at least such an activity would help keep his mind occupied so he did not despair so much over Kairi.

The rest of us found shelter beneath a clump of trees that grew on a level area of ground next to the waterfall. The ground was thick with pine needles making it a comfortable place to sit.

Mulenda, Edbersa and two of the leading Bathlayan soldiers sat apart from us, deep in conversation. It was difficult to know what Mulenda would do. He had vowed to defeat the priests, but the presence of the Castra and Gilgarius made his quest far more difficult, if not impossible.

A little while later, Edbersa signalled me to join them. For some reason I can't explain, I hesitated and it took a gentle push from Nyxes to make me respond. 'Go on, Han,' she said laughing. 'It looks like they need someone with brains.'

Osbin, who had been sitting quietly on his own, had also been called over.

'Well, my young friend,' said Edbersa as I settled on the ground next to him. 'I reckon you know Gilgarius better than anyone. What do you think the evil beast is up to?'

'He desires children to eat,' I replied. 'And I fear I'm the one he most hungers for.'

'Do you believe he has no interest in doing battle with men?' asked Mulenda.

'I can't say,' I replied. 'I suspect he will try to kill anyone who comes between him and his desired fare.'

Mulenda shot a glance at Edbersa. When his eyes returned to me, he said, 'But if we do not interfere with Gilgarius's desire, we will be free to pursue the priests and the Castra when more of my men arrive.'

I was confused by Mulenda's words, though Edbersa quickly grasped their significance. 'You can't abandon these children,' he said, genuinely aghast. 'Without your protection, they will stand no chance against Gilgarius.'

'Playing nursemaid was not the purpose of my mission,' Mulenda retorted.

'Please, stop this,' I said, fearing they would end up fighting.

Osbin placed a calming hand on my shoulder. 'They are both right, Han,' he said.

'I don't see it,' said Edbersa. 'Either Mulenda and his men pursue the priests and the Castra, or they remain with these children to protect them and help them flee from Gilgarius. They can't do everything.'

'You don't understand,' said Osbin. 'Gilgarius, the priests and the Castra are an alliance of evil. You can't defeat one in isolation. They help each other achieve whatever they desire.

Gilgarius will do whatever the priests ask of him as long as he is given children to feed on. He might not care to eat the tough flesh of a soldier, but he will kill one nonetheless if it pleases the priests and helps fulfil his own needs.

'If you attack the priests, the Castra will also be called upon to defend them. These mercenaries are prepared to range far to steal children who can be fed to Gilgarius, as long as they are given gold as their reward. In return for this treasure, they will also fight you and your men, Mulenda.

'For their part, the priests desire to be all-powerful – and they are amassing more power by the day. This is partly because they possess a huge store of gold and hold sway over the Castra and, therefore, Gilgarius. But it is also because they have evolved a way of draining strength and power from other beings in ways that can only be imagined.

'You might ask what Gilgarius does for the priests in return for the children he feeds on. I will tell you: he creates fear and exploits differences between peoples, so they can be kept divided and controlled. And he tears down mountains to get at the gold buried in their depths. That's why the priests are in league with Gilgarius.

'The creature is just one head on a three-headed monster. If you destroy the Castra, Gilgarius will not get his child fare; if you destroy Gilgarius, the priests will not be able to instil fear and exercise power over all the lands around, nor add to their stocks of gold which they pay to the Castra so they can perpetuate this evil.

'But ultimately you must destroy the priests because they have spawned all this. If you don't, they will soon entice another Gilgarius to this land and another tribe of mercenaries who will tear children from their mothers' arms in exchange for a golden reward.'

There was profound silence after he had finished speaking as his words sank in. I hoped what he had said would persuade

Mulenda not to abandon us, as he was clearly thinking of doing.

'So, nephew,' said Edbersa at length. 'What do you propose to do?'

Mulenda stroked his beard. 'If I was minded to kill Gilgarius, it would not be easy. I've already engaged in one fight with the creature and lost good men. We assailed the him with spears and arrows and they had about as much effect as a flea landing on the hide of buffalo.'

He was right. For the same reason Garia's father, General Sperius, had been afraid to commit our Akben soldiers to fight the creature. There had to be another way.

Then, as another silence descended upon us, the sky darkened and we could feel a wind getting up. Very soon it was so powerful we became drenched by spray blown from the waterfall, as if a heavy rain storm had arrived.

I peered out from the trees to try and work out what was causing this odd event, only to see the terrible shape of Gilgarius obscuring the sun as he swooped towards our hiding place. He flew so low over the gorge that his giant wingbeats created a tempestuous wind that whipped the waterfall into a frenzy.

We were well hidden, yet even if our terrible adversary could not see us it was possible he would smell us or sense our presence – our fear – in some other way.

Gilgarius let out a series of weird roars as he rose high and circled around us, then he swooped slowly over us as if he knew we were there. At any moment I expected to see the creature's giant claws penetrating the canopy to tear up the trees and pluck us from our hiding place.

But the spray whipped up by the creature's powerful wingbeats must have doused our smell, for suddenly he rose, circled once more and, with a final roar, soared away back towards the mountain peaks and beyond them to the Valley of Havilon. When we were sure he would not return, we came out of our hiding places, slowly and uncertainly at first, but with a profound sense of relief.

Mulenda put a hand on my shoulder and squeezed it gently. 'With a bit of luck, Gilgarius will have given up on eating you lot and will seek child victims in other lands,' he said with a growly laugh not unlike Edbersa's. 'You now have your chance to flee while I focus my attention on defeating the priests and their Castra mercenaries.'

At that moment Garia appeared from the trees carrying a large halibom, which he dropped to the ground next to us.

Mulenda knocked his foot against the fruit. 'I'm sure it will taste good enough, but fare such as this will not help us win battles,' he said, shaking his head. 'What we need is meat.' With that, he left us.

'Well, Han, I see you managed to scare off that monster again,' Garia said, half attempting a smile. 'I mean Gilgarius, not Mulenda.'

I saw this humour as a recovery of sorts, but my companion still didn't look like the Garia of old – the brave, proud soldier. Instead he looked like a man much burdened by despair. I knew why, of course: fear about Kairi's fate was still weighing heavily upon him.

'Yes, well – the creature knows not to mess with me,' I said.

Garia produced a knife from his belt and cut into the halibom while I explained what Mulenda intended to do and asked him if he would join their fight. 'My duty is to remain with you, Han,' he said sombrely. 'But don't think I have a fear of fighting. I'll be happy to fight and die doing my duty.'

I couldn't help but think Garia's willingness to sacrifice his life was in no small part due to his belief – at least I considered it to be his belief – that Kairi was dead. But I pondered this only a little before being distracted by Nyxes who had chosen to join us.

'Do you think Gilgarius was looking for us?' she asked, settling on the ground beside me.

'No doubt,' I replied.

'It's a good job you half-blinded the monster, Han. When he came closest to us, I could see his good eye was looking the other way.'

'I fear we have not seen the last of him,' I said.

'Then what are we to do?'

'I'm not sure. Mulenda may soon leave with his men to meet up with his reinforcements so they can attack the priests and the Castra. It looks like we must make our own way to safety and do it quickly before Gilgarius comes back.'

I turned to Garia, feeling this would be an opportunity to draw my dear companion out of himself. 'What do you think we should do?'

But he didn't answer and instead stared over the forest to the broad plain beyond as if in a trance. His silence left me as confused as ever by his state of mind.

I returned my attention to Nyxes. 'If Mulenda and his men go off to fight, we must fend for ourselves.'

'But we have no spears or bows and arrows. How will we find food?'

'We will just have to collect fruits from the trees,' I said.

'I'm sure you would rather tuck into a nice juicy ledbuk that has been baked in an earth fire?' The voice, that unmistakable voice, came from above and behind us.

Garia lifted his head and his eyes widened with joy. 'Kairi!' he exclaimed, springing to his feet.

I turned my head to see our wild friend appear, smiling broadly. He bounded effortlessly down to us and straight away enclosed Garia in a powerful hug before reaching out to draw me into their embrace. I could see tears streaming from Garia's exhausted eyes.

Nyxes probably felt quite out of it but, if she did, the

expression of delight on her face masked it well. Later she said to me, 'You'd believe they were brothers, the way they embraced.'

'Danger has brought them very close,' I said.

Nyxes had no idea, of course, about the true nature of the relationship between Garia and Kairi and it was not my business to tell her.

With Kairi back, my spirits rose immeasurably. Edbersa joined us as soon as he heard our excited exchanges, greeting our wild friend with his familiar affectionate growl. 'Well,' he said. 'I trust you're going to explain the reason for your absence from our company. You've missed some interesting moments.'

'Believe me, Edbersa,' said Kairi, 'I've had a few interesting moments of my own.'

'Then tell us all about them.'

And that is what our friend proceeded to do.

* * *

Garia has probably told you that he and I had been entrusted with finding a safe place to hide those horses that had survived the encounter with Gilgarius, Kairi said. In addition to Melemari and Fermansa, there were twenty-one mounts belonging to Mulenda and his soldiers; that number had survived with their riders out of the thirty or so that had galloped into that ferocious fight with the creature.

Because the gorge beneath your cave hideout was so deep and thickly wooded, it was an unsuitable place to keep the surviving horses. We volunteered to find a better grazing area where the trees were less dense and the ground not so steep.

The mounts were gathered and Garia walked ahead of them, leading Melemari. The Bathlayan horses were accompanied by two of Mulenda's men, who would help us settle the mounts before taking two of them and riding on to Bathlaya for reinforcements.

I scouted ahead of the procession, watching out for any signs of the Castra.

After leaving the gorge behind, we soon came across a suitable grazing area on a sort of plateau. There were enough trees to ensure the horses remained hidden from view and enough grass for them to eat. Some of the trees had parasitic vines growing around them which we cut to make hobbles to stop the horses wandering too far, although we had already decided to stay and guard them anyway.

When the last mount was hobbled and Mulenda's men had left, Garia set off to find Mulenda and report where the horses were and that they were safe. He hadn't departed long when I heard the crackle and spit of the forest fire. I clambered to the top of the nearest tree to see flames, driven by the wind, devouring everything in their path. I realised that the fire was heading in the same direction as Garia and that it could quickly overtake him.

I clambered from the tree to run after him, shouting for him to turn back. But it soon became clear that the fire was raging far too fiercely for any man to beat it, even one so fleet of foot as I. Nor, among the roaring flames, would anyone hear my warning cries. All I could hope was that Garia had heard the flames or smelled the smoke and that he had managed to turn from his deadly path.

I was still fretting about this when the wind suddenly changed direction, sending the closest flames and sparks swirling and leaping towards me, embracing me in their unbearable heat and choking me with the foulest smoke.

I turned and ran and the flames roared after me. I could only think of the horses and that I would not have time to release them from their hobbles before they would be engulfed in the fire. But before I could reach the mounts, the wind changed again and took the fire in a completely different direction.

This had the effect of creating a swathe of burnt ground; if the flames were to blow towards me again, there would now be nothing for them to devour.

I had no idea how the blaze had started – at least not until I found another tree to climb. When I did so, I saw a group of about ten men on a rocky outcrop, some still holding flaming torches, delighting at the destruction they had wrought. I descended the tree and made my way through the undergrowth to try and get closer to them and hear what they were saying.

The Castra – for that is what they turned out to be – were so distracted with joy at their fire-making that I found it easy to sneak up to them without being detected. I crouched behind a rock and heard their excited shouts, and I quickly realised their deadly purpose was to smoke us all out of our hiding place. I did not know then that setting fire to the trees was just one attack upon you, Han, and that Gilgarius was also playing a part by tearing up the remainder of the forest to leave you exposed as you fled from the flames.

After a little while, the Castra extinguished their torches and went away. I resolved to follow them, to find out what else they were up to. I tried not to imagine what fate had befallen Garia but I had to believe he had made it safely to you – which, of course, he had.

The Castra moved slowly, laughing and sometimes stumbling as if they were drunk. They must have felt in no danger, for they stopped to piss and joke and indulge in delighted back-slapping.

I kept a safe distance, ascending convenient high points to get a better view of them. Before long, I saw other torch-bearing Castra join this group, until many more of them ended up gathered together in the lush, broad Valley of Havilon. The Castra continued along the valley until they came to a large building made from stone blocks. From the nature of its imposing construction, I took this to be the priests' main temple.

The building was set against the base of the mountain, almost as if it were growing out of the rock. To one side a waterfall cascaded from a great height and I had to find a way to cross it before I could get closer to see what was going on. I climbed higher, using rocks for cover, only to see the stream which fed the waterfall was wide and so fast-flowing over many cataracts that it seemed impassable.

It took me a good while to find a way to cross at a point above where the water separated into two distinct flows, one heading to a series of waterfalls and the other disappearing into the mountain behind the temple. Just above this split, the water tumbled into a gorge and in one place this was narrow enough for me to leap across.

I made my descent, again using rocks as cover, until I found myself directly above the temple. I made another leap, this time onto the lowest part of the temple roof which sloped upwards away from me. At the roof's highest point, a stone construction thrust skyward in the shape of a broad arrowhead. I could hide behind this, yet still view the main temple square below which the Castra had assembled.

I crept forward and crouched to peer over the parapet. I had barely settled in this position when I found myself with surprising company. A large eagle with a white tail appeared as if from nowhere and landed upon the temple roof, so close to me I could have reached out to touch it. The bird bobbed and swivelled its head in an agitated manner.

My people traditionally use eagles for hunting, taking a great deal of time and trouble to train them, so I would normally feel at ease being so close to one. But there was something about this bird that unnerved me at first. It stamped its feet and gurgled in its throat, a sound that I feared would quickly become a screech and attract attention to me.

I began to make a series of guttural noises that I hoped the eagle would be familiar with to show I was not a threat. They appeared to calm the bird. Then, as if suddenly bored with the attention, it launched itself into the air and settled in a tree beyond where the Castra had assembled.

I returned my gaze to what was going on below. Within moments, a procession of priests emerged from the temple almost directly beneath my perch. There were perhaps twelve of them, led by one priest taller than all the others. He had the longest beard and carried a staff with a golden orb upon it. I assumed he was the one known as Kolak. I also recognised Asdur, from Bathlaya, who walked at Kolak's side.

The priests were accompanied by twenty guards armed with spears or swords. They all looked like each other and dressed the same, which was strange to see.

Among the Castra I recognised their leader, the one called Gostopo. Curiosity overcame caution; I was determined to get closer to hear what was being said. I slid down the slope of the roof until I came to its lowest point. From there I worked my way around its edge, then lowered myself onto a second roof which sloped more gently and much closer to the ground. I crawled to the edge of this so I could peer over its edge just as Gostopo stepped forward to address Kolak.

'The forest is burning,' he said. 'Now we have come for our gold.'

'But your task is not complete,' the priest replied in a severe voice. 'You should have stayed where you were. Mulenda and his men are a threat. If they do not perish in the fire, they will be driven into the open. You and your men must hunt them down and kill them.'

'You can get your tame monster to do that,' said Gostopo. 'Again I say that we have come for our gold.'

'And the gold will soon be yours. I'm giving you the chance to earn more of it.'

'We were promised payment for bringing the boy, which we

did. We also set fire to the forest when called upon. I say we have already earned our gold.'

'A greater reward is in prospect,' the priest replied.

Gostopo shook his head. 'We have been away from our own land for too long. We would need a vast reward indeed to stay longer and risk our lives in battle with Mulenda's men.'

Kolak said, 'Your men outnumber the Bathlayan soldiers. There is nothing to fear in pursuing them.'

'The fire should finish them off.'

'We cannot depend upon that. We need to hunt every last one down or they will cause us trouble. You must do it.'

'You already owe us gold for the boy.'

'That you will be paid when everything we ask of you has been done.'

There was a short period of silence as Gostopo mulled over the priest's words. Then he said, 'It is possible we could help you – but only if you double the gold promised to us for bringing the boy, and if you double it again when Mulenda is lying stricken or dead before you and all his men slain. What say you?'

'Two hundred horses' worth of gold? You ask a very high price.'

'We provide a service of very high value.'

'Indeed,' said Kolak. 'And we have always paid you well. But there's the question of Gilgarius's needs.'

'What of them?'

'You must find the children who escaped. Gilgarius will expect nothing less. And, of course, the Havilon server who betrayed us.'

'And when this is done, will the creature demand more children?'

'Yes, as we will require him to find us more gold.'

Gostopo shook his head. 'You do realise that the supply of children around here is exhausted, requiring us to venture much further afield – maybe even as far as Dhagani. That would put us in direct conflict with your king, Pediv.'

'It is true, yet Gilgarius still has to be considered. He is already angry that those we held escaped his jaws – especially the boy Han.'

'That's not our problem,' said Gostopo. 'We brought the boy and the other children; you can't blame us for them escaping.'

Kolak took a few moments to respond as he weighed his options. Then he said, 'If I agree to your inflated request for gold, will you do everything I ask?'

Gostopo also contemplated for several moments, stroking his fiery beard. 'It can be done. But maybe Gilgarius should fight with us.'

'It is possible if he knows you are intending to help recapture the children but I cannot say for certain. I have not had a conversation with the creature since their escape. And you must bear in mind that he was wounded severely in the eye. He could be difficult to deal with.'

'Perhaps not if we guarantee him the Akben boy,' interrupted Asdur. 'He is the child Gilgarius wants more than any other.'

'You may be right,' said Kolak. 'We must engage with the creature on the subject.'

With that, he raised his staff and the white-tailed eagle rose from the tree beyond the Castra. The bird circled the gathering before settling upon Kolak's outstretched arm. Stroking its feathers, the priest spoke to it softly and the eagle bobbed its head as if understanding what was said. Then Kolak raised his arm and the eagle launched itself into the air. Intrigued, I watched the bird swoop low over the Castra, its talons splayed menacingly, before it flew along the valley and out of view.

Kolak returned his attention to Gostopo. 'Gilgarius will be with us shortly,' he said. 'In the meantime, your men should return to the forest to see who has been flushed out by the fire.'

Gostopo hesitated. 'And our gold?'

'Do not worry about the gold. What you ask for will be yours.'

Seemingly reassured, the Castra leader turned and addressed his men in their own tongue as the priests looked on. But I saw that many Castra were not happy with what they heard, shaking their heads and appearing to mutter beneath their beards. Even so, there appeared to be no mood for rebellion. As soon as Gostopo finished speaking, they picked up their weapons and shields and set off along the valley towards the smoking remains of the forest.

Kolak turned to Asdur. 'What do you think?'

'We have an unreliable ally in Gostopo,' said Asdur. 'I know him well, but he cannot always be trusted.'

'It is only the promise of gold that keeps him in order,' replied Kolak.

'That is true and it is why Gostopo must not have too much of it at once. Otherwise he will disappear with his men and not be seen again.'

'Yes, that is a risk,' said Kolak. 'And we need Gostopo to help us fulfil our destiny. Gilgarius, too, of course. It is vital Mulenda is disposed of before we take on Pediv.'

'Indeed. For all his self-assertion, Mulenda is still loyal to the king.'

'And he could be a problem when our surrogates in Dhagani rise against him.'

'Will you give Gostopo the gold he demands?'

'Yes, of course,' said Kolak. 'I'll give them everything they ask for. It is important to keep them satisfied. I shall have need of them when we move against Pediv.'

Asdur grunted his admiration. 'If it is truly possible to conquer all and possess everything, then you are the one who can do it.'

'That may be true, although gold and the power it brings are but tools to me. What I desire to conquer most of all is death.'

As he said this, the priests' attention was distracted by a giant shadow moving across the valley. Everyone looked up to see Gilgarius flying over the rim of a jagged peak towards them. Kolak's eagle was gliding in his powerful wake.

Quickly realising my position was greatly exposed and that I might easily be seen by the creature, I retreated to the rear of the roof. Below this was a short drop on to a rocky ledge which formed the edge of a water channel. I lowered myself onto it, a fortunate and timely move for moments later Gilgarius swooped low over the temple roof, shaking the building as if the very earth had quaked and cracked beneath it.

I decided it was too dangerous to remain where I was, even though I desired to overhear the conversation between the priests and Gilgarius. I lowered myself into the channel to see where it would lead me. The water came no higher than my waist and, working against its flow, I soon discovered it was spilling over from a small lake

Stretching out from the side of the temple, the waters lapped on to a shore of lush grass. Beyond that, the ground rose steadily towards a clump of trees. At its remaining edges, the lake was bounded by a high rock face, sheer and for the most part unassailable. I crouched in the channel at the very edge of the lake, the water lapping against my chin, to ponder what I should do.

I remained there for some time, weighing up the risks of my position and how I might escape without being detected. Suddenly I felt a powerful draught of air, more like a swirling wind, and I quickly realised it was being made by Gilgarius's giant wingbeats.

The creature had taken to the sky, any exchange with Kolak apparently ended. I watched him circle the temple before he settled on the grassy lake shore barely a few strides from where I was hiding. I tried to become as invisible as possible, pressing myself into the channel and just managing to hold my nose and mouth above the water.

Just as I thought I could make my escape the way I had come, Gilgarius plunged his huge head into the lake to take a drink. The action created an explosive wave that completely swamped me, first pushing me back up the channel before the force reversed and dragged me in the opposite direction and into the lake.

As I tumbled in the maelstrom, Gilgarius lifted his head to gulp down the water he had taken in. I was spinning, unable to rise to the surface to take a breath. I struck out desperately with my arms to find calmer water, but Gilgarius plunged his head back into the lake to take a second draught.

I found myself being drawn irresistibly towards the creature's jaws.

I truly believed my end had come. I'd swallowed lot of water and was struggling to swim away, but I was trapped in a terrible whirlpool. I knew that if I didn't break the surface I would drown, yet if I did I would be at the creature's mercy.

I was forced to kick against Gilgarius's head to avoid being sucked into those terrible jaws but if the monster felt this, he did not react. Instead he lifted his head again to gulp down his fill of water.

By this time I had risen to the surface, breathless and thrusting out my arms in a desperate attempt to swim clear. That is when Gilgarius saw me and reached out with his giant claws to retrieve the strange, thrashing human. I knew at once what my fate would be so I gasped as much air as I could and plunged beneath the surface, swimming as fast and as deep as I could.

Gilgarius's claws tore at the water, stirring up a frenzy of foam. At first I was pulled back towards the surface by the power of it and I felt the sting of a foreclaw as the creature tried to hook it around my spinning body. Gilgarius's desperation to catch me caused the water to churn ever more violently. Still spinning, and my lungs about to burst, I found myself buffeted against underwater rocks.

***

Kairi paused at this part of his story, as if not daring to carry on. He looked at Garia, who draped a comforting arm around his shoulders. None of us spoke, we just waited until Kairi felt able to carry on.

'So, there I found myself,' he said at length. 'About to die – either by drowning or being impaled by the monster's claws and crunched in his jaws.'

'But you are here to tell your story,' I said. 'You survived. How?'

'Something remarkable saved me, Han. You see, the turbulent water dragged me onto submerged rocks. I grabbed the jagged edge of one and pulled myself away from Gilgarius's claws. There was a gap between this and the next rock, a gap just wide enough for me to squeeze between, and I hauled myself through into a black void.'

Kairi said he had chosen to drown rather than be torn apart by Gilgarius. Unable to breathe, he allowed himself to float freely in what seemed to be an underwater cave.

'It was strange but I felt serene,' said Kairi. 'I had no air, save the used air left in me. I couldn't keep the water out any longer. I'd resisted to the end and knew I had to let go, to open my mouth. To die on my terms and not as Gilgarius's fodder.'

Again there silence from Kairi – and from the rest of us. We must all have been thinking the same thing: how could he now be here with us? How could he have escaped such a certain watery grave? What miracle had saved him?

Kairi smiled, as if taking delight in how suspenseful his story was and how we longed to know the nature of his salvation.

Edbersa, who had joined us part way through Kairi's testimony, broke the silence. 'So, you chose to drown?'

'I did.'

'Mmm. There is quite a big flaw in your tale, Kairi,' said Edbersa, caressing his beard thoughtfully. 'Either you are lying and there was no danger of you drowning, or you are an apparition, the ghost of a drowned man.' He reached out and put a hand on Kairi's head. 'No, solid enough; you're not an apparition.'

'But how did you save yourself, Kairi?' I asked.

'Well, Han, this is how it happened. I had, as I say, resigned myself to death by drowning. I didn't have time to think about it. I closed my eyes and opened my mouth to expel the last bit of used air inside me. At the same moment the bubbles left me, my feet found the rocky floor of the cave. I don't know why I did it, for I expected in my drowning state to just sink and die, but without thought I pushed my feet against the rock to propel myself upwards. Although I believed I was dying, I must have still had an instinctive will to live.' He paused and shot a glance to Garia.

'But Kairi,' I said, 'I still don't understand how you managed to escape from your watery grave.'

'Because the grave, dear Han, was not so watery. Within a moment or two of pushing myself upwards, I found I was not drowning but gasping for breath above the level of the water. There was just enough room for my head between the water and the rocky roof. Though all was black and I couldn't see a thing, I knew then that I would live. I probed around and found that I was in a tunnel rather than a cave and I wondered where, if anywhere, it would lead.'

I was about to make another remark, when Edbersa put a hand on my arm. 'No more questions, Han,' he said quietly. 'Let our friend continue with his story.'

Kairi then explained how he was able to make his escape.

***

Carefully I began working my way away from the lake, fearing Gilgarius might tear up the rock to find me. My main aim was to find the source of the breathable air which had saved me because it might lead to a way out. Progress was slow and at times, when the roof dipped sharply, I could barely keep my nose and mouth above water.

It soon became clear that the tunnel was getting wider and the air space deeper. Eventually I could stand with my head totally above the water, then my upper body. The further I progressed, the more turbulent the water became, suggesting to me that the underground stream which fed the lake was itself fed by the waterfall I'd previously seen disappearing into the mountain.

I waded along the tunnel with my hands able to touch both its sides. To my left I could feel the uneven rock of the mountain, while to my right was a wall, flat and smooth. that seemed to have been built by the hands of men.

On the wall side, there was also a ledge wide enough for me to stand upon. I scrambled on to it, dripping and shivering and moving cautiously. Here the tunnel was no longer totally black and I could discern a series of orange glows just a few strides ahead of me at about the height of my knees. I approached cautiously to see the flickering lights of torches shining through the wall in four places.

I crawled to the first hole, which was the size of a milking pail and covered by a bronze grille. From inside, I could hear tapping and scraping sounds. I peered through and saw at least five priests hunched over stone tables, working at a variety of tasks by candlelight. On each side of them were stacks of Kolak's gold, glinting in the flickering light.

Although intrigued by what I saw, I did not wish to linger. I was soaked and shivering with cold, and I realised I had to

249

quickly find a way out of my underground prison.

After a few steps, the dry ledge came to an end and I was forced to slip back into the water and make my way against the ever more deafening torrent as I neared the point where it entered the mountain.

Ascending a series of cataracts, three times my hold failed and I ended up tumbling backwards and half drowning myself in the process. But at the fourth attempt, I managed to reach a point where I could crouch on a narrow ledge away from the water's full force. I looked up and spied a shaft of daylight sparkling and dancing on the spray at the point where the stream tumbled into the mountain.

The final climb proved not to be steep. With a renewed sense of purpose, I scrambled up the remaining cataracts, fought my way through the swirling water spout and made it, safe but exhausted, to the surface.

I found a place to shelter among the rocks where I could dry out and regain my strength. It was there, while I was resting, that I began to detect a terrible stench brought to me by a sudden change in wind direction. I scrambled to a vantage point to determine what could be causing the smell and, in the distance, saw among a jagged formation of rocks a large rock which appeared to be moving from side to side. I realised I was looking at a back view of Gilgarius's giant, jagged head. The creature was squatting among the rocks and scree, wings outstretched, emitting groans and rumbles and issuing a series of putrid farts, fouler than anything I had ever smelled. I had found Gilgarius's shitting place.

Thus occupied, the creature appeared to pose no threat but I had no wish to hang around being bathed in that terrible putridity and so I set off on my quest to find you.

***

It had been a lucky escape, especially from the clutches of Gilgarius, and a respectful period of silence followed the end of Kairi's story as we took it all in.

***

Arkis slid down from Rashi and looped her rein around a branch of the large tree which provided welcome shade for drinkers at Goman's tavern.

'Well, if it isn't our traveller friend Arkis,' the tavern keeper said with a booming laugh. He was a big man, a full head above Arkis and most of the other men. 'How is old Han? Still spinning his yarn?'

Arkis shook his head and smiled tolerantly. He knew what would come next.

'You don't still believe his tale, do you?' the tavern keeper asked. The other men laughed.

This was fifth time Arkis had called at the village to be greeted as if he were an old acquaintance by the tavern keeper. By now the sun was high and it was too hot to work, so other village men were also gathered in the shade of the chatka tree.

'So, what can we get you?'

'Water for the horse and beer for me,' Arkis said.

Goman snapped an order to a young girl inside the tavern.

'It's all a fantasy,' said another man. 'Han's never been right in the head. But he's harmless.'

'All that family are odd,' said Goman. 'Mind you, old Han's daughter, Akona, and that husband of hers, Mercon, had the sense to get out.'

'What about the granddaughter, Pelia?' This was Goman's brother, Rofold. 'She must be mad to stay there. She used to be pretty. Given up any chance of a husband, that one.'

And it continued along a similar vein, as it had on Arkis's previous visits when he had called after spending a morning committing elements of Han's story to parchment.

The men's voices became increasingly excitable.

'Do you think the old man's giving her one?'

'More likely an old billy goat's giving her one.'

'There are many who'd like to be in there. How about you, stranger?'

'I bet he already has.'

'They say old Han has powers. He looks you in the eye and tells you something and you believe it.'

'Has that happened to you, stranger?'

'My father knew him as a boy. He said you always ended up believing what he said. He had this way.'

'*My* father said he was a nutter.'

'How can you believe something you haven't seen?'

'There's never been any proof.'

'Aye, we've to rely on his word. The word of Han.'

'There's no one been round long enough and is still alive to contradict him.'

'It's just a legend. What old Han did – or says he did – it's just a story.'

'Mind you, I'd like to believe the bit about the gold is true. Now it would be something if we could find that. What do you think, Arkis?'

***

It was I who impatiently broke the spell of silence after Kairi had finished his story, said Han. 'But how did you know where we were?' I asked.

'I guessed that if you got out of the cave alive you would want to put the mountain between you and the fire. This gorge seemed the only route to safety.'

'The problem is, the priests are likely to make the same assumption,' said Edbersa. He stroked his beard distractedly, clearly troubled. 'Well, my friend, you've certainly brought some disturbing intelligence from your eavesdropping. It seems from his talk of Pediv that Kolak has ambitions to control the whole of Polastia. I think you'd better come with me and tell Mulenda what you heard.'

This Kairi did, accompanied by Garia, whose mood had lifted considerably upon our friend's return.

Nyxes turned to me, putting her arm through mine. 'What do you think Mulenda will do?'

'I don't know. He's thinking of leaving us to fend for ourselves as he goes off to fight the priests and the Castra.'

'What about Gilgarius? Will we be left at the creature's mercy?'

'Almost certainly. Even if the monster is diverted by the priests to defeat Mulenda, he'll still come looking for us when he gets chance.'

'You believe Mulenda will be defeated.'

'I'm sure of it. Even if more soldiers come from Bathlaya, there are too many Castra and the priests have their own powers. And Gilgarius might not have to become involved. All he'll need to do is sit on his haunches and watch the slaughter.'

'Then he'll try to find us.'

'Yes. And we'll have no one to protect us – unless we can find a way to help Mulenda, to give him an advantage.'

Nyxes smiled and gently squeezed my arm. 'I have a feeling you're working out a plan.' She was right.

'Gilgarius will have to be tricked,' I said. Thoughts were coming to me quickly and in a jumble, and I shook my head as if it would help me put them in some kind of order. I must have started to act strangely because Nyxes put her arms around me.

'Are you all right, Han?' she asked.

'I don't know… I mean, I'm not sure…' I was floundering in a sea of possibilities, but through it an idea surfaced – the sort that came whenever I was faced with difficulty or danger – yet

I had no notion where such ideas were conceived. It was as if they were born beyond me, beyond anyone and anything known to me.

Nyxes urged me to go over to Mulenda, who was deep in debate with Osbin and my three companions. For a while, we stood quietly by listening to the conversation.

'Kolak is ambitious,' Osbin was saying grimly. 'I'm not surprised he is harbouring a desire to depose Pediv and take over the whole of Polastia. That's why the gold is so important to them. It enables them to buy those who can help them.'

Osbin went on to describe how ingots of gold were stored in a vault beneath the temple. No one but the priests ever went down there. The Castra would certainly not be allowed to know where the gold was stored in case they got ideas about stealing it; as far as Gostopo knew, the gold could be concealed anywhere in the Valley of Havilon. Osbin said some of the priests spent hours each day in the gold vault turning the precious metal into adornments and ornamental objects. He also revealed that the underground holes Kairi had seen in the vault walls were for ventilation.

'How do the priests enter the vault?' I asked.

'Steps from inside the temple lead down into it,' said Osbin.

'And who guards it?' asked Edbersa.

'No one.'

'There are no guards?'

Osbin smiled. 'Entry is prevented by a huge slab of stone laid over the steps to the vault. Only the priests can move it.'

Edbersa was intrigued. 'By employing some ingenious mechanism?'

'No, by their sheer strength. You have to understand the true nature of these priests. They are physically very powerful – all of them. Kolak has the strength of five men. To the priests, moving a huge slab of stone is no problem.' Mulenda shut his eyes and pressed a hand to his temple as if to ease his troubled thoughts.

'It's obvious from what Kairi saw that there are too many Castra to fight,' Edbersa was saying. 'And that's without the priests, their guards and Gilgarius joining in.'

'There will be a way,' Mulenda replied defiantly. 'We just need to think.'

'The gold could be a key,' I said, but I don't think anyone heard me.

'We will find a way to defeat all of these enemies,' said Mulenda. 'As soon as we have reinforcements from Bathlaya.'

At this point I stepped forward, determined to be heard. 'Excuse me, but I have a plan.'

My uninvited contribution was met with a brief silence, except for an exasperated laugh from Mulenda. 'Why should we heed you, boy?'

'Because what I'm going to say makes sense.'

Mulenda snorted disdainfully.

'You would do well to listen to him, nephew,' said Edbersa.

'Then proceed, young Han,' said Mulenda with another exasperated laugh.

'Very well,' I said, nodding gratefully to Edbersa. 'This is what I think. If Gilgarius, the priests and the Castra are too many to take on directly in battle, we must get them to fight each other.'

'And how do you propose we do that?' There was more than a hint of distrust in Mulenda's voice.

'First, we must separate Kolak from his gold,' I said.

Mulenda shook his head and spat on the ground. 'You make no sense, Han,' he said. 'How will stealing the priests' gold help defeat this evil coalition? It is a mad idea – and it would only be a dangerous distraction. I will apply my mind to Kolak's treasure after our victory.'

'Actually, I haven't said we should steal the gold.' By now my plan was forming more clearly.

Mulenda grunted sarcastically. 'Please, make up your mind. What exactly are you proposing?'

'We should stop the priests from giving any more of their gold to the Castra.'

'So, are we going to steal it?'

'Only in the sense that we can deprive the priests of it.'

'I'm intrigued, but not optimistic,' said Mulenda. 'Please share with us the detail of your plan.'

'Oh, I'm still working that out but the principle is settled.'

Mulenda shook his head in disbelief. 'This boy is mad. He has no plan.'

Edbersa placed a hand on his nephew's shoulder. 'I suggest you allow Han to explain before you judge his state of mind.'

'Very well,' said Mulenda with a condescending bow of the head. 'Please explain, young Han, what you think we should do next.'

And that's just what I proceeded to do. As I spoke, the plan formed more clearly. Everything I said was greeted in complete silence but I was sure there would be challenges and questions. In particular, there was no certainty Garia and Kairi would consent to be involved in such a dangerous adventure.

When I had finished speaking, Mulenda nodded slowly and stroked his dense beard. 'If it works, it would indeed be a good plan,' he said. 'But you can't be sure how each of our adversaries will react.' The doubt was not unexpected.

'If they do not react as I hope they will, the situation would be no different to that we already face,' I said confidently. 'All I ask is you delay going into battle. If I fail, you can still fight with your men. Nothing would be lost but a day.'

Edbersa grunted. 'The lad's right, Mulenda. What he suggests involves little or no risk to you. Although I'm not happy about Han putting himself in danger.'

'He will not be alone,' said Garia. 'Kairi and I will be with him.'

Mulenda thought for a while. 'Very well. It is madness, but there is time to try it while I wait for fresh men to arrive. After that, if there is no change in the situation, we will attack the priests at their temple and whoever else they call upon to help them – whether that be man or monster.'

By this time, the sun had begun to set. Mulenda's men were returning from the forest bringing an assortment of fruits and small dead creatures – tree rodents, frogs and the like – borne aloft on shields. Several fires had already been lit and the meat roasted quickly over hot cooking stones. Most of it went to Mulenda and his men, with only leftovers for the rest of us. Nevertheless, there was sufficient to go around, especially the fruits, which the soldier's appeared to treat with a measure of disdain. Not one of us was left wanting for more.

Soon after our meal was finished, the children settled themselves in the softest of beds they made from pine needles while all the men, including my three companions, sat around the various fires and conversed in low voices. Nyxes and I decided to search for a sleeping place away from the others and we made our way further up river, above the waterfall, where we found a suitable place among the rocks.

As we gathered ferns to sleep on, I tried not to think about the danger I would face the next day; having boldly declared my plan, I had no choice now but to proceed. I didn't want Nyxes to sense I was scared – which I most certainly was – so it was good that we distracted ourselves by talking more about our lives, our hopes our desires, anything but our fears.

The next morning, before the sun was fully risen, Nyxes and I re-joined the others in the cave. Garia and Kairi were sitting quietly while Edbersa was entertaining the younger children with an old tale from his youth, gesticulating with his powerful arms and making the children laugh by using strange voices.

'Are you sure you want to go through with this mad plan of yours?' Nyxes asked me as we breakfasted on the remains of the forest fruits.

'I am nervous about it, but it's the only way to defeat the priests and the Castra.'

'What about Gilgarius? Have you a plan to defeat him?'

'Something will come to me,' I said, feigning confidence.

All too soon it was time to leave. My two brave companions declared themselves ready to meet whatever challenges lay ahead. I sought out Mulenda and he assured me that he and his men were prepared to play their part. 'I don't know why I agreed to this,' he said gruffly.

'Because if it works, you will not have to fight,' Garia replied coldly.

Nyxes led me to one side and took my hand. 'I want to go with you.'

I placed a finger across her lips, shaking my head. She knew I would never allow it. She kissed me quickly on the cheek and turned away so she need not see us leave. By this time, Edbersa had halted his storytelling to watch us. He said nothing, though his troubled expression spoke for him.

I didn't look back as Kairi led the way upwards. He effortlessly found a way through the rocks and thorns until we reached a point where the jagged mountain summit rose sheer above us. We skirted around it, largely shielded by vegetation, but when we were forced to cross the open areas I found myself nervously scanning the sky in search of Gilgarius.

Once at the other side, we could see how much of the forest in the shadow of the mountain had been destroyed by the fire or uprooted by the creature. In stark contrast, the Valley of Havilon beyond was lush and bathed in sunshine.

Kairi halted and pointed to a peak ahead and to our right. 'There's the temple mountain and beyond it, sitting in its shadow, is the temple itself,' he said. 'But to reach it we have to cross the gorge I told you about. Below this is where the water divides in two.' He looked at Garia, then at me. 'Are you sure you're ready for what is to come?'

I said nothing but nodded. Garia slapped me on the shoulder. 'Then let's show that monster and those idiot priests we mean business.'

We set off again, picking our way carefully through a thick forest of thorn and gorse until we reached the lip of the gorge at its narrowest point. Kairi was the first to leap across, landing on a flattish ledge, and Garia followed.

I stared down at the torrent deep below as it thundered through the gap, unsure I could make the leap. But, with the encouragement of my companions, I took a run and hurled myself into the air, legs flailing. Although my leading foot made it firmly on to the ledge, the other slipped from it and I felt myself tipping backwards. Fortunately, Kairi and Garia were quick to grab my arms and haul me to safety. They had surely risked being pulled by me into the gorge, but before I had chance to thank them Kairi was on the move and Garia pushed me after him.

By the time we reached the place where the stream disappeared inside the mountain, the sun was at its highest. We found a shaded place away from the water's roar and ate the little fruit we had brought with us in a goatskin bag Garia had stuffed inside the blouse he wore beneath his tunic.

I reflected on my plan and tried hard not to doubt it would be successful. If my companions had similar thoughts, they did not declare them. There could be no certainty that Gilgarius would appear before us or how he would react upon seeing me so there was nothing else to do but wait. Each of us sat quietly with our own thoughts, frequently scanning the sky as we anticipated the creature's arrival.

Kairi, with his keen eyes, was the first to see him appear on the horizon, casting a huge shadow over the priests' lush valley. Gilgarius's flight was not high and nor was it swift, but it was certainly purposeful as he headed towards us.

I clambered on to a large slab of stone just above the point where the stream tumbled into the mountain while Garia and Kairi found a hiding place among the rocks close by. Although by now I was shivering with fear, I kept my eyes fixed on the approaching monster. When I deemed him close enough, I started to wave my arms wildly to attract his attention. He appeared not to see me at first, even though I was on the side of his good eye, so I continued waving frantically whilst also jumping up and down upon my slab of rock. This worked and Gilgarius turned his head and locked his giant eye on to me.

Faced with the precocious child who had twice escaped his digestive juices, Gilgarius let out a deep rumbling sound as he circled my vantage point, perhaps unsure whether I was real or a phantom. Then he settled upon an expanse of scree, his powerful wingbeats creating a wind that nearly blew me off my feet. Still rumbling like distant thunder, he lowered his enormous head so his huge eye was level with mine.

I had by now stopped waving and jumping but continued shivering with fear. I had to keep my nerve.

The creature turned his head so I could clearly see the eye into which I had plunged Osbin's knife, which now wept a green pus. He fixed me again with his good eye. 'Am I deceived?' he growled. 'Or do I spy the elusive Akben boy?'

'Yes, Gilgarius,' I shouted above the roar of the water, mustering as much bravado as was possible in the circumstances. 'It is Han, come to see how life is treating you.'

'Very badly,' the creature grumbled. 'Life is treating me badly indeed. I have had no children to eat of late – and you know the reason for that.' He opened his huge mouth to show off menacing rows of umber teeth. At the other end, he let out a thunderous fart.

'I know the reason well,' I said. 'You have ended up with no children because you are a stupid creature. Stupid and evil.'

Gilgarius blinked his good eye. 'No! You are wrong! It is

humankind that is stupid and evil. As I believe I have already told you, I would not be in this world had I not been called into existence by men who are greedy for land and gold and other riches. Men who desire all-consuming power.'

'Are you not greedy for the flesh of children?'

'Do not try and make me feel guilty, Han. As you well know, I can only take what is given. You were given and I consider that you remain given, so now you can be taken. But first I need to know why you made yourself so conspicuous on this mountainside, exposed and able to be so easily plucked, like a piece of tempting fruit a human might find hanging from the branch of a tree.'

'Because I wish to prove that you are nothing, that you have no place in this world. I wish to prove that you can be defeated and prove to the children of this land, and all other lands, that they need not fear you. They can play and grow and marry and have children of their own in the knowledge that none will ever be stolen from their mothers and fathers and so terribly abused, as too many children are.'

'It is hardly my fault, boy. If you need to blame anyone, you must blame the priests. They want dominion over all lands and the peoples within them. Your Akben priests are no different.'

I thrust out my chest defiantly and jabbed a fist at the monster. 'You are lying. My country's priests are good people, not like these evil gold-worshippers and child-stealers.'

'It's a shame that you will never go back to Akbenna to ask them now that you are finally to be consumed.'

'You will never eat me.'

'Oh yes I will.'

'I've defied you twice before and will do so again.'

Gilgarius shook his enormous head and snorted arrogantly. I was drenched in a fine pungent spray expelled from his nostrils. 'You are so close,' he said. 'One movement of my well-practiced claw is all it will take.'

'Never!'

'You are alone on an open mountainside. You have nowhere to hide.'

'There are many hiding places among these rocks.'

'I will simply pick them and throw them aside, as a child would pluck and throw a pebble on the seashore.'

'No, you are too stupid. You will never take me. I'm too clever for your feeble brain.'

Gilgarius lifted his head from the scree and spread his huge wings. 'I will debate with you no more. Your time has come.'

Just as he made to lunge at me, claws splayed, Garia and Kairi sprang from their hiding places and positioned themselves between me and Gilgarius, creating a fleeting distraction. Then, before the creature realised what was happening, the three of us launched ourselves into the gushing stream and disappeared inside the mountain. As we tumbled down underground cataracts into the black abyss, I heard the creature howling and stamping and clawing at the very rock that now entombed us.

***

Arkis had slept fitfully, wrapped in his bearskin and listening to the wind dancing with the chatka branches above him. At one point in the night he heard Han coughing and Pelia's soothing words. He heard her rise to get something, probably milk or maybe even beer to send her grandfather back to sleep. The goats must have detected the old man's discomfort, for they became restless and their restlessness unnerved Rashi and she whinnied pitiably.

Arkis found it difficult to return to sleep even after all the sounds died down. There was too much going through his mind. Han's story had prompted him to remember his own childhood, to try to recall events in the same detail that the old man could. Most of Arkis's memories were vague, wrapped in a fog.

There were no clear lines for Arkis, no blacks or whites, rights or wrongs. He had watched Han telling his story, hardly taking his eyes off the old man. He watched him closely to detect even the slightest flicker of a lie, that the tale was being made up, but nothing in Han's eyes or general demeanour or in his words and way of speaking hinted of untruth. Despite the implausibility of it all, especially the implausibility of a boy thinking, reasoning and speaking like a wise man, and conversing with an even more implausible monster, his story was so eminently believable. When you looked at Han and he spoke, you had no choice but to accept what he said as truth.

Arkis thought of his own mother. He smiled at the memory of her and the wonderful warmth of her and the stories she had told. Like Han, she made you believe. Then Arkis slept and dreamt of her.

The next morning he rose early and visited his writing place. When the sun reached the top of its arc, he put away his paraphernalia and set out to explore more of the surrounding land. Today he would not go to the tavern; he'd had enough of inane conversation.

He returned to Han's farm when the sun was already well into its decline. The old man was sitting in his favourite spot beneath the chatka tree. He didn't ask where Arkis had been. 'Have you guessed yet what my plan was?' he said immediately.

'I have an idea,' said Arkis.

'Then tell me.'

'You wanted to make Gilgarius angry.'

'That's obvious. But to what end?'

'I trust you are about to reveal that.'

'Rest assured, my friend, you will find out. But you have left little time for storytelling today and my cot beckons.' The old man got up with difficulty and shuffled barefoot through the dust to his little round house. He seemed to be shrinking before Arkis's eyes.

Arkis had noticed with each new day that Han needed to lean more heavily on his stick and to pause more often to take in breath; he was exhausted by the increased frequency of his coughing fits and hardly touched any of the food Pelia brought him. Yet when he was telling his story, Han's eyes shone and his voice was unfaltering.

***

So you have worked out my plan, said Han. At least the first part of it, which was to make Gilgarius so angry that he would do anything to capture and devour me.

As you might recall from Osbin's story, demolishing mountains was something the creature was quite capable of. In the past, he had demonstrated this ability as he satisfied the priests' greed for gold in exchange for the child-food he so craved. I was determined to provide a similar opportunity in the hope that the creature's desire to devour me would drive him mad if he was deprived of the prize just as he was about to take it. Yet I couldn't be certain that his desperation to acquaint me with his digestive juices would make him mad enough to tear down a mountain.

But that's what my crazy plan was all about and, as the waterfall flushed the three of us deep into the mountain, Gilgarius could be heard screeching and wailing and stamping and tearing apart the rock above us in pursuit of his escaped dinner.

Being washed underground proved a bruising experience. We encountered a number of waterfalls, and I feared my wound might reopen when it had begun to heal so nicely, but soon we found ourselves in a pool of deep water.

'Follow me and keep close,' said Kairi. 'We are not out of danger.'

He was right. Earth and rocks from Gilgarius's work had already begun to tumble into our underground escape route. We wasted no time in hurling ourselves over the final waterfall, to be swept away with what natural light there was rapidly fading behind us.

We were carried around a curve in the passage and soon could see above us the faint orange glows of the ventilation holes Kairi had seen in the temple vault wall. Priests were probably in there carrying out their fine gold craft and it occurred to me that, if everything went as I hoped, they were about to get a terrible shock. It did not concern me that they would almost certainly be drowned because of my plan.

We continued to be swept along, by now in complete blackness and with the space between the water and the roof ever smaller. I hit my head frequently on the rock and took in water but thankfully we soon reached the point where the underground river fed into the lake.

'Feel for the gap in the rocks,' said Kairi. 'Take a lungful of air and dive. When you get through, aim for the light. You go first, Garia, and then Han. I'll follow.'

But it didn't work out in that order. Kairi had barely finished speaking when a sudden surge of water came from behind us, almost completely filling the tunnel. We had no space or time to take the deep breath needed to make it through to the lake. We coughed and spluttered and gasped for the little air available and I found myself being pushed down by strong hands.

Imagine my fright, Arkis, in the blackest black imaginable, as I was completely immersed in the swirling water. But the hands that pushed me down also propelled me forward and I frantically reached out to find the space between the rocks. I made it through just as my lungs felt like they would burst.

Sunlight was shimmering on the surface of the water above me and I kicked hard and motioned my arms like a bird might use its wings to reach it. I broke the surface, gasping for air; then, still flailing wildly, I struck out for a group of rocks jutting from the water at the lake's edge.

Moments later, Garia surfaced and quickly after him came Kairi, both spluttering and gulping as they struggled to exchange water for life-saving air.

'Over here,' I called and they quickly swam to me.

Then we heard Gilgarius's huge roar as the creature clawed further into the mountain, gouging out huge rocks that tumbled down the jagged slope to crash upon the temple and into the lake where we were sheltering. The ground quaked and the water around us boiled. We were not out of danger.

Amid the thunderous noise and shaking ground, and struggling to keep our heads above the turbulent water, we began to make our way along the edge of the lake to find a place of safety.

Although we remained undiscovered, there was a great risk of being crushed by the falling rocks that Gilgarius was now hurling in all directions in his desperation to find us. The lake continued to boil and swell until it could no longer be contained. Without warning, a great wall of water rose up and fell upon us; it swallowed us whole, churning us over and over, washing us across the rising ground until, exhausted of power, it could carry us no further.

As the foaming water receded, it left the three of us entangled in the branches of a clump of trees well away from the lake's edge. Although in a precarious situation, we were at least fortunate enough to have been swept beyond the range of the flying rocks. I looked around and saw that we were each clinging to the branches of the same tree.

'Can you see what's happening?' asked Garia, who had been caught in the lowest branches and was already lowering himself to the ground.

Kairi and I climbed higher, where we could see that the

temple had been completely buried beneath the shifted mountain and the overflowing lake had begun to flood the entire Valley of Havilon. By now Gilgarius had ceased the major part of his destruction, which had created a wall of rocks across the far edge of the valley, preventing the outflow of water from the mountain streams. The creature was crouched upon this, snorting and growling as he picked over the smaller rocks as a cat might claw at pebbles to expose a mouse.

Then he suddenly rose into the air and headed away down the valley, screeching in his anger and frustration.

So, it seemed we were safe – for the time being, at least. Yet danger still lurked in the form of the priests and the Castra.

I looked around for any sign of them and it didn't take me long to see them. Across from the destroyed temple, I saw a gathering of priests and their servers on the hillside. Three figures were standing upon a rocky outcrop, staring at the destruction Gilgarius had caused, the water rising before them. I easily made out Kolak and Asdur but it took me a few moments to realise who the third priest was. I squinted to better focus, for I could not at first believe what I saw.

There, in his unmistakable scarlet robes, was Medzurgo – the head priest of my own motherland.

I left Kairi and clambered down the tree to Garia. 'I've seen Medzurgo,' I told him, hardly able to contain my emotions.

'What? Are you crazy?'

'Please believe me,' I said. 'He's with Kolak and Asdur. See for yourself.'

Garia obliged, swiftly climbing the tree to join Kairi in the uppermost branches. After a few moments he returned to the ground, leaving Kairi observing all that was happening from his perch.

'Did you see him?'

'Yes.'

'So I didn't imagine it.'

Garia shook his head. 'But what do you think he's doing here?'

'I don't know,' I said. 'But he's obviously a traitor.'

'Traitor?'

'It's something Osbin said.' I hesitated, allowing the dancing thoughts in my head to settle.

'Go on,' urged Garia.

'Osbin said he thought we'd been betrayed by someone in Akbenna.'

'One of our own people?'

'Yes – and it must have been Medzurgo. Seeing him here proves it. He betrayed our mission to the Polasti priests.'

'It would seem so. But why?'

'I can't say – but there's something else I'm now sure of.'

'And what is that?'

'It's when Gilgarius came to Akbenna…' I hesitated again because my reasoning seemed so ridiculous, so improbable.

'And?' prompted Garia.

'Well, you may think I'm stupid but I'm convinced the creature didn't just descend on our land by accident or chance – it must have been because someone sent for him. I believe that someone was Medzurgo.'

Garia was silent as my words sank in. Then, just as he was about to respond, we heard a rustling in bushes behind us. I pivoted in time to see a flash of burnished bronze followed almost instantly by a loud crack as the blade of a spear embedded itself in the tree from which we had just descended. Instinctively I threw myself to the ground, as did Garia.

My companion drew his sword but no more spears followed. Instead, the bushes parted and out stepped a large, fierce-looking man with flowing red hair and beard, adorned in a broad gold belt and with golden bracelets encircling his forearms. It was Gostopo.

Other Castra emerged behind him, grasping spears and

swords and bows ready charged with arrows. It was clear that if we tried to escape, we would be slaughtered without ceremony.

We had no choice but to surrender. Surrounding us, the Castra disarmed Garia then they bundled us into the open in the direction of the place where the priests and guards – their human statues – were assembled.

I turned and raised my eyes to see where Kairi was but Garia tugged at my sleeve. 'Don't give him away,' he whispered.

I froze as my shock at our capture turned to terror and despair. Then a Castran prodded me in the back with the point of a spear to force me on.

Oh, Arkis, I thought I'd been so clever by trying to show everyone what a wonderfully wise and resourceful boy I truly was. But now, as we were led to what I believed would be our certain deaths, I realised I'd deceived myself into thinking I had all the best answers. I'd thought that no plan could be better than my plan and I would never fail to triumph. Now death stared us in the face. How could we escape such a fate?

I could not see how we would survive. Garia must have known my thoughts, for he put a hand upon my shoulder and squeezed it as if to reassure me.

As we pushed towards the assembled priests, terror and despair turned to anger and defiance as I anticipated the forthcoming confrontation with Medzurgo. He would probably be as surprised to see me as I had been to see him. Perhaps he thought no one would ever discover his treachery; perhaps he had travelled to the Valley of Havilon believing Edbersa, Garia and I were already dead.

The priests, who had been surveying the destruction wrought by Gilgarius intently, and with it the rising floodwater, remained unaware of our capture until we were almost upon them.

Gostopo pitched me forward with such force I ended up sprawled on the ground at Kolak's feet. If the priest was surprised, he did not show it. He jabbed at me with his staff then he waved it over the devastation that once was his temple. 'Are you the cause of this?'

'You must have done something to anger Gilgarius,' I said precociously. Frankly, I was baffled why the priest was not in a terrible rage given the destruction of his temple and the drowning of his gold. But his expression was well hidden behind his beard, giving nothing away. Yet I could see there was anger in his eyes.

I looked up at Medzurgo. 'You are a traitor,' I spat.

No reaction.

'And you are a young fool,' said Kolak, raising his orbed staff and scanning the horizon. 'Doubtless Gilgarius will be delighted to be re-acquainted with you, boy.'

I kept my eyes fixed on Medzurgo. 'Why did you betray your people?' He looked at me scornfully but said nothing. 'Why?' I persisted.

Asdur stepped between us and bent his head to mine. 'Can't you see?' he said.

'All I can see is evil,' I said, rising to my full height and inflating my chest in defiance.

Asdur laughed. 'Your precocity knows no bounds, Han. You have been deceived by a misguided sense of self-importance.'

'Perhaps the boy is entitled to an explanation before he meets his end,' said Medzurgo.

Asdur tilted his head in a bow of respect. 'Of course, although I doubt that he will understand.'

I bristled at this assumption. 'I understand only too clearly,' I said. 'Sacrificing children to Gilgarius is an act of pure evil.'

Medzurgo responded with a laugh more menacing than humorous. 'Evil is a word that can be so easily be misused,' he said. 'In many lands, making sacrifices is a long-standing tradition to please the deities. In some lands it is children who are sacrificed, in others animals or old people.'

'Not in Akbenna,' I said. 'As well you know.'

Medzurgo shook his head and, with a fleeting a glance at Kolak, continued, 'You will never be able to understand, Han, that satisfying Gilgarius's desire for child flesh is merely a means to an end, that harnessing his power is just one step towards achieving a greater glory.'

I was having none of that. 'You pretended to be as distressed as the rest of us when Gilgarius descended upon our land but it was because of you that he came to take the children. Why?'

He was about to answer when Kolak, no longer tolerant of the exchange, interrupted. 'It is sufficient for you to know that we have to keep the creature happy so he will do our bidding.'

'I'm not talking to you,' I retorted. 'This is between me and him.' I jabbed a finger at Medzurgo. 'I deserve to know the truth.'

The words were barely out when I felt the back of Asdur's hand crack against the side of my head. It sent me sprawling. 'Show respect, boy,' he growled.

I winced but didn't wish to show how much the blow had hurt me.

By this time Kolak had raised his staff and appeared ready to bring it down upon my skull. Garia leapt between us to protect me, even though he had no means of defence but his bare hands. Fortunately Kolak stayed his hand, probably believing Asdur's assault upon me to be sufficient punishment.

After several moments during which I dared not move, he lowered his staff. 'It is a shame I am unable to beat out your impudent brains,' he said, 'but I cannot feed you to Gilgarius if you are already dead. He desires to relish your squeals as he sinks his fangs into your upstart flesh.'

With that, Kolak raised his eyes to range the horizon beyond Havilon. Then he waved his orbed staff in the air, in the wide circular motion I had seen him do before. After a few moments, we heard a sound like a howling wind produced by this movement – the sound Kolak used to call his white-tailed eagle.

I wanted to shout out in my anger and fear, to continue railing against the evil these priests and this valley had spawned, but my eyes were irresistibly drawn to Kolak's eagle, which had responded to the haunting call and risen from among the temple ruins.

It circled overhead before swooping down to rest upon the priest's outstretched arm. The priest preened the bird's neck feathers with his long fingers as he eyed me closely. 'I have to say, Han, it is a shame you have been so troublesome. Had you been more amenable, you might have made a great priest.'

I was tempted to spit in his face but didn't fancy another blow to the head. I just stood there, glowering silently.

Kolak turned to Medzurgo. 'Perhaps the boy does deserve an explanation before he dies,' he said.

Medzurgo inclined his head respectfully in agreement. 'Perhaps.'

Kolak resumed his gentle preening of the eagle and looked at me. 'Then I could begin by asking Han why he might think there are so many conflicting beliefs among different peoples.'

I realised it was a question I wasn't really being invited to answer, so I didn't respond.

The priest quickly pressed on. 'It seems every land has its own deity,' he said. 'In Bostratis, for example, they worship the sun, the wind and the rain. In Akbenna, your people revere a turbulent mountain. In Polastia, people bow down before the creatures of the forest. I have heard that in some lands they worship their own ancestors, and in others the moon and the stars. I have even received reports that some peoples do not address their devotions to any of these visible deities but to something that cannot be seen or heard or touched.

'People who worship do so in the belief that they have found the true way to eternal life. Life beyond death. But they cannot all be correct in their chosen paths. Indeed, it is my belief that not one of them has it right and there is no life beyond death. The only way to counter that terrible scourge is to harness life itself through what Nature offers.'

All the time he spoke, Kolak continued preening his eagle.

'It did not come to me in an instant, Han,' he continued. 'It took me time to realise where the true path lies. But gradually I turned against traditional forms of devotion and set out to found a new faith based not on fanciful notions but on the here and the now – on the power that existence on this earth affords us, if only we could learn how to harness its life-enhancing possibilities.'

Kolak straightened his tall frame and lifted his staff, pointing it down the flooded valley. 'So, I founded Havilon to be a paradise on earth where life can be endless – but only for the chosen few. The secrets of the valley should only be known by those who prove themselves worthy. They certainly cannot be shared with one such as you.'

He lowered his head towards me. 'Do you not feel cheated, Han, that you are about to die when others who have already lived long will continue living forever?'

I said nothing. Osbin had already given me a good idea what those priestly secrets might entail. I simply stood there, glaring my hatred.

'So, there you have it,' Kolak continued, raising himself to his full height. 'The reason why Havilon exists and why Medzurgo did what he did in Akbenna. It was for a greater good – everlasting life for those worthy of it. Such an achievement is worth all the sacrificed children, including you, young Han. When old people can live forever, there is no need of children.'

With that, he lifted the arm upon which his eagle perched. The eagle would be sent to summon Gilgarius. It was clear that time and hope were now running out for us. Surrounded as we were by priests and Castra, there appeared no chance of escape. And sure enough, Kolak murmured his command to the eagle before it launched itself skyward with a screech. The bird circled and rose ever higher before disappearing from our sight.

But I was determined not to submit meekly to my fate, certainly not without challenging Medzurgo again. I was about to do just that when Gostopo stepped forward to address Kolak. 'We have delivered the boy a second time. Now you must give us the gold you promised.'

A humourless smile cleaved Kolak's beard. 'What of Mulenda?'

'Some of my men are still searching for him. We found his horses and my men are lying in wait to see if he returns for them. We will do no more until we have our gold for the boy.'

I felt Garia stiffen at my side. That meant they would also find Melimari.

I stared defiantly at the Castra leader. 'You have wasted your time – the gold is drowned.'

Gostopo turned to Kolak. 'What is the boy talking about?'

'It is lost,' I said with a laugh.

'Don't listen to him. You will be rewarded as promised.'

But I wasn't going to be silenced. 'Your gold is beneath that,' I said, pointing to where the temple once stood. Now there was just huge pile of rock with part of the roof still visible, an island in the flooded valley.

Gostopo glared at Kolak. 'You should have given us our reward when we first demanded it.'

'You must be patient, Gostopo. You have had gold before and you will have it again. Just bring me Mulenda.'

'We have done enough and will do no more without our due payment.'

'There is no problem with the gold,' insisted Kolak. 'It will just take time. Gilgarius will dig out that which he has buried in his anger. The creature will regret his hasty act of destruction and wish to help us.'

'What if he refuses?'

'I am sure he can be persuaded now we have the boy to give him.'

Gostopo stared at the altered Valley of Havilon and the water still rising. Then, after contemplating Kolak's words for some moments, he growled, 'If you are trying to trick us, you will know what it is like to make an enemy of the Castra.'

Kolak took a stride towards Gostopo, his eyes wide and blazing with anger. 'You are a fool to threaten me,' he said.

'No! You are the fool. My men are tired of doing your bidding. They have not seen their homes for two summers and a winter. You are in danger of losing their goodwill.' As he spoke, Gostopo grabbed the hilt of his sword and drew it from its scabbard. 'If we cannot have what we are owed, we will have the pleasure of revenge.' He turned to his men. 'Maybe it is time to show these priests that we are not to be messed with,' he said

His followers murmured their approval of these words and one began to drum his shield with his sword. Other Castra quickly joined in the drumming, while some also began stamping and chanting. Soon all were drumming, chanting and stamping in unison.

If the intention was to intimidate, it didn't work; the priests appeared unfazed by the Castra demonstration. All them, including Asdur and Medzurgo, stared arrogantly. At their head, Kolak raised his orbed staff aloft in defiance and contempt at the Castra show of strength.

By now Gostopo, his hair like a flame, was grasping his sword two-handed, stabbing the air directly in front of Kolak. The stand-off seemed to slow down time, while the Castran clamour of spear and sword against shield, and foot against ground, and voice against air echoed ever louder around the flooded valley. It seemed clear that something must happen to break the tension and all eyes were fixed upon Gostopo and Kolak to see who would be the first to make a move.

All eyes, that is, except Garia's. For while we were all mesmerised by the stand-off, his eyes were desperately seeking a way of escape.

The first I knew of his intention was when he lowered his head to mine. 'We're getting out of here,' he hissed as he grabbed my arm and began dragging me backwards through the forest of Castra.

I couldn't believe the Castra did not try to stop us but they were so preoccupied supporting Gostopo with their warlike clamour that none appeared to care what we were doing.

Once clear of the throng, we turned and scrambled up the steep bank towards where we had left Kairi. But before we reached the shelter of the trees, we had to cross an exposed stretch of ground in sight of all those below if they chose to look.

I shot a glance behind to see if our escape had been noticed and immediately realised that it had. Asdur had seen us and was waving an arm in our direction. I had no doubt he was ordering the priests' servers to pursue us. They would have to be swift, for they would not be able to push their way through the Castra horde but must find a way around them. Even so, I was petrified they would catch us up. They were big and powerful and would pursue us relentlessly.

There was some relief when we found the cover of trees yet we could not slow down. I struggled to keep up with Garia. We might have made our escape despite the pursuit but, in my haste and fright, I tripped over an exposed root and ended up sprawling on the dusty ground. Hearing the thud and my wimpy shriek, Garia stopped and spun around.

'Keep going, Garia!' I shouted. 'Run! Save yourself.'

But he came back to help me. He had barely pulled me to my feet when three of the servers were upon us, two brandishing knives and one a spear. Faced with these weapons glinting menacingly in the sun, we had no choice but to surrender. A painful prod from one knife got me moving back the way we'd come. Garia glared angrily until he, too, was forced to comply by a spear pressed into his ribs.

We descended quickly and soon emerged from the trees onto the exposed hillside, where our captors forced us at the point of their weapons to sit upon the ground while they observed what was happening below.

The confrontation was just as we had left it: Gostopo and Kolak were still facing each other in a tense stand-off and the Castra drumming, stamping and chanting continuing unabated. In stark contrast to this warlike clamour, the priests and their servers were standing motionless, unperturbed by the assertive Castra.

In an instant, all that changed. With a bear-like roar. Gostopo lunged, thrusting his sword towards Kolak's heart but the priest deflected the blade as though it were a mere stick. Almost in the same movement, Kolak grabbed his assailant by the throat. The Castra leader tried to push the priest away but quickly found himself suspended above the ground. Astonishingly, Kolak held him there one-handed with little effort while Gostopo wriggled like a worm on a hook.

Then Kolak hurled him through the air and into the floodwater, an act which spurred Gostopo's shocked men into action. Almost as one, the Castra surged towards the priestly rank.

Garia and I had no choice but to sit there watching while our captors, alarmed at the assault upon their masters, exchanged hushed but urgent words before two of them set off down the hill to join the fray. That left just the server with the spear to prevent any thoughts we might have of resuming our escape.

For now, we were transfixed by what was unfolding below. For all their number, Gostopo's men didn't get the better of the encounter. We saw many of the Castra being hurled into the floodwater to join their leader, whose distinctive flaming head was bobbing about, his arms flailing. It seemed that he was unable to swim.

Aided by their guards, Kolak and the other priests, who also possessed enormous strength, set about picking off the remaining Castra and hurling them into the air as if they were tiny children.

Soon all the spearmen were dead or drowning, leaving a clear view for the Castra bowmen to fire off their arrows but these were swatted away by the priests as though they were nothing more than biting insects.

Standing over us, the remaining server could not take his eyes off the fighting. I could see Garia watching him closely. Suddenly, he sprang to his feet and threw himself at our captor's legs, wrestling him to the ground. Instinctively I joined in the assault, grabbing his spear hand to prevent the weapon being used.

Instead of fighting back, the server remained meekly impassive. I was surprised he gave in so easily, then I looked more closely upon his face and realised who it was. 'Let him go, Garia,' I said.

But Garia continued to grip him firm. 'Are you crazy, Han?'

'He'll do us no harm,' I said. 'He's not our enemy.'

I released my hold of the spear. 'Can you help us?'

He nodded.

I got to my feet, but Garia was still holding on to him. He said, 'What's going on, Han?'

'Release him, Garia,' I said. 'This is Drago. He is Osbin's friend.'

Although reluctant, Garia let him go and Drago got to his feet. 'There is no time to waste,' he said. 'You have to get away from here.'

'Will you come, too?'

Drago was about to answer but was suddenly distracted by something on the horizon. I followed his gaze and saw a distinctive shape emerge from behind a solitary cloud. 'The creature!' he said. 'You have little time.'

Garia tugged at my sleeve. 'Come on, Han. Hurry!'

We set off. Then I halted and spun round to face Drago. 'What will you tell the priests?'

'That some of Mulenda's men came and freed you. I could do nothing to stop them.'

'What shall I tell Osbin?'

'Tell him I will find him.'

'We'll be by the sea!' I shouted. 'Beyond where the gorge ends.'

'Go!'

'Come on, Han!' Garia called.

Even though the Castra appeared defeated, every moment I expected to hear a cry behind us and feel a spear or an arrow in my back. But no hindrance to our escape came. Very soon we were climbing fast, hidden by the woodland, which soon gave way to thickets of dwarf trees with very little clear ground to run on.

We had reached the top of a steep rise when we saw a movement in the vegetation ahead. Garia grabbed my arm and we both watched nervously, fearing the presence of other guards or Castra spearmen. Then from out of the bushes leapt Kairi, a broad grin upon his face. 'What kept you?' he said.

Garia wrapped him in a quick hug as I beamed with relief.

'We must move quickly,' said Kairi. 'Gilgarius...'

'We know,' said Garia. 'The creature's going to be very angry – again – when he finds Han's not there to greet him.'

Kairi led us into a dense clump of spiky bushes that scratched and punctured us terribly but we had to push on regardless, climbing ever higher, our lungs near bursting with the effort. Only when we cleared the summit of the first rugged peak did we dare stop to take a breath. The wind was strong and cold so we clambered down a short way and found a stand of dwarf pine trees to shelter in.

Garia rested a hand upon my shoulder. 'Well, Han, it would seem your plan is working out,' he said grimly.

But I wasn't so sure. My first aim had been to cut the priests off from their gold and that was done; my second had been to get the Castra and the priests to fall out and that, too, had been accomplished. But the result of their clash was not what I expected.

It is true that I believed the Castra and priests might fight over the gold – or absence of it – but I did not imagine the priests would come out on top. Yet that's what seemed to be happening in the flooded valley beneath us. Even though Osbin had told me of the priests' strength, especially that of Kolak, I hadn't understood how powerful an opponent he might be. I had simply assumed that the two sides would deplete each other's strength and resilience to the point where Mulenda, with his reinforcements, could enjoy an assured victory over what was left of them.

Now we were faced with a grave prospect. If Kolak completed his rout of the Castra, as now seemed likely, he would surely make easy meat of Mulenda and his fighters.

Then there was Gilgarius. Although I would have liked to seal his fate, there had been no time to consider how he could be destroyed once and for all. In that sense my plan was incomplete. I suppose I hoped that, without the Castra to bring him children, he would have no reason to remain as a threat to us. But it seemed the creature had been sent mad by his desire to consume me. If that were truly so, I could imagine him tearing up the entire Valley of Havilon to finally devour the elusive flesh he hungered for.

As we took our all too brief rest, I realised how hungry I was. Where we sheltered there was no offering from Nature, not even the smallest clutch of berries. Kairi must have read my mind, for he said, 'We will be better placed to find food when we reach the sea.'

He looked up to check position of the sun, shading his eyes with both hands. 'But it will be dark before we get there,' he concluded. 'And even I cannot hunt in the night.'

Garia, too, was checking the sky and he suddenly gave a start. 'What's that?'

I followed his eyes to see a large bird soaring above a ridge about a league behind us. 'Kolak's eagle!' I gasped.

'It could be any eagle,' said Garia.

'I fear Han is right,' said Kairi. 'We must not let the bird see us. It is obvious Kolak has sent it to track our escape. We must remain hidden here until it is gone or night has fallen. An eagle will not fly in the dark.'

'Nor Gilgarius,' said I with some relief.

The eagle circled above and around us, sometimes unnervingly close to our hiding place, until dusk forced it to return to the Valley of Havilon.

There was no moon that night but stars enough to ensure the first part of our descent towards the sea was not too treacherous. However, we were soon forced to halt at the edge of a jagged ravine, narrower but deeper than the gorge where we had left Edbersa and the others. We contemplated our situation.

'It's too dangerous to continue,' said Kairi. 'We must wait until the light returns.'

By this time hunger was gnawing desperately at my innards. Water would have helped fill our bellies but we had encountered no stream. To add to our discomfort, the wind was getting stronger, making our position by the ravine treacherous.

We reversed our steps and scrambled around collecting kindling and pine cones and dried moss to make a fire. Kairi soon sparked one into life and we settled to rest. But I could not sleep; I was exhausted beyond sleep.

My companions sat together a little away from me, leaning against each other, talking in hushed voices. They had no idea, of course, what I had previously witnessed between them and I had no wish to dwell on it. Thankfully, they did not attempt to repeat their strange combat. As for me, I could only take comfort in thoughts of my mother and my father, even though part of me feared I would never see them again.

Eventually I did sleep but it was restless and dream-laden and, when Garia shook me awake, I felt just as exhausted as before.

Dawn had barely broken but we anxiously checked the cloudless sky before setting off, thankful to see no sign of Kolak's eagle. We retraced our steps to the ravine and climbed down its precipitous face, clinging onto branches and tree roots and jagged rocks to prevent us from plummeting to our deaths.

At the bottom, a narrow stream flowed over mossy boulders and we dropped to our knees eagerly to drink the chill water. On its narrow banks we found a variety of bushes bearing berries and trees with low-hanging fruits, and Kairi showed us which ones were safe to eat. We took our fill, sheltering under an overhang of rock, shielded from eagle eyes.

'We are safe now,' said Kairi. 'All we have to do is follow the flow of the stream.'

'Will this lead us to the sea?'

'All water leads to the sea eventually, Han,' said Kairi. 'The river in the gorge where we left the others also flows into the sea. As you know, they will follow it to the shore. Once we also come to the edge of the land, it will be easy to find them.'

'What is it like?'

'The sea?'

I nodded.

'Well, it's like a lake but much broader and deeper and it never stops swelling and shrinking. It is forever moving.'

Kairi's description of the sea excited me. Despite the danger we still faced, I couldn't wait to see this wonderful thing.

The stream flowed out of the ravine into a dense, dark forest, and we continued following its course. We found more food among the trees and even heard the scurrying of prey animals that had taken fright at our approach.

Very soon the trees thinned out, allowing shafts of bright sunlight to penetrate the canopy. For some strange reason – probably out of concern that Kolak's eagle might be somewhere above us – we hesitated before stepping out into the open. But when we did, I beheld the sea for the first time, stretching out all the way to the far horizon.

I hadn't believed such an amount of water could exist anywhere. I was mesmerised by the gentle surge of the waves, the salty smell of the air and the sound of the surf washing onto the pebble shore.

Since that day, the sea has held an abiding fascination for me although it's a long time since I rested my eyes upon it. But even now, after all these years, it returns in my dreams as a most wondrous memory.

You will probably understand how I feel, Arkis. You, like me, will doubtless have seen the sun rise and fall over mountains and forests and over deserts and cities. But I'm sure you will agree, my friend, that the sight is never more beautiful than when the sun rises and falls over a shimmering sea.

That day the sea was quite calm, even serene, and I couldn't imagine it boiling in anger. Of course, I now know how treacherous such waters can be, how violently the waves respond to storms, how the sea can swallow anything that dares to venture across its surface and what violence can erupt from its depths.

It was also Garia's first encounter with the sea and we both stood there, transfixed, until Kairi reminded us of our precarious situation. 'We'll follow the shore, but must stay in the shelter of the trees,' he said, pulling at my sleeve. He was right, of course. The eagle could return at any time and if it spotted us, Gilgarius would doubtless quickly follow.

It had been our intention to return to Edbersa and the others by a more direct route but the nature of our escape from the Valley of Havilon had led us much further away than we desired. However, we knew our companions would be waiting for us somewhere along the shore. All we had to do was follow it, keeping the sea to our left, and we would come to where they were sheltering.

After a while we arrived at a stretch of particularly dense forest, which slowed our progress. The trees grew in strange shapes and sizes; the roots of many of them were raised above the ground, sometimes embracing the trunks of neighbouring trees, while above us their branches intertwined as if engaged in some static mating ritual.

As the forest thinned out, our progress was easier. We kept going until we could see by the shafts of bright sunlight that the sun had reached its highest point almost directly above us. Eventually the trees petered out completely and we were forced to cross open ground, all the time craning our necks for any speck in the cloudless sky that could signify an eagle's presence – or worse, a much larger creature that could only be Gilgarius.

By this time a strong wind had got up off the shore and we pushed hard to cover the open ground as quickly as it would allow us, only breathing easier when another wooded area was reached. But any shelter it afforded was short-lived for, after scaling a small hill, we emerged from the trees to find the sea directly in our path and the wind, if anything, stronger.

Beyond water, about half a league distant, we could see another swathe of forest. 'That is where our friends should be waiting for us,' said Kairi.

Above this forest, the bare rock was cleaved by the gorge we had left the previous morning and flashes of sunlight reflected from the tumbling cataracts we had followed after our escape from the mountain.

But reaching our companions would not be easy. Below us the sea's encroachment upon the land was no gentle caressing of the shore, as I had witnessed only a short while before, but a violent assault upon it, whipped up by a strengthening wind. We made our way back to the shelter of the trees.

'I have seen this before,' said Kairi, shaking his head. 'It is a bay. Sometimes it is dry and can be walked across but sometimes, as now, it is filled by the sea.'

'Maybe we should walk around it,' said Garia.

'We could, but it might take a long time,' said Kairi. 'I believe it would be better to wait until the sea goes out again so we can cross directly. And it will give us a chance to rest and take food.'

'What makes the sea come and go?' I asked.

Kairi laughed. 'It's truly a mystery,' he said. 'Many people believe gods live within the sea's depths and the violent waves are caused by those gods fighting among themselves.

Garia laughed. 'And when the waves are gentle, they are just bickering.'

'You may well be right,' said Kairi.

'Are there monsters like Gilgarius in the sea?' This was me.

'I've heard there are,' said Kairi. 'Some say they hunt and fight like land creatures do and that's what disturbs the surface.'

'Perhaps the gods keep these creatures for their amusement,' offered Garia.

'I've not heard that one,' responded Kairi. 'Although I've heard some say that the sea is not the domain of underwater gods or monsters but a plaything of the moon.'

Garia shook his head. 'How could that possibly work?'

'I don't know,' said Kairi. 'It's just what I've heard.'

I was amused by this exchange between two men who, not

so many days before, had almost ended up killing each other.

'What's got into you, Han?' Garia must have noticed me smiling.

'Nothing,' I replied, slightly embarrassed. 'I was just thinking how good it will be to see Edbersa again.'

'Not to mention Nyxes,' said Garia with a gentle laugh.

I felt the heat of a blush. It was true. Nyxes was very much on my mind.

As we waited, I could see the waves gradually receding from the limit of the bay, coming in and going out, each time encroaching less upon the land. The whole process was mesmerising and I wondered what it would be like to live by the sea, to see and hear this every day.

Sooner than I had anticipated, the waves had abandoned enough of the bay for us to walk across. With cautionary glances skyward, we set off, scrambling over green, slimy rocks until we could walk upon the sand with its curious swirls and ridges formed by the outgoing tide. Fortunately, there were plenty of exposed rocks, some of them as tall as I was, behind which we could hide were Kolak's eagle to make an appearance.

We were perhaps half way across when Kairi saw that very bird soaring into view over a mountain ridge. He signalled to us to take cover but I saw a movement that distracted me. Appearing from the trees on the edge of the bay ahead of us were perhaps five or six children. They had ventured out into the open and were turning over stones in the rock pools looking for crabs and other creatures.

And among them was Nyxes.

They were concentrating so much on their search that none had seen the eagle. But even if they had, they would probably not have considered the bird's significance.

By then we had found cover behind one of the larger rocks and I turned to Kairi. 'They will be seen,' I said, unable to hide the panic in my voice. 'I must make them go back.'

I didn't wait for a response from Kairi but lurched forward, keeping low, darting from rock to rock, some big enough to hide me, others barely up to my knees. I glanced back to see both he and Garia watching anxiously.

I'd barely made half the distance to the children when I heard Nyxes cry out. 'Han! It is Han!'

'Go back,' I shouted. 'There's danger!'

But Nyxes was already hurrying towards me.

I looked up to see the eagle had ended its circling and was swooping towards us.

***

Starlight still illuminated Han's farm as Arkis rose the next morning, intending to begin the day's journeying by first sunlight. As he approached the stockade, he saw that Pelia had risen before him and was feeding hay to Rashi, singing gently just as she did when milking the goats. Arkis hesitated to enter, unwilling to break the spell.

After finishing her song, Pelia rested her head against Rashi's head and stroked her mane. The horse snickered with delight.

'Well,' said Arkis, stepping into the stockade. 'It seems I have a serious rival for my horse's affections.'

Pelia lifted her head. It was too dark even by starlight to see whether she had blushed at his intrusion. 'Rashi is a beautiful horse,' she said.

'I've had her since she was a foal. The most loyal friend a man could wish for.' Arkis joined Pelia and patted Rashi's neck. 'Maybe you would like to ride her,' he said.

Pelia reached down and picked up her milking pail, smiling demurely. 'I cannot,' she said hesitantly.

'Haven't you ridden a horse before?'

'No. We've never had horses, only goats and dogs – though

once, when I was young, we had a cow. I would be afraid of falling off.'

'I shall teach you how to stay on.'

'I don't know.'

'Think about it. I shall be away most of today and will listen to more of your grandfather's story on my return. Maybe tomorrow.'

'I don't know.'

'Maybe I should ask Rashi if she would like you to ride her. She is a lady and sometimes needs to be coaxed, as ladies do.'

'Really?'

'Trust me.'

Arkis leant towards Rashi and spoke softly into her ear, at the same time stroking her mane. After several moments, she began to move her head up and down in the manner of a graceful nod.

Pelia laughed. 'What have you said to her?'

'I asked Rashi if she would like you to ride her – and it is obvious she said yes. Now how can you refuse?'

'We'll see.'

The sun was above the horizon by the time Arkis had saddled Rashi. He coaxed her out of the stockade with a wave towards Pelia, who had begun milking. She smiled back but quickly dipped her head as if regretting doing so.

***

Kairi and Garia were soon at my side just as I reached Nyxes, said Han. I grabbed her arm. 'Kolak's eagle!' I shouted above the sound of the waves.

Nyxes followed my eyes. Her expression indicated she now understood the danger, that Gilgarius would soon be led to us.

'We must get away from here,' I said.

By this time my two companions were urging the other

children back into the shelter of the trees. Nyxes and I followed and we soon found Edbersa, Osbin and the others in a small clearing. Edbersa greeted me with a generous embrace, an expression of relief upon his face. And did I detect tears bubbling in those usually brooding eyes?

'What happened, Han?'

'We left the Castra and the priests fighting,' I said. 'But there's no time to tell you all. We have to get away from here for Gilgarius will soon be upon us.' Then I realised Mulenda was not there, nor any of his warriors.

'They have gone to retrieve the horses,' Edbersa explained.

'Then they will encounter the Castra,' said Garia grimly. 'Or worse, the priests.'

Edbersa pondered a little, pulling at his dense beard. Then he placed a hand upon my shoulder. 'There's nothing we can do about that. We have to think about ourselves – and the children.' He turned to Osbin. 'Tell Han about the boats.'

Osbin said he knew of a fishing village close by that had been deserted after the villagers were driven away by Gilgarius to slave and die in Kolak's gold mines. 'Afterwards, I visited this village with the priests to ensure no one remained,' said Osbin. 'They had all gone and their boats were just left there. It was terrible to see this desertion and even worse to imagine the fate of the villagers. Yet maybe some good can come of it. We can make use of the boats if they are still there.'

'But we must hurry,' I said. 'Gilgarius will surely come now the eagle has seen where we are.'

Edbersa was already gathering the younger children together. 'Come, my young friends,' he said with an incongruous cheerfulness. 'It seems we are going to try our hand at sailing.'

Nyxes watched, distracted by the children's willing response. She turned to me. 'Edbersa is good with the little ones,' she said, apparently shrugging off any thoughts of the danger we faced.

It was true. Although we were in a difficult situation and all surviving in varying degrees of anxiety, it was heartening to see how the youngest children responded to Edbersa. Nyxes said he had spent the whole time waiting for our return telling stories and singing songs to them, sometimes imitating forest animals with his growly voice – anything to keep the children entertained and from thinking about Gilgarius.

I should probably have been surprised to hear this but I remembered what Edbersa had told me about his mother singing to him when he was a boy. I concluded that his gruff manner had been but a crust, perhaps a defence against memories of his own sad family story. Beneath it he was as warm a human being as anyone could be.

I must have smiled for Nyxes looked at me. She reached to cup my chin in her hands. 'What's making you so happy, Han?' she asked, although in the circumstances 'happy' was not the most appropriate description of my state. She must have known thoughts were flitting in my head.

'I was just thinking about Edbersa,' I replied after a little hesitation. 'He would make a wonderful father.'

'What about you, Han?'

'What do you mean?'

'Do you think you could also make a wonderful father?'

I didn't answer, but reached for her hand, giving it a gentle squeeze.

By now the others were gathering up some of the fruit and other food Mulenda's men had left. We set off into the forest with Osbin and Edbersa at our head and the youngest children immediately behind them. Nyxes and I were last to leave the clearing with Arkemis just ahead of us.

Despite the urgency, we hung back a little. I kept hold of Nyxes' hand to steady her as we made our way through the dense vegetation, which conspired to trip us up at every step.

At one point she leaned against me. 'I was afraid I'd never

see you again,' she whispered.

I managed to contrive a reassuring smile. I wanted to say something but couldn't put sound to the words in my head.

Arching back her neck, she kissed me on the cheek, as if telling me she knew what I was struggling with. At that precise moment, Arkemis turned to say something to us. Seeing the kiss appeared to amuse him. He tried but failed to suppress a mischievous smile. 'Be careful, Han,' he said. 'She'll make a husband out of you yet.'

Nyxes pulled away from me, flustered. 'Mind your own business, brother!' she snapped.

After that, she made her own way, purposefully and seeming no longer in need of my support.

Nyxes' sudden anger against Arkemis and her change in demeanour disturbed me, but I had to shut it from my mind. I was being an idiot, thinking of things that should be the furthest from my mind when we were in such a dangerous situation. At that very moment, the eagle would be returning to Kolak and would soon lead Gilgarius to us. Although we were sheltered by the forest, the creature would make short work of tearing up every tree to expose us.

As it happened, the trees began to thin out of their own accord. The sea could be heard once again and, in the gaps between the trees, we could see the waves breaking upon the rocks. We halted at the forest's edge.

'The waves will soon begin their return,' said Osbin. He pointed directly ahead of us across the exposed shore to where a huge arch of rock jutted out into the sea, rising sheer above the waves. 'Beyond there is where the boats will be.' There was a sense of urgency in his voice. He glanced skyward. I shaded my eyes as I, too, ranged the horizon.

Osbin set off with the rest of us following in much the same order as before, picking our way along the shore over exposed rocks and clumps of slimy seaweed.

Once again, Nyxes held back until she resumed her place by my side. She put her arm through mine. 'I'm sorry about before,' she said quietly. 'It's just…'

'Just what?'

She laughed nervously. 'It's just that Arkemis annoys me. He's always annoyed me.'

'He's just being a brother,' I said, wondering for the first time in my life what it would like to have a sister. Would I, too, be an annoying brother?

We left it at that. With our closeness restored, what did it matter what other people said or thought?

By the time we made it to the rock, the incoming tide was lapping around our feet. Passing through the arch, we found ourselves at the edge of a small bay, bound on its three landward sides by wooded cliffs. Osbin pointed to a small stretch of sand on the far shore. 'See there, the fishermen's boats,' he said.

I counted three boats tilted on their sides, their masts jutting out like bare tree branches. The sight fascinated me yet I was afraid. They seemed so insignificant and vulnerable in the face of such a large and unpredictable sea. Could we really use them to escape? Or were we about to exchange one deadly danger for another?

Rather than cross the bay in the open, we skirted its edge, keeping to the shelter of the trees. By the time we reached the other side, the returning tide had half-filled the bay.

None of the boats appeared large enough to carry us all. Indeed, one was so small there would not be enough room for more than two or three of us.

Kyros and Arkemis, who had sailed on the sea with their fishermen fathers, examined the vessels closely and shook their heads at the state of the largest boat, which had a half-repaired hole in its hull. They also rejected the smallest of the three boats because it wouldn't carry us all. The third boat of intermediate size seemed pleasing to them.

'Will it carry all of us?' Edbersa asked.

Kyros shook his head. 'No, but we could tow the small boat behind us. That would give room for everyone and any food we can gather to take with us.'

Everyone agreed.

There were no obvious holes in the chosen vessels but, to make sure the wood was sound, Kyros picked up a rock and tapped the planks in various places. When he seemed satisfied, we all retreated to the shadow of the cliff to await the returning tide and ponder the perilous challenge that lay ahead.

Garia was keen to set sail right away. 'Gilgarius won't follow us,' he said confidently. 'It is said the creature fears the sea.'

'Why is that?' I asked.

'I don't know, but that's what is said.'

'Even so, can we risk it?' asked Kairi.

'We could sail in the dark,' suggested Osbin. 'We know for certain Gilgarius will not fly at night.' He turned to Edbersa. 'What do you think?'

'Both sailing in the light and the dark have their dangers, with or without Gilgarius,' he said.

'Can you sail the boat?' I asked Kyros.

'There is little difference to Caspi boats, so I can't see why not. The hull is sound and shouldn't sink. The sail cloth is good, too.'

We fell into silence as we contemplated the prospect of venturing onto the sea, which at that moment was calm. But what if the gods or monsters beneath it started fighting while we were sailing on the watery roof of their domain? If they resented our intrusion, they could swallow us up, boat, mast, sail and all.

We had not resolved the question of when to sail. Should we venture on to the sea immediately, putting faith in Garia's assertion that Gilgarius was afraid of the sea and would not pursue us? Or would it be better to wait until it was dark because we knew the creature would never take to the skies at night? Yet sailing in the dark had its own perils.

One thing was certain: we risked being assailed by the creature if we remained where we were. It seemed to me that danger lurked whichever option we took. There was no certainty any of us would survive.

After much discussion, we decided we would sail a little before dawn, the precise time to be governed by the incoming tide. The sun was already starting to set and we calculated that if Gilgarius did not seek us now, he would wait until a new day dawned before taking to the sky. By then our voyage would be well under way; we had to trust the creature was truly afraid of the sea and would not follow us.

In silence we ate a little food. I tried not to think of the perils that lay ahead.

Suddenly, there was an exclamation from Kyros. 'Someone's coming!' he said, pointing along the shore.

I followed his gaze to see a tall figure approaching across the sand. It was Drago. Osbin ran to greet him. They exchanged a few hasty words before he led Drago to our hiding place in the shadow of the cliff, where he settled in our midst and took a little food and water.

'Have you been followed?' I asked, looking out anxiously across the bay, then to the sky.

'No,' Drago said, still eating. 'Not by priest, beast or Castra.' Then he shook his head as if trying to make sense of jumbled images in his head.

'What is it?' asked Osbin.

Drago paused to order his thoughts. 'You will not believe what I'm about to tell you,' he said at length. 'I cannot even believe it, though I saw it happen.' Then he commenced his story.

Instead of returning to the priests after Garia and I had left him, Drago remained on the hillside, finding shelter among the bushes where he couldn't be seen but would still be able to observe what was happening below.

By this time, the only Castra remaining were those dead or drowning in the flood water. The priests gathered around Kolak, who was triumphantly holding his orbed staff aloft. Then a strong wind got up and the huge dark shape of Gilgarius rose from behind what was left of the temple mountain and settled upon that building's ruins. The creature began to slaver and grumble and claw at the rock.

'We can all guess who he was searching for,' said Drago, looking directly at me.

The priests and the other guards – none of whom had suffered so much as a scratch in their combat with the hapless Castra – watched the creature's strange behaviour in silence. After a while, Gilgarius appeared to tire of his slavering, grumbling and clawing and he lifted his huge head to bellow across the water, 'The boy, Kolak! Where is the boy?'

Asdur grabbed Kolak's arm and whispered into his ear. It was obvious that the priest had been so preoccupied with disposing of Gostopo and his men that he hadn't noticed our escape.

Gilgarius glowered at Kolak through his one good eye and snorted, 'Once more you promise me the boy, but I cannot see him and I cannot smell him. Where is he?'

'I can only guess what Asdur told Kolak,' said Drago, 'but I am sure it was to reassure the priest that you and your companion had been recaptured and were at that moment being guarded by me upon the hill.'

'Were you not afraid of being discovered?' I asked.

'Of course, Han. My situation was precarious. Kolak immediately shouted an order that you be brought to him. If I was discovered, I would be severely punished, perhaps killed, for allowing your escape. But I was captivated by what was unfolding below me and determined to remain watching for as long as possible.'

Drago said that by this time Gilgarius had become extremely agitated, stamping his huge feet so the ground, the rocks and the trees trembled and the flood water, with its floating bodies of Castra, swelled and boiled.

Then Kolak addressed the creature.

'I could not hear what was said because Kolak's words were lost on the wind, but he must have assured the creature you were close and would be quickly brought.'

We were all hanging on every word, impatient to know what had happened, but Drago paused. No one dared prompt him. After a few moments, he looked directly at me. 'Gilgarius will destroy the world to find you, Han,' he said.

I didn't respond. It was no surprise to hear this. Drago's eyes ranged our entire group, settling upon the smallest of the children. 'None of you will be safe while ever the creature is alive and commanding the skies.'

I asked, 'Did my escape make him angry with the priests?'

'Obviously,' said Drago with the kind of laugh that carries no humour. 'My fellow guards scoured the whole of the hillside, although I managed to evade detection. It soon became clear that you and your companion were truly gone. They must have realised that I was complicit in this and assumed I had fled with you.' Drago stopped speaking and again shook his head.

'When did Gilgarius realise I was no longer there?' I asked.

'Obviously when those sent to fetch you returned without you.'

'What did the creature do?'

'Can't you guess?'

I could indeed. 'I can imagine what the creature is capable of,' I said.

Drago paused, allowing his gaze to take in all of us as if to prepare us for the drama of his coming words. 'Everyone dead,' he said at length. 'Everyone.' He now looked only at Osbin.

'Gilgarius destroyed them all. The priests, our fellow guards and even those few pathetic Castra who had managed to drag themselves from the flood water.'

'Kolak?' This was Garia.

'Yes. Him, too, with Asdur and the Akben priest, Medzurgo. All dead. Despite their collective strength and power, the monster crushed them into the ground like flowers. Kolak was the last to succumb. He fought powerfully, no doubt believing in his own invincibility. He tried to choke Gilgarius with his staff, thrusting the golden orb into his slavering jaws, but it was like attacking the creature with a toothpick. Against such might the priest did not stand a chance; his bones were crunched as though mere sticks and his head devoured in one mouthful.'

We were stunned into a long silence. Even I could hardly comprehend that my plan had worked so wondrously, that the evil priests had been killed. And the Castra, too.

But if we thought Drago had finished with his testimony, we were mistaken. After allowing all he had told us to sink in, he said, 'But that was not an end to the killing.' He paused and looked at each of us in turn, his eyes finally resting on Edbersa.

'Mulenda and his men, swelled by reinforcements, appeared just as Gilgarius finished his murderous attack. They charged from the hills; there must have been a hundred or more of them, fully armed with spears and swords and axes. Whether they thought they were about to confront the Castra or the priests I cannot say, but the only enemy they faced was that terrible creature.'

He didn't need to tell us what happened; it was obvious. Yet he continued, nonetheless. 'They did not stand a chance,' he said. 'Gilgarius destroyed all of those in the attack, tearing them apart like we humans might pull the wings and legs off an insect. Then he flew over the scene of his destruction, picking off those of Mulenda's men who had been left to guard the horses. There was no one left alive.'

'I fear Gilgarius will not rest until he has destroyed us all,' I said.

'But the creature will have to find us first,' said Edbersa.

'And that he will do if we remain here,' I replied. 'I believe Kolak's eagle will lead him here.'

Edbersa was not convinced. 'But with Kolak is dead, who is there to command the bird?'

'Han is right,' said Osbin. 'The eagle was reared from a chick and was trained as soon as it could fly to find Gilgarius whenever Kolak wanted. He did this in the days of mining, when the creature terrorised the mountain villages. I have no doubt the eagle is continuing to act in concert with the beast.'

'The eagle saw us crossing the bay,' I pointed out. 'I've no doubt Gilgarius will follow.'

'Then we must hope the creature is afraid of the sea, as legend supposes,' growled Edbersa.

I doubt any of us slept that night. Nyxes and I found a place a little away from the others and settled into the sand which made a comfortable bed. There were no clouds and the heavens were perfectly lit by a rich display of stars. I felt a warm glow from our closeness as we lay on our backs staring up at the twinkling formations.

'Do you know any star stories?' Nyxes asked.

'Just one. Do you?'

'We were told star stories as children,' she said. 'Our fathers rely on the stars when they go out to sea to fish so they can return safely to our village. They know a lot about them.'

'My mother only told me one story about the stars. I suppose that's because we didn't really need them like your people. We never used to go anywhere.'

'What's it about?'

'Oh, it's about the star children. Do you know it?'

'Star children? No, I don't think I was told about star

children. Will you tell it?'

And so I did.

***

'I believe, Arkis, that I've already told you the story of the star children,' said Han, blinking back a tear.

'Yes, Han. It's a lovely story.'

'That's what Nyxes said. She said she would never forget it.'

Arkis nodded distractedly and made as if to speak, but changed his mind.

Han shook his head and closed his eyes. 'Please forgive me,' he said. 'I am weary and need to sleep.'

'Of course,' said Arkis. 'Maybe you can resume tomorrow, if you feel up to it.'

Arkis went in search of Pelia and found her making cheese. 'As I promised, I shall teach you to ride Rashi tomorrow,' he told her.

'I'm not sure it's a good idea,' she replied with barely a glance towards him.

'And why not?'

Pelia was stirring a pail of milk and kept her eyes firmly on the swirling liquid, which was just starting to curdle. 'Fine horses are not for the likes of me,' she said.

'That's nonsense!'

'It isn't. I'm just being realistic.'

'I see.'

'I'm not sure you do see.'

'Please then, you must explain why you will not learn to ride Rashi.'

Pelia stopped stirring the milk and looked up. With the back of her hand she brushed a wisp of hair from her eyes.

'Go on,' Arkis prompted. 'Tell me why you won't ride Rashi.'

She returned her attention to the curdling milk. Her reply

came almost in a whisper. 'Because I might like it too much.'

Arkis tried to find a reply but stopped himself before turning and walking away.

***

Before dawn we all gathered by the boats, said Han. Our first task was to get them closer to the water by dragging and pushing them. For the larger boat this required the involvement of all of us, even the youngest children, who were cajoled and encouraged by Edbersa. The smaller vessel, which we loaded with as much food and as many gourds of freshwater as we had collected, was hauled alongside it.

Once Kyros and Arkemis were satisfied with the position of the boats, we could do nothing but sit and eat some of the fruit while we waited for the incoming tide. Nyxes and I remained together the whole of this time, talking quietly so no one else would hear.

Once the tide began to float the boats, Edbersa and Osbin lifted up the youngest children. Nyxes climbed in with them, offering reassuring hugs and soothing words as they settled at the prow. I desperately wanted to remain close to her but, as the last person to climb on, the entire length of the boat separated us.

The boat couldn't have taken another person and, with our combined weight, it no longer floated. To ease the burden, Kairi and I climbed into the small boat, which had been attached by a rope and was floating freely. We all waited anxiously for the tide to lift the larger boat from the sand once more. Meanwhile, Kyros and Arkemis seemed unconcerned and were already raising the sail, impressing me with their confidence as they skilfully worked ropes and tied complex knots.

My concern was the wind, which was not coming directly from the shore behind us but across the bay. It seemed impossible that such an ill-directed wind could take us out to sea. Nor, in my opinion, was it blowing with enough force to move a heavily laden boat with another one in tow. Yet Kyros and Arkemis remained unworried. Indeed, they seemed exhilarated by our enterprise as they tugged at ropes and used a pole to turn the sail this way and that way to test how the cloth might catch the wind.

Very quickly the boat began to move. I couldn't believe it was happening. The wind wasn't behind us, yet our companions' skills were such that the boat caught enough of it to ensure that we went where we desired to go. The turning tide helped, of course. We'd boarded close to its highest point and both boats were now in deep enough water and being carried along by its retreat from the shore.

The sun rose quickly and, apart from a few isolated clouds, the sky was clear. But my joy at getting underway soon turned to discomfort as the motion of the small boat upon the waves left me feeling ill. Kairi, crouched next to me, looked to be suffering no ill effects, but on the larger boat I could see some of the others looking the way I felt. Edbersa, in particular, had ceased growling words of encouragement to the youngest children and was now gripping the rim of the boat, staring blankly ahead of him.

Arkemis realised what was happening. 'Concentrate on the horizon and it will stop you feeling sick,' he shouted.

My own horizon-staring was not out to sea but upon the shore we'd just left. I was as much on edge as I'd ever been, convinced that every large seabird I saw swooping low over the breaking waves was Kolak's eagle or that every dark cloud rising over the mountain tops was Gilgarius.

As the mountains grew smaller, I began to feel less anxious and to believe we'd finally escaped the monster's claws. I convinced myself he had not made an appearance because he was truly afraid of the sea. And with each gust of wind, my confidence grew. We were now being carried across the waves at such surprising speed I dared to hope we would reach the safety of the far-off shore without incident.

But I was a fool to put my faith in hope; a fool to believe Gilgarius could not try to thwart our escape. I should have realised the monster was so desperate to wreak revenge upon me, he would disregard any fear he might have of the sea. I'd humiliated him too many times; I should have known that his desire for retribution had grown beyond any sense he might have possessed.

As you can probably imagine, Arkis, I've relived this perilous time over and over throughout my long years. I remember each thought and every fear as if they first entered my head only this morning.

Many terrible images invade my mind but the one that I recall most vividly, that haunts me even to this day awake or dreaming, is that of Gilgarius rising above the distant mountain and fanning a great wind with his huge wingbeats as he comes to find me.

I cursed Kolak's eagle.

Had Gilgarius not learned we'd taken to the sea, he might have flown forlornly along the deserted shore, his one-eyed vision hampering his search for us. In his anger and frustration, he might have torn up huge swathes of forest, demolished more mountains but, for all his desperation, he would likely not have ventured after us over those turbulent waves had it not been for that eagle.

As you probably know, Arkis, eagles have the best eyesight of any bird so they can see small prey from great heights. Without this help, Gilgarius might never have strayed from the land, might never have been tempted to conquer his own fear of the sea – if indeed he'd ever been truly afraid of the sea. And he might never have sought to fulfil his desperate quest to acquaint me with his digestive juices.

I cursed that eagle, Arkis. From the moment I saw it appear, as if out of nowhere, soaring high over us then circling back over the land to pass intelligence to the monster, I cursed that terrible bird.

We were out of sight of the shore when the creature cast his huge shadow over us, his powerful wingbeats fanning the waves, whipping them up as if a storm. Our boats tossed and dipped and rolled as Gilgarius circled us, his solitary eye searching for me. It seemed I had no chance of escape for if the monster didn't have me, the sea surely would.

In the larger boat the youngest children began to cry with fear when they realised Gilgarius was pursuing us.

I grabbed Kairi's arm. 'Go, friend!' I shouted. 'Get back with the others. Leave me on this boat and cast it free.'

'No, Han! I cannot.'

'You must! You have to help save the children. Gilgarius is only interested in me.'

'You're wrong.'

'If I am, there's nothing to lose. I'll ask him to consume me on the shore. It may be enough to satisfy him or it will at least delay him and give you all a chance. But if I'm wrong, and he does come back for the rest of you, we've neither gained nor lost.'

Kairi reached to take hold of me. 'No, Han!'

I rolled away from him and stood up unsteadily, gripping the side of the pitching boat. 'Then I shall throw myself into the sea.'

I don't know how long it took for Kairi to realise what he had to do, for time seemed to stand still even as the sea tossed and rolled. Then Gilgarius let out a terrible roar and I knew he'd seen me. 'Go!' I shouted to Kairi. 'He's coming.'

And sure enough, the creature's shadow grew ever blacker as he descended to take me. Kairi hesitated too long; before he could leap free, Gilgarius had taken our little boat in his claws as if a plucking a fish from a lake.

But we were still attached by rope to the larger boat, whose stern was already lifting out of the water. Almost in one movement, Kairi drew his knife and severed the tow rope with a powerful blow. Instantly, we were borne skywards, clinging to the boat and each other for life as Gilgarius glared at us through his good eye and bathed us in his pungent breath.

'This time, boy, you are truly mine!' he roared.

'Jump!' shouted Kairi. 'We must take our chance with the sea!'

It was, perhaps, sound advice; to drown would be better than having your bones crunched. But I knew that if Gilgarius took me to shore it would give the others time and a chance to stay alive. Would the monster do this? Or would he devour me there above the sea, in flight and within sight of my terrified companions?

Even to this day, I don't know why Gilgarius acted the way he did. Why did he delay returning to land, where he could have crunched my bones at leisure. Perhaps he believed this time there was no way I could escape, that I was a prize to savour and flaunt, a singular triumph to make up for all the past humiliations.

Whatever was going on in the creature's head can never be fathomed, of course. All I do know is that Gilgarius caged me in his claws and I was drawn upwards towards his gaping mouth. His huge fangs bared, ready to tear me apart, while beneath me the little boat spun wildly as it plunged towards the sea, ejecting Kairi and the rest of its contents in the process.

I prepared to meet my fate, to be drawn into that terrible mouth, to be entombed and suffocated and pierced within a slavering cave. Perhaps, if I was lucky, the creature's poisonous breath would render me unconscious so I wouldn't feel the pain and hear my own bones crunching inside me. I would face death with fear – I was a boy in a constant state of fear – but I would also die with defiance. So I kept my eyes open and, for the second time in my all too-young life, stared into the gullet of hell.

Oddly, I was fleetingly distracted by a glint of gold. I saw that it had come from Kolak's golden orb, which was wedged between two of the creature's molars. Even in the face of death I took solace in this reminder that the evil priest had already passed the same way to be digested. So much for everlasting life.

But as you can plainly see, Arkis, I'm here now telling you my story so it's obvious that death did not take me. I was not drawn into that foul mouth to follow Kolak; I was not entombed and suffocated and pierced within the slavering cave. I wasn't even rendered unconscious by Gilgarius's poisonous breath.

So, what saved me? What caused the creature to free me suddenly from his grip before he could crunch me in his jaws? If you will bear with me, Arkis, I'll explain the sequence of events so you will learn them in the order I experienced them.

My salvation began when a huge wall of water rose up, as if an undersea Mother Mountain had erupted and lifted the waves into the sky. Gilgarius's claws unclasped and the creature let out a painful screech as I was hurled into the air to fall, spinning into the turbulent water. I sank as a rock would but fought through the swirling, rolling sea to regain the surface. It was like climbing a waterfall with nothing solid to cling to.

I floundered, arms flailing, unsure of where was up and where was down, until a strong hand clamped over my arm. I felt myself drawn through the water until I broke the surface, fighting for breath within Kairi's grip. 'Hold on!' he shouted.

I wrapped an arm around his neck and Kairi started swimming, even though it was virtually impossible to do so in such a violent sea. It quickly became clear that we would sink together if we stayed like that, so I let go of Kairi and tried to strike out on my own.

As you know, Arkis, I'd never learned to swim except out of necessity and then only for a short distance. This time I had no idea how long I must swim for. Could I make it all the way to the shore? I would almost certainly drown. I couldn't help but think it was a most cruel irony that I had escaped Gilgarius's jaws only to face being consumed by the waves. I determined that would not happen and fought to stay afloat.

I hadn't got far when I saw Kairi waving an arm to indicate he had located a saviour – our little boat, which was miraculously floating the right way up. Kairi reached it quickly, clinging on while I caught up. We scrambled aboard and made it just in time, for the precarious craft was suddenly thrust skyward on top of another huge swell.

From this elevated position we quickly learned the true cause of the sea's violent eruption. This was no submerged Mother Mountain but a giant creature that had risen out of the sea and now locked Gilgarius in a death struggle. An enormous sea monster!

Gilgarius was huge but this creature from the depths was half his size again, with a jagged ridge of peaks running along its back and on to its enormous head. Its tail thrashed in the water; its claws, the thickness of chatka branches, were holding Gilgarius in an unyielding grip, preventing him from rising into the air.

Gilgarius screeched pitifully, desperately clinging to the sky with his giant wingbeats, but the sea dragon gripped his head in its huge jaws. It was an unequal struggle; the more my erstwhile opponent fought, the less he was able to resist the sea monster's greater strength.

In moments Gilgarius was floundering on the surface, his head still held in the jaws of this greater adversary. But my old enemy fought to the end, thrashing the waves with his sodden wings in a futile bid to resist being dragged beneath them. It was a vain struggle.

Kairi and I watched in awe, clinging to our precarious little boat as Gilgarius, now half-submerged, ceased his resistance.

My last image of that hated creature before he was hauled to his undersea hell was a solitary eye staring at me in abject fear. I couldn't help but think of the frightened eyes of all the children the monster had devoured.

Justice was finally done. I'd escaped once more from the jaws of Gilgarius – and this time would be the last. But my relief was not joyful for, though Kairi and I had survived in the most miraculous way imaginable, we faced a new and terrible reality. We were alone, surrounded by an empty expanse of water.

We stood unsteadily in the boat to get a better view, holding on to each other to counter the rolling, but there was nothing to see in any direction. There was, Arkis, no sign of the other boat or anyone who had been in it. While our little craft had miraculously kept afloat, the violent eruption of the sea, now subsiding, had swamped the larger boat and sent our friends to join Gilgarius in his watery grave.

Kairi and I didn't speak, so gripped were we in shock and disbelief. Overcome by emotion, I repeated Nyxes' name over and over in my mind. I can only imagine what Kairi was thinking.

But, in spite of our distress, we couldn't remain like that, alone in middle of a sea, floating aimlessly and waiting for fate to deal us another blow. What if the sea monster returned? We had to make it to the shore; grieving would be for later.

Our boat had no sail and no paddles, and I feared we could easily be dragged further out to sea by ill-favoured currents and winds. By now the sun was high, its heat beating down upon us unmercifully. In the boat there was no way to escape and we had no food or water. Thirst was already taking hold of me. Instinctively, I reached over the side and scooped my hand to take a little water to drink.

'Don't!' Kairi gripped my wrist. 'Drink that and you'll die,' he said. 'Don't you know about seawater?'

I shook my head.

'It will make you even more thirsty.'

'What can we do?' I asked.

'I don't know,' said Kairi. 'We must think.'

We sat down, facing each other across the width of the boat, and pondered our newly perilous situation. I tried not to believe that Nyxes and everyone else had perished and I kept checking the sea in all directions for any sign they might have survived. My heart was heavy.

After a while the blazing heat got the better of me and I fell asleep. When I woke, Kairi wasn't there but I could hear the gentle lapping of water and feel the boat in motion. I scrambled to the prow to see him in the sea, swimming with slow purposeful strokes, his arms taking it in turns to blade the water, a taut rope tied around his naked body, pulling the boat along.

I shouted his name and he stopped swimming, spinning in the water to face me. 'It's the only way,' said Kairi.

'But I can help,' I said. 'You can't do this on your own.'

'I need you to watch out for me. Tell me when you see land.'

'How do you know we're going in the right direction?'

By now Kairi was swimming on his back, sweeping with both arms and legs. 'Don't fret, Han, we'll make it,' he said. 'The sun is guiding me.'

Night began to fall without any sight of land. Kairi was exhausted and I helped him back on the boat. He stretched along its length, saying he would sleep a little; the boat would have to drift. Eventually I, too, fell asleep, thinking of Nyxes, my mother and father and all I had lost.

I would have cried but I was so dry I had no tears.

Dawn was just about breaking when Kairi shook me awake. The first thing I noticed was that the boat had stopped floating freely. A scraping sound could be heard beneath us and the water was growling around us. 'It seems we have found land,' said Kairi, peering over the side.

I sat up. True enough, the boat had foundered on a stony shore, driven by a miraculously favourable wind and tide. I felt relief but little joy as we clambered out, eager to find food and fresh water.

But where were we? Not where we had sailed from, that was clear. We were grounded at the mouth of a narrow inlet with towering rock walls bathed in rich, cascading vegetation. Kairi climbed a little way to find a place where freshwater seeped through the plants. He signalled me to join him and we eagerly cupped the water in our hands to drink.

When our thirst was satisfied, we sat and stared out to sea, each of us imprisoned in our own thoughts and certainly not able to celebrate our miraculous survival after losing so much.

'We can't stay here' said Kairi after a while.

I started to sob, unable to hold back an overwhelming feeling of despair.

Kairi draped an arm around my shoulder. 'We're safe from enemies now,' he said.

'But what shall we do? Where shall we go?'

Kairi simply shook his head and settled into silence. I decided not to prompt him further.

I don't know how long we remained like that. I knew we would have to leave even though part of me wanted to stay as close as I could to my lost companions: Nyxes, who should have lived to become my wife; Edbersa, that gruff bear of a man whom I'd grown to love like my own father; noble Garia and my new friends, especially Arkemis, who could have been the brother I'd never had.

Eventually Kairi dragged me to my feet. 'Come, Han, we must find food.'

He was right. Hunger was gnawing at me and, while we

might find fruit to help sustain us, we desperately needed meat. Kairi still had his knife to hunt with, though I doubted it would be as effective as a spear when it came to bringing down a ledbuk. But at least it gave us a chance.

We decided our best hope was to stay as close to the sea as possible; that way, if we couldn't find ledbuk or kolaki, we might be able to search for crabs and other creatures among the rocks. But which direction should we take? Should we keep the sea to our left or our right? I don't suppose it mattered too much to Kairi where we went because he was used to wandering, but I desired to return to my Akben home. I said as much.

'Very well, Han,' said Kairi. 'To head that way, we must go where the sun comes from.'

Our journey started slowly as we foraged for fruits among stands of trees that came close to the shoreline. They offered very little, so we began searching among rocks freshly exposed by the outgoing tide. I managed to catch two crabs while Kairi busied himself prising shell creatures from the slimy rocks. We didn't waste time trying to make a fire but ate everything raw. 'When sea meat is fresh it's safe to eat without cooking,' said Kairi by way of reassurance.

We resumed our journey when the sun was at its highest, but there were plenty of trees to shade us. We'd barely gone a league when we heard a piercing screech that drowned out all other sound.

I looked up to Kolak's eagle hovering above us. I felt anger well inside me. 'Why is that evil bird following us?'

Kairi shook his head. 'I don't know. Let's keep moving and see what she does.'

We carried on our journey with the eagle watching us, sometimes circling, sometimes hovering, occasionally swooping low as though we might be its intended prey. Then, after seeming to tire of its aerial activities, the bird flew out of view and I assumed that would be the last we would see of the cursed creature.

We made good progress along the shore, especially when the tide was out and we could walk on firm wet sand. As we covered league after league, the land became less steep and forested and sloped more gently. During this journey we saw not one human and I assumed all the people been driven from the land, or perhaps been killed by Gilgarius at the behest of the priests.

As the sun began to hide beyond distant hills Kolak's eagle reappeared, this time ahead of us. It swooped low over our heads and I was sure it was about to attack us but, instead of falling like a stone and digging its talons into our skulls, the bird gave out a chattering call. This was accompanied by a thudding noise just behind us. We spun round to see a dead kolaki on the ground.

The eagle circled again before settling upon the branch of a tree, bobbing its head and making a strange sound as if trying to tell us something.

Kairi picked up the kolaki. 'The eagle has brought us a gift,' he said.

'But why?'

'I don't know, Han. Maybe it's sorry for what happened, what it did by leading Gilgarius to us.'

'You mean it's trying to be friends?'

'Maybe. Would you want that bird as a friend?'

'No,' I said emphatically. 'I could never befriend such a creature.'

'What about its gift of food?'

'It would choke me.'

Nevertheless, Kairi held on to the kolaki. 'If you won't eat it, then there's more for me,' he said.

I felt betrayed at his words. This bird had caused the loss of our companions; surely Kairi understood that.

We walked on in silence until darkness fell. We found a

place among the rocks, sheltered from the cool breeze blowing off the sea. Kairi set himself aside from me and fashioned a fire to cook the kolaki. Even though I could smell its enticing flesh as he roasted it on heated stones, even though I salivated and my body desired to feast upon the eagle's gift, I resisted reaching out to take even a morsel. I ate a little of the fruit we had gathered and eventually fell asleep to confront my nightmares.

When I awoke, Kairi was nowhere to be seen. I was alone and immediately believed he had despaired of me and returned to his ways of wandering. How would I survive?

I rose and walked down to where the sea washed upon the shore. I saw the eagle perched upon a large round boulder, watching me, taunting me. I wanted to kill that bird, to catch it and drag it into the water and drown it just as Nyxes and all my other companions had been drowned.

I was about to act on this unrealistic whim when, from the corner of my eye, I saw the shadow of a human form cast by the strong morning sun. It was Kairi. He said, 'Han, you must not blame a natural creature for the evils of men.'

I did not reply.

Kairi crouched by my side. 'It's just a bird,' he said.

Again, no response from me.

Kairi put a hand upon my shoulder and I tried to shrug it away, but he gripped me hard. 'Have you not thought why the eagle might be seeking to help us?'

'No. Why would it?'

'It needs us. The bird has grown up in human company, trained to do human bidding.'

I turned to face Kairi. 'I thought you'd left me.'

'I couldn't do that,' he said.

We remained like that in silence for a while, the eagle watching us, moving its head from side to side.

'We should forgive the bird its past allegiances,' Kairi said at length.

'But I don't know how to forgive.'

The eagle stretched out its wings and fanned them so it rose a little into the air, then it settled once more, dancing with its feet upon the rock.

'So you believe birds are capable of being evil,' said Kairi, his voice and manner patient.

'That one is,' I said, pointing.

'But what of other animals, Han? When wolves hunt a defenceless ledbuk fawn are they being evil? Is it evil for a bear to open up a kolaki nest with its eager paws and consume the still-blind kittens?'

'No. Of course not,' I said. 'They are doing it to survive.'

'Then what is it to be evil, Han?' His words confused me.

'I don't know. I only know if it hadn't been for that bird, we wouldn't have lost our friends.'

More silence followed, intolerable silence, and I couldn't stand it. I turned to Kairi, reaching out to place a hand upon his arm as if I needed to remake a bridge between us. 'What you're saying is that humans are the only living things capable of being evil.'

'That is precisely what I'm saying, Han.'

'But what about Gilgarius? He was no human, but we all know he was evil.'

'Perhaps he's an exception. But even so, I would say it was more that he was used evilly by the priests, the very people who should decry all evil acts. In every other respect, Gilgarius was simply an animal that liked to eat human children.'

'But to do that is still wrong.'

Kairi's laugh was joyless. 'Wrong, maybe, from the way we see it but not evil, Han. As you know, a bear or a pack of wolves will readily eat a human child if there's no one to protect it. It's the way of the animal world.'

But I didn't readily see Gilgarius as animal. For a start, he could speak like a human; he could argue and justify his actions and, as I'd already learned, he could teach us lessons about our own faults and frailties. Where, then, is evil spawned?

Unprompted, Kairi seemed to provide an answer. 'You see, Han, it's not evil for an animal to kill a human to survive, nor for a human to kill an animal for the same reason. It's not even evil when an animal kills one of its own kind, as sometimes they do. But humans are higher beings, and if one person kills another without justification then that's an evil act. In other words, the ability to be evil is a purely human thing.'

I thought a while about that and Kairi waited patiently for my response. 'Well,' he prompted finally. 'Are you prepared to forgive the eagle and accept her help?'

If Kairi was right and evil is a purely human thing, it was clear I should acknowledge that other creatures who share this world with us merely act out of instinct. They are unable to control their nature and, therefore, ought not to be condemned for doing so.

I got to my feet. 'I don't know,' I said, almost beneath my breath.

As Kairi and I resumed our unpredictable journey, I didn't look back to see if the eagle was watching us but I knew it would follow. Even so, I would refuse to eat any fare it cared to bring to us.

We kept to the shore for two more days, living mainly off sea flesh foraged from rock pools. Sometimes we found streams tumbling out of the forest that provided us with fresh water. Most of the time the heat bore down on us, so we were forced to shelter among the trees when the sun was at its highest. We slept at night, listening to the tide washing upon the shore, watching the stars, keeping our innermost thoughts to ourselves.

The eagle did follow us and occasionally brought offerings of creatures it had caught. Once we saw it pluck a large flapping fish from the sea, which it dropped at our feet and which Kairi ate raw. Although desperate to eat flesh, I could not bring myself to share it.

All this time we saw no human, which showed how extensive the evil of Kolak's priests had spread. On our fourth day we turned inland, walking upon higher ground where we saw more birds and animals than on the shore. The eagle hunted them for itself and for Kairi, who did his best to get me to eat something from the offerings, but I couldn't relent.

Then, early one morning it began to rain and didn't stop the entire day and most of the night. We were forced to find refuge beneath an overhang of rock at the base of a cliff, which was partially shielded by bushes and bracken. Everything around was so wet that there was no prospect of starting a fire, so we huddled together, hungry and shivering, talking to keep up our spirits until we were too exhausted to resist sleep.

We woke to find ourselves overlooking a sunlit plain and our spirits rose. The eagle brought a tiny ledbuk fawn, which Kairi immediately commenced to gut and skin, throwing the bird some of the less appetising pieces of flesh as a reward.

As he worked I explored a little, scrambling about the higher bushes to distract myself from the thought of meat and to collect whatever fruits and berries might be available. It was then I saw something below us in the far distance, something rising over a ridge in the plain like a wave rolling on to the shore. As it got closer, I realised this was an army of men on horseback, their spears and shields flickering like flames in the sunlight.

I scrambled back down to Kairi. 'Castra are coming!' I yelled. 'We must not let them find us.'

It was understandable, perhaps, that I was nervous and distrusting given all that had happened.

Kairi shared my concern. 'Stay here,' he said. 'I'll take a closer look.'

He set off down the hill, leaving me alone with the eagle, which was perched on a shelf protruding from the rock face, preening itself. But soon the bird took to the sky and disappeared in the same direction as Kairi

I wished my friend had taken me with him and I was contemplating whether to follow when I heard the rustle of bushes to one side of me. I turned to see four horses emerge from the foliage, three of them carrying fully-armed warriors and one packhorse being led. Two of them quickly dismounted, while the other warrior remained in the saddle, thrusting his spear towards me.

It was obvious from their appearance and weapons that these were Castra. As I faced their spears, I recognised two of them from my initial capture. I wondered how they could have escaped Gilgarius and acquired four horses. Then I realised that one of them – the packhorse – was Melemari.

The mare snickered when she recognised me and reared a little, but one of the Castra drew his sword and beat her across the flanks. An image of Garia flashed in my mind. If he had been there, that man would not have survived a moment longer.

Another rider slid from his mount and came over to me, prodding my ribs with the point of his spear. He grabbed my arm, squeezing my flesh hard, then he turned to his companions and said something in their native tongue. They all laughed.

My first thought was they were proposing to kill and eat me and I stood there, frozen with fear, when I should have at least tried to flee. Well, Arkis, you can imagine the profound sense of hopelessness I felt. I'd managed to escape the jaws of Gilgarius, only to find myself being sized up as a meal for the Castra. Yet it seemed this prospect might be delayed as one of the men grabbed the butchered ledbuk fawn and, with a laugh, threw it across the neck of his mount.

I looked around in the hope that Kairi would suddenly

appear from the trees to rescue me; I even contemplated calling his name but I realised doing so could put him in danger. Brave as he was, he would not be able to take on three fully-armed adversaries.

I was dragged towards Melemari and made to climb on to her, sharing her back with the burden she already bore. She whinnied pathetically, as though lamenting the plight we both found ourselves in. The Castra bound my head and body so tightly to her with rough vine that I could scarcely move.

Dread mounted inside me as I was led away, unable even to cry out. And so began another terrible journey.

***

Pelia was sitting close to the top of the knoll behind the farm as the goats foraged around her. Just like on that first day of the traveller's arrival, when her grandfather had started to tell his story, she could see Arkis reclining against his saddle, listening intently.

Over the days little had changed in that scene, except Han's breaks from storytelling had become more frequent as the effort of reliving the painful past took a toll on his health. But Pelia knew that nothing would stop her grandfather from completing his story as long as he had breath in his body.

Even so, during the middle of the previous night when he was in particular distress and coughing up blood, she had pleaded with him to stop. 'You are killing yourself, grandfather,' she said, as she washed away the bloody sputum he had coughed into his hands.

'I am dying anyway,' Han replied. 'Telling my story is the only thing that's keeping me going. I have to tell it to the end – whether Arkis deserves to hear it or not.'

Pelia had risen that morning determined to ask Arkis to leave so her grandfather would have no reason to carry on. But, when she saw their visitor, she could not bring herself to do so. Her grandfather needed Arkis and in a way she did too. He had brought the outside world into their little farm; for Pelia nothing would ever be the same again.

Yet she harboured some measure of suspicion. Maybe when her grandfather's story was ended, she would have the courage to demand of Arkis that he tell a story of his own – one that revealed why he had really journeyed to Akbenna. Pelia knew that their visitor had at least one secret and it truly worried her. It was something she'd witnessed, some odd ritual she had never seen before, which led to a fear that Arkis was just like all the others – her mother, her father, Gorman and everyone else in the village and the surrounding farms.

As she watched Arkis reclining against his saddle, listening intently to her father, Pelia desperately wanted to believe he was not feigning interest in her grandfather's story merely to find clues to get what he really wanted. Gold.

***

The horses were coaxed along the base of the cliff, said Han. And then we went higher, away from the plain, away from Kairi. I feared the more distance was put between us, the harder it would be for him to find me, even though any prospect of rescue truly appeared hopeless.

My only comfort was being so close to Melemari, which brought me closer to Garia. I whispered to her that we would get out of this, that Kairi would come to find us, and she snorted and tossed her head as if she understood my words.

We halted when the sun was at its highest, beating mercilessly upon my back. I was unbound and dragged from Melemari. I was desperate for water but, like before, I was given none and knew once again I would have to suckle sweat from the horse's neck when our journey resumed. However, my discomfort was eased when I was hauled into the shade of a large tree to which I was bound by a vine. It was, perhaps, a sign they wanted to keep me alive.

That's when a thought occurred to me: they must surely know who I was. Could their plan be to use me in some kind of trade? Maybe in the hope of gaining some of the gold that had evaded them? Perhaps these Castra didn't know their comrades and leader had all been killed and the gold they craved was buried beneath a mountain of rock in the flooded valley.

The men ate some bread they carried with them and drank from a gourd but offered me nothing. Ultimately, I expected to be killed. Even if the Castra didn't eat me, there would be no reason to keep me alive once they realised there was no golden reward.

Faced with this new danger, I couldn't see any way out. I had no hint of an ingenious plan to fashion my escape. Also, I had very little fight left in me after enduring so much in such a short space of time. I would probably have to resign myself to a terrible end. My only consolation was that because death had taken Nyxes, through my own death we would be reunited.

I dozed off and only woke when the Castra dragged me to my feet. Once again I was strapped to Melemari's back and the wretched journey resumed.

My captors seemed to be in no hurry and I realised they must believe we were not being followed. The thought distressed me, for it could only mean one thing – they'd encountered and killed Kairi before capturing me. The thought was both terrifying and confusing. I was now alone, the only survivor of all those I'd travelled with or befriended on my mission. It seemed ironic that the purpose of my journey was to bring peace and harmony between neighbouring peoples and I had ended up seeing little more than death and destruction.

Soon my own death would complete the picture and there would be no one left to tell the story. Except as you can see,

Arkis, and as I have pointed out before, I did live to tell the tale.

So, what happened?

Well, it was obvious that at some point my captors would have to find somewhere to camp for the night. We'd already crossed a range of hills from which we descended steeply along a grassy track until we reached a fast-flowing river. We followed its bank until we encountered an outcrop of rock where we halted. Presumably this was chosen because it would give some shelter from the cool breeze that had begun to blow off the hills. I was hauled from Melemari's back and my hands and legs bound.

A fire was made and the ledbuk fawn cooked on heated stones, just like Kairi would have done. While the Castra busied themselves, I took in the surroundings. We were on a broad treeless plain, surrounded by distant rolling hills. The sun was descending rapidly and a bank of clouds had blown in, drawing an eerie gloom towards us.

It was then I saw it – Kolak's eagle. Or should I say Kairi's eagle, for it had obviously established a special relationship with my companion. The bird occupied a part of the sky not yet taken over by cloud so I saw it clearly, silhouetted against the orange glow of the sunset.

It's strange, Arkis. The sight of the creature I had once dreaded now brought me an odd sense of comfort. It could have been any eagle, of course, but somehow by its behaviour – its way of hovering, plainly watching us – it was clear to me which bird this was. The Castra were too busy focusing upon their feast to notice our aerial visitor. Then, as quickly as it came, the eagle flew off.

The Castra offered me not a morsel of the ledbuk fawn and I fell asleep, hungry but somehow strangely calm. Dawn had barely broken and it was raining when I was roughly shaken from my sleep and bound to Melemari at the point of a spear.

We crossed the river where it ran wide and shallow and followed the steadily rising open ground. Soon the rain cleared and once again the sun's heat relentlessly beat down upon me.

All this time I'd spoken no word to the Castra: no protestation at my treatment; no condemnation of their evil ways, and no demand for my immediate release from their bonds. It was as if I were resigned to certain death.

Believing this state was soon to come, I felt strangely at peace. I was, as I have already said, exhausted both in body and mind and truly wished it could all end. Not that I would have shunned salvation; I simply couldn't imagine being rescued and did not want to burden my weakened thoughts with a hope that could so easily be dashed.

Whether Melemari sensed my thoughts and feelings I can only guess, but she snickered and snorted and occasionally swayed her head from side to side, as if frustrated at being roped to the horse in front when she would far rather be cantering free across the open grassland. Whatever the reason, the movement of her head rocked me gently like a baby in its mother's arms.

I was asleep when the eagle struck.

The bird screeched as it descended out of nowhere, and I felt the caress of its feathers as it swept over my head. My eyes opened in time to see the bird's splayed talons striking the head of the rider directly in front of me, its claws immediately drawing blood from the man's scalp. The rider screamed in pain and his horse reared in confusion. Then the eagle rose once more into the air and circled before repeating its assault, this time upon the horse's rump. The animal bucked wildly, throwing its rider to the ground.

The other Castra appeared stunned by the eagle's work and their horses whinnied pitifully as the bird continued rising and swooping and threatening with its vicious talons. The Castra lashed out with sword and spear but the eagle proved too quick and agile to be caught by them.

Only Melemari and I were spared harassment, so the eagle's purpose was obvious. I dug my heels into the mare's flanks. 'Fly, Melemari!' I shouted.

And she needed no more of an entreaty. As the eagle continued harrying the Castra, Melemari reared and snapped the rope that tied her to the lead horse. She set off across the grassland, true to her name and flying like the wind.

I was so firmly lashed to her that there was no fear I would fall off but, of course, I had no idea where we were heading. I simply had to trust Melemari knew what she was doing and that the eagle would continue harrying the Castra to delay any pursuit.

It didn't take long for us to cross the open plain and move into a gently rising bank of trees. Melemari must have sensed we were out of danger because she slowed to a walk. Soon we came upon a stream, where the mare halted to take a drink.

I, too, was desperate to slake my thirst but was obviously unable free myself from her back. Her thirst satisfied, Melemari continued up the bank, following the stream, picking her way deliberately. The ground rose more steeply and I could see the stream cascading over ever-larger boulders. Before long I heard a much louder rush of water and knew it to be the sound of a waterfall.

What happened next, Arkis, I've never been able to satisfactorily explain but Melemari must have known that I was in danger of dying of thirst if she did not devise a means of helping me. Without hesitation, she entered the stream, which was now flowing very fast, and carefully, surefootedly, made her way towards the deafening sound of the waterfall. By then the spray was dancing over me and I could feel the cool, sweet water upon my face. I reached as much with my tongue as I was able, though at that point you couldn't call it drinking. Then Melemari changed her stance until she was positioned across the width of the stream. Slowly moving sideways, she eased us into the cascading water, which soaked me in a moment. I twisted my head as much as I could and drank my fill, while Melemari held steadfast against the torrent.

After my thirst was satisfied, I gently squeezed my heels into her flanks. 'Can you find Kairi?' I asked her, desperately hoping rather than really believing he was still alive.

The mare snorted and picked her way carefully from the stream, retracing our way downhill and back to the open grassland. She hesitated before leaving the cover of the trees, as if wary that the Castra might have tracked us. But, though I couldn't see properly to confirm it, there appeared to be no evidence of their presence at that point.

Melemari grazed upon some bushes as I contemplated my new situation. Unless we found a friendly person to free me, there was still a chance I could end up dead upon the mare's back. Human contact of the right kind was urgently needed so, after allowing a short time for Melemari to browse and with the encouragement of soft words and the gentle prompting of my heels, we set off again.

Melemari kept at walking pace, following the edge of the plain where occasional tree cover was to be found to shade me from the worst heat of the sun. Soon the motion lulled me to sleep – but not for long.

This time I was woken by the clamour of shouts, then came the whistle and zip of arrows flying close to my head. Melemari reared and set off at a gallop. My bound position limited my vision but I could hear the thunder of hooves behind us.

Melemari didn't need encouragement to flee. I felt sure she would beat our pursuers in a test of speed but no way could she outpace a speeding arrow. We'd barely gone half a league when I heard more shouts, this time ahead of us, and I feared we were about to be cut off by other Castra.

Arrows soon flew overhead from this different position,

yet Melemari didn't swerve to change direction. Instead she seemed to gallop directly towards those who were firing them. I couldn't believe that, after she had done so much to save me, this wonderful horse was about to commit a terrible act of betrayal and deliver me directly to the enemy.

Such seemed to be confirmed when Melemari slowed to a canter and then a trot. I dug my heels into her flanks to make her go faster but she continued decreasing her speed until we were barely above walking pace. Suddenly, I felt a swift movement close by. A hand grabbed at my bound arm and I tried to wrestle it free, though within the confines of my bonds it was an ineffectual resistance.

Then I heard a familiar voice. 'Han! It's me, Kairi!'

I have to confess, Arkis, that I immediately wept.

After I was unbound and able to slide from Melemari's back, Kairi held me in a relieved embrace. 'You're safe now, Han,' he said. 'We're among friends.'

He released me so I could see what he meant. I'd been so overcome with joy at our reunion, and my eyes too clouded with tears, to notice men and horses assembled just a short distance from us in the shade of a stand of trees.

Kairi smiled and answered my unasked question. 'They are some of Pediv's men,' he said. 'Others have gone with the king in pursuit of those who captured you.'

His voice trailed off as he suddenly realised the horse that had borne me to him was Melemari. He said nothing, simply leaned towards her and rested his head against her neck.

'Melemari saved me,' I said.

Kairi led me into the shade where we sat. I explained what had happened and how both horse and eagle had played their parts in my rescue. Then Kairi told his own story, explaining that the horsemen I'd seen appearing like a wave at the edge of the plain were hundreds of Polasti soldiers with King Pediv at their head.

'After leaving you, I found a vantage point in the branches of a tree and watched their approach,' said Kairi. 'At first I had no idea who these warriors could be but, when they stopped to water their horses in a stream in a dip below me, I was able to creep close enough to two of them to hear their talk. From what they said, I knew they were Pediv's soldiers.

'If you remember, Mulenda had dispatched two of his men to the capital to alert Pediv to the priests' treachery. The king responded by gathering an army and setting out to join with Mulenda but, as you know, the Bathlayan leader rashly decided to launch an attack upon the priests and their allies without waiting for the king's help. Perhaps if he had been more patient the outcome would have been different, even with Gilgarius to contend with.

'Anyway, I approached Pediv's men openly and asked to be taken to the king, saying I had urgent news to impart. Pediv's reaction to hearing what had happened to Mulenda and the priests was disbelief and he ordered his soldiers to surround me, saying I could be a Castra spy.

'It is understandable, perhaps, for what had happened in the Valley of Havilon must have appeared far-fetched. Fortunately, both Mulenda's messengers recognised who I was and sprang to my defence, swearing I was no enemy.'

It was then that Kairi told the king about my role in what had happened and that I'd been sent as an emissary from Akbenna. Pediv said I should be brought to him but, as you know Arkis, the Castra got to me first. From the disturbed ground and evidence of hoof prints where he had left me, Kairi could see I'd been kidnapped but by which enemy, he could only guess.

When he returned to tell Pediv, the king immediately organised a detachment of his best horsemen, with himself at its head, to pursue my captors.

'With the eagle's help, we were able to keep track of you,'

said Kairi.

This intrigued me. 'But how can you make a bird understand you?' I asked. 'And why would it wish to help rescue me after all the trouble I caused its old master?'

Kairi laughed. 'Like with humans, maybe she realised the error of her ways and wished to make amends. Perhaps you should reciprocate by offering forgiveness – and not being too fussy when she brings you food.'

I looked around and skyward but saw no sign of the eagle. 'Where is she now?' I asked.

'Helping Pediv in his pursuit of your captors,' said Kairi. 'Anyway, you must be hungry.'

I confessed I was and so Kairi brought me some left-over dried kolaki to chew on. 'Did the eagle catch this for you?' I asked.

Kairi nodded. 'Does that mean you won't eat it?'

I smiled. 'I suppose not.'

Kairi handed me the meat and dropped a gourd of water at my side. 'I've given her a name,' he said.

'The eagle?'

'Yes. I'll call her Aipo. In my tongue it means to rise above.'

I could see the sense in that.

After drinking and eating a little I settled into some soft grass and didn't take long to doze off, but it wasn't a restful sleep, rather one in which I was haunted by images of terrible violence. I awoke to find no respite for, as I rubbed the sleep from my eyes, Pediv's soldiers were returning to the camp, bearing evidence of their own brutality.

At the head of the column were five riders, each carrying a spear with a Castra head impaled upon it. The bloody sight sickened me but I had to believe my kidnappers deserved their fate. I turned away.

Kairi must have detected my distaste for this display. 'Victors will always desire trophies,' he said with a disapproving shake

326

of his head.

One of those brandishing a Castra head was the Polasti king, a broad man of noble bearing, who rode a majestic white stallion. Later I was called to meet Pediv as he held court sitting upon an elevated rock, surrounded by his attentive warriors. He looked me over for a few moments, saying nothing, then a broad smile cleaved his beard.

'Your friend with the eagle told me who you are and your purpose,' he said. 'Although I cannot believe someone so young would be sent as an emissary. Perhaps you should enlighten me as to how this has come about.'

And that I did. I told him about my first encounter with Gilgarius in Akbenna and how he was defeated with help from our new friends, the Bostrati. I explained Karmus's desire that I should travel to spread the same message of peace and goodwill to Polastia. I heard my voice rising in condemnation of the Castra and the evil priests we had encountered. I felt myself shaking as I revealed how we had lost our companions to the sea. Finally, I said what Karmus told me to say: that Akbenna that would welcome emissaries should he wish to send any. I added that I hoped he would, because there was too much mistrust and evil in our lands and only when people learned to understand and befriend each other could evil be defeated.

Pediv listened patiently, nodding sagely at various points in my speech. I felt myself liking him, believing that he admired my courage and tenacity, that he understood the importance of my message of peace.

When I'd finished, he said, 'It is a remarkable story. You have experienced so much for one so young.' Then he raised his voice to address his men. 'I am minded to accept Han's ministrations of peace on behalf of Akbenna and I agree that our two lands should become allied in friendship. Never again shall we be enemies as we have been in the past.'

He paused, then turned back to me. 'You have done all that Karmus asked of you, Han. What would you like to do now?'

I found myself struggling to reply, for I was suddenly struck by the realisation that I had indeed completed my quest yet also I had lost so much in the achievement.

Patiently, Pediv awaited an answer to his question while I was trying – but failing – to hold back a tide of emotion. My shoulders began to heave as I was swamped by an overwhelming sense of release and with it came a flood of tears. Kairi, who was standing by me, draped a comforting arm around my shoulders.

'Well, Han?' prompted the king.

I looked at him through the mist of my tears, struggling to finally find the words I'd so long wanted to use but had been forced through circumstance to repress.

Kairi squeezed my arm before addressing the king on my behalf. 'I believe, sir, that Han would like to go home.'

And so my quest was finally ended. Pediv treated me with good standing, as if I had come as a prince of Akbenna rather than a lowly farmer's son. That evening I was invited to dine with the king and he asked me to tell him more about my adventure and the ills that had befallen me and my companions. When I got to the part where Gilgarius pulled down the mountain and buried Kolak's gold, Pediv shook his head and smiled.

'Will you try to recover the gold?' I asked.

There was a pause as Pediv pondered this. Then he said, 'I would have thought it an impossible task to try and recover gold that is hidden beneath a mountain of rock at the bottom of a flooded valley.' He laughed and added, 'No, let it lie there as a monument to folly. That gold, for all its worth, has cost too much in human suffering. There's plenty of gold in the Polastian mountains without taking on a fool's errand.'

I could not help but smile at his answer. 'But people may still try to find it,' I said. 'They might attempt to drain the lake and dig out the rocks.'

'But only if they know where it is,' Pediv replied. 'Let us make a bargain on the subject, Han – if you don't tell anyone where the gold is, then neither shall I.'

He reached out and grasped my arm in a snake grip. I beamed at the king. Our deal was struck.

After that we fed on succulent meats and fruits and drank strong beer, which seemed to allow me to speak more freely. Through the fog of my drunken thoughts, I recall at one point using the opportunity to harangue the king about the Bathlayans' treatment of their elderly, driving them out of the city to fend for themselves in their own vulnerable communities just because no one could be bothered to look after and provide for them. Pediv stroked his beard thoughtfully as I made this criticism but said nothing.

I fell asleep while still in this royal company but woke briefly as I felt myself being carried by Kairi to my sleeping place in the bracken.

I woke in the heat of the night, my head hurting terribly and with a desperate thirst. Kairi was not at my side. Somewhat incoherent in my movements, I headed to the river to take a drink. Close by, the horses had been hobbled and, after satisfying my thirst, I decided to check on Melemari.

As I approached I could see her, black against the glow of the horned moon. That's when I heard a strange, muffled sound. A little closer and I could see a human shape leaning against the mare, arms wrapped around her neck, head resting against her muzzle. It was Kairi. He was sobbing like a child and repeating Garia's name over and over.

I returned to my sleeping place, believing that I would never again witness such a love one man could have for another.

I woke with a heavy head and churning stomach and could not face eating breakfast, which was really a continuation of the previous night's feasting. Pediv explained that I would journey home to Akbenna with one of his most trusted generals acting as the Polasti emissary. We were to be accompanied by two of the king's personal guards and would leave before noon.

I asked Kairi if he would travel with us and there was a long silence before he answered. I was patient but the silence unnerved me. I already knew the answer before he clothed it in words. 'I can't go with you, Han,' he said.

'Why?'

'It will be too painful.'

I think I knew what he meant. Perhaps if Garia had been alive he might have returned with us. Going to Akbenna without our dear companion would not seem right and probably be too much for Kairi to bear.

'You must take Melemari,' I said. 'Garia would have wanted you to have her.'

'No,' he said firmly. 'You must ride her. She came with you and she'll take you back. That is something Garia would certainly have wanted.'

'Where will you go?'

Kairi looked away from me towards a distant hill, which was glowing orange in the fierce sunlight. 'Somewhere something is waiting to find me,' is all he said.

'Will you take Aipo?'

Kairi returned his eyes to me. 'She is a free spirit now and will never belong to anyone, though I expect she'll accompany me for a while.'

By noon my heavy head had been replaced by a heavier heart as the king and his soldiers gathered to see us off. Kairi drew me into a farewell embrace while Pediv's top general, Doloman, waited patiently to lead us from the Polasti camp.

Fingers interlocked, Kairi formed a makeshift stirrup with his hands to help me on to Melemari's back; then he wrapped his arms around the mare's neck one last time, whispering something to her in his own tongue. I tried not to look back as we rode out with Doloman at our head on a big grey-dappled stallion and the two guards flanking me on less impressive mounts, each of them leading a packhorse loaded with provisions.

My eyes were drowning and I turned to wave a final farewell to my dear companion, only to see Kairi walking out of the camp in the opposite direction, the eagle upon his shoulder. I shouted his name; the sound I made was thin and plaintive but Kairi heard me and halted. He turned and stood there, watching us, lithe as a sapling and perfectly still. I twisted some more in the saddle to give him one last wave but at that moment Doloman urged his mount into a canter and Melemari, without any prompting from me, chose to follow the stallion's example.

All too soon, we disappeared from my dear friend's view.

Our journey to Akbenna lasted many days as Doloman took detours to stop at each Polasti community to issue edicts and conduct business of varying kinds on behalf of the king. We eventually arrived at Bathlaya, where Pediv's envoy had the solemn duty of informing the people that their tribal leader, Mulenda, and his soldiers were dead and that Asdur had been responsible for bringing this about.

An angry crowd descended upon the temple and rounded up those priests who had remained in the city, about ten in number. They were preparing to beat them to death in a frenzy of vengefulness but Doloman intervened, telling the Bathlayans it was up to Pediv to decide the priests' fate and they should be detained in the temple while this could be determined.

Then, upon the king's edict, Doloman ordered the citizens to go out into the land around and to bring their elderly people back into the city. 'The king desires that you take care of your mothers and fathers and grandmothers and grandfathers, just as they took care of you when you were young children,' he said. 'No more shall they be banished to fend for themselves.'

It seemed Pediv had not been insulted by my precocity after all. I later learned from Doloman that the king had long been unhappy with the Bathlayans and their treatment of the old, but he had been reluctant to interfere, not wishing to test the loyalty of a strong tribal leader who protected Polastia against potential invasions from the south and east. Now, with Mulenda dead, he had an opportunity to impose his direct rule on Bathlaya.

Before we left the city, Doloman issued a final warning to the people to obey Pediv's edict for the king planned to journey there in the coming weeks and would expect to see a positive response to his wishes.

After Bathlaya, there were fewer settlements to call upon and we were soon travelling through land I had journeyed across with Garia and Edbersa. Each familiar landmark brought back unnerving memories, not least the mound of sun-bleached skulls. By the time we encountered Akbenna settlements, it seemed such a long time had gone by from when I last saw them, but it can only have been the passing of three full moons at the most.

We entered Ejiki as the sun was setting. For the first time I was at the head of our small party, coaxing Melemari through streets familiar to both of us. As we approached the central square, a small crowd gathered out of curiosity. At first, no one recognised me, for I received no wave or greeting. Perhaps my experiences had wrought a great physical change on me.

We halted outside the complex of buildings that housed the most eminent of our citizens, Karmus. Finally, one of the guards did recognise me and he ran excitedly inside.

Karmus emerged, his kindly face beaming with delight at my return, but his expression quickly became solemn when he realised Garia and Edbersa were not with us.

I slid from Melemari and ran to him to explain tearfully how my brave companions had lost their lives. Karmus placed a trembling hand upon my head and said he would send a messenger to General Sperius to tell him his son had died a hero in the service of his people. I then told Karmus about Medzurgo's treachery and he nodded gravely but said nothing.

Later I learned that, after our expedition had left Akbenna, Medzurgo had tried to turn the people against Karmus, proclaiming him to be a weak and corrupt leader. He had said that the priests should rule the land in his stead. But the people had great respect for Karmus and Medzurgo was driven away. Karmus had no idea where he had gone but seemed mightily relieved when I told him the errant priest's fate.

I introduced Doloman to Karmus and the two responded to each other with dignity and warmth. We were led into the leader's hall where food and drink were brought. The two men soon got down to talking and I felt thankful to be left out of their exchange.

All I wanted to do was to go home but it was too dark to begin that final part of my journey. We settled for the night in a chamber off the main hall. Before I fell asleep, Karmus came to my cot side. He smiled benevolently, yet it was a grave smile. 'I have some sad news of my own to impart, Han, which I should have told you earlier. Your father died two full moons ago.'

'I know,' is all I could bring myself to say.

The next day I set out alone on Melemari. Karmus had assigned two soldiers to travel with me but I declined their companionship. 'I have to do this journey my own,' I said.

As I rode along the track to this place with Mother Mountain at my back, I struggled to hold back tears as I once again beheld my home. All was quiet but for the bleating of a goat. Melemari snorted as I climbed from her and the sound alerted my mother. She emerged from the stockade, a tiny, frail woman now, her face sunken and skin parched, as though she'd had many lifetimes of woe heaped upon her. I ran to embrace her, sadness and despair mutating with joy and hope.

As my freed tears washed her hair, she clung on to me in fear that, if she let go, I might be lost to her again.

I did not want her to know what had happened to me. I resolved to tell any story I could make up about a joyful adventure where there were no dangers and good people didn't die. But she knew. My mother knew the dangers and despair I had encountered.

'I heard your cries for me, Han,' she said, clinging to me with all the diminished strength of her frail body. 'I heard them on the wind and felt them in my heart.'

***

'There is something I would like you to tell me before you leave.' Han looked up from the clay bowl which contained the small portion of goat stew he had hardly touched. In the last few days he had struggled to eat at all and drank only a little beer.

Arkis took the bowl from the old man's hand and placed it on the ground. He had been wondering when more questions would come. 'What do you wish to know?'

Han pulled his cloak more tightly round his shoulders; he swallowed hard to suppress another cough but failed. He heaved and shook with the pain of it and the blood could not be held back. He held a piece of cloth to his mouth, which was already crimson from previous coughing bouts.

Arkis reached out a hand and gripped his arm. 'Shall I get Pelia?'

'No, no. Don't disturb her. I'm all right now.'

Arkis gave a despairing shake of his head. 'Very well, but you should rest.'

'No, my friend,' said Han. 'What I wish to know can wait no longer.'

'Then I shall do my best to answer you.'

'Good. You see, Arkis, I'm curious about when you've ridden off to visit places around. What of the people you meet – have you asked them about me?'

Arkis didn't allow his eyes to meet Han's. 'I've mentioned your name. People seem happy to declare they know you and your story.'

Han's face appeared pained but there was no further coughing. He closed his eyes. 'Yes, I'm sure they are happy,' he said. 'I'm also sure they will have told you that I'm a mad old man who imagines things, who rambles incoherently about times gone by. Perhaps they've told you not to believe my story.'

Arkis slowly shook his head but said nothing.

Han continued speaking, eyes still closed and in a subdued voice, as if he were merely thinking aloud. 'How does anyone else know what the truth is? I've reached an age beyond all of them. Most of those with whom I was a child are long dead. People who grew up with my own son and daughter are ignorant of the past, and today's young people – those of Pelia's age – are only interested in finding out what exotic wares merchants are carrying along the trade road. They all see the land around holding its own against drought and other curses of nature and can't imagine what it was like those years long ago.'

Han opened his eyes and fixed Arkis with a stare, as if questioning whether his visitor was also a disbeliever. 'Almost all the others who knew what I know about the terrible times that befell Akbenna are dead. The priests, the elders, the soldiers from those days, they have been turned into dust and dispersed to nothing by the winds of forgetting.'

'Almost all? Who else may be left?'

'There was a boy I worked with in the fields,' said Han. 'He always said I saved his life. He became a hermit and went to live in the hills. It is a long time since I've seen him. He may be dead. In any event, he never spoke of those days other than to me.'

Han smiled now, ironically. 'Only I have decided to reveal our terrible history and I would urge you not to listen to those who pour scorn on my story.' His voice had taken on an incongruously stern tone.

Arkis shrugged. 'What do you suppose their motive might be for scorn pouring?'

'You would have to ask them. What I can say is that they have no way of knowing the truth. Although it happened such a long time ago, every memory is vivid to me. I made a difference, Arkis. My young life counted for something. As a result of my perilous journey, there was a peace treaty between Polastia and Akbenna. And, of course, Bostratis. We showed other lands the way and the peace still holds good to this day. That's why traders like you can travel across these lands and all the others between the place the sun rises and where it sets. With peace has come prosperity, though life for such as me is still hard. But that's because I chose it to be. I never wanted to leave Akbenna again and I never wanted praise or glory for what I did. Only, perhaps, recognition.'

Han paused for what seemed a long time, staring into the distance beyond the gently smouldering summit of Mother Mountain, looking back in time, appearing to be both repulsed and drawn by his memories in equal measure.

Arkis reached out to press a hand on his trembling arm. 'Please rest.'

Han smiled weakly. 'I may be an old man,' he said, 'but as long as I have breath in my body, no one will keep me from telling the truth.'

'I'm worried that you are very ill,' Arkis said. 'I hear you coughing in the night.'

'I have an affliction of the chest, which is always worse when I lie down. It doesn't seem to be getting any better, despite all the goodness that Pelia puts into me.'

Arkis thought that ironic, given the rapid decline of Han's appetite. 'I really think you should rest.'

'Perhaps, but I still have things to tell you. And I also know, my friend, that you have things to tell me.'

***

It was early. Arkis was saddling Rashi when Pelia emerged from the little house to milk the goats.

'Are you leaving us?' she asked.

'I'm going to Ejiki for a little while.'

'Will you go back to your homeland?'

'Not yet. I shall return here, but not for long. As you say, the rains will come and the tracks over the mountains will become more difficult. I can't delay too long.'

'Will you go back to your own land?'

'Perhaps. Eventually.'

'What will you do in Ejiki?'

'I'm curious about what I might find.'

'Is there something particular?'

He couldn't look at her. 'I'm curious about everything,' he said as he tugged at Rashi's saddle strap.

'Why did you seek out my grandfather?'

Arkis hesitated. This was not the time.

'Why?' persisted Pelia. 'Your visit here – it didn't come about by chance.'

'Because I heard people talk about Han.'

'People?'

'Yes, people.'

'What manner of people?'

'Well, the first person was someone in my own land.'

'But that's so far away.'

'Yes, I suppose it is.'

'And the other people?'

'On my travels, I heard stories about your grandfather.'

'You must have been asking about him.'

'I was.'

'There must have been a reason.'

'Yes, there was a reason.'

'Won't you tell me it?'

'I can't … not yet. But I shall do so, I promise.'

They left it at that, but Arkis had detected something mistrustful in Pelia's questioning, something edged in bitterness.

***

Arkis's route to Ejiki involved negotiating a way through the foothills to the east of Mother Mountain before joining the trade road. Occasionally the volcano belched stinking, sulphurous smoke into the air but without the accompaniment of fire.

It was late afternoon when he got to Ejiki. A caravan of traders had arrived ahead of Arkis and the main square and surrounding streets were already thronged with merchants and their horses and camels and braying donkeys, heavily laden with merchandise.

Young Ejiki boys – few girls were to be seen – pestered the merchants for treats in return for looking after their horses and donkeys. Not all the boys appeared keen to hold the rein of a camel, however, probably out of fear of receiving a cantankerous kick or a foul dose of phlegm.

At the temple steps, one ragged boy with a mischievous grin reached out for Rashi's bridle. 'I'll look out for your horse, mister,' he said eagerly.

Arkis slid from the mare but held on to the rein. 'How do I know you won't ride off with her?'

'I can't ride,' the boy said forlornly, probably intending to elicit sympathy.

'Very well, you can look after her for me. She's called Rashi. Speak to her nicely and she'll behave herself.'

'What'll I get for it?'

Arkis slipped fingers into his pouch and disgorged a pink translucent object, the size of a pebble, polished smooth.

'What is it, mister?'

'This, my young friend, is a magic stone which will keep you safe and bring you luck.'

The boy stared at the object. 'I can see inside it,' he said.

'If Rashi is happy with your care, you can have it.'

Arkis returned the stone to his pouch and handed the boy the rein. Entrusting the mare to him was more an act of goodwill than a necessity, for Rashi would never stray from where Arkis left her and would make a terrible fuss if anyone attempted to lead or ride her away. Also, there was nothing in the saddlebags worth stealing. Arkis had his coins about his person and he'd hidden his remaining possessions in the base of a hollow tree behind Han's farm.

'Don't worry, mister,' said the boy. 'I'll make sure no one steals her.'

From their appearance – narrowed eyes and pinched noses and small stature – Arkis could see many of the traders had come from the east. They wore brightly coloured clothes and spoke to each other rapidly in high-pitched voices, more like bird chatter than human conversation. These merchants led camels and donkeys which carried bulging sacks or were almost buried beneath richly-patterned cloths. Although they were just passing through, they had taken this opportunity to break their journey and trade with the Ejiki citizens.

The haggling they embarked upon was carried out with much noise and waving of arms, jabbing of fists and counting of fingers. Arkis was not a haggler; he entered no combat with any of the traders, merely asking those who interested him to show examples of their wares. When at last he found what he had hoped to find, there was only the briefest exchange of words. Arkis produced two silver pieces and the deal was done.

Before returning to Rashi, he climbed the steps to the temple, sidestepping the beggars who tried to grab at his arm or tug at his tunic. Inside, the temple was so poorly lit that he couldn't comprehend the extent of it.

There were voices chanting and he approached the direction from which the sound came. As his eyes adjusted to the dull light, Arkis could see four men whom he assumed to be priests, one dressed in scarlet robes with gilded trimmings and the others garbed in white cloth edged with purple braid. A dozen or more rush lights flickered behind them, sending the priests' shadows dancing as they engaged in their ritual.

Arkis remained in the shadows, watching as the priests took turns to chant unintelligible words, their voices rising and falling and contrasting as if engaged in a devotional duel. When this ceased and the ceremony appeared to be over Arkis stepped towards the scarlet-robed priest, who seemed affronted by this sudden presence and appeared to be searching for words of admonishment.

The traveller bowed his head deferentially before addressing the priest in a voice barely above a whisper.

***

Where the goats would wander could not always be predicted. They usually went wherever the matriarch, a stubborn red-haired nanny with a white saddle-patch upon her back, felt inclined to lead them.

Pelia had followed the animals as she always did, keeping her dogs close, remaining ever-watchful for wolves and bears and wild cats. Such predators tended to live in the hills but, when food was scarce and streams disappeared beneath the ground, preying animals were tempted to venture to lower lands in search of water and vulnerable livestock.

Pelia's goats instinctively knew, depending upon the season, where the best browsing was to be found. On this day – the day Arkis went to Ejiki – they were in a dry stream bed in the lee of a stony hill, finding wizened shoots of vegetation or dexterously using their lips to pluck leaves from the scattering of thorn bushes. Like every other creature in those arid parts, they survived on anything that could be browsed as they waited for the autumn rains in the hills to bring the land to life.

The goats picked and probed and occasionally contested feistily with rivals over the choicest shoots. Pelia, ever watchful, rested on a fallen tree, the dogs panting in the heat at her feet. Rarely did other living creatures venture into this disobliging landscape, so when the dogs began to bark at an approaching human Pelia jumped to her feet. It was her grandfather.

Han was slowly picking his way around stones and bushes, stabbing at obstacles with his stick as if he was blind. Pelia remained standing, watching, puzzled, but when he appeared to stumble she called out and ran to help him. 'Grandfather, what are you doing?'

It was many months since Han had ventured so far from the farm but he seemed to have retained the same instincts as the goats, for he had rightly guessed where they had gone. 'Let me sit and I'll tell you,' he said.

Pelia led the old man back to the fallen tree and held his arm while he lowered himself on to it. His breathing was laboured and he struggled to contain a coughing fit, tapping his chest with his fisted hand in an attempt to diminish its effect.

'I need your help,' he said, after the coughing subsided. 'There's something important you must do for me – and also for yourself. And it must be done right away.'

'But the goats…'

'Never mind the goats. What I'm going to ask you to do has to be done today ... now, while the sun is high.' Han looked to the mountains. Clouds were gathering. Not enough for rain, but he knew it would soon fall in the hills.

'But grandfather, the goats must feed and I can't leave them to fend for themselves.'

'Please, Pelia – while the light is good. I'll help you with the goats.'

They stayed there a while in silence, Pelia unnerved but unsure what to do. After a while, Han reached out so she could help him to his feet. 'What I'm asking of you is not just important for me but for your own future,' he said.

The goats, used to their routine, did not respond well to the untimely end to their foraging. Pelia ran back to the stockade to fetch a pail of grain and it took more fruit than she felt comfortable expending from their meagre store to entice the animals.

Only when the goats were safely in the stockade and feeding on hay did Han reveal more about the help he needed. He led Pelia to the well. 'We must do this while the sun is high and the water is low,' he said, pointing his stick at the well-head. 'There are steps and handholes cut into the side. It is many years since they were used, but if you are careful...'

In all her life Pelia had never known a need to climb into the well. Sometimes after the rains the water level was high; sometimes, as now, after a long dry summer it was so low that the goat-hide pail she lowered by a hemp rope would only half fill even if she left it lying on its side an entire morning. Yet water at some level had always occupied the well and there had been no requirement to descend it to gouge a deeper sump out of the sandstone. Now, as Pelia, faced climbing down there, she contemplated disobeying her grandfather for the first time in her life.

She looked at him, old and frail and breathing with difficulty, leaning on the boulders forming the well's raised rim. Her eyes questioned him. She had thought it for some time but now she truly believed he was suffering an aberration of the mind.

She had wanted to tell Arkis her true feelings about the things her grandfather said but had worried that would be a form of betrayal. The stories the old man recounted seemed to become ever more implausible yet, when he looked at her, it was as if he was projecting some wonderful truth. His eyes fixed you; they convinced you what he was saying had really happened. He mesmerised. That was it – he mesmerised you with his eyes and with his voice, for once he started on his tales his eyes sparkled and his words became strong and sure and compelling. Believable. That was it – the stories he told were made believable by those eyes and the resonance of his voice.

Now he had told her another story, one connected to the tale of Gilgarius from all those years ago, yet which for the first time would mean something tangible for her own life. Could it really be true?

'Please, Pelia,' Han implored.

And so, with the sun at its highest point, its light penetrating directly into the well, she climbed over the boulder rim and positioned herself ready to descend.

'The footholds are there, to your left,' said Han. 'There are smaller holes either side so your hands can grip.'

With some difficulty Pelia found the first hole with her foot while hanging on to the rim, then she liberated her right hand so she could locate the first handhold. This done, she had a little more confidence finding the next with her other hand.

The depth of the well was about the height of four men and she descended, still with some trepidation, probing warily with fingers and toes to locate illusive recesses that had been chiselled into the rock long before she was born. These, Han said, would lead her to the truth.

Rashi snickered affectionately when Arkis emerged from the temple. The boy was sitting cross-legged on the dusty ground, head slumped on his chest but still holding the mare's rein. He jerked awake when she impatiently stamped her hooves upon her master's appearance.

'Well, my young friend,' he said. 'I take it you weren't sleeping but merely resting your eyes.'

'I was trying to keep out the dust out of them,' the boy said.

Arkis happily accepted the lie and retrieved the rein. 'I shall ask Rashi if she's satisfied with the service you have provided.' He whispered into the mare's ear, gently stroking her neck, and she bobbed her head in response. 'It would seem that Rashi is indeed pleased and she is happy for you to have the magic stone.'

He handed the translucent pebble to the boy, who beamed with delight. The transaction was noted by other children, who crowded excitedly round to see what he had been given.

When Arkis returned to Han's farm, he found the old man brighter than when he had left him. He was sitting among the chatka roots abstractedly making marks with his stick in the dusty ground. 'I trust you've had a fruitful time in Ejiki,' he said, without looking up.

'Indeed,' said Arkis.

Han stabbed at the earth as if impaling some imaginary creature. 'Have you been talking to people about me again?'

'I sometimes mention your name. You're a legend; people have an opinion about you.'

'I hope you haven't been talking to ignorant farmers who who've nothing better to do than tittle-tattle as they watch their crops wither and their goats die for want of good husbandry. Or perhaps you've mentioned me to a drunken soldier who's afraid to fight but not to demean an old man's reputation which puts his in the shade. Maybe you came across a priest who calls my story slanderous because it exposed their evil ways.'

Han's words, incongruously vindictive, took Arkis aback. 'I don't judge people's motives,' he said. 'Nor should you concern yourself with what people say. If they haven't the imagination to understand your story it's their problem, not yours.'

Han opened his dry mouth and ran his tongue round his lips to moisten them. Arkis could see the few teeth that remained were still stained with a bloody residue from his last coughing fit. There were several moments of awkward silence between them before Han spoke again. 'Please, leave me alone,' he said, closing his eyes.

With a heavy heart, Arkis went in search of Pelia but she was out with the goats. He saddled Rashi and rode to the hollow tree to retrieve his belongings, then to the flat stone where he worked carefully on his symbols, fearing more than ever that the old man's story would be lost to him if he allowed himself to be distracted.

That night he stayed away from Han's farm, sleeping beneath the spread of the hollow tree. He returned the next day when the sun was close to its highest point to find Pelia in distress. 'What's happened?' Arkis asked as he slid from the saddle.

'Grandfather – he's gone.'

'Gone? Where?'

'I've no idea otherwise I would have followed and stopped him. I decided to bring the goats back early because the sun was so hot. After I put them in the stockade, I went to take him some food and he wasn't there. I looked everywhere I could think of and he's nowhere to be found. I'm worried because he's now so frail.'

'Has he done this before?'

'He's not been away from here for a long time. I've no idea where he could be.'

'I think I know,' said Arkis, reaching out a hand to Pelia. 'Come, ride with me on Rashi.'

***

Gold. That's all the people of the village were interested in. They had goaded him about it for years, claiming in one breath that he was a fool who made stories up, but in the next imploring him to reveal the location of the flooded gold. How could they believe one part of the story and not another?

Han had vowed long ago never to reveal the secret to them. He alone had survived to tell the truth; if they didn't wish to honour him for his past, they would never get to know where the gold could be found. Why had they not been able to learn such a simple lesson?

And Arkis, who had been so attentive to his story – did he truly believe him? Pelia had told him something about the traveller, something that should have alerted him to Arkis's true motive for travelling to their little farm. Was he only interested in finding golden treasure?

Among the villagers, the coarse innkeeper was the ringleader. Han knew that. He knew also that Goman had long desired Pelia but she had rebuffed him and, in his bitterness, Goman had said terrible things about her. She had done the right thing in rejecting Goman's attentions and those of other hot-headed men from the village. She had remained aloof from all the spite, as Han himself had been above it over the years.

But now it seemed from what Arkis said – or perhaps more accurately from what Arkis didn't say – that the villagers were talking again. They probably still desired to know more about the gold and, in all probability, continued to say things about Pelia. Hurtful, demeaning things. Han now believed it was time they were confronted. The nonsense needed to be ended once and for all.

When he entered the village, he saw that the innkeeper was sitting with a group of men in the shade of a chatka which had twice the spread of his own tree. They were idle men, content to let their wives and children care for the goats and raise what crops they could while they drank and ate and slept in the hot sun. Han had never compared himself with such men, even though it would be correct to point out that he, too, left a woman to do all the work on his little farm. But at their age he'd never been afraid to care for goats and crops and would have been happy to continue doing so were his lungs not being eaten away.

At first the men failed to notice Han. They were playing a game in the dust with small round stones, one he was not familiar with, which might have been taught to them by some passing trader – someone like Arkis. It got him thinking that the stranger could be in league with the villagers; perhaps they'd encouraged him to find out where the gold was while feigning interest in the story of Gilgarius.

Han watched as Goman lobbed a stone a distance of four or five strides into the dust. The innkeeper went to the point where the stone had landed and drew a circle around it with a stick. The other men – there were four of them – took it in turns to flick their stones towards the circle, getting ever more excited the nearer they came to hitting Goman's target stone.

When the game was concluded and one villager declared the clear winner, with the most stones inside the circle and one nearer than any other to Goman's, Han moved towards them, leaning heavily upon his gnarled stick.

Goman's brother Rolfod was the first to notice him. 'Now look what we have here,' he said with a chuckle.

The other men turned their heads.

'It's mad Han,' said one, smiling toothlessly.

'Eh, Han – have you come to tell us a story?' cackled another. Han said nothing but seemed bewildered as he looked around, as if suddenly realising he'd arrived somewhere he never expected, or really wanted, to be.

'Now then, old man,' said Goman. 'What a pleasant surprise, you walking all this way in the hot sun. I reckon you'll be ready for a beer.'

'Aye,' said Rolfod. 'And you can pay for it with some of that gold you've been hiding.'

'Maybe that granddaughter of yours should pay,' said another man. 'Would you accept something in kind, Goman?'

'Depends how kind she wants to be,' said the innkeeper.

The men laughed in unison.

Han pointed his stick at Goman. 'Why?'

The innkeeper stepped towards him, long arms spread. 'Why what, old man?'

'The truth,' said Han. 'Why can't you see it?'

Goman shook his head. 'We know the truth, Han. That you're mad. You were odd enough before but after your son-in-law beat you about the head, you turned proper mad. You might think it unkind that I point it out, but that's the real truth.'

Rolfod stepped from the group and draped an arm around Han's bony shoulders. 'Come on, sit down and have a beer. My brother doesn't have any hard feelings about Pelia turning him down so many times. A hard something, but not feelings.'

Han wriggled unsuccessfully to free himself from Rolfod's disingenuous embrace. 'Why?'

'He's off again,' said Goman. 'Listen, old man. If you want to know why no one believes you, it's because your story is too fantastic. There's never been a Galgari – or whatever it is you call it. No such creature has ever stalked this land or any other, least of all to eat children. It's all in your mind, old man. Your mad old mind.'

Han lifted his head defiantly. 'What if I told you where the gold can be found? Would you still think me mad?'

Goman nodded, twisting his mouth into an odd smile. 'Gold is a persuasive word,' he said.

'If I told you where it was, you would go looking for it, wouldn't you?'

'Maybe. It depends.'

'So, you are prepared to believe the gold exists but not Gilgarius, even though both are part of the same truth.'

'I've seen gold,' said Goman. 'I've felt it, touched it. The traveller who's been visiting you, he's paid for beer and food with tiny pieces of it. But you'll never convince me about a monster that eats up children.'

Han jabbed his stick in the air. 'Did none of your fathers or mothers tell you about Gilgarius? About my part in his end?'

'I only heard that our ancestors made the creature up to scare children into behaving themselves. That's all.'

'Yes, old man,' said Rolfod, dropping his arm from Han's shoulders. 'How come you thought Gilgarius was real when everyone else knows he's made up?'

Han didn't answer. It was not that he couldn't but because he realised now it wasn't the time – that it would do no good.

Suddenly, Goman became distracted by something he saw over Han's shoulder. 'Well, old man, if I'm not mistaken this could be our mutual acquaintance.'

Han turned to follow Goman's stare and saw a horse being ridden towards the village, kicking up a cloud of dust. When it slowed to a walk and the dust settled, he could see the mare carrying Arkis and Pelia behind him, his granddaughter's arms encircling the traveller's waist. Han shuffled uncomfortably.

'This is a rare sight indeed,' said Goman. 'A rare sight.'

Han was horrified. Pelia should never have come.

When they were close, Arkis pulled up the mare and Pelia slid from her back and ran to him. 'Grandfather!'

Goman stepped towards them. Han raised his stick and he stopped. Pelia took her grandfather's arm. 'Come, grandfather, let's go home.'

'They don't believe me,' said Han. There were tears in his mournful old eyes.

'They're idiots,' said Pelia.

Han turned his attention to Arkis, who had dismounted and was walking towards them, Rashi following obediently. 'Everything is true,' Han said. 'You must know that.' There was a sad ache in his voice.

Arkis placed a hand gently on the old man's arm, noticing that he felt hardly any flesh. 'I believe you, Han,' he said.

Goman laughed. 'Then more fool you.'

'I know who the fools are,' said Arkis. 'And I'm not one of them. Neither is Han.'

'Very well,' said Goman. 'If you believe this mad man's fantasy to be true, let's have the proof of it.'

'Certainly.'

Arkis pulled Rashi's rein to draw the mare closer then he lifted a flap of the nearest saddlebag and reached inside. When he withdrew his hand, he was holding a curved object which had the hue of old yellowed bone. Han shrank from it. Goman and the other men were silenced by its production.

'What is that?' asked Pelia.

'I'm sure your grandfather can tell us,' said Arkis.

Goman took a step towards the proffered object and squinted. 'It's a cow's horn,' he said. 'What does that prove?'

'You couldn't be more wrong,' said Arkis. He turned to Han. 'You know, don't you?'

'Yes,' said Han.

'What is it?' This was Pelia again.

'One of the creature's fangs,' said Han.

'Are you sure, grandfather?'

'When you've been as close to one of those as I have, you never forget.'

'You're all mad,' said Goman. 'I tell you it's the horn of a cow.' He turned to his brother. 'You have a look, Rolfod.'

But Rolfod remained where he was. 'It does look like a cow's horn from where I'm standing,' he said.

'A cow's horn is hollow,' said Arkis. 'A Gilgarius's fang is not. See – take hold of it. Feel its weight.' He held the object closer to Goman to show it was of solid structure. 'Hold it, Goman, if you don't believe me. It weighs much more than a cow's horn.'

Goman threw his hands in the air. 'All right, so it's not from a cow. It must be from some creature I've yet to encounter.'

'Precisely,' said Arkis. 'Gilgarius.'

***

Han was silent all the way back to his farm, carried on Rashi's back with Pelia up behind him and Arkis leading the mare on foot. The sun had almost set when they arrived. After helping her grandfather down, Pelia led Rashi into the stockade to feed her and milk the goats.

Han looked up at Arkis. 'I deserve an explanation,' he said, half closing his eyes and inclining his head wearily.

'Yes, of course,' said Arkis contritely. 'I've been silent about certain things – but there was never an intention to deceive.'

'Then tell me who you really are.'

'I really am called Arkis,' the traveller said. 'I did not mislead you in that regard. What I didn't tell you is that I'm named after my mother's uncle. Arkis is a shortened version of Arkemis.'

Han nodded almost imperceptibly, but there was no other expression of emotion, not even in the flicker of his half-closed eyelids.

'Yes,' Arkis continued. 'The very same Arkemis you knew all those years ago and who you believed had perished in the sea.'

Han said quietly, as if to himself, 'Arkemis was the brother I never had. And Nyxes...' His voice trailed off.

'She was my grandmother,' said Arkis. 'She lived to a fair age.'

Han shook his head as if finding it difficult enough to order thoughts, let alone words. When he returned his gaze, Arkis discerned tears forming in the corners of the old man's eyes. A dewdrop of mucous bubbled from his nose, which Han wiped away with the back of his sleeve.

'I'm sorry. It's just...'

'Maybe you should sleep now,' said Arkis. 'You walked a long way to the village.'

'No, I can't rest until you've explained...'

'Very well.' And Arkis did.

'The children did not drown as you supposed,' he said. 'I don't know precisely what happened because my great-uncle was old when he told me. He was more than a bit vague, which was sad because it was said he had a sharp mind when he was young.'

'Yes,' said Han with a smile.

'Anyway, shortly before he died my great-uncle said there was a story I should know. His memory was not as good as yours, Han, for he was not able to recall his experiences in great detail, unlike you.'

'Perhaps he wanted to spare you the horror of it.'

'Perhaps.'

'So, what did he tell you?'

'Well, he first told me about the Castra, how they raided their fishing village and took away many children. He told me how those children were forced to march for days until they came to the Valley of Havilon. He told me how they were held prisoner and that terrible things happened, but he declined to say what those things were. He said only a few children were left by the time a boy called Han was brought by the priests' men.'

'Now you know I was speaking truth,' said Han.

Arkis acknowledged this with a nod. 'My great-uncle said you raised their spirits and devised a means by which they could escape.'

He paused, watching Han closely, trying to discern in his eyes what thoughts his words might have provoked. Han simply stared into the distance, unrevealing.

'He described how you persuaded two of the priests' men to help you flee into the forest. He said you were wounded and that a Polastia chief helped you when they came to attack the priests. He told me that Nyxes nursed you and how eventually you all made it through the mountain and came to the sea – just as you described.'

'But Gilgarius. Did he tell you about Gilgarius?'

Arkis gave a little shake of his head. 'He didn't need to. I could see by the fear in his eyes that something terrible had happened to the children. The events still haunted him.

'He said you all set sail in two boats, one towing the smaller boat as you described, and that something terrible happened. A great sea rose up and threatened to capsize the boats. It was like the greatest storm that could be imagined. He said the two boats became separated and you were in the smallest one. No one had a chance of surviving in such a small boat and you must have drowned.'

'And my companions, Edbersa and Garia?'

'They perished saving two of the youngest children who'd been unable to hang on. My great-uncle said the older man managed to reach one little girl but was struggling in the churning sea. The younger man dived in to help and between them they got the children back to the boat, where they were pulled on board by the others. Then a great wave came and swept the rescuers away. Just moments later, another wave capsized the boat and children were trapped beneath the boat in a pocket of air, which kept them alive.'

'Osbin and Drago – did they survive?'

'My great-uncle did not say but I assume they must have drowned. All I know is that my grandmother and Arkemis and the other children all survived.'

There was a long period of silence while Han absorbed what had been revealed.

'I know you will have many questions,' Arkis said at length. 'I may not be able to answer them all.'

Han reached out and touched the traveller's sleeve. 'You are right. So many questions, but one more important than any other. Did Nyxes live a good life?'

'Yes, Han. Long enough to see her grandson born and know him a little.'

'You?'

'Yes.'

Han closed his eyes. 'I see,' he said quietly.

'I suppose I should tell you how she and the others managed to survive.'

'Yes, it would be good to know.'

'Well, Han, as the sons and daughters of fishermen they were used to the sea and knew that no storm lasts forever, no matter how violent. Before too long the waves calmed and they managed to escape from underneath the boat just as the air started to become poisoned. They clung on to the upturned hull as best they could and trusted that favourable currents would carry them to safety.

'In the night it began to rain heavily. They climbed on top of the hull, licking desperately needed drinking water from the planks of the boat or squeezing it into their mouths from their saturated tunics.

'The rain cleared as dawn came and, in the clear light, they could see waves breaking on a distant shore. They knew it wasn't Polastia because of the shore's position in relation to the sun. It turned out that they'd crossed the entire sea to the place of the Avensians. But they were still not out of danger. As they were carried to the land, they saw how the violent waves crashed upon a shore edged with jagged black rocks. To safely land on this would be impossible.

'Fortunately, they were seen in time by local fishermen who managed to throw a line from their boats and tow them to a safe harbour. They were given food and water and stayed for some days with the fishermen, who righted the boat and carried out repairs so it could be sailed again. They told Arkemis and Kyros that if they continued along the coast with the sun at their backs, they would eventually reach their own land.

'When the Arkemis and Kyros finally brought the boat into the harbour of their home village, they were greeted with not just astonishment and joy but also terrible grieving because so many children taken by the Castra had not survived. Not so long after this Nyxes married Kyros. And not long after that, my mother was born.'

Han squeezed his eyes tight shut. 'I see,' he said again, his voice hardly above a whisper.

Arkis could imagine the impact his story was having on his host, but he pressed on. 'As I say, Arkemis grew to be an old man, even though his young life had been very hard and with little comfort. He was clever with numbers and became good at trading, which made him prosperous in later life. But he never married or had a family.'

Han looked away from Arkis, adopting his habitual gaze towards Mother Mountain and the dark plume of smoke that hung over her. 'There's something I don't understand,' he said. 'You tell me that Arkemis and the other children believed me to be dead. If that is so, why did you come to find me?'

'An understandable question,' said Arkis. 'And hopefully I can provide an acceptable answer. You see, as a merchant my great-uncle established many contacts along the trade routes.

When I was old enough, I was allowed to accompany him on some journeys. I encountered many important people from surrounding lands and we used to gather in city markets or in camps along the way, where we shared food and drink, bought and sold our wares and exchanged stories.

'Eventually Arkemis grew tired of travelling, so I took on these journeys in his stead, accompanied by our servants and packhorses laden with cloths and dyes and other goods to trade. Mostly we travelled in the lands to the north and west, but one day my great-uncle suggested I return to our old land as a new trade route had opened up. As usual, we traders gathered in the evenings by camp fires to exchange stories. It was at one of these, underneath a beautiful night sky, that I heard someone telling one particular story. A story about the star children.' Arkis paused and looked directly into Han's curious eyes.

'It's a beautiful story,' the old man said with a wistful smile.

'Yes, indeed,' said Arkis, 'and one I had heard once before.'

Han said nothing but closed his eyes as if to capture something more clearly in his mind.

Arkis continued, 'You see, the person who first told me the story was my grandmother.'

'I see,' said Han softly.

'I was very small but I have never forgotten the story of the star children. My grandmother said it was told to her when she was young by a boy she loved very much, a boy called Han. And she said something else I've never forgotten, something I know you would like to hear.'

'Oh, and what was that?'

'She said that she'd never stopped loving him.'

Han blinked back a tear. 'And I never stopped loving her,' he said in a barely audible whisper.

Arkis smiled and reached out a gentle hand to squeeze his thin arm. 'So, when I heard the story of the star children a second time, I was compelled to ask the storyteller its origin.

He said it had been told to him as a child by his mother in Akbenna, and that she'd been taught it by her mother. I explained I'd heard the same story from my grandmother, who'd been told it by someone who was also from Akbenna – someone called Han.

'The man said, "Han? Why he's known for his stories."

'I said, "Then he's still alive?"

'"Alive! The Han I'm talking about has lived two lifetimes and is well into his third."

'"So, he didn't drown in the sea."

'"If he did, he must have talked his way out of it."'

Han made a fist and pressed it to his chest. 'How cruel fate has been,' he said forlornly. 'Each of us believing the other was dead when our hearts should have told us the truth.' He was speaking as if to himself. The ache in his voice stabbed at Arkis. 'Why didn't you tell me all this when you first came here?' the old man asked.

'You have to understand that I couldn't be sure if the storyteller's Han was the same Han my grandmother and my great-uncle spoke of. That's why I had to come and find you and hear your story. To be certain.'

'You could have told me at any time. Why did you really wait?'

'I was seeking confirmation about something.'

'Did I provide it?'

'Not exactly.'

'What happened to your grandfather Kyros?'

'He died before I was born, so I never knew him.'

'And your grandmother?'

'When I was a boy, a great pestilence was visited on our land and both she and my mother Assentia died. My father, Kamos, was one of my great-uncle's merchants. He took another wife and went off somewhere and never returned.'

Han slowly shook his head and smudged away another

emerging tear with his sleeve. He feigned something that resembled a smile but then masked it with a gentle stroke of his wispy beard. 'Was your mother like Nyxes?'

'She was very beautiful, but it makes me sad to think of both of them now because I can no longer picture their faces in my mind. I cannot recall my mother's voice, nor even remember the scent of her.

'I remember my great-uncle the most because he lived so long, so fruitfully. But he never used to speak about the past. He always seemed to find revisiting old times very difficult; to him, the present and the future were all that mattered. As I say, he spent his much of his life travelling and trading, building riches. He eventually settled among the affluent Archae, who occupy islands over where the sun sets where they are noted for their voyaging to distant lands. After my grandmother and mother died, I went to live with him there.'

'Did he ever marry?'

'No, but it never seemed to make him sad. He would laugh and say he was always happy never to have been nagged by a bitter wife. But he was just as happy that his sister had produced two children, my mother and a younger brother – my uncle – named Kyromis, after Kyros.'

Arkis explained more about his life: how, after his great-uncle died, he and Kyromis inherited his wealth and how Kyromis's sons accompanied him on the first part of his journey to Akbenna. He did not elaborate on the reason for their premature return home, save to say that they were not cut out for travelling.

Han appeared to be listening but Arkis could see in the old man's eyes that he had once again returned to the past to find Nyxes. Arkis could have told him more, and he felt he must, but with Han becoming lost in his memories he went to check on Rashi.

For Han, those memories were both sweet and painful.

Now, knowing that Nyxes had survived and never stopped loving him, he only wanted to remember the sweetest of them all. On that last night together, after he had finished telling the story of the star children, he and Nyxes had lain on the seashore facing each other, her arm draped over him. He could feel her breath on her face. The only sound was from the gentle roll of the waves and they had stayed like that, in still silence, letting time go by but willing it to slow down because they both knew these were precious moments.

'Has your wound properly healed?' Nyxes asked at length. 'Is it still painful?' She reached out her hand to touch his side.

'Just a slight ache,' Han said.

She moved her hand to his face and with the back of it gently stroked his cheek. Then she traced his face with her fingers – his eyes, his nose, his mouth. He began to say something but she pressed a finger against his lips and shuffled closer until their knees touched.

It was then that he began to shiver, as if stricken again by fever. Nyxes must have detected this, for she put her arms around his shoulders and pulled him towards her, straightening her legs so their bodies touched more fully. She kissed his neck.

Han wrapped his arms around her waist and felt the exaggerated arch of her back. With one hand, she reached down and gently stroked him until he felt he would explode. Although he wanted this as much as anything he'd ever wanted – ought ever to want – he knew there was more that should happen before his passion could be released. He sensed Nyxes' warm breath on his neck as he lifted her smock to feel her silky soft nakedness. She moaned and kissed his lips as he pulled her closer. She helped him. With her hands, she liberated and guided him. Her breath quickened and she moaned again as she rolled on to her back and brought him into her.

The night ended all too soon.

***

Pelia could have let it happen. So easily. She could have let that bear of a man smother her with his paws and fill her with his children. It nearly happened.

When she was a young girl, he would call round with his cart to pick up milk and cheese and he would linger to talk. Pelia didn't mind too much in those days, and at least he was more amenable than his weird brother, Rolfod, who leered at her and smiled crookedly.

Goman could speak kindly in those days. He would hang around, soft-talking her mother, getting her to giggle like a girl when her father wasn't about. But Pelia knew his designs were not on her mother but her. And her father seemed to think Goman would make a good husband for her because he made good beer. But though Pelia did not dislike Goman in those days, she never wanted him. Not in the way a wife should want a husband.

After Pelia's mother and father left during that terrible time when too much was said and regretted, the innkeeper would spend time talking to her grandfather, listening to his stories as if he believed them.

One day he approached Pelia when she was alone, milking the goats in the stockade. He watched her quietly for a while then, rather quaintly for such a big man, asked her coyly if she would be his wife.

Pelia had laughed, though she didn't think she did so mockingly, and shook her head. 'I cannot marry you, Goman,' she said. 'I do not want to be an innkeeper's wife, surrounded all the time by drunken men.'

'They'll not bother you, Pelia. I'll see to that.'

'But I don't want you.'

By that she meant she didn't desire him. He seemed to know that's what she meant and his demeanour changed in an instant. His voice grew angry and he jabbed a big, fat finger at her. He called her terrible names and stormed off back to the village.

That's when it started. All the hatred. Before then, Han was loved by everyone in the village. They delighted in his stories, even if they might have believed they were made up. Before, no one had ever said that's what they thought. But Goman changed all that. He convinced the villagers and all the other farmers around that Han was deceiving them.

If the story of Gilgarius was true, then a vast hoard of gold really existed in a vault beneath a lake – a lake that might be drained – and Han knew where it was. But he was too mean and selfish to share his knowledge with the rest of the village. If his story was false, then Han was a stupid old liar who thought the villagers must be idiots.

It always came back to the gold. Was that why Arkis was here?

Pelia decided it was time to confront him. She would start by telling him that she'd watched him working with his parchment at the flat stone, standing on a small hill, the goats foraging in the dip behind her.

She had described to her grandfather what she'd seen when Arkis was on one of his visits to surrounding places. Han recalled Garia's map with symbols scratched on it to show where things were in the landscape. Maps were used by people to find places, he said. He had seemed angry and muttered something about 'deceit'. Yes, that was the word he'd used.

He had said it was obvious their visitor was scheming to find the gold, recording clues to its whereabouts that he had discerned from Han's story, just like many Akbens had wanted to do over the years. They, too, had once listened to Han's story, good-naturedly, tolerantly, but they only wanted to know where the gold was hidden and whether it would be possible to retrieve it. When he refused to tell them, they derided him as a liar.

But Pelia, too, had humoured her grandfather, never questioning his story. She wished her mother and father had responded in the same way but they hadn't, and Han was beaten because he would not take them to the place where the gold was buried. That was a terrible time, when her parents sided with the village against her grandfather, but Pelia remained steadfastly by his side and believed him and cared for him and loved him.

Now she was worried about the traveller's intentions. Was he, as her grandfather had suggested, just like everyone else and only interested in finding gold? Why else would a stranger spend so much time tolerating an old man's rambling story?

Now Pelia watched them from a distance, unnoticed. Arkis got up and left her grandfather so as to check on Rashi. Then he returned and she saw her grandfather reaching out a trembling hand to him. Things were being said that she could only imagine. The traveller, it seemed, must be finally revealing what he had been hiding from both of them.

Pelia had already milked the goats and drawn water from the well to make a stew from the meat of a nanny she had slaughtered after it grew too old to produce kids. She'd fed the dogs on the raw lights and had given Rashi hay. There was nothing left to do but wait for Arkis to come to see her as she knew he would.

They walked in silence, stopping only when they came to a steep drop at the edge of a dry stream bed. Arkis turned to face Pelia. They were close enough to touch without needing to reach out, though each seemed to find comfort in the space between them.

'I must ask your forgiveness,' Arkis said.

'Why should you need it?'

'Because I did not declare my true motive for coming here.'

'The gold?'

Arkis's expression of surprise seemed genuine. 'Gold?'

'Well, that's what everyone else is interested in when they hear my grandfather's story – the gold buried in the Valley of Havilon.'

'Believe me, Pelia, I have no desire for gold. I have wealth enough.'

'Then I, too, must ask forgiveness.'

'Why?'

'I spied on you when you were writing symbols on your parchment. I told my grandfather and he said you could be making a map so you could find the gold.'

'I see. That's why he seemed angry with me.'

'Yes, it did make him angry. He said you were just like everyone else. Only interested in riches.'

'My dear Pelia, the symbols I scratched on the parchment are intended as reminders of what Han has told me to preserve the most important things that happened. It isn't a map – it is a history.'

'Then both my grandfather and I have misjudged you.'

'You have, Pelia. I was searching for something far more valuable than gold.'

'What is that?'

'To know who I truly am.'

'I don't understand.'

'You see, Pelia, I needed to find the truth and now I can say it without any doubt: Han is my grandfather.'

***

Arkis's great-uncle might not have remembered everything about those times long ago, but he knew one thing for certain and he had revealed it as he lay just hours from death with his nephew kneeling at his cot side.

'The truth has been kept from you for too long,' Arkemis

said as he struggled to take in enough breath to fuel his words. But the words did come, slow and laboured and hardly believable.

After he returned from checking on Rashi, Arkis knelt at the side of another dying man. It was his duty to reveal the same truth that had again been too long hidden.

Han's breath rattled in his chest and blood bubbled in his mouth. Arkis soaked a cloth in water and squeezed it so that drops fell on the old man's parched lips. He said, 'Before my grandmother and Kyros were married, Nyxes told Arkemis that you, Han, were the father of her unborn child.'

Arkis hesitated. The old man stared blankly at him. Did Han understand what he was saying? He feared his revelation had come too late but he pressed on. He had no choice. 'My great-uncle revealed that he was not surprised. He knew something was going on because you and Nyxes spent so much of your time alone. He always suspected the true nature of your intimacy. Indeed, he made a joke of it.'

Han blinked as tears bubbled in his eyes. He parted his desiccated lips as if to say something but the words did not come.

'Kyros knew the truth,' said Arkis. 'My grandmother would not have been able to keep such a thing from him. He was a good friend and an honourable man, totally devoted to both Nyxes and my mother – your daughter Assentia – until his dying day.

'When eventually Nyxes became pregnant with Kyromis, Kyros was understandably delighted, but he never treated my mother any differently to his own child.'

Han was unable even to lift his head from his cot and he could barely open his eyes except to blink back tears. He began to mouth words, struggling to make them audible. They were more seen than heard. 'I should have known.'

Arkis shook his head and felt his own tears forming. 'I

ought to have told you earlier. But I had to know everything. Anyway, I wasn't sure…' He let his voice trail off.

Han reached out to claw at Arkis's sleeve, his eyes still closed. 'There is little time,' he said, barely above a whisper. 'I have to ask you to do something for me.'

Arkis placed a hand on Han's trembling arm. 'Of course. Anything.'

'Promise me that you will take care of Pelia.'

By now Arkis was unable to hold back his own tears. 'Yes, Han – I promise. And will you do something for me?'

Han nodded and tried to smile. He mouthed, 'Yes'.

Arkis gently squeezed the old man's arm. 'Please take care of Nyxes and my mother.'

Han's eyes flickered briefly and he gave a barely perceptible nod.

He died in the night.

Pelia was too numbed by grief to shed tears over his thin, lifeless body. She had to be purposeful and set to helping Arkis dig a grave in the hard, stony ground beneath the spreading branches of the chatka tree. Even with metal-bladed mattocks, once used to turn the arid, stony soil for crops, it took them most of the day.

They laid Han facing Mother Mountain and placed flat stones over him before refilling the grave. They stood in silence for a few moments. Then Pelia reached out to take Arkis's hand. 'When will you leave?' she asked.

'Soon. But I'm more concerned about what you will do.'

'I have the goats to look after.' Pelia sighed, then added with a thin-lipped smile, 'It seems I will always have goats to look after.'

'But you can't stay here on your own.'

'Why can't I?'

'You have no one to protect you.'

'I've had no one capable of protecting me for a long time.'

'I promised Han I would take care of you.'

'Then stay here.'

'I can't. I have to return to my home. My uncle Kyromis is not such a good trader and…'

'Then I'm happy to relieve you of the obligation you made to my grandfather.'

'But life will be more difficult for you once the villagers hear of Han's death. You will be taken advantage of.'

'I don't fear the villagers Anyway, how will they find out my grandfather has died unless someone tells them? I certainly won't do that.'

'Neither will I. But they'll find out eventually, then what will you do?'

'I have no reason to leave. Anyway, what do you think I should do?'

'You could come with me.'

'Why?'

'It's something you could do without needing a reason.'

Pelia shook her head and laughed. 'And what would be done with the goats and the dogs?'

'We could take them with us.'

***

The cave wasn't difficult to find; the priests in the temple said some villagers still went up there with food for the hermit and they'd created an obvious route. Arkis took with him bread and beer. He led Rashi much of the way on foot as the track hugged the jagged hill slopes with menacingly sheer drops.

He found the old man sitting cross-legged at the entrance to his shallow cave on a pile of rags. He was probably naked, but it didn't seem so because his long hair hung over his torso like silver drapes. What portion of the hermit's skin that could be seen had the appearance of cured goat hide and the bones were ridged and knuckled inside it. His beard had grown in patchy wisps and he was toothless save for three top incisors. His possessions appeared to amount to no more than a bowl, a jug and an old bearskin cloak.

At first he stared at Arkis and didn't answer his questions, as though he considered him an intrusion. He ate the bread, though, so his visitor was not totally unwelcome. The hermit soaked the hard crust in beer and then drank the beer, too. Afterwards he talked.

Yes, he remembered Han. He remembered when they were children together, working side by side in the fields, helping each other, when the Akbens were more co-operative. They were good days, when people didn't care too much for personal possessions. They were happy just to eat and mate and drink beer. Of course, they were hard days and dangerous days because there were constant wars between neighbouring peoples. Wars were bad, he said, but the threat of them brought oppressed people together.

Yes, he remembered Han's journey and he knew about Gilgarius. 'Legend has it that sorcerers made that creature,' he said. 'They started with a giant lizard which possessed poison in its mouth, then they took the largest lion they could find, the most majestic eagle and a humble goat. They took the reproductive organs from each animal and blended them inside different hosts but the creature they created was not as fierce and powerful as they wanted it to be. Its behaviour was tempered by the part of it that was goat; so they made others, gradually breeding out the goat and leaving Gilgarius three creatures made one.'

'Maybe that's why Gilgarius preferred odd numbers,' said Arkis.

The hermit said he would never forget Han because, thanks to him, no more children were sacrificed. He remembered when Han came back from his travels. 'He seemed so different even though it was only a few months, no more than three, since he had left with the general's son and the temple servant. He went out a boy and came back a man.

'Han was accompanied home by emissaries from Polastia, although his return was subdued. He went back to his farm and shunned attention. Very soon people began to forget what he had done. In those days Han didn't want to talk too much about his experiences because they had affected him so terribly.

'I saw him once out with his goats and sat with him and asked him what had happened and he told me some things. He told me about the evil priests and the terrible things done in the name of worship. We sat and watched the goats and he said he had seen things no child should see, had learned things no child should learn. We looked at Mother Mountain and he reminded me of those terrible days when we were betrayed by Medzurgo.

'Talking to Han changed me. I thought so hard about the priests and what they had done. Although I still considered Mother Mountain was worthy of respect, I began to believe this was because of what she represented and not what she was – a huge lump of rock with a fire in its belly. Akbens believe it is a furnace that created our lives. But we should not make the mistake of worshipping the furnace, only the life force it makes possible – and that begins even before the fire.'

The hermit did not expect Arkis to respond and they were quiet for a while. It was getting cold in the mountains and hermit pulled his bearskin tight around his shoulders. 'You probably wonder why I spend my life sitting here watching a mountain I do not believe is sacred.'

'It does make me curious,' said Arkis.

'She has slumbered for a long time and will soon show her anger. I can feel the rocks beneath me vibrating more frequently. I see more powerful belches of fire. I watch the birds and other animals and how they react. Many are frightened and have gone. There are few creatures remaining. That tells me I am right. Mother Mountain is preparing to show her power. She will destroy all the life around, perhaps even Ejiki.'

'Will you leave?'

'No, I must stay. I must face my fate, whatever it is.'

They were silent awhile, staring at Mother Mountain and the plume of dark smoke which seemed now a permanent presence above its cratered peak. Then unexpectedly the hermit slowly uncrossed his legs and pushed himself with difficulty to his feet. Arkis reached out to help him.

'I have something to show you,' said the hermit. 'Something Han gave me many years ago, when we were both young men. He said it should be kept safe from people who might become corrupted by it. Perhaps it is time to entrust it to someone else.'

***

Was Arkis serious? Whether he was or not, Pelia dismissed the suggestion she should go with him, even if that meant his promise to Han would not be kept. She could not imagine abandoning the little farm, with or without the goats. And she could not leave her grandfather.

The morning after they buried Han, Arkis said he would travel on one last piece of business. He would return in two days and made her promise to think about leaving.

After he left, Pelia stood over Han's grave and told him she felt alone and vulnerable and that she didn't know what to do. Could he give her a sign? She raised her eyes to Mother Mountain but the summit merely belched into the sky, as it seemed to be doing more and more.

Pelia attended to her work, trying not to break down over her grandfather's passing or dwell on Arkis's absence. On the second day, she was preparing to liberate the goats from the stockade when she saw a cloud of dust in the distance, rising from the track leading to the farm. She ran to the brow of the little hill to get a better view. The dust was certainly being kicked up by a horse, but not a fast-moving one.

Pelia froze when she realised it was a heavy lumbering animal with a heavy lumbering bear of a man upon its back. Goman.

She retraced her steps to the stockade. Inside, sensing her unease, the goats whirled and bleated and the dogs growled. Pelia remained outside, the gate still closed, staring at the innkeeper's approach, dreading each dusty horse step. She folded her arms defiantly, if only to bolster her confidence. What did he want? She dared not think beyond the question.

As Goman rode by the chatka tree, his attention was taken by the mound of earth with stones laid upon it. He stared down at it, scratching his beard. Then he eased his horse to within a stride of Pelia.

She squinted against the sun. 'What do you want?'

'The traveller? Has he gone?'

Pelia did not answer.

'Where's your grandfather?'

'None of your business.'

'I think I know,' Goman said with another glance to the disturbed ground. His mouth formed a lopsided smile. 'So, you're on your own.'

'Please leave.'

'It's not safe for a woman to be alone when there are so many dangers.'

'I'm not alone.'

'The traveller has left you.'

'Arkis is not far away. He'll be back.'

'My brother saw him in Ejiki,' said Goman with a smirk. 'It looked to him like Arkis was leaving. He was thick with some merchants.'

'I want you to go.'

'Leaving you alone and vulnerable? That wouldn't be nice, would it?'

'I tell you, Arkis will be back soon. You'd better go.'

'If he does come back, I have some serious words for him.' Goman reached into a leather pouch tied around his distended waist. He pulled out an object, curved and pointed and yellow. 'You recognise this?'

Pelia said nothing.

Goman laughed bitterly. 'You would think it was the fang of some fantastic creature. That's what it looks like – except it's not a fang at all. Granted, it's not a cow's horn either. It's solid. But most certainly it isn't the fang from mad Han's made-up monster.'

Pelia stared at the object. It was exactly like the one Arkis had produced in the village.

'What could it be, Pelia, if it's not from the creature?'

'You tell me.'

'I shall.' Goman eased his mount towards her and she stepped back until the animal had her pinned against the stockade wall. He laughed. 'It's a horn sold by merchants to our friends in the east. Yes, a horn that comes from a strange creature – but no Gilgarius, no flying monster that goes around eating children. My brother bought it from a merchant in Ejiki, just as Arkis bought his. The merchant told Rolfod it grows out of a creature's head. There are people who grind these horns into powder and they use it to cure ills or make men better with women.'

Goman leaned from the saddle and reached out a hand as if to take hers. He smelt of stale beer. 'I don't need such help,' he said.

He forced another smile as if to reassure Pelia he intended no harm, but it came across as sinister. She slid to the ground and scrambled between the horse's legs. Then she was on her feet, running. Her dogs, sensing danger, yapped and snarled and clawed at the stockade wall to be let out.

Goman swirled his horse and dug his heels hard into its flanks. Pelia was running quickly and had already reached the well. If she could get behind the farmhouse, where the ground rose quickly and was strewn with boulders, it would impede the innkeeper's pursuit.

But the horse was soon was upon her. Belying his bulk, Goman slid quickly from the saddle and grabbed her hair. 'Why are you afraid of me?'

'Get out of my way.'

The innkeeper pushed a big bear hand on to Pelia's breast; his other hand slid down her belly. The goats were bleating wildly, the dogs still yapping and snarling. They knew wrong was being done.

Pelia tried to push Goman away and started to scream, but the sound was smothered by his big bear mouth while his fingers clawed between her legs.

Then she heard a bone-breaking crack and Goman let go of her. With a grunt, he dropped to his knees, his eyes open wide in shock. He opened his mouth as if trying to say something but no sound came. Arkis was standing behind him, the mattock that had been used to dig Han's grave raised aloft, ready to strike again.

Another blow wasn't necessary. Goman was a big man but he died without resistance. As he slumped into a bloated heap, Pelia could see that his skull had been cracked open by the force of Arkis's blow. For several moments they stared at Goman's body then at each other.

'I didn't think you'd come back,' Pelia said.

'I had to,' said Arkis. 'And it's a good job. You must leave with me. When Goman doesn't return to the village, they'll come looking for him.'

'I can't.'

'You must.'

Pelia said no more. She knew he was right.

Arkis opened the stockade gate and Pelia shooed out the goats. They used Rashi to drag Goman's roped body inside. The dogs sniffed at the remains, one of them licking the blood that was congealing at the back of the innkeeper's skull. Pelia called them and Arkis dragged the gate closed.

He shot a glance at Goman's horse, now tied to the chatka tree. His own mount was snorting affectionately as she nuzzled the stallion's neck. 'It seems Rashi has a new friend,' he said. 'And you a horse of your own to ride.'

'It wouldn't be right,' said Pelia. She had no desire to become attached to the animal.

'Don't worry,' said Arkis. 'You can ride Rashi.'

By now the goats were out of sight. They would doubtless return to the stockade when night fell; it would take some time for them to realise they had their freedom. It would take Pelia a good while, too. Maybe it was a freedom she didn't deserve.

She watched Arkis preparing the horses. Despite all she now knew about him, the traveller was still a stranger. Is that why she now consented to leave with him? Not to escape the wrath of villagers but to stay close to the man who intrigued her, who had made her feel so changed. To know him more.

While Arkis was distracted, Pelia remembered the horn Goman had shown her still lying, unseen by Arkis, where he had thrown it on to her grandfather's grave. She retrieved it and disappeared into the farmhouse where she set about filling a sack with bread and cheese. In a second sack she placed the horn, a shawl and one other item, which was wrapped in a fold of goatskin. Then she retrieved two bladders of beer hanging from the rafters of the porch. Arkis shared the load between the two horses while Pelia drew water from the well and filled three more bladders.

They began their journey in silence, Pelia's dogs running ahead of the horses. She cast one last look at the farm where she had lived, more or less contentedly, since she was born. She resisted the urge to cry.

They journeyed towards the bare hills, avoiding the track that led to the village. Arkis deliberately chose stony ground to make being followed more difficult. He was in no doubt they would be pursued once Goman's body was discovered.

They stopped in the shelter of the last stand of pine trees before the land rose to a scrubby, exposed plateau. The sun was eager in its decline over the western peaks and the cold had begun to bite. Arkis gathered thistledown and dry grass to start a fire. Pelia collected wood and pine cones then watched as Arkis dexterously fashioned two lighting sticks, one with a groove along its length against which he vigorously scraped the other to make the first spark. Then they sat mostly in silence, eating a little and drinking beer, squeezing it into their mouths from the goat bladder.

Pelia watched the crackle and spit of the fire, mesmerised by its playfulness. The flames lit up Arkis's face. He turned to say something and caught her watching him. She blinked and rubbed her eyes to hide her embarrassment, as if the smoke had stung them. It allowed her to avoid Arkis's gaze.

He seemed unnerved by her silence. 'What is it?'

'What is what?'

'I know you're upset about what happened, about leaving…' He could sense she was holding something back.

'I am,' Pelia said without looking at him. She reached into her sack of belongings from the farmhouse and extracted Goman's horn.

Arkis scratched his beard and said nothing. Pelia tossed it to him. The horn landed at the edge of the fire, sending up a flurry of ash. Arkis made no attempt to pick it up.

'Goman's brother got it from a merchant in Ejiki,' she said. 'Maybe the same merchant you bought yours from. Why did you deceive us?'

Arkis picked up a stick and poked the fire. Sparks exploded. 'It seemed a good idea at the time,' he said at length.

'I don't mind you making fools of the villagers, but to deceive our grandfather…'

'I was trying to defend his reputation, to make his story seem credible.'

'But you don't really believe it is credible, do you?'

'Whether I do is not the point. Knowing about Gilgarius was not the main reason I came to Akbenna. All I wanted to do was to find my grandfather, to be with him, listen to him. To know him and understand him.'

'How do you feel about knowing him now? Did you believe the villagers when they said he was mad old Han?'

'He wasn't mad. Anyway, there are different kinds of truth, Pelia. Han had to tell his story and the story of the other children in the only way palatable to him. There's no doubt they all had terrible experiences and it's perhaps best that we never truly know what those really were.'

'What if our grandfather wasn't fantasising, Arkis? What if everything he said was true about Gilgarius?'

'We all believe what we want to believe. If it helps answer your question, I found his story compelling.'

There was silence, too long a silence it seemed to Arkis. A gust of wind animated the flames and the smoke stung his eyes. 'There is something I need to tell you,' he said.

Pelia was staring at the fire, appearing mesmerised by its all-consuming power. But she was listening.

'I went to the temple in Ejiki and spoke to a priest. He told me about the hermit.'

Pelia looked up, but said nothing.

'He said if I wanted answers I should speak to the hermit. And I did.'

Pelia said she knew about the hermit but it had been many years since she last thought about him. People from the village would take him food and drink and listen to his ramblings. Pelia had long since stopped mixing with the villagers and she did not know how long they had carried on doing this. The hermit was old, like her grandfather, and she was surprised to learn from Arkis that he was not dead.

'I have something to show you.' Arkis reached out to his saddlebag and retrieved a fold of goat hide. He handed it to Pelia.

'What is it?'

'Open it and you'll see.'

Pelia did, revealing a thin scroll of animal hide, similar to the parchment on which Arkis had been scratching his own symbols at the flat rock. She opened the scroll, holding it in both hands, studying in silence, angled to the firelight.

'It's a map,' said Arkis. 'Han told the hermit it was the one carried by Garia. He found it in Melemari's saddlebag after his return. He said that over the years he added things to it from his memory, scratching symbols with goat's blood, showing the places where they'd stopped or been attacked by the Castra and the Valley of Havilon, where the temple was buried – and beneath it the gold.'

Pelia squinted. The detail was not clear by flame light but there were marks – circles and other shapes, some of them scrawled in a dark red that could have been blood. They depicted a body of water and what appeared to be a pile of rocks in a valley encircled by mountains. Beyond one range of mountains was a forest and beyond that the sea. It seemed to fit with Han's description of his adventure.

She scrolled up the parchment. 'Now I have something to show you,' she said. She reached into her sack and pulled out a hide bag. She handed it to Arkis.

Arkis tilted the bag and a golden orb rolled on to his lap. The fire reflected upon its burnished surface and danced on the precious stones encrusted in a band around its circumference.

Arkis picked up the object and turned it slowly, deliberately, in his hands. The orb was badly dented at both its poles.

Pelia said, 'Do you know what it is?'

'I think so, but where did you get it from?'

Pelia threw more pine cones on the fire and pulled her shawl tightly around her shoulders. It would be a cold night. She said, 'It's the golden orb from Kolak's staff. Our grandfather brought it with him when he returned to Akbenna.'

'He never told me he had it.'

'He wouldn't. He didn't trust anyone to know he had such an object.'

Arkis nodded slowly. 'Just like he didn't want people to know he had a map which could show people the Valley of Havilon where Kolak's gold is buried.' He lifted the orb; he could see in the firelight where a hole fashioned in the dented bottom was still plugged with splintered wood from its staff. 'Han told me he saw this glinting in Gilgarius's mouth, wedged between his molars.'

'That's also what he told me,' said Pelia.

'But how did he get hold of it?'

'It came to him as if it was meant to belong to him. At least, that's what he believed. When the storm ended and the sea calmed, as he and Kairi were adrift with no land in sight, he saw it floating towards their little boat. He said he leant over the side to splash water over himself to cool down. That's when he saw it. He said it came right up to the boat as if he was meant to have it.'

'Did he show it to Kairi?'

'I don't know. He said he kept it folded in his tunic but I can't imagine Kairi not noticing it. Later grandfather transferred it to Melemari's saddlebag. He probably thought it would be something to keep as proof of what had happened.'

'Did he tell anyone else about it?'

'Only my mother when she was young but she never actually

saw it or knew that he kept it hidden in the wall down in the well. Later my mother told my father about it. He tried to find out where it was and also wanted to know where the gold was buried. He was just as greedy for wealth as the rest of them in the village. Grandfather refused and that's when they fought.'

Arkis lifted the orb to his eyes. He clicked his tongue. 'How did you find it?'

'Grandfather asked me to go down the well to get it. He said it was mine now and I should keep it safe as it was proof that Gilgarius existed.' Pelia got to her feet and kicked a pine cone on to the fire. 'I've made a mistake,' she said.

Arkis said nothing; he knew what she was referring to.

'I have no future. Not without the farm,' she said. 'It's not my lot to travel and see far-off lands. I need my goats. I need to be near to my grandfather. I am afraid.'

Arkis got to his feet. 'You can't go back now. You'll never be safe.'

Pelia turned her back to him. The tears came in a flood. She had held them back since her grandfather's last breath but now they came, and her shoulders heaved with the pain of it all.

Arkis pulled her to him and spun her round. She soaked his tunic with her sobbing. They stayed like that for an age, Pelia now clinging on to Arkis as if her life depended upon it. He stroked her hair and whispered soothing words. She lifted her head and blinked away the tears.

He kissed her eyes.

Acknowledgements

I am greatly indebted to Karen Holmes, my editor at 2QT Publishing, for her invaluable support and insightful guidance.

Also to my wife Natalja, without whose faith and encouragement this novel would probably not have been finished, let alone published.

About the Author

Allan Tunningley is a retired journalist who has worked for newspaper titles in Yorkshire and Cumbria over five decades. He has also carried out numerous freelance writing assignments and in 2002 was awarded a Masters degree in Creative Writing by the University of Leeds.

He is married to Natalja and lives at Kirkby Lonsdale in South Lakeland.

Gilgarius is based on a short story Allan first wrote almost forty years ago. It is his first published novel.